by chandler baker

HYPERION

Los Angeles   New York

First Edition, June 2015
3 5 7 9 10 8 6 4 2
FAC-020093-15267
Printed in the United States of America

This book is set in Bembo
Designed by Tyler Nevins

Library of Congress Cataloging-in-Publication Data
Baker, Chandler.
    Alive / Chandler Baker.—First edition.
       pages cm
    Summary: After finally receiving a heart transplant, seventeen-year-old Stella throws herself into her new life, but her recovery is marred with strange side effects and hallucinations, and when she meets Levi Zin, a mysterious new boy at her Seattle prep school, Stella soon realizes that she and Levi have more in common than she could ever imagine.
    ISBN 978-1-4847-0683-1
[1. Heart—Transplantation—Fiction.   2. Love—Fiction.]   I. Title.
    PZ7.1.B35Al 2014
    [Fic]—dc23   2014028082

Reinforced binding

Visit www.hyperionteens.com

SUSTAINABLE FORESTRY INITIATIVE   Certified Sourcing   www.sfiprogram.org   SFI-00993

THIS LABEL APPLIES TO TEXT STOCK

To my grandparents, for love and wisdom

"The death's been made official. That's it."

"Are you sure?" my mother whispers. I keep my breath steady. I don't want them to know I'm awake.

"Positive. Family went in to say their good-byes. I just got off the phone. They pulled the plug."

"And, will she . . . ?" My eyes pop open. The shadows of my hunched mother and Dr. Belkin stretch over the wall of my hospital room.

The cardiac monitor beeps softly, once, twice, three times. "That's the plan."

Transplant NTE   CROSS, STELLA M.

Preliminary Report

Document type:	Transplant NTE
Document status:	Auth (Verified)
Document title:	Pre–Heart Transplant Note
Performed by:	Belkin, Robert H.
Verified by:	Belkin, Robert H.

Preliminary Report

Pre–Heart Transplant Note

Patient:	Stella Cross
Age:	17 years
Sex:	Female
Associated diagnosis:	Acute cardiomyopathy
Author:	Belkin, Robert H.

Basic Information

Reason for visit: Measurable deterioration of the myocardium; dilated &
   dyspnea with peripheral edema
Transplant diagnosis: Transplant match
Transplant type: Deceased donor heart transplant
Allergies: Amoxicillin
Blood consent signed: Y

History of Present Illness

Acute cardiomyopathy potentially leading to heart failure; irregular heartbeat;
   risk of sudden cardiac death

chapter one
71 BPM

I was fifteen when my heart betrayed me. Like with all truly masterful betrayals, I didn't see it coming.

I had my eye trained on the outside world—bad grades, horny teenage boys, college admissions—and all the while the real danger was lodged square between my rib cage and spine. It hatched its plan, welcomed the poison in like a Trojan horse that pumped the disease through every artery, atrium, and valve until it turned my whole body against me.

That was two years ago. Life really isn't fair.

The hospital bed mattress squeaks beneath me as I try to wriggle my way upright, digging my heels into the paper sheets. Even that makes me tired. I feel my breath get short and wait, still, until my pulse slows. A *Bachelor* rerun blares in the background. I've been on a two-day bender—the hospital only gets a handful of channels—and I'm holding out hope that DeAnna wins this season, only I'm not sure I'll be around long enough to find out. I suppose I can Google it, but even the thought of that feels self-defeating.

I've been joking with Mom that I'm contestant material now. My athletic five-foot-nine frame has shrunk to a frail 112 pounds, burning calories overtime to keep the rest of my body functioning. Turns out not dying takes a lot of work.

I drum my fingers on the plastic side rail of my bed and Mom glances up from the magazine she's been pretending to read. She's been doing that a lot lately. I can tell by the way she keeps glancing toward me or the cardiac monitor—anywhere but actually at the magazine. She's put on makeup for the first time in days. Blush sweeps across her cheekbones and the bridge of her straight nose. She must have snuck out her compact while I was sleeping. Wisps of her black hair still stick out at her temples, though, and she looks the most tired I've seen her in ages.

Dad took Elsie downstairs fifteen minutes ago, since she'd been crying like it was *her* heart that was about to get ripped out. That kind of attention-hoarding behavior is what makes Elsie the perfect replacement child. She fills up practically every nook and cranny of my parents' attention.

I'm getting antsy when Dr. Belkin walks in, white tennis shoes squealing along the speckled tile floor. "How's the patient?" he asks, making a beeline for the little digitized screens that will tell him exactly how "the patient" is doing. I don't say anything, since I don't really know. For the two years since my diagnosis with cardiomyopathy, computers have proven a much more reliable indicator of my overall health, seeing as I feel pretty much the same as always—kind of crappy, but not terrible.

"Her color's good." Mom folds the magazine without

marking her page and sets it on the table next to her. She puts a lot of stock in my color. She adjusts the trendy Kate Spade glasses perched on her nose and reaches mechanically for her big stack of research, the voluminous file she keeps on Yours Truly. Career criminals have case reports that are shorter than my medical records.

Dr. Belkin offers a thin smile. "Everything's still on track," he says kindly, which is nice of him to say and all—only one problem: which track? The one where Stella Cross goes on to stay up late nights watching reality TV, attend college, and lose her virginity, or the one where she dies, like twenty-five percent of other transplant patients, but in utter teenage obscurity, having never done a single thing with her life? Ever? "Are you ready, Stella?" he asks, apparently unable to read my mind. Dr. Belkin has bushy blond eyebrows and reddish skin, the face of a man who would sunburn in Alaska.

My rotten heart hammers at the inside of my chest. "So . . . I'm going to be dead?" I ask, even though I know the answer. "As in, one hundred percent not living?"

"Stella!" Mom shushes me like I've said something offensive instead of totally true. She's always on me about asking too many questions.

"Yes, technically." Dr. Belkin checks the tube that trails out of my left arm. I can't say I like him much—not personally anyway—but we reached an understanding a long time ago. We're on the same team, he and I. It's my job to maintain a pulse and his job to see that I do and, believe me, I'm all too happy to be another bump in his success rate.

"What we'll do is prepare the cavity in your chest. A spot for the new heart to sit." Dr. Belkin draws a circle in the air and I picture a bunch of people in white face masks hovering over me at an operating table, scraping out my insides like I'm a human jack-o'-lantern. My palms start to sweat at the thought of the foreign heart. I dig my fingernail into the white flesh underneath my forearm, the spot where the blue veins push up into a plump little bulb at the base of my wrist, and scratch a cherry-red line. A nervous habit I picked up during my sickness. Illness upon illness, that's how it works. "Once your new heart is positioned, we'll sew it in place and stitch together the arteries." He locks his fingers together to demonstrate and my stomach performs a flip-flop.

"I'll look like Frankenstein." I feel the sting on my skin leftover from my fingernail, and picture it fading away from red to pink to white. Then gone.

Dr. Belkin forces a chuckle that doesn't reach his eyes, which are cold and calculating, as always. "Maybe a little. But at least you'll be walking and talking." The man makes a good point.

"And what if you put it in wrong?" I ask. This time my mom doesn't interrupt me.

"We won't put it in wrong."

"But my body could reject it. The heart, I mean?"

Dr. Belkin frowns. "We're going to do our best to make sure that doesn't happen."

There are more questions on the tip of my tongue, but I let them sit there unasked. Instead, I chance a look at my mother, whose expression is unreadable, and take a deep breath, thinking again about how there are fifteen dead people in the history of the world for every living one and wondering which end of the chart I'll wind up on.

On the nightstand next to me, there's a vase full of daisies from our neighbors and a big pink teddy bear sent by my teachers. Dozens of cards line the windowsill, some from my best friends, some from people I've never met.

My ears start ringing now, and I'm getting a tingly sensation in my toes, and I'm watching the room and my mother and Dr. Belkin, and suddenly it feels like there's a piece of glass between me and the rest of the world. I swallow hard: the glass evaporates, but the ringing is still there.

The moment hangs there a second too long before Dr. Belkin asks me again if I'm ready and pats my knee under the thin hospital blanket. He's awkward when he tries to have a good bedside manner, but I don't mind, because I can barely feel the spot where he touched me. It's as if this body is somebody else's. "Three o'clock," he says, glancing at the clock on the wall and then back at his clipboard. "We better get going."

"Ready." I lie.

Dad strolls in, holding the hand of a teetering Elsie, who toddles over the threshold and into my room looking frustratingly adorable, as usual. Big pink bow, soft brown curls, and chubby cherub fingers you can't help but get the urge to lick icing off of.

Dad scoops her up and places her on the side of my bed. "Tell your sister we'll see her soon," he coos. He's all scruffy beard and smiles and his calming presence spreads over me like a warm bath. When Mom's watching Elsie he winks at me, and I know it's a secret meant for just us two to share.

Elsie pats my arm and laughs. A lump grows inside my throat as I look at my baby sister. She was brought into this world a short ten months after I found out I'd probably be making an early exit. As if I was a replaceable doll that happened to be back-ordered by a few years. I wonder if she'll grow up to look like me, with stick-straight black hair and green eyes that are too wide, or whether her hair will stay brown and curly, like Dad's, her skin the same tan color. I wish someone could promise to send me a postcard in the afterlife just in case I die.

"Are you nervous, sweetie?" Big fat tears line my mother's eyelashes as she slides off the bed and studies me with her head tilted.

I shake my head and force a smile. "This body ain't big enough for the both of us," I tease, donning a thick Western accent. My parents like when I joke around about my condition. That sort of humor is sick-kid gold. It makes adults think we're resilient, when really, my limbs have that shaky feeling I get just after I throw up.

What I really want to tell her is that I'm terrified. Terrified I'll miss high school and my friends and a normal life. Terrified that Elsie will take my place in the family and I'll be forgotten. Terrified that I'll never have a real boyfriend.

Dad ruffles my hair with the hand that's not clinging to Elsie. "That's the spirit, kiddo." The creases lining the corners of his eyes are damp.

For a brief moment, my heart physically aches and I think maybe there's some good left in it after all, but I catch myself right away, since now isn't the time to get tricked all over again. There's only one punishment for treason and it's death. And if I have to wrestle my stupid, defective heart all the way into the depths of the underworld, then that's what I'll do, and I swear to God, if only one of us can survive, it's sure as hell going to be me.

I slide my iPhone out from underneath the back of my

hospital gown. I've been clinging to it—my only connection to the outside world—but now I'll have to give it up. My hands shake as my thumb slides across the screen. The nurses are unhooking me from machines. My family is staring at me. Orderlies are busy clearing a path. And yet I've never been so alone. My bed is a planet around which everyone else orbits. It must be this realization that plants inside me the sudden desire to tell one person in the world how I feel. It's a need that takes hold like roots in soil.

I've been avoiding Henry, but with trembling fingers I type one sentence: *I'm scared*. The words appear one letter at a time until I'm left staring at them all spelled out in front of me. If nothing else, I think, they're true, and there are worse ways to end things. So I hit send and try to imagine I've mailed the fear along with it.

Mom pulls my head to her lips and pushes my hair back, so the scrub nurse can put a shower cap over it. Mom takes my phone and the jewelry that I'm wearing, along with the stuffed puppy I keep for good luck.

Before I know it, they're starting to roll me away. Panic wells up inside me and I just barely get out, "See you soon," even though I'm already facing backward as Dr. Belkin and the nurse push me out of room G216. Of course, Elsie's crying again.

The double doors rush at me, swinging open at the last second. I stare up at the ceiling tiles instead and watch them whiz past one by one. We're in a new room now, with a giant light overhead and a crowd of masked clinicians. From somewhere behind me, an anesthesiologist is telling me to count, so I do it, and I'm counting out loud: "Ten, nine, eight..."

I see myself holding Elsie, right after she was born.

Seven . . . Covered in blood, she's sticky and screaming, but brand-new and strangely beautiful. She stretches her fingers up, clasping at nothing. Her tiny mouth sucks the air.

Six . . .

I watch as black water closes over the top of her head, submerging tiny wisps of baby hair. My eyelids flutter. Or at least they try to. Bubbles break the surface.

Five . . .

Only I'm not sure if I'm counting anymore. There's a boy. His eyes are shaded. His face is a flash and then it's gone, replaced by a body. I can't see whose. The face is turned, hair splayed out like it's floating in the ocean. I should tell someone. I should.

But I can't because *four.* The word is announced as if over a loudspeaker.

On cue, the room goes dark, or at least it's dark for me. There's a tight squeeze against my lungs and then—

chapter two

95 BPM

Spoiler alert: I'm not dead.

I know there are people at school wondering, wanting to ask one of my (very few) close friends, but not sure how. They've probably tried checking my Facebook page for signs of life—or death. They can't. It's locked unless I let you in.

The truth is, I'm superstitious. In the weeks after surgery, every day was a waiting game, breath held, an anybody's-guess version of Russian roulette—will my body accept the new organ or not? Staying at the hospital was a routine step in the surgery, but it felt like purgatory.

Days turned into weeks and still my clock kept ticking. My parents are still the last holdouts, even more hesitant than I was to make the big *Stella's okay* broadcast. Nobody wants to show our hand, to publicize that we cheated death. The weaker hand has won. Only you can't live that way forever. Can you?

I snap shut the lid of a yellow marker and admire my handiwork. On the wall of my bedroom hangs a calendar. Between this year and the year before there are a total of 237 red x's, one for each day of school I missed. The five weeks are a solid block of angry crosses. I slashed each over the date, often pushing so hard the ink bled onto the page beneath.

"Are you sure you want to do this?" Mom leans in the doorway, warming her fingers with a steaming mug of coffee. "Dr. Belkin said—"

"Dr. Belkin said it was *fine*." The red marker lies in the garbage can beside my nightstand. With the yellow, I've colored a bright sun on today's date to mark my return. *At last,* I think, unable to suppress a smile. My skin practically crawls with longing to get out of this house. Four weeks ago I'd have said I had cabin fever. By now it's escalated to full-on cooped-up pneumonia.

"Fine." She stirs her coffee with a miniature spoon and concentrates on the cream swirling into milky brown. "But that doesn't mean advisable."

"I was ready to go back weeks ago." I tie a ribbon around the base of my ponytail and admire my reflection in the mirror. On my last visit to Dr. Belkin, I'd petitioned for a clean bill of health, but he'd sentenced me to another seven days. I would have invoked the rules of the Geneva Convention if I'd thought it'd convince anyone that I deserved an early release. But I waited. Patiently. So that no one would question my judgment the moment I was cut loose.

My recovery hasn't exactly been a straight line. There've been side effects. Painful ones. In the mirror the remnants of dark, bruise-like circles peek through the concealer underneath my eyes. Bones protrude from my thin wrists. I keep these things hidden from my mom. They're only distractions. I'm lucky she can't see the worst of it. My chest has been feeding me a raw, incessant ache ever since I returned home from the hospital. Sometimes I peek underneath my shirt, certain that I'll find pus oozing out of the wound. I never do. That's the thing about pain: it's invisible.

"What are the rules?" she asks.

I sigh, retucking my shirt. "Wash my hands frequently. Maintain a bland diet. Don't elevate my heart rate unless I want to malfunction. Happy?" I say, grabbing my bag off my bed.

"I'd prefer not to think about my daughter *malfunctioning*." She trails me down the hall toward the entryway.

"I figured it sounded nicer than the real word—*dead*." I stop at the front door and turn to face her. The corners of her eyes crinkle like tissue paper under her wire-frame glasses. "Mom." I try to sound firm, adult. "I'll be fine. I promise."

My mom's cheeks cave as she purses her lips. "Another week at home wouldn't kill you."

I push open the door, letting in a burst of fresh air, which isn't steeped in sun like I'd imagined, but slick and soggy. I breathe in a heaping mouthful and smile. "No, Mom. It would."

Seven o'clock. I push the lock button one more time on the keys to my black Jetta before looking up at the school I never thought I'd see again. It's already been in session for six weeks. The late September air's filled with a million crystallized droplets so minuscule they seem to hang suspended rather than fall. They clog up my pores and pull at the strands in the hair-sprayed ponytail I spent fifteen minutes combing this morning.

Everything's deadly quiet here. The gravel parking lot's empty and the sky is still gray, making outlines fuzzy and out of focus. The oak trees, portables, and the American flag that droops limply from the pole all loom in the murky air like abandoned carnival rides. It's my favorite time, these stolen minutes in a place normally teeming with people.

I take a sip of coffee from a silver travel mug, and as if in response, my heart performs a kick. I rub at the spot on the outside of my chest where it feels as if my new heart may have left a bruised rib. I push on one of the bones to feel it. The muted pain spreads up my breast and I knead it with my fingertips.

Relax, I tell it. First-day jitters. I trudge through the parking lot to the mist-soaked grass alongside the library's edge. Through the fog I see someone cut across my path. His figure is obscured by the gray dripping from the sky, but sharpens as our trajectories converge. He's tall, with hands shoved into his pockets as he walks briskly in the opposite direction.

"'Morning," I mutter when we're only a few feet apart. His head tilts and he nods before brushing by without a sound.

I take another swig from my coffee mug and resist the urge to glance back. Our school is two redbrick buildings with cement trim framing a grassy quadrangle that's dotted with picnic tables and black-and-white checkered benches. An arched covered walkway connects them, and portables lie on the outskirts like shantytowns for student body overflow.

The school itself backs up against a thick stand of pine trees that Duwamish High students call simply The Woods. Where lazy prep school boys in wrinkled polos cut out to smoke cigarettes between classes and sneak their hands up the plaid skirt of any girl who's willing.

It's early still. Too early to head to class. The main entrance will be locked while the teachers try to enjoy their last few minutes of peace and quiet. But the janitor always props open the back door of the west-side building, the one closest to the woods and, conveniently, nearest to my locker. That's where I head.

Inside, the hallway smells as damp and musky as the outdoors. My shoes squeal against the linoleum. My locker's close enough to the open door that the early fall breeze plays with my hair.

The halls are silent except for the faint trickle of music from a teacher's radio. In front of my locker, I slide off my book bag and plop down cross-legged on the ground. I've packed a copy of *The Awakening*, a book I was supposed to have finished the last week I was in the hospital. I almost did, but my life got pretty busy what with twice-daily naps and finishing up that last season of *The Bachelor*. It's funny how the more time you have, the more nothingness there is to swallow it up.

I turn to the dog-eared page near the back of the book. I'm not sure what to make of this Edna character. She's very whiney for someone who's had three lovers in the past two hundred pages.

I lick my finger and flip the page, trying to see Edna's life the way she sees it. I'm about to finish the chapter when a strong gust blows in and ruffles the pages. I rub my hands together and blow into them, cold. The wind howls as it sweeps through the long hall. I trace the direction it traveled with my eyes.

The tiny hairs on the back of my neck prickle. Reluctantly, I cast my eyes around, twisting my neck without moving. A creepy sensation inches its way up my spine. My fingernail finds the fleshy part of my forearm and I scratch into the smooth surface. Not enough to leave a scab, but the line stings like a mouthful of Listerine.

The feeling that I'm not alone makes me want to bolt. I peer down the hallway to the point where I can't see around the corner. Someone's watching me. Maybe I should leave.

No, I'm being silly. I force myself to settle down by rubbing my fingertip against the skinned patch on my arm. I push down. The stinging flares. Eventually, though, it calms me and I take a deep breath and return my attention to the book.

I pick back up with Edna, who can't understand why Robert doesn't love her. As far as I can tell, it'd be a lot easier if Edna just asked him. People in old books don't communicate well.

But then there it is again. The watched feeling.

This time goose pimples spring up on my forearms. There's a squeak—the sound of sneakers on a basketball court.

I tuck my heels in and slowly rise to my feet, new heart thumping. I tiptoe to the end of the row of lockers and peer around. Nothing.

A loud thump comes from behind me and my heart leaps clear into my mouth. I whirl around, hand clawing at my chest.

"Holy shit." The words rush out in one long whoosh of air. A mangy Siamese cat peeps its head out of a trash can and stares at me with blank eyes as colorless as melted snow. I let my head droop, trying to catch my breath. "You've got to be kidding me," I say out loud. "How the hell did *you* get in here?"

The cat hooks a bony limb over the top of the trash can and pulls itself onto the rim, balancing. Its cream-colored fur is both greasy and matted. The cat tosses its head and a puff of fleas—or maybe dander—flies from the ridges of its back, its skin pulled taut over a scrawny skeleton. Usually I love animals, but this one smells foul and looks diseased. It blinks at me once, slowly, before pouncing and slinking out the door to the woods. I breathe a deep sigh of relief but am compelled to check my pulse just like Dr. Belkin instructed. It's fast. Faster than it should be, but not so fast as to tax my new heart in a serious way.

Brushing dust off the back of my pants, I stuff *The Awakening* back in my bag and swing it over one shoulder when I hear—

"So?" The voice is low but chipper. "How do you feel?" I jump at the sound of his voice and spin around.

Henry's head is tilted slightly to the side. He's wearing his stained Washington Huskies hat with the ripped brim and his curly brown hair pokes out underneath. He's not laughing hysterically at me, so he must have missed the whole cat incident. Small blessings, as Mom would say.

I tuck my hair behind one ear and swallow hard, trying to steady myself. "Well, I feel like I've got about a zillion weeks of class to catch up on and an AP Euro exam next week that's going to kick my ass."

"I'm sorry, I thought you were Stella, but you must be the Grinch, here to steal all of the first-day-back cheer." Henry leans a skinny shoulder against my locker. There's an awkwardness that lingers between us. I know since he didn't hug me right away. I haven't given him an answer, not since my surgery. Not since there became a future to speak of, one that I could actually plan. Back then I couldn't talk future *anything*. I couldn't even think about what Henry and I could be when he asked. But now everything's changed. I just need to catch up.

"Sorry, this is the first time in almost a month I've had to wake up pre-ten A.M. Be warned. Plus I barely made it out of the house without my mom forcing a surgical mask on me. Honestly, you'd have thought I was marching off into a nuclear war zone."

Henry's cheek dimples when he smiles. "I've always thought that's what our uniforms were missing—surgical masks." Without thinking, I touch the collar of my white polo, conscious again of the angry scar that runs up the entire length of my torso. It's the first time in almost ten years I've been thankful to go to a school where uniforms are required.

"You know Ms. Johnson would *probably* give you an extension on that exam if you asked." He's not going to press the issue. He's not going to rush me, I realize, and relax.

"Um, let me stop you right there. No." I peer up at him, curling my thumbs under the padded strap of my book bag. "I absolutely can't fall any farther behind than I am now. Not if I want to graduate with you guys." I'd decided before any of this that—if I lived—I wasn't going to finish my high school career with the lowly juniors below us. No way. "Plus, anytime my parents take a break from pill patrol, they switch right over to hyperscientific grade analysis. I'm not joking. There's a chart where my mom has calculated how many more points I'll need on my SAT to offset the fact I'll no longer be recruited for swim team so that I can still get into Stanford. It's frightening."

"What about the Replacement Child? I thought she was occupying most of the free space on their mental hard drives."

"Elsie? She already has Stanford onesies, socks, and matching hair bows. Trust me, she's a shoo-in."

"Well, don't count yourself out of the running just yet. You may have a better shot than you think. I"—he scoots back, knocking at my locker door—"have a present for you. Open up."

I glance sideways at Henry. "Okay, weirdo." I spin my combination lock. "You didn't have to get all mushy on me." What if he's planned some grand romantic gesture for my return? I'm not sure I'm ready for that.

He shrugs.

Inside my locker is a new binder tied with wrinkly pink ribbon. I pull it out, cradling it with one arm. "Gee, thanks, school supplies. Can never have too many of these." I drum my fingers on the white plastic. Okay, definitely *not* romantic.

He rolls his eyes. "Look inside, Stel." God, I hate when he calls me that.

I tug at one end of the messy bow and stash the ribbon in my locker. Unfolding the binder, I peek. Scratchy handwriting is scrawled on pages of leaf paper. I immediately snap it shut. "It's the homework I missed, isn't it?" I squint up at him. I've always found Henry's height comforting.

He sighs. "Oh God. Please don't make a big deal out of

this. My new number's in there, too. See?" He flips to the inside cover. "Had to get a new phone. So don't"—he points at me in mock seriousness—"throw this away."

I stare at the cover. A binder full of all the work I need to make up. Of course it's tempting. A fast track to senior-year fun. I shake my head, ignoring the devil on my left shoulder. I've come this far.

"Henry . . ." I say, drawing out the word a little too long. "Thank you. Really." I stretch up onto my tippy-toes and wrap my arms around his neck. My nose squishes into the rough fabric of his uniform and I'm caught up in the familiar fresh scent of Dove soap and Ralph Lauren cologne.

He pushes away and holds me out at arm's length. "Okay, what's wrong?"

"Not to be *that girl*"—I curl my fingers into air quotes— "but I feel a little, I don't know, icky, taking this. Like I'd be cheating." My shoulders pinch up toward my ears.

"Oh, come on, Stella." He wraps his palms over the bill of his baseball cap, tugging it down over his eyes. "I knew you were going to do this. Weren't *you* the one complaining that your incessant rule-following hadn't gotten you anywhere? That *was* you before surgery, right?"

"Yeah, but . . ." I bite my lip. He's right. If I made it—and that was a big if—I'd promised myself I'd try not to be so uptight.

"And besides, it's not like anyone thinks you can't do it on your own. You're, like, number one in the class."

"Correction: *was* number one in our class." I feel my lips curl into a scowl. Missing a couple hundred days of school doesn't exactly work wonders for your academic record.

"Whatever. You know what I mean. Everybody missed

you. It'd be nice to actually get to see your face now that you're back for real."

"Henry. Nobody missed me. I've been practically invisible in this school since, like, my diagnosis."

"I wouldn't say nobody."

I stare up at him, trying to give him my best puppy-dog eyes. For good measure, I thrust out my lower lip, too. "Look, I'm sorry. I know I'm lame and I swear I'm going to change that, but . . . I just have to do this my way, okay?"

Henry tilts his head back and stares up at the locker pod ceiling for a good five seconds. "You, Stella Cross, are too good for your own good."

"True," I say, this time giving him a playful punch in the gut. "But that's why I keep you around."

Just then, two clammy hands reeking of cocoa butter and chlorine cover my eyeballs. "Guess who-oo?"

"Oh my God, Brynn!" I squeal, spinning to wrap her in a big hug, too. Brynn's auburn hair is swept into a messy bun and she's wearing a blue zip-up hoodie over her uniform. When Brynn and I were little, we'd once tried to count the freckles on her cheeks but kept losing track, so we decided she must have infinity freckles, which at the time didn't make sense, but ended up being sort of true, since she seemed to keep getting more every summer. I haven't seen her since post-op at the hospital. Once home, my parents had adopted the title of "Germ Nazis" and hadn't allowed visitors.

"You look ah-mazing!" She twirls me around. "Here I was thinking you'd be all like zombified with stringy hair and fingers falling off. But nope. Good as new."

As hard as I try to keep up—which until now hasn't been very—Brynn continues to outpace me on everything, whether it's rounding third base with the captain of the cross-country team or getting caught with a cigarette after last period. I really shouldn't be surprised anymore when I come back from a long absence to find she's not the same freckle-faced kid I knew growing up. For instance, she seems to have a new piercing every time I see her, and this time it's her eyebrow, a neon-green barb that looks like it hurts, threaded through the skin above her right eye.

"I think to be a zombie, I'd have to have been bitten by a zombie. You don't just spontaneously become a zombie by dying and coming back to life."

"Not necessarily," says Henry. "You could be Patient Zero. Like, you could have been the first person infected and the zombie disease was just lurking inside of you so that when you died and reanimated, you'd be total walking dead. Don't you guys ever watch TV?"

I stick my tongue out at him.

"See?" Brynn crosses her arms. "For all we know, you could be about to start the apocalypse."

"Noted," I say. "Then I guess you two better stay on my good side."

I spend the rest of the day fighting to keep my eyes open. Recovery is still exhausting, and there are several times when I have to creep along like an old woman. I try extra hard not to fall asleep in calc, and, in AP lit, and I finish reading *The Awakening* while the rest of the kids in my class take a quiz on *All the King's Men*. By lunchtime, I'm so tired, I'm not even hungry. I'm seriously considering finding a picnic table to crawl under to nap. Ever since the surgery my appetite has shrunk to zilch, probably because I spend half the day worrying about the time I'll be met with my next lightning-round burst of pains. If side effects were baseball cards, I'd have a half-million-dollar collection. I stayed late to talk to Dr. Schleifer, my government teacher, about my makeup work, and by now, I've missed the lunchtime crush of students. I walk down an empty hall where every classroom door has been sealed shut until the time when the next bell rings. Through the blinds of the classroom windows, I can make out the students, trapped inside, faces aimed at whiteboards, human specimens entombed inside a series of glassy terrarium tanks, all lined up one after another. I pass through a cold spot on the way to the cafeteria, a not-so-rare phenomenon in Seattle, where the coldest air seems to pool into invisible ice pockets—even indoors. I guess it happens because of the uneven amounts of moisture in the air, but when I was little, my neighbor told me that if you found yourself passing through a cold spot, it meant you'd just passed through a ghost. The image always stuck.

I pause to lean on a set of lockers. Being up for an entire day has left me feverish. I feel red and sticky at the base of my neck and behind my ears. The locker cools my skin and I allow myself a few minutes to breathe. I don't have a firm grasp on what would happen if I overworked my new heart, but I imagine it heating up under pressure before exploding like a bloody pile of spaghetti in a microwave.

A boy my age who I recognize as Harrison Miller rounds a corner down the hall, whistling, with a book in hand. He stops when he sees me. "Are you all right?" he asks. "You lost?"

I smile wanly. "Fine, yeah, thanks. Just catching a

breather." I stand up straighter and push the fallen wisps of hair out of my face. Though it's sweet he asked, I take his comment as a context clue about the rest of my appearance and, to put it in medical terms, the prognosis isn't good.

"You must be new here. I'm Harrison." He extends a hand. "You're a senior too?" He points to my copy of *The Awakening*. Harrison, who I've known at least in passing for six years, is built like a screwdriver, knobby head attached to a rod-straight body.

My eyes widen. I don't know when the last time we talked was. Maybe never. But at a small private school, you *know* people. "I—I—" I stammer, unsure of what to say. I've been in and out of school for over a year, but could people have possibly forgotten me? I pause for a second. Nobody takes this long to answer with her name. Then, on instinct, I answer, "I'm Veronica Leeds." I use the name Brynn and I once invented to talk to boys online. I couldn't bear the embarrassment of introducing myself as Stella—he'd surely recognize the name and afterward realize he was talking to a girl who's completely unmemorable.

We shake hands and—after exchanging a few excruciating niceties about how friendly the people are here and how the class ranking system blows and how the worst thing about Duwamish by far is the uniforms—part ways. By now I feel confident that I've turned an unattractive shade of Pepto-Bismol pink, so I duck into the women's restroom, which smells unmistakably of Lysol and French fries, just as I remember.

It's hushed. The sound of running water trickles in from the boys' restroom next door. Feeling all but invisible in this school, I'm halfway relieved to see a reflection in the mirror.

I unzip my bag and take out a travel-size Clinique makeup carrier. I lean over the counter to apply a soft layer of lip gloss and a dash of blush. The last thing I want now is to look sick. I've done the whole sick thing and I'm so over it.

At first glance I think that I spilled my compact on my shirt. The hint of color on my white polo draws my gaze downward. Tucking my chin, I frown at a glob of red on the fabric. I try to scrape it off with my nail. No luck. I feel my eyebrows squinch into a *V* at the top of my nose.

When I step back to look in the mirror, crimson hand-prints cover my shirt from my stomach all the way to my chest. My hand flies to my mouth and I catch a whiff of something metallic.

"Oh my God." My voice is a whisper. I stare at the blood. "Ohmygod." I repeat faster. "What *happened*?" my voice shrieks.

I turn on the faucet and pull my shirt underneath it, where I scrub furiously at a handprint. It stays put. Blood crusted on fabric. Smelling like spare change. Blood in the shape of hands. Grabbing at me. Gore. Plasma. Bodily fluid. *Get off me. Get off me.*

Beginning to panic, I flee from the bathroom, walking fast the rest of the way outside to the lunch area.

It's only when I'm surrounded by other people in the quadrangle that I let my stride slow. My pulse throbs in the two glands at the top of my throat and my hands tremble even though they're clenched into fists at my sides. I glance down at the gory blots, ready to find someone to tell, but when I do my breath hitches in my chest.

They're gone.

As in, they're not there.

I thumb the fabric, looking for even one of the stains, but the only thing remaining is a giant wet spot where I'd doused myself with water from the faucet. Even my fingernails are clean. It doesn't make sense.

I press my knuckles into the side of my head and take a deep breath. I'm tired. I must be tired. I rub the heel of my hand into my eye socket and try to shake off whatever it is I thought I saw.

I was wrong. Confused. Meanwhile, the teeth in my chest gnaw at the new heart in response.

chapter three
80 BPM

"How was your first day back at school?" Mom shouts as soon as my foot crosses the threshold into the entryway. She has the uncanny ability of a golden retriever to know exactly when any member of the family will be getting home. For my dad, that hasn't been often since the surgery.

"Exhausting," I call back, plopping my backpack next to the large South African man-sculpture my parents bought on their honeymoon. I've always loved our house because it isn't all Pottery Barned out—except for our coffee table, which Mom got on sale and which she insists looks like an authentic frontier piece. My parents used to travel a lot before I was born and sometimes after, too, right up until the time when I'd gotten sick. They had a one-week trip to Santorini planned, but had to cancel on account of the fact that my heart started giving out.

Who knows? Maybe they'll go now.

I drift into the living room, where Elsie's busy knocking blocks together on the floor and Mom's supervising from the kitchen, looking at one of those fifteen-minute-meal cookbooks filled with recipes that will inevitably take her, like, forty-five.

"Stel-lah!" Elsie shouts at me. Lately, she only has one volume, and she punctuates it by slobbering all over her chin. "Lah! Lah! Lah!"

"Hi, Elsie." I plug my ears until she stops repeating the last syllable of my name. Remind me what's cute about baby talk again?

"Shhh, Else," Mom says. She's been reverse-aging *Benjamin Button*–style since I woke up from surgery. She looks at least ten years younger without all the worry. Makeup's part of her daily routine again, and she uses the curling iron to tame that patch of frizz around her temples.

For me, the memory of a briefcase and high heels cling to my mother like the Ghost of Christmas Past. But Elsie will never see that. It's a piece of my mother that was carved away, yanked out the same way my heart was yanked out of me. It's simply no longer part of her, like swimming is no longer part of me. Another victim of the aftermath of my surgery.

"Come sit down and let me make you a cup of tea." The familiar worried look flashes over her face, wrinkling her forehead. I must look tired. But she doesn't say anything, and I sit in one of the whitewashed kitchen chairs and try to look more spirited. She turns down one full-color page and gets up to start rattling around the kitchen.

"When's Dad coming home?" I ask, trying not to sound resentful.

Mom levels her chin and peers over the top of her glasses. "He'll get home when he gets home."

I blow at a strand of hair that's getting in my face. "Will he be home for dinner tonight?"

Mom pulls out a ceramic mug from the cabinet. "I'm sorry." She lifts her eyebrows. "I guess we just assumed you'd want to go to college someday." There's a sly twinkle in her eye. "Or would you rather just live with us for the rest of your life? Because your dad and I would be happy to arrange that, you know."

I bury my forehead in my arms. "Fine. Fine. Gratitude. I get it." My dad used up more than his allotted time off during my surgery. He's a lawyer at a midsize firm in town, but lately you'd think he was on the brink of curing cancer, given how much they're making him work to catch up. Sick-girl consequences... and yet another thing for me to feel guilty about, I suppose.

"Any headaches today?" she asks, as if offhandedly. Her look's practiced. Face perfectly relaxed, not even a crease of worry. But I know better. This is how she asks the questions that keep her up at night. Light and airy, so as not to startle the patient.

"I told you. They're not headaches." I pick at a hangnail.

I can feel Mom tense. She hates when I snap at her. She hates the fact that she can't understand what I'm going through and hates it even more when I point it out.

"I called Dr. Belkin. Are you getting enough rest? He wants to know if you're getting enough rest." My "head-aches" are probably already a three-page entry in the Stella binder. Google searches have been run. Doctors have been phoned. And all the while, she's still calling the pain that lights my body up like a Christmas tree a freaking "head-ache." But that's my mother. She's got to turn each part of my illness into something she understands. A one-word label. Honestly, I can't really blame her. She cocks her head. "Maybe you're back in school too soon. Do you feel it was too soon?" This again?

"Mom. I was already having the . . . the *pain* before today. Remember?" I put my elbows up on the table. "It's fine. I'm sure it's fine. Now can we please talk about something else?" If my parents had their way, they'd swaddle me up in Bubble Wrap and stick a FRAGILE sticker on my forehead. If there's one realization I've settled on since my surgery, it's that I can't let this happen. Not even figuratively.

Of course, the first time I had the pain, it was terrifying. We rushed back to the hospital. I cried. My parents cried. They ran tests. Nothing. But now . . . now I just do my best to forget about it each day. At least until it's time.

"What about college applications?" I say. Since I joined the swim team in sixth grade, I'd had one goal: a scholarship. And once I hit ninth grade, it became more specific—the top-ranked Stanford team, which suited my parents, it being their alma mater—and we all became part of the same team. We were going to get me into Stanford. That all changed the day of my diagnosis. "Can we talk about those? Deadlines are coming up in a few months." While it hasn't been officially opened for debate, now that we're subtracting swimming from the equation, I'm not sure I'm dead set on going to Stanford. Not sure I'd get in now either.

Mom frowns, pausing at the sink with one hand on the faucet. "Stella, we're not finished here. If you insist on continuing with school right now, we need to get a handle on these headaches, on what's causing them."

"Mom, please," I whine. "Not now."

"Then when?" She sets the timer on the microwave to thirty seconds so that she has to talk over the radioactive hum. "I've read about this. All transplant patients suffer a certain amount of acute rejection. The biggest risk of hyper-accute rejection falls between weeks one and twelve."

"Does everything have to be so life-and-death? I'm not a ticking time bomb."

Just then, there's a big belch—a sound somewhere between what might emanate from a frog and an overweight fifty-year-old—coming from the living room. Mom sets the mug down on the counter and freezes.

"Elsie?" she says, eyes wide.

But it's too late. The next noise is more liquid, like the gurgle of a toilet unclogging, followed by a sickening squelch. Mom rushes into the living room, wiping her hands nervously on her jeans.

I turn around to see Elsie, covered in yellow slime. Mom kneels beside Elsie, taking her shirt and blotting at Elsie's chin. "It's on the carpet, too."

Before I can get out of my chair, Mom has whisked Elsie off the floor and is scrambling to the closest bathroom. The door clicks shut behind them and I hear the bathtub start to run and Elsie begin to cry. Meanwhile, my cup of green tea sits untouched on the counter.

I snag my bottles of Avapro and Imuran from the cabinet and my backpack from the foyer, and trudge down the carpeted hallway to my bedroom.

"Great talk," I call over my shoulder, knowing Mom won't be able to hear me. Even though she means well, it's exhausting being the subject of my parents' containment strategy while Elsie reaps all the cutesy baby nonsense.

My bedroom smells like vanilla. Mom must have lit the candle in it before I came home from school, which softens my mood slightly. Plus my bed is made, the fluffy lavender comforter tucked underneath the pillows. The yellow sunflowers Brynn's parents sent are starting to droop on the nightstand but are still pretty, and I make a mental note to water them so they don't die. The rest of my room still shows signs of the fact that I've been living in it nonstop for the past month. Magazines are stacked on the floor. The trash can's filled with Starburst wrappers and empty Doritos bags. A short stack of books is piled near the foot of the bed, either finished or almost. None of them are on the school reading list.

In the far corner is a bin filled with trophies and medals. I asked Mom to take them off my shelves because I want them thrown away, but she says I'll regret that when I'm older. Honestly, I doubt it. By now, my legs and arms have atrophied beyond the point of recognition. Sometimes I dream about swimming, about the smell of chlorine and the way it feels to churn up a frothy path with your feet. About the moment when you pass a girl in the next lane who's two years older and should be five seconds faster but isn't. Not that it matters, since I'll probably never swim again and I don't think anyone—even Future Stella—will be super impressed that I won All-County in a swim meet freshman year.

I check my watch. I've got less than an hour, so I slide my laptop out from the bottom shelf of my nightstand and log on. There's a green circle next to Henry's screen name, so I click on it. I need to have some sort of human interaction before the pain starts.

stelbelle022: Hey.

I unscrew the caps of my prescription bottles and empty two pills of Avapro and one of Imuran into my open palm. The medicine doesn't even make me throw up anymore. If that's not progress, I don't know what is.

huskiejones8: hey

huskiejones8: i'd have thought u'd sworn off the whole internet thing now that uve reentered the human race.

stelbelle022: The Replacement Child struck again.

I take a swig of water from a leftover cup on my nightstand.

huskiejones8: lol

huskiejones8: what was her diabolical plan this time?

stelbelle022: Puke. Again. An oldie but goodie.

huskiejones8: zero points for creativity. she must be getting lazy.

stelbelle022: I think it's more, don't fix what ain't broke.

stelbelle022: I swear, she's only 1 and she's already an evil villain mastermind.

huskiejones8: aw, sibling love.

stelbelle022: haha. Let's see how you'd feel if your parents decided to replace you with a younger, cuter model.

stelbelle022: Too bad I screwed things up and didn't kick the bucket.

Right as I hit "enter" I wish I hadn't. My parents would die if they saw that and, besides, my entire existence has caused enough pain as it is.

huskiejones8: speaking of which, did u survive ur first day back?

I'm glad he ignored my comment. I was lucky that Brynn and Henry let me tag along with them all day. In the past year and a half, Henry has gotten popular. Like really popular. The kind where girls doodle his name on notebooks. Sometimes I swear I'm just a fixer-upper project for him. Take pity on the sick girl. A plot out of one of those '90s teen flicks where the homecoming king tries to be nice to the misfit. But I know I'm only being cynical.

stelbelle022: Ish.

I don't mention the bloody handprints. Or the fact that they made me feel as if I'm losing my mind.

huskiejones8: a rousing endorsement.

A couple minutes pass without the chime of a new IM and I take the opportunity to check my celebrity blogs, but no one famous has either broken up or gotten back together within the past twenty-four hours. It's a real downer.

The window containing my conversation with Henry flashes with a new message.

huskiejones8: well, i'm glad ur back . . .

It's the dot–dot–dot that worries me. I'm still not ready for this conversation. I'm not ready to decide what Henry and I are yet. It's too soon. And what if it ruins our friendship? I've only got two and a half friends as it is. I can't stomach losing another.

Henry and I became friends over a stringy-haired girl with dated clothes and telekinetic powers. Her name was Carrie and she was a character in a Stephen King novel that Henry and I both read at age twelve, well before either of us was old enough. We'd call each other in the middle of the night: *Are you sleeping? What page are you on?* Both too frightened to keep going but too competitive to stop. Pretty soon we were challenging each other to see who could out-scare the other. First there was *The Exorcist*, followed quickly by

Hell House, Rosemary's Baby, and *The Amityville Horror,* until we were no longer freaked-out little kids but connoisseurs.

We began mainlining episodes of *The Twilight Zone* in the basement of Henry's house, and we eventually discovered this crazy paranormal conspiracy podcast called *Lunatic Outpost* via a superfan message board. We would spend hours coming up with our own nutty theories about ghosts and dead presidents, and I could almost forget I was sick.

I return to the window.

> *stelbelle022: I should probably get started on this homework.*
>
> *huskiejones8: and get to work planning your next stage stealer from the Replacement Child*
>
> *stelbelle022: It's weird...I'd have thought the whole heart transplant thing would have done that.*
>
> *huskiejones8: chubby cheeks are a hard card to trump.*
>
> *stelbelle022: True.*

I sign off and ten seconds later, the screen goes dark. So much for that distraction. Now all I have to do is wait.

It's four thirty-five. Thirty-three minutes left.

I navigate to YouTube and watch a couple of stupid cat videos, which are only mildly amusing. When I've run out of attractive links there, I flip on the TV. I like the background noise. Plus there's a *Friends* rerun I haven't seen in a long time.

I do my best to avoid checking the time, but with seven minutes to go, my hands start to sweat. *Relax,* I try to tell myself when I notice my fingers digging into the comforter. My dad has a theory. He says I anticipate the pain, therefore get stressed about the pain, therefore cause the pain. I'm a walking, talking self-fulfilling prophecy—or, as my dad claims, a Pavlov's dog.

I looked it up. The term refers to an experiment performed by Ivan Pavlov. Every day, Pavlov rang a bell at the exact same time he presented a group of dogs with food. In time, the dogs began to salivate at the ringing of the bell, whether or not the sound was accompanied by a side of Kibbles 'n Bits. They'd been conditioned by the anticipation. In other words, I'm the equivalent of a German shepherd with a drooling problem.

Yeah, it's not the most flattering comparison.

Two minutes to go.

I try to laugh along with the laugh track, but it's hard to concentrate on the silliness, you know, to really buy into it. In another minute, I know why.

It starts out small. An itch under my ribs that gradually becomes discomfort. That discomfort spreads from my back all the way through the top of my intestines. My breathing gets heavy. While I can still move, I tear down my covers and crawl underneath. Cradling my pillow, I pull it against me as if that will be able to stop the thing that's growing inside.

A deep breath.

Five oh eight.

That's when it hits. The pain spikes through my entire body and races up my neck and into the base of my skull, a white-hot light that blinds me. It scorches everything it meets. Incinerates my insides. My back arches. I scream into my pillow.

I'm torn in two pieces, and out from the brokenness pour words. Only I can't make them out. They're hushed—no—muffled. I strain against the pain. Against the pressure in my ears.

Waves lap at the edges of my mind and I try to haul myself out. But nothing washes away the pain. And the words hover out of reach.

The moment lasts seconds and forever and not at all. All I can see is the light, glaring and dazzling.

It hurts. God, it hurts.

Tears streak my face and soak my pillow. As the light backs away from the edges of my vision and of my mind, the pain subsides, dwindling until it fades into a pinprick in the cavern of my chest.

And then it's just me left at the end. Slumped and ragged.

chapter four
116 BPM

"Cross, Cross...Come in, Cross!" My eyes flit up from my turkey sandwich on pita when Henry snaps his fingers underneath my nose.

It's been a week, and I'm worn down by the process of trying to catch up. There's never enough daylight, sleep, energy, concentration, never enough *time* to break even on all the work I've missed. Henry's binder taunts me from under the nightstand in my bedroom. One tiny peek? I'm just stubborn—or stupid—enough to resist.

I've been picking at my food for twenty minutes and Brynn's already accused me of being anorexic twice. It's not like I'm *trying* not to eat. I just haven't been hungry since the transplant. It's most likely a totally normal side effect and Brynn just hates that I'm finally skinnier than she is.

"Huh?" I say thickly. I've been doing that blank stare-y

thing again, and Henry's looking at me across our lunch table, eyebrows raised, clearly waiting for me to say something. Anything.

I clear my throat. "Sorry . . . can you, um, can you repeat that?"

Brynn snorts but doesn't look up from her math book. She's scribbling down the last few answers to an assignment due today. Her hair's still wet and wadded up into a bun and she's bitten the drawstrings of her sweatshirt until they're a darker color of red at the ends. Lydia's sitting with us today, too. Lydia's a floater. She sits with us some days and with another group other days. Technically, she's Brynn's friend from swimming. She's kind of quiet in a way that seems purposeful, and I sometimes wonder if she hates standing out as the only black girl in our school. For someone who barely talks, it's funny that she's the one who feels the need to split her time between social groups.

"Sorry." I kick Brynn under the table. "I was to-do-listing in my head." Brynn holds up her middle finger but keeps her eyes on the glossy page, muttering numbers under her breath. Charming.

Henry removes his baseball hat and flips the bill backward. It's a nervous habit of his, backward, forward, backward, forward. I've watched him do it a million times in Calc, which I know for a fact is definitely not his thing.

"We're all going to do something tonight." His glance flicks over to Brynn before returning to me. "You wanna come, maybe?"

He said "we," which means he's not asking me out again. It's a friends thing. Friends are good.

Brynn slides her textbook off the table and rams it into her crammed backpack. "He's asking if you're officially off house arrest."

"Who's 'we'?" I ask. "And go do what?"

Lydia giggles, her lips parting into a wide, sheepish smile. Brynn stares at me like I've sprouted tentacles out the top of my head.

"What's wrong with that?"

Brynn exaggerates a sigh. "Do we have to put all our cards on the table?"

I look to Henry for help. He shrugs. "She's right. We can't let you become a hermit. Not on our watch."

"But—"

"Stel." Brynn slaps her forehead. "We're trying to surprise you, moron. That's it. You're coming."

A smile tugs at the corners of my lips. "Fine. You guys are so strict."

"You ready?" Lydia asks me. We have the same period after lunch and usually wait to walk together. She shuffles a stack of notes she'd been looking over and places them in a red folder.

"Be ready at eight," Brynn calls after me. "We'll grab you on the way."

"On the way to where?" But she's not listening. She's already turned her attention back to Henry.

Lydia and I walk to Anatomy. Each time she speaks I have to strain to hear her over the school's normal hustle and bustle.

"Are you coming?" she asks.

"To what?"

Her giggle is melodic and she looks at me only out of the corners of her eyes, through a feathery arc of thick eyelashes. "To Michelle Boerne's."

I realize I must have missed a chunk of her conversation, but I put together that Michelle's having a party either next Friday or the Friday after that.

"Oh. Sure, I guess so." It's not like I've got plans for any Friday night in the near future. Lydia smiles, but her eyes are trained right back at the ground and I know I won't be getting much more out of her. Still, I take this as an invite. Or at least close enough.

Somewhere between the cafeteria and our classroom it occurs to me that Lydia, who tends to total only three sentences every hour, is probably my third-best friend in the world right now.

Inside Ms. Birkbauer's anatomy class, Lydia and I weave our way through the rows of empty lab tables and find a two-top near the back of the classroom, where the beakers are lined up next to the sink.

At the front of the classroom Ms. Birkbauer gets up from her computer credenza and rings the teacup-size bell she keeps on her desk. "As you get settled, please retrieve the pig hearts we were working on earlier this week. We'll try to finish up with the dissection today so that you all can have plenty of time to write your lab reports by next week." Plenty of time? As if.

Lydia shudders. "Ew, that stuff smells like brain juice."

"*Brain* juice?" I giggle and get behind her in the line forming behind the refrigerated case. "Is that a smell you're well acquainted with?" I ask.

She levels her chin, moving one step forward in the line. "No, but I think that's like what Hannibal Lecter preserves the brains in before he eats them. You know?"

"Okay, disgusting. I prefer my brains preservative-free." I slide the covered tray marked CROSS from the thin refrigerator shelf and trail Lydia back to our lab table.

"I don't care either way, as long as there's no gluten."

I snort. That may be the first funny thing I've ever heard Lydia say. I set the tray down on the black countertop. The smell hasn't fully hit me with the lid still on, but I know exactly what Lydia's talking about, only to me it smells like sickness and old people. Or maybe like those big morgues where they perform autopsies.

I dig out the lab sheet from my backpack while Lydia doles out toothpicks for the two of us. I'm not sure what they're for, but they're on the supply list, so I set mine aside in a neat pile. "'Step one: Locate the aorta,'" I read from the sheet. That should be easy enough, I think, remembering what it looks like from our textbook. "'Step two: Locate the veins.'" Okay, slightly more difficult. "'Step three: Cut the heart in half to expose the chamber. . . .' Shall we?"

She shrugs and we both remove the lids from our containers, revealing the sad, limp, yellowed hearts. I wrinkle my nose at the smell and pull plastic gloves over my hands.

Gently, I poke my finger against what I think must be the aorta and then walk my fingertips over to the different veins, making chicken-scratch notes in my black-and-white-speckled composition book about each of their locations—*interventricular, sulcus, brachiocephalic.* They're embedded in the fleshy heart like shallow grooves in a shriveled-up brain.

Pinching the scalpel between two fingers, I roll the heart onto its side and pick the spot closest to the center. " 'Cut the heart down the center to reveal the chambers,' " I read under my breath. The scalpel sinks into the organ. There's a glitch in my vision and the world in front of me rocks, knocking me off balance. The blade narrowly misses my fingers as it slices vertically all the way through. Cradling my forehead, I shake my wrist out, alarmed at what a close call it'd been.

That's when I notice slick, red liquid leaking onto my gloved hands.

I choke once. This time the lab table in front of me seems to jump sideways. I stumble right, then stagger back. It's like trying to walk in a fun house.

As I hold onto the black countertop for balance, my head swims. I rub my eyes. It's fine. Totally fine. Deep breath. The scalpel sinks deeper. Metal through puffy flesh.

Blood sprays up at my face. Several droplets dangle in my line of vision. They cling to my hair. Gagging, I cover my mouth.

Only, my wet fingers slip across my skin, leaving warm patches of blood on my face. Blood that pours out onto the table.

Quickly, I flip the pages of my textbook to the diagram. Bloody fingerprints appear on the white pages. My ears fill with a singular, high-pitched ringing. At the beginning of the chapter is an illustration of a pig heart side by side with a human's. The shape of the human organ is abstract, odd, irregularly contoured, like an asymmetrical trapezoid. But the pig heart has the familiar curves of a valentine.

I look from the page to the flimsy tray, then back again.

Even though the textbook has only a drawing, the scholarly version bears no resemblance to the gaping organ in front of me.

My chest contracts like a little kid has slapped his hands on either side of a blown-up plastic baggie causing the air to burst out in one loud clap. Impulsively, my hand clutches at the spot over my heart.

As if in return, the bleeding arteries throb. Another round of hoarse gasps. The classroom's spinning so fast now, I'm certain I'll hurl.

Pain shoots through me like tree branches. I double over. "No," I mutter. Not my heart.

Light flashes off the lethal point clutched tight in my plastic-gloved hand. The heart sputters for life out of every open orifice. Gushing and burbling, droplets cascade to the floor. Bile burns at the back of my throat.

I hear a scream.

Spots sneak up around the edges of my vision.

I try pressing my nails into my wrist, but my head's floating, high over my shoulders, and the screaming won't stop. It pushes through into a splitting headache and I'm horizontal now. How did I get this way? Down on the floor, I see faces converge around me.

Hands reach for me. Reach into me. I try blinking. The spots multiply.

More screaming. The sounds stretches out, spirals.

"Stella?" The voice is Auto-Tuned, fake. "Stella?"

It's only at the last second that I realize where the screaming is coming from.

Me.

And by then, it's too late.

chapter five
121 BPM

I nearly stabbed myself. All those years of Mom telling me
not to run with scissors and I narrowly miss puncturing a
lung when I fall on top of a scalpel. Thankfully, the only
thing punctured was the right side of my shirt, which I can
confirm firsthand is much easier to replace than vital organs.

"I'm going," I say.

"You're not." Mom flattens her palm against the kitchen
table and leans toward me. The breakfast nook in our home
has morphed into the negotiating room, and I've been told
that, back in the day, my mother was a force to be reckoned
with when it came to closing a deal. Good thing I've brought
my A-game.

My dad, who shaved his scruffy beard since his return
to work, wraps his arm around her. "Your mother's right,
Stella."

I lean back in the stiff wooden chair. "Why?"

Mom scoffs. "Do we really have to explain this to you? Two hours ago you were writhing in pain. And this afternoon? What about this afternoon?"

"What about it?" *What about it?* I can barely say this with a straight face. If topics could trend at Duwamish High, this would top the list. Headline news.

What happened, Stella? I thought you were better, Stella? I can still feel the twenty-six pairs of eyes on me as I was led, red-faced, out of the classroom.

Dad casts a nervous glance toward Elsie's room, where she's supposed to be taking an unscheduled nap. "You fainted." His voice rasps.

"So? That could happen to anyone. I hear nineteenth-century girls fainted whenever a hot guy walked into the room."

He scratches at the stubble on his neck. "And did a hot guy enter the vicinity that we don't know about?" Annoyed. Clearly annoyed.

"Unfortunately no, but—"

"Well, then do you honestly think that's healthy?" The last time I saw my dad this flustered was diagnosis day.

"I'm breathing, aren't I? It's all relative." The key is to come off calm, nonchalant. *Healthy.*

My phone vibrates again. This time it's Henry. It's his turn to relay the message: *We can do this another time. No big deal.*

No, I type once more, while my parents pass exasperated looks between them. *I told you. I'm fine.* It's not as if I haven't already had this conversation with Brynn and Lydia. Passing out in school is embarrassing enough without everyone rushing to treat me with kid gloves.

"That's not funny," Mom says through her teeth.

"It wasn't meant to be." I'd been sent home from school in a rush after the incident in Anatomy. Nobody wants a girl dying on campus. Not that I was in danger of dying. Not really. My heart just went a little wonky.

And now, according to Brynn, anyone who was in the classroom during my breakdown is being grilled for details, including Lydia. "I had a *heart transplant*. Given the circumstances, I think things have gone pretty smoothly, don't you?"

"Dr. Belkin's worried about you. And the psychiatrist."

"No." I puff my cheeks out. "The shrink said my teacher was an idiot—okay, unwise—for letting me do a heart dissection weeks after my own transplant. Of course I had a freak-out. It was too close to my own personal circumstances. Pure mental anxiety. There's nothing wrong with me physically." I repeat the doctor's words in my most sensible tone. "I was in the doctor's office. I *know* what he said."

Major life stressor. I guess that's what you call it when you almost die then are saved by somebody else's vital organ. Things are bound to get a little freaky.

My parents' lips press into matching straight lines.

I light the screen on my phone to check the time. My friends should be here any minute and I'm starting to worry that negotiations are breaking down.

"I'm the one who has to live with this stupid condition." I hate to do it, but I reach for the trump card. "You guys can't put me in a freaking glass box. Otherwise what was the point?"

"Watch your tone," Mom snaps.

Dad removes his arm from around her shoulder, which

sends my heart skipping with hope. He puts his hand over hers. "Maybe she's right, Donna." I knew it.

Her eyes threaten to burn crop circles into his forehead. "What?" He shrinks back, pulling his hand with him.

There's a long silence. Followed by an equally long honk coming from our driveway. I hold my breath.

When Mom peels her glare off Dad, her jaw is stiff. "If you and your father have decided..." She trails off.

My chair screeches across the tile. "Thanks," I say. And before she can change her mind, I shove my phone into the back pocket of my jeans and head for the front door.

Outside, Brynn's behind the wheel of her silver Jeep Cherokee. The heel of her hand is still jammed against the horn. I make out the heads of Lydia and Henry in back. Shotgun's reserved for me.

I cover my ears the rest of the way to the car. She doesn't quit until my seat belt's buckled.

"Was that necessary?" I ask.

She shrugs. "Thought there might be some parental tension to diffuse."

I slump against the headrest. "You're right about that."

Lydia pops her head between the two front seats. Her hair has been pulled into two French braids that weave down either side of her part. "How are you feeling?" Her braids smell like mango. She witnessed my entire meltdown. I cringe and pray that I didn't do anything more humiliating than scream. As if that's not mortifying enough.

I try to offer a smile. "Fine. A little shaky maybe, but mainly I wish everyone would quit asking me."

She disappears into the backseat, muttering something about being sorry, and I feel a stab of guilt for brushing her off, especially since Brynn told me she'd been tight-lipped when anyone asked her what happened in anatomy today.

I look back at Henry. "Cat got your tongue?"

"Hey," he says. But instead of looking happy to see me, he shakes his head—almost imperceptibly—and stares out the window.

Who made it his job to worry about me?

"So, where are we going?" I ask. My first big outing since my surgery. And, if we're being honest, since quite awhile before that.

Brynn drives too fast along the neighborhood's roads. "You'll see."

I sit on my hands in the front seat and try not to get carsick while everyone talks over each other about the quarterback on the Huskies this year and whether his girlfriend is hot enough for him. Henry thinks definitely yes, while Brynn thinks no way, and I'm not sure until Lydia pulls up an image on her cell phone and I agree with Brynn that he could do better. Sure, I know it's shallow, but I can't remember the last time I had something utterly frivolous to gossip about. Next, I wouldn't mind going for a long, detailed discussion about the merits of the sock bun.

I'm distracted enough to be surprised when Brynn finally pulls into a parking lot near the waterfront. There's a single car, but otherwise, the lot is empty.

The Cherokee's headlights reflect off the black water as we all scramble out of the car, our shoes crunching on gravel and dirt. A short distance over, a pier looms out over the water, marked at intervals with glowing industrial lanterns.

"What is this place?"

Henry appears at my elbow, a tall, lanky shadow in the

darkness. Together, we follow Brynn and Lydia down to the water. "An old fisherman's pier. It's abandoned now. Except for a few old folks who still like to cast for catfish up here."

Speaking of, the air reeks of dead fish and garbage. "Okay, but why are *we* here?"

We trudge after Lydia and Brynn down a set of soggy stairs made out of railroad ties.

"Police never check around here." Henry's fingers lightly graze the small of my back as he guides me down the dark path.

"It's like a scene out of *Duma Key*," I whisper. Our favorite Stephen King novel, one of his most obscure, is set alongside a creepy, forgotten shore. In one chapter that particularly terrified me, a red-hooded woman lures twin girls into the ocean surf to drown. I can still picture vividly the whitecaps foaming over the tops of their blond heads until the pair are so filled with water that they sink in unison down to the sandy seafloor.

"Only with less murder and mayhem," he replies.

"Fingers crossed."

We curve around. Underneath the pier I see a flicker of light. Then a full campfire swarming with bodies comes into view. The glow of the flames flicker across the faces of several kids I know from Duwamish. Three of them I recognize immediately from Henry's lacrosse team—Ty, Connor, and Brandon—I wonder why he didn't ride with them. Tess, a diehard devotee of Burberry headbands and tabloids, is draped over Brandon's lap, suggestively sucking on a lollipop while he watches, mesmerized.

I tense at the sight of her. She and Henry used to date

and I swear she's never liked me since. Not that the feeling isn't mutual.

A bass thumps softly from a portable stereo. Near the water's edge other kids skip rocks onto the glassy surface. I have to kick through scattered beer bottles to reach the bonfire at the center.

"Look who's here." Brynn throws her hands in the air and struts into the circle of those gathered at the fire. Warm flames cast shadows that mask the freckles on her face. She pauses and beckons for me to join her. "Miss Stella Cross, back from the dead and ready to attend her very first pier party. She's kindly requested that nobody ask her about . . . yanno . . . today. All other questions and requests may be honored on a case-by-case basis." She curtsies. "Carry on."

I don't know what I was expecting, but it's not as if anyone applauds when Brynn twirls me around. Instead, the conversation falls to a hush.

I stumble awkwardly out of our little pirouette. My hands hang limply at my sides while everyone stares at me like I'm from another planet.

There's the gentle crashing of waves onshore. Out of the corner of my eye, I notice a few of the other partygoers looking over in our direction with curiosity.

Unsure of how to proceed after my anticlimactic entrance, I slink to the perimeter.

Lydia grabs an unoccupied camping chair and Henry high-fives and backslaps his pals. Meanwhile, I hover. I've never even heard of a pier party. Since when is this a thing?

Finding me, Brynn comes over and latches onto my left arm. Her eyes glitter in the firelight. "Well?"

I bite the inside of my cheek. I still feel eyes on me. "Thanks," I say at last. "You know, for not treating me like a cancer patient."

Brynn opens her mouth as if to say something but apparently decides against it and, instead, makes her way over to the ice chest and blankets folded on the outer corner of the circle. She's never been the touchy-feely type. What else would you expect from a girl with six piercings by the age of seventeen?

She's loud and brash, more fiery than her muted auburn hair. In sum, she's life personified, while I wear the trappings of death around me like an invisible cloak. If she had her way, she'd prefer to ignore my illness—unless she's teasing me about being an invalid. In fact, I can't recall ever having a real conversation about it. Not even once.

I remember lying on the roof of her house where we used to go tan and telling her I might die. That was the last time she ever so much as acknowledged the possibility. But then again, she's never abandoned me. It's as if I'm there to ground her and she's there to infuse life into me. The yin to my yang.

I trail after her, as I do so often, and tug the edge of a blanket from the pile and lay it out on the dirt underneath the pier.

Before I can get my feet tucked cross-legged, Henry plops down on the quilt beside me.

"I'm glad you came," he says, staring at the smoke coiling up into the night air. Lydia's come up with a bag of marshmallows from the cooler and is passing them out while Ty searches for sticks.

I hold my palms out to warm them. "Told you I was fine." I bump my shoulder into his. "You don't have to always be my protector, you know." It's funny. I used to want to be protected.

He nods. "I know."

I watch as Tess takes a swig out of a flask and scoots off Brandon's lap. Clearly tipsy, she sways to the music in front of Brandon, toying with the hem of her shirt. The spectacle draws several guys into the vicinity, like mosquitoes to light. She tips her head back, long hair falling over her shoulder blades. Her belly button peeks out when she raises her hands over her head. I swallow. I could never dance like that in front of everyone.

Henry takes a deep breath, probably making a herculean effort to ignore Tess and her flat stomach. "So, anyway. I was wanting to talk to you about next Friday. I have two tickets to Action Hero Disco." His words pour out. "If, you know, you might want to go."

I register his question, but barely. Despite the carnival atmosphere going on around me, my attention is caught by movement in the distance, beyond the reach of the firelight. I raise myself up onto my knees and cup my hands over my eyes as a visor. "Did you see that? I think there's someone over there."

Henry leans forward, peering around me. "I don't see anything."

I strain to see a moment longer, worried that a homeless person is lurking at the edge of our group. Or worse, the cops.

"Stel?"

"Yeah, sorry," I respond idly, giving up. Must have been a raccoon or something.

"Concert tickets?"

"Really? I look at him sideways. "But you don't even like Action Hero Disco. How the hell did you get tickets?"

Brynn plunks down on the blanket beside Henry, balancing a charbroiled marshmallow on a stick. "Don't mind me." She winks at Henry.

I shift my weight.

Henry huffs and angles his body away from Brynn. "Hold on. I don't dislike them. I just hadn't listened to much of their music and—" He hunches forward to rest his elbows on his knees. "Matt had a couple tickets and asked me if I wanted them and I figured, why not?"

"Matt who?"

"Matt Akin."

"From cross-country?" I ask. Why's he so chummy with Matt Akin?

Brynn snorts and Henry glares back at her. "Jeez, Stella. Yes, from cross-country." His fingers curl around his knees and he rocks back. "Can you call off the interrogation now? Do you want to go or what?" I can't be sure, but I think Henry's holding his breath.

"Okay, okay, my bad. I was just asking." I nod once decisively. "Yes, I want to go. One thousand percent, I want to go." As if I'd miss a chance to see my favorite band.

A crooked smile creeps across Henry's face. "Really? Okay, cool." He glances at Brynn again, and I feel like a secret passes between them, a secret that leaves me out.

"It's at Neumos. We can figure out whatever else before then." He's talking too fast. It's kind of adorable, actually.

"Get a room," Brynn hoots.

This catches the attention of a couple of the boys seated by the fire. Connor chucks an empty aluminum can at Henry's head. My cheeks flush.

Brandon twists around. He gently prods Tess's leg to move her to the side so that he can see me. She teeters to her left and her locks brush across her face, sticking to her mascara. Her lips work themselves into a pout as she glares at Brandon.

"By the way, Stella." His words slur as he tilts the open flask precariously. "I was wondering, do you have, like, a pig heart now or something?" He flattens his nose into a snout, as if we all need a refresher course on our basic barn animals.

"Shut the fuck up, Brandon." Henry throws the can but misses. It clatters against a pile of rocks.

"Her tongue still works, doesn't it, Jones? Let her answer."

The gratitude I felt toward Henry only seconds earlier falters. Brandon may be an ass, but he's right. It's not Henry's job to speak for me, and besides, I'm sick of having so many handlers. I'm not a child star with a drug habit.

I clear my throat. I hate talking in front of groups. "Uh, no, just a regular one. All human."

"Damn. So some poor sap had to eat it before you could get cured?"

Henry grinds his teeth next to me.

"You're on thin ice, Delancey." Brynn points her finger at him.

"Basically," I say quietly.

"Brandon . . ." Tess raises her eyebrows as if she's been kept waiting. Now that she's not dancing, she's been orphaned, off-center from the group's attention. He ignores her.

"Shit." Connor pierces another marshmallow and holds

it over the fire. "You know anything about whoever's heart it is?"

"I'm sure she'd rather not think about it," Henry growls.

"That's not true," I jump in. "But no, I guess I don't. Know anything, I mean. The family asked not to be identified, so it'll have to remain a mystery." I inch closer to the fire, trying to fend off the dampness that's seeping into my vulnerable backside. A classmate cuts between Brandon and me on his way to the cooler and back.

"Come on," Brandon prods. "You must be curious about it. I mean, you literally have someone's heart beating inside you. What if he was, like, a psycho or something and it, I don't know, somehow infects your brain."

"You're an idiot." Lydia takes a break from blowing on a hot marshmallow.

I tug at the sleeves of my sweater. "Not sure that's how it works exactly," I say, attempting to sound nonchalant. "But yeah, of course. I think about it. Mainly I wish I could thank them." I try to brush off the line of questioning, but without wanting to be, I'm taken back to that night in the hospital bed, as I listened to Dr. Belkin tell my mom that my potential donor had died. My family never talks about my match. But that doesn't stop me from wondering.

"Survival of the fittest," Brandon muses, taking another long pull from the flask.

Tess's glower shifts to me. She narrows her eyes. "Well, at least you get to be the center of attention for once. That's got to be a pleasant side effect, right?" Her tone is sugary enough to give me diabetes.

I pull my knees into my chest. "I'm not sure what you

mean. There are a lot of side effects. I wouldn't call any of them pleasant."

"Oh, I mean just like the whole surgery thing, then the in-and-out-of-school dance, and now, well, of course the stunt in anatomy today."

My cheeks burn. "That wasn't—"

"No, no." She waves her hand as though I'm misunderstanding. "I totally get it. Go big or go home."

Henry stands up, brushing off the back of his jeans. "Let's go, Stella." He reaches down for me, but I push his hand away and stand up on my own. Is this what people think of me?

Brynn stands up and flanks me on the other side.

Tess cocks her head and flutters her long eyelashes. "After being gone so long, I mean, it makes total sense that you'd feel the need to act out. I think we all understand." She nods her head like a guidance counselor.

"*Act* out? There's no acting involved." My stomach clenches along with my fists. Just then a familiar head breaks through the ring. Harrison Miller has an easy gait as he walks to the cooler stuck in the sand nearby. He swings his arms as if he's never had a care in the world, smiling warmly, unthinkingly, at the faces he passes. The type of kid who's always class something—president, student council representative. This year it's treasurer.

At the sight of him, my mouth goes dry. I try to look down but it's too late. When he sees me, his eyes brighten. "Hey, Veronica," he says.

Brynn's and Henry's heads both snap toward me. "Veronica?"

"Veronica Leeds. She's new." He looks back at me. "We met in the hall. Remember?"

All at once, my night is going in for a crash landing. Unable to avoid him, I look up. My eyes sting like I just got out of a pool. "Hi, Harrison," I begin. I wonder if I look as different to everyone else as I must have to Harrison, whether my weight loss has been that dramatic, whether my eyes have sunken in as much as I think they have whenever I look into the mirror.

His forehead wrinkles. "Wait a minute. I know you. You're..." He snaps his fingers and, for some unknown reason, I wait for him to come up with the right answer. "Stella. Right? You've been out, but why—"

A snorting burst of laughter comes from behind him. Tess covers her mouth, giggling into her hand. "You gave him a fake *name*? That's so *weird* and *embarrassing*."

I struggle not to hurl on his shoes. Harrison just sort of shakes his head brusquely as though confused, then wanders away.

Brynn laces her fingers through mine and smiles sweetly at Tess. "Better than having a fake personality."

Tess snatches the flask out of Brandon's hand. "Why don't you go take a leap off the pier, Brynn? Go on, I dare you. Oh wait, didn't you already chicken out on that dare, like, months ago? Still scared?"

And just like that I'm invisible again. Forgotten. Brynn's warm hand drops mine as she steps toward Tess. "Oh, like you would even dip your toe in that water."

"What are they talking about?" I ask Henry.

"Brandon dared Brynn a few months ago to jump off the pier in her underwear."

Brandon smirks at the girls. "I'd actually be fine with any of you doing it. Rule one of the game: One cannot call out the daree, if the darer is not, in turn, willing to accept the dare."

"Because we're not morons," says Lydia.

"I'll pay you fifty bucks to do it." Brandon fishes for his wallet as if to prove that he's serious.

Lydia just glares at him.

"Chicken." Brandon snaps his wallet shut. The group's chatter dies down and we listen to the fire crackle. Connor rummages around the cooler for a fresh beverage.

"I'll do it," I say, surprising myself. I wait for a reaction, but everyone's gone silent, and before I know what I'm doing, I stand up and dust off the back of my jeans. "I'll do it. I'm serious."

Adrenaline pumps through my veins, coupled with a high-pitched ringing in my ears.

Ty's eyebrows spike up to his mop of blond hair. "Do what?"

"Jump off the pier." I tilt my chin and stare up at the warped planks, through which the light of faraway stars shines.

Henry's fingers wrap around my wrist. "Stella. Stop. It's dangerous. Not to mention freezing."

"I'm fine. How many times do I have to tell you?"

He drops his voice low. "You don't have to try to look cool in front of them. I don't care about any of that."

My muscles go rigid. Acid burns my throat. He thinks I'm worried about embarrassing *him*? I wrench my wrist free from his grip and look to Brynn for help. Gently, she touches Henry's arm and shakes her head.

I can't put into words exactly why I need to do it. All I know is this: I'm sick of being sick. And I'm even more sick of people treating me that way. I'm tired of being left on the sidelines while everyone else is busy living their lives. I promised myself I'd stop doing that. I promised myself I wouldn't be invisible.

I brush past Henry and start kicking off my shoes. For a brief moment, I think I see someone moving on the outskirts of our group again, but the movement's stilled by the time I pull off my sweater and am left stripped down to jeans and a flimsy black tank top.

"Holy crap, she's going to do it." Connor springs from his chair.

With the group following behind, I climb the railroad-tie stairs barefoot and tiptoe onto the pier. The wood is moist and rough underneath the soles of my feet. I run my hand along the railing as I walk farther out. Underneath the landing, we'd been protected from the wind, which now whips spray off the water and onto my face. I wipe it from my lashes and squint against the gusts. The breeze lifts the hair off the back of my neck and I stare down at the water as I walk. Frothy whitecaps dot the sea.

The voices of the group sound distant, carried off by the wind. When I reach the end of the dock, I hoist myself up on the railing and crawl over so that I'm standing on the opposite side. The drop is farther than I expected.

I look back. The whites of Brynn's eyes stand out against the night.

I'm an excellent swimmer. I have been since I was five, and teenagers have done things far more stupid than jumping off a pier at night. A list of all the things I've never done scrolls at rapid speed through my head.

Not anymore.

The swelling throb of my heart pounds inside me like dramatic background music that nobody else can hear.

Without another thought, I release my grip on the railing. The air rushes up to meet me. My stomach leaps into my throat. A shriek escapes just before I plunge into the ocean.

The cold water clenches around my chest. I open my eyes and stare up. The blackness is complete. My legs beat and my arms churn. I struggle upward.

My mouth breaks the surface in a loud, ugly gasp. I tilt my head back. Everyone is cheering and shaking their fists in the air. My teeth chatter uncontrollably as I tread water. Exhausted, I let my head fall below again and then bob back up.

Salt stings my eyes. I toss my head and then, underneath the pier, next to our campfire, I spot the outline of a person. In the smoke and shadows, he feels familiar and, although all I can make out is the silhouette, I have the unmistakable feeling that he's watching.

chapter six
100 BPM

After the lab incident—not to mention my leap from the pier—whispers follow me around school. They snake around me, cling to my clothes, and get tangled up in my hair. Stepping through them is like passing through a cloud of buzzing gnats; all I can do is keep my mouth shut and hope that none fly up my nostrils.

I'm making my way down the covered archway with Brynn. The morning fog has turned to drizzle, and the smell of wet grass and mud fills the air.

"Do you think she just snapped?" I hear someone murmur behind me. I fight the urge to look back.

"Were you there?" another voice responds.

I chew the inside of my cheek to keep from smiling. I know this isn't what one would call good publicity. But people *noticed* me.

Brynn must misread my worried cheek-chewing, because

she wraps her arm protectively over my backpack. "Jack-asses," she says loud enough for the culprits to hear.

"It's fine," I mutter, not wanting her to cause a scene. Scratch that. Not wanting her to *stop* the scene. It's as if I've turned a key and unlocked the secret chamber. *Click.* I've become visible again.

My hands tingle like they've been zapped with electricity. I'm buzzing with the same energy I used to feel poised on top of the dive stand. Goggles locked over my eyes, swim cap pointed toward the water.

Brynn unfurls her arm. Her blue-polished nails disappear into the pocket of her sweatshirt. "You have one public freak-out and all of a sudden you can't catch a break, am I right?"

I let out a soft snort. "I know. If I was on reality TV, that wouldn't even make the filler reel."

"My thoughts exactly. I mean, I think people should at least wait until you're running around naked before making a big deal out of it."

Brynn drops me off at Calc, where two girls are already sitting a row back. One of them is Tess, and with her elbow propped up on a desk and not a drop of makeup on her face, she must be nursing a wicked hangover. Can't say she doesn't deserve it.

I slide into my desk and begin copying down our teacher's notes from the whiteboard. From behind, clipped, tittering whispers reach me. I think they're talking about me. My shoulders tense. Being noticed is one thing, but if Tess Collars forgot I lived on this planet, I'd be totally okay with that.

I sit back in my chair to listen.

"Where do you think he's from?" I hear Caroline ask.

"How the hell should I know." Tess's voice is thick, as if someone's playing a recording of her in slow motion. "He just got here."

Definitely not talking about me. A flush rises in my cheeks. Since when did *I* become so egotistical?

"He might have just gone to public school before."

"Who cares?" Tess hisses. "As long as he's at least passably attractive. I could use some new scenery around here."

"He's more than passable," Caroline confirms. "And he must have money, too, if his parents got him in this late in the year."

So, there's a new kid in our class. And apparently he's quite dashing. Already a bigger conversation-starter than I am. Mr. Conway stands up and asks everyone to pass up their assignments from last night. It's sort of strange to be starting at a new school partway through senior year, though. Did he get in trouble? That has to be it. After spending a few minutes pondering what dark past our new classmate must be harboring (drugs, probably, I decide), I go back to trying to listen to Mr. Conway explain limits and continuity, but mostly I just watch the rain outside.

I'm startled out of my reverie by the sound of the door slamming. My elbow nearly falls off the edge and I sit up with a jolt.

"Shut up. He's in our class," Caroline says a bit too loudly.

"He sure is," Tess whispers. "Somebody hand me a camera, because this suddenly became a room with a view."

I pivot in my seat. There's a boy. An oh-my-god-gorgeous boy. He takes long strides in a pair of faded blue Converse, laces untied—and not uniform-sanctioned—to the front of the room, where he hands Mr. Conway a yellow slip of paper.

The sight of him makes me asthmatic. In a good way I didn't know was possible. There's a distinct tightening of the chest, like I'm battling the effects of a peanut allergy.

"Sorry I'm late. Some confusion at the front office," he says. Mr. Conway slides his reading glasses up to the bridge of his nose.

"Welcome, Mr. . . ." Conway holds the slip closer.

"Zin," he offers. "Levi Zin, sir."

Thick dark eyebrows frame his almond-shaped eyes, half-covered by slick black hair that hangs low over his forehead. He's clinging to an end-of-summer tan that hints at liquid sunshine and honey dripping off the comb. A damp polo sticks to his chest. I find myself wanting him to look at me so that I can grasp the whole picture at once. I have an idea that the full effect can't live up to the bits and pieces I've been cobbling together through sideways glimpses.

I lean forward on my elbows, hoping that I'm not too obvious, but not willing to be more discreet. One look, I tell him with my mind. A stray, stupid thought I'm sure I wouldn't have if I wasn't so completely bored in class, but for now, it feels like a game. Notice me, I tell him.

"Please, take a seat. We're on section five." Mr. Conway gestures to an empty seat in the front row.

Levi turns, slipping his backpack off one shoulder. For a split second our eyes meet, and in that moment it's like two streaks of lightning converge in the sky. My heart leaps out of my throat and firmly attaches itself to him and I have a fleeting sensation that he read my mind.

He noticed.

chapter seven
105 BPM

"I heard he's dreamy," says Brynn, mouth stuffed full of Cool Ranch Doritos.

It's just Brynn, Henry, and me at lunch today since Lydia's switched over to her other group. It's stopped raining for a second, which means the cafeteria is only half as crowded as usual. I suppose we should be taking advantage of the "nice" weather in the quadrangle, too, only I guess I'm not as keen as the rest of my class to walk around the rest of the day with the back of my khakis soaked through. After all, it's still Seattle. Just because it's not raining doesn't mean it's not wet.

"Okay, hold up. Do people say 'dreamy' anymore?" I ask while Henry makes a big show of pretending to beat his skull against the lunch table. "Drama. Queen." I poke him in the shoulder. "Cut it out before your forehead smells like ketchup and cheese fries."

"They do when they're talking about Levi Zin," says Brynn, arching her eyebrows. "He's brought dreamy back."

Zin. Levi Zin. I roll the name over on my tongue. It has a nice ring to it. "He's okay," I say, staring down at the table and suddenly having an I-saw-him-first moment.

Brynn narrows her eyes. "You little liar!" She chucks a Dorito that I manage to bat away. "You totally want to jump his bones, don't you?"

"Brynn, please." I stuff a bite of peanut-butter-and-jelly sandwich in my mouth to avoid answering her question..

She lifts one pierced eyebrow and crunches through another chip. "I'll take *that* as a yes."

The back of my neck is on fire. It's not as if Levi would be a bad first choice.

"You're totally picturing it in your head." I jump when I realize she's been staring at me.

"Am not." I frown while at the same time deliberately avoiding eye contact with Henry. "Why do you have to"—I want to say *be so crude* but instead say—"make such a big deal about it?"

She rolls her eyes. "I wasn't. If I were trying to make a big deal out of it, I would have said you want to—"

But before she can finish Henry jumps in. "Enough! It's not like Channing Tatum came to school. Can we please talk about something else? Please? Something of *mutual* interest, maybe?"

"Touchy, touchy," Brynn chides. "Jealous much?"

"Please. I'm just not quite as interested in the state of Levi's pectorals as you seem to be."

"Then maybe you shouldn't sit with a bunch of girls at lunch all the time. Ever think of that?" counters Brynn.

Henry rolls his eyes. The truth is that Henry has a bunch of guy friends, but all of them have the lunch period before us, so he's stuck. Except I think that he actually likes it. Either that or he likes me.

I feel my face go white. Well, first white. Then there is the burning rush of what must be bright, fluorescent pink as my neck and ears feel as if they've been shoved inside a microwave.

"Shit, Stella. What? You look like you're about to hurl." Brynn looks at me and then follows my gaze up to none other than Levi-of-the-amazing-pectorals Zin. And he's standing right beside the empty lunch table next to ours with a lunch tray full of mini-carton milk, pizza, and two apples, smiling at us. "Oh, crap," says Brynn, not in a whisper.

I force my face into something I sincerely hope captures a nonchalant-hipster-meets-Parisian-snob vibe, although I'm stuck with a sneaking suspicion that I look as soppy as I feel. His beautiful brown eyes narrow to a squint. He's squinting at me and I'm thinking, What does that mean? . . . until it dawns on me that there's no way it can be good when a guy squints at you, can there? This runs through my head all the while we're locked in a grin-off until finally, he sits down at the other table and opens up his carton of milk. I let out a huge sigh of relief.

"Um, what was that?" Brynn asks in a hushed voice, leaning over on her elbows.

"What do you mean, what was that?" I snap. "I had to cover for your big mouth." I can't shake the sense that looking at Levi brings on a very specific feeling of déjà vu.

Brynn chances a glance in Levi's direction. "Well, you looked like a snaggletoothed tiger."

Henry laughs and I glare at him. "Sorry." He wipes tears from his eyes. "Sorry." Henry sniffles. "I mean, you did, a little."

"Shut. Up," I giggle, feeling flushed with embarrassment all over again. "And it's *saber*-toothed tiger, you idiots."

"Ohhh." Brynn holds her palms up like she's scared. "Somebody's feeling feisty."

"It's your fault." I glare at her, only half-jokingly.

"Hey, I'm not the spazoid."

I rest my chin on my fist.

"It wasn't that bad," adds Henry. "And also, who cares what he thinks?" Probably every girl in the senior class, I could tell him, but that would be like telling a five-year-old not to believe in Santa Claus.

"I've heard he's a trust-fund kid," Brynn says, making me feel as though the entire school had been involved in a game of telephone.

"You know, he can probably hear you," I hiss. But in truth, he probably doesn't, because Tess and Caroline are on their way over to his table right now in that hip-swinging way that screams *Look at me*, and, to my deep disappointment, it seems to be totally, completely working.

"Incoming," says Brynn.

Since last period, Tess has undergone a miraculous makeover. The lingering signs of her hangover have been replaced by pink lips, sparkly blush, and a fresh layer of gold-flecked eye shadow. At the next table over, she's so close to me I can smell the floral perfume wafting off her skin.

From where I'm sitting, I can only hear Tess and Caroline clearly. They exchange pleasantries, with Tess acting like she's the cruise ship director of the school.

"Ten bucks one of them sleeps with him before the end of the week." Brynn pops another Dorito into her mouth and licks the orange dust off her fingers.

I whip my head around. "What? Why? Why would you say that?"

She jerks her chin back. "Um, have you seen the welcoming committee over there? Here's your student-body handbook, a plate of fresh-baked cookies, and a box of condoms."

"My money's on Tess," Henry says.

I feel a spike in my temperature. "Well, you would know."

Henry freezes mid-bite into a cheeseburger. "What's that supposed to mean?"

I'd never asked whether Henry slept with Tess when they were dating and he'd never volunteered it, so if I had to guess, it would be a firm yes, that totally happened. And now the sight of her falling over Levi is enough to make me need a Xanax.

Maybe the better question is, Why do I care so much? It was almost imperceptible, something I could only notice in the absence of a thing rather than in its presence, but as soon as Levi sat near us, I felt a weight lifting from my chest.

The constant ache that has been gnawing at me for weeks slipped away and I felt a peace in my bones that had gone missing.

Henry and Brynn are talking, but I'm barely listening. I nod. Henry's annoyed with me. I try to care, but is it just me or is Levi sneaking glances this way?

"Why don't you just pee on him, Stella? That would be less obvious."

"Shut. Up," I say, and without meaning to, I slam my

fist on the table. I should apologize, but I still can't focus enough to do it.

Brynn slides her books off the table into her bag. "Come on, Henry. Stella's clearly having some issues of the feminine variety."

I scowl at her with no worthy comeback. Henry pushes his chair back and fixes me with a look that seems more pitying than angry. "Stella, we're all willing to give you a bit of a pass, but—"

"Don't."

"Don't what?"

"Don't give me a free pass. I'm fine." Then, in a lower voice. "Look, I'm sorry. Brynn, are we still on for after school?"

She peers down her nose at me. "Yeah, just leave the attitude at home, where it belongs, okay?"

I attempt a feeble smile, but when I return my attention to Levi, certain that now that I'm alone, he'll perhaps venture a smile or a wave or come over to chat, I see that he's already following Tess out the door. My heart butts painfully against my rib cage in protest.

chapter eight
104 BPM

Whoever said child labor was banned in the first world forgot to tell my parents.

I hoist a top-of-the-line stroller, aka baby tank, out the side of my Jetta. The wheel crashes into my big toe and I hop around the parking lot on one foot. "Ouch! Jesus Christ!"

Elsie giggles and slaps her hands on the sides of her car seat. "Uh-oh!"

I scowl at her through the open window.

"If you spit up on my leather, I swear I'll leave you here to rot," I warn my sister, who throws her sippy cup onto the car floor in response.

I study the stroller. Who are these designed for, rocket scientists? Peering underneath the carriage, I think I spot the problem and kick at its back to try to unlock the folding mechanism. Eventually, it comes loose and the stroller snaps open.

"You make that look so easy," comes a sarcastic voice from behind me. "Didn't know you were bringing a friend."

I wipe my forehead, pushing the stroller around to the other side of the car. Brynn sips a Frappuccino.

"My parents have an interview at some fancy preschool they're trying to get Elsie on the waiting list for. Good thing they have a free babysitter on speed dial." I unhook Elsie from her car seat and straddle her over my hip. She's sporting a newly laundered ladybug dress, given that she managed to slobber all over the jumper Mom had her in beforehand. Elsie's the reason we're running late. Brynn better keep this quick.

Brynn shudders. "Thank God *my* parents never get it on anymore."

I lower Elsie into the stroller. "I'm sure you're all the birth control they need."

The streets are crowded as Brynn and I start to trudge up the steep hill toward the giant golden hog statue with red lettering that reads PIKE PLACE MARKET. A salty breeze carries the smell of the ocean off Elliott Bay.

"You know where we're going?" I ask. The wheels of the stroller bounce off burgundy bricks.

"We have to make a stop here every year before my mom's birthday. She goes crazy for these pistachio macarons at Le Panier. Seriously, it's like soccer mom crack." Brynn smirks.

Poor Mrs. McDaniel. She's got all the components of a grade-A soccer mom. The cream cable-knit, the pearls, the perfectly symmetrical orange slices. Only problem? Her daughter is Brynn.

I chase after Brynn, who's walking too fast. A group of tourists snap photos outside the market, and all around, vendors dart in and out of the covered arcades selling fresh produce, pencil sketches, and I ♥ SEATTLE T-shirts. We thread our way through the crowd and I try not to mow over the backs of anyone's heels with the Elsie Mobile.

"One year my dad couldn't get off work in time to get them and, no joke, she almost bit his entire head off," Brynn explains.

"Well, she didn't have a macaron," I point out.

"Apparently, the South Beach Diet has a very narrow exception for small, ridiculous-looking cookies."

She guides us past the seafood stalls where tattooed men in grimy aprons sling fish over the counters, and I narrowly miss getting slapped across the face by a flying silver-finned tuna.

I'm relieved when we find ourselves walking alongside the glassy storefronts. We pass a half dozen or so before Brynn spots the black-and-yellow sign marking Le Panier Very French Bakery.

A tiny bell jingles above the door as we enter. Turns out we're not the only ones with this idea—the tiny bakery's stuffed fuller than a jelly doughnut. And no wonder. The aroma's nothing short of heavenly, a mixture of the scent of freshly baked croissants, sugar glaze, and a wood-burning oven.

Brynn wedges her way in between a fat man in a suit and a woman yelling into a cell phone on her way up to the counter, while I wield the stroller as a bumper car. Brynn waves her arm erratically, trying to get the clerk's attention. "McDaniel," she shouts over the bakery's hustle and bustle. "Order for McDaniel. Over here!" I maneuver next to her. "I called ahead," she says. "Shouldn't take long."

"Cookie," Elsie says, pointing up from her stroller at the broad assortment of pastries and, yes, cookies in the display case. Her fingers smudge the glass over a waistline-busting moon pie.

"No, Elsie," I tell her firmly, pushing down her chubby arm. "Not before dinner." The thought of a one-year-old on a sugar rush is enough to make me want to grab Brynn and hightail it out of here.

Not to mention—I check my watch—it's already four thirty.

"Hello!" Brynn jumps up and down, flailing her arms. "McDaniel for pickup. Anybody?" She pushes to the cashier and leans over to talk to a girl with flour dashed over her cheeks and a matching white cap on. The girl disappears into the back but returns shaking her head.

Brynn turns to me, throwing her hands up in the air. "They lost my order."

A woman in high heels balancing a cake box bumps into me, nearly tripping over one of the stroller wheels. I catch her elbow right before she topples over. "Sorry about that," I mutter. She casts me a dirty look over her Le Panier box. "I think I better wait over there," I tell Brynn, retreating to the front of the store with the stroller.

With luck, I manage to find a chair and try my best to stay out of the way. Elsie's still demanding that cookie and seems to think that she can ask anyone and everyone who passes by with a bakery bag, "Cookie?" Of course, she knows all of ten words, and *cookie* has to be one of them. The girl has her priorities straight.

I watch Brynn gesticulate at the cashier and then prop herself up on the counter and peer over it. Typical Brynn.

"Hi!" I'm startled by Elsie's increase in volume. "Hi," she squeals again. Her hand stretches out and I follow her reach.

In the crowd of people all pushing toward the counter, I spot a single eye peeking out from behind two teenagers murmuring into one another's ears. The eye blinks, then disappears behind the young couple. I lean for a better view and think I spot a swatch of dark brown hair. That was . . . I think, biting my lip. But, no, it can't be.

"Got them." Brynn appears, brandishing a red bag. "Must have mixed up the names. You'd have thought I was trying to leave with a national treasure. Shall we?"

I chance one last glance at the wall of customers and follow Brynn outside. "Let's shop fast," I tell her. "I need to get home."

"Before you turn into a pumpkin?"

"Something like that."

Elsie cries only a little once the bakery is out of sight, at which point she realizes there won't be any cookie today. After that she seems to forget—one of the big pluses of being one.

I take deep breaths in the open air as I follow Brynn. There's no place better for people watching than Pike Place. When I was younger, my dad would take me to the market. I remember he'd lift me up and let me touch all the fruit and veggies until I found the ripest ones. We'd watch the show at City Fish Co. and he'd let me get ice cream—a vanilla/chocolate swirl cone. Then we'd bring our finds back to Mom, most of which we didn't really need, and she'd concoct some sort of creative dish for dinner. I, of course, had the most important part, since I'd done all the finding.

I know it's been years, but somehow you never expect your family to change.

Brynn and I amble past the produce and all the other fresh-food stands to the section of the market where vendors sell handcrafted jewelry. I can't help but sneak glimpses over my shoulder, but after a few quick scans, I join Brynn's hunt, slipping on a few bauble rings with fake gems and a leopard-print scarf for good measure.

Nothing's catching my eye. Except for the time. How did it get away from me? My phone reads five o'clock.

"Are you ready?" I ask, tapping my toe to let Brynn know she's taking forever.

She holds up two barbs, one blue and one hot pink. "Which one?" She holds each up to her ear.

I huff. "Who cares? They're rods you stick through your flesh, Brynn."

"I can't decide." She ducks so that she can better see her reflection. The number of people is starting to feel overwhelming. I check the time again, and my knuckles go white around the handles of the baby stroller.

"Brynn?" I try to say as evenly as possible. "Do you mind watching Elsie for a sec? I need to find a restroom."

She nods, tilting her face one direction then the other to study her reflection. I can feel the seconds tick by.

"Watch her, please!" I call over my shoulder. I hate to trust Brynn with my sister, if only because my parents would kill me if something happened.

Stepping outside, I follow a path along the bricks toward the waterfront. Maybe the breeze will help. I'm already flushed. I spot the bay through a gap in the shops. My neck's sticky and I stagger to the railing that separates the market from the sea below. I take a deep breath of ocean air and slump onto a stone bench. Why does this happen to me? And why won't it stop?

Salt sticks to my cheeks. The breeze sweeps across the water, whipping my ponytail into my face. I peel it back and pull out my cell. I watch as the digital lines on my clock arrange themselves into different numbers. A one becomes a four that becomes a six. My muscles are tense and alert, as if being ready will change anything. I'm alone out here. Away from the human traffic of Pike Place.

Five oh eight.

I shut my eyes. Maybe today it won't come. Maybe today it's different.

But I'm only halfway through the thought when it begins. Small at first. I wonder, for an instant, if I can ignore it. But it grows.

My heart abruptly squeezes like a sponge being wrung dry.

The shock of the compression doubles me over and sweat springs up on my neck. The pain is minor at first. Tricky. Slight but still enough to allow me to lie to myself. This will be it. This isn't so bad. I can deal with this much. Even this much, I bargain.

But it grows, and before I know it someone has lit a sparkler inside me.

I imagine my brain on a CT scan exploding with color. Pain everywhere. I bite into my fist and crumple into the fetal position.

Then, before the pain reaches its crescendo, it disappears all at once. "Stella?" The voice is boyish. Clear. "Stella?"

The pain is gone so fast it seems it was never there. Someone pats my face and it's as if I've been saved. "Are you okay?"

My eyelids flutter open. I blink once, twice, and stare up at what should be the gray sky.

"Can you hear me?"

Dark, almond eyes stare down at me. He cradles my head in his lap and wipes sweat from my forehead. I can hardly believe the clean, smooth feeling in my chest.

"Levi?" I can't believe I just said that. He'll think I'm a stalker.

He chuckles. "Good, you know who I am. I was worried you'd think I was some bum off the streets."

I stare at him blankly. Words, Stella. Any word will do. Say something. Anything, I plead with myself.

"Um, yeah, calculus," I say, crawling upright. Brilliant, Stel.

His smile, though, is megawatt. "Yeah, I noticed you in there." There's a tiny bead of water hanging from a tuft of hair on his forehead, like he must have walked through pouring rain earlier today or arrived from a photo shoot under a waterfall. Meanwhile, I probably have mascara smudged underneath my eyes and the stringy hair of a wet shih tzu.

"What are you doing here?" I ask.

He raises an eyebrow. "I'm rescuing you. Do you have a habit of shrieking and passing out on public benches?" I don't remember making any noise at all.

"Low blood sugar," I lie. "Started feeling faint and then—"

"Then I saw you lying here white as a sheet and panicked." He shakes his head and stares out at Elliott Bay. "I was about to call the damn coast guard."

"Seems like a lot of people for one girl," I say dryly.

"Well..." He winks. "You gave me a scare, Cross."

I squint at the glare from the clouds. He knows my last name, too? He hands me my purse and my wallet, which had slipped out. My hopes take a nosedive.

I swallow hard. He must know the effect he has on girls, right? "So." Unsure of what to do, I figure I ought to at least make conversation.

"If you don't mind me asking, what brings you to Duwamish after the start of senior year? Can't exactly be the easiest time to switch schools."

He bends his head down, wrinkling his forehead. "You sure you're okay? That looked pretty serious. Can I—?"

I wave him off. "I'm fine." And it's the truth. I actually feel perfectly well. Amazing even. "School?"

He narrows his eyes and lets his gaze linger on my face another moment before continuing. "Bit of a life change, you could say."

I play with my shoelaces. "Is that code for 'got expelled'?" I ask before I can stop myself.

"No, it's not code for 'got expelled.'" He runs his hands through his hair. That had to be him in the bakery, I realize, but, if so, why did he hide? "Be honest. Is that what everyone thinks?"

"I'd say roughly seventy percent."

This time he actually laughs. "Super."

A seagull swoops in close and pecks at some chips scattered on the ground. I try to focus on that instead of how close I'm sitting to Levi Zin. Just being next to him makes me feel like spilled grape juice on white carpet.

"You're not exactly answering my question," I point out. He looks straight at me, his mouth pinched to the side. "Well, I *have* known you for approximately three minutes, Stella Cross."

"I—I'm sorry. I didn't mean to pry. I just—"

He cracks his knuckles using the side of his knee. "That's okay. Let's just say not everything or everyone can last forever." He picks a pebble off the ground and tosses it into the bay.

I nod, biting my lip to keep myself from asking yet another question and then, because my brain has to know the answer to everything, I mentally recategorize Levi from troubled dropout to a kid grieving the loss of someone close to him. I fight the urge to reach out and give him a hug.

"So, do you like it so far?"

He hums at a level that's almost inaudible—a sexy baritone. The tune is familiar but I can't place it. "Could be worse. I had friends at my old school. You know, guys I grew up with since elementary. I don't exactly love the idea of jumping into that dynamic somewhere else, I guess."

"I know the feeling," I say without thinking.

Levi cocks his head. "Are you new also?"

I shake my head quickly. "No, but I had to take some time off—and, I don't know, it's hard to get plugged back in."

He lets a few moments slide past in silence. "Mono?"

I let out a breathy laugh. "Something like that."

"I feel like there's something you're not telling me." I know that he's teasing, but the intensity of his stare still makes my toes curl.

"Well, I *have* known you approximately three minutes,

Zin," I reply. The contents of my stomach perform rhythmic gymnastics.

Something passes over Levi's face. Sadness? Anger? It's a flash of an expression that leaves an imprint like the white spots beneath your eyelids the moment after a photo's been taken. One moment, that's it, and then it's gone. "Do you want to go out Friday night?" he asks.

It's a good thing I'm sitting down.

I find Brynn leaned up against my Jetta with a big wet stain stretching from her collarbone to the top of her bra. I grimace. Three guesses how she got it.

"Do I look like a thirteen-year-old girl with no job and braces?" she demands, fists rammed into her hips. "I am *not* your babysitter." She tosses the car keys at me. "You left them in the stroller pouch. Your little devil is inside. Enjoy."

"Wait!" I all but shout at her. The thought of having to keep this inside for even one more moment will kill me. "I have a good excuse. Promise."

She halts her revolution and lifts the pierced eyebrow.

I'm sure my face is bright red, but I feel it turn maroon as I say, "Two words, Brynn: Levi Zin."

"I'm listening."

I hop onto the trunk of my car and put my head in my hands, ruffling my hair because I still can't believe it. "He asked me out! He asked *me* out."

"Where the hell did you go? I thought you went to the bathroom."

"I, uh, I ran into him. On the way." I'm not ready to share the whole story. I don't want anyone else knowing that I'm not one hundred percent better. Not yet anyway.

"He asked you out?" she says, as if finally registering it. Then she smirks. "On the way to the bathroom?"

"Shut up." I wrap a strand of black hair around my finger and twirl. I'd forgotten what it felt like to talk about normal girl things. News other than what my iron levels were and how I was feeling that week. "He asked me out," I repeat. "But it'd be okay to tone down the surprise just a hair."

"Sorry. No, I mean why wouldn't he?" She rolls her eyes. "Come on, you know that's not how I meant it."

"I know, I know." I peer through the back windshield to check on Elsie. Thankfully, she seems to be engrossed in a serious chat with her stuffed penguin, Mr. P.

"So, details, please!"

"We're going out Friday night." Brynn sucks in a mouthful of air. "What?" I ask, suspicious.

"I hate to break it to you, but that's the night you're going to the concert with Henry."

Her statement takes a moment to sink in, and when it does, I groan. "Ugh, you're right," I say, smacking my forehead with my open palm. "How could I have forgotten?"

"I have a few guesses."

"What do I do, Brynn?"

"Do you really need me to tell you?"

I glare at her and jut out my lower lip. "No."

"It's Henry, Stel. You can't blow him off." Yes, it's Henry, I want to say, but what does that mean? "If you still feel this way after the concert, then—"

"Then you're implying it's a date with Henry, when I don't think that's the case."

"Don't be an idiot. It's a date and you knew it when you agreed. You can take your naive ingenue routine elsewhere, thank you very much." Brynn unfolds her arms and takes pity on my pouting face. "Look, Levi asked you out once. I'm sure he'll ask you out again."

"Not if someone else gets there first." I pout. He's only just started at Duwamish. Running into him out here was pure luck.

Wasn't it?

And what happens when he realizes I'm not the most popular girl at school. Or the prettiest?

"Come on." Brynn shoves my shoulder playfully. "They have nothing on you." But she's only being nice.

"Since when did you become the moral police?" I huff.

"Please, I'm an angel." At that, I laugh out loud, because there's nothing angelic about Brynn McDaniel. "You should have just told Henry you weren't interested, Stel."

Through the back windshield, I see that Elsie is now beating Mr. P's head against the seat. "But I'm not *not* interested." The truth is, I was excited when Henry asked me out before my surgery, but the last thing I wanted was some sick-girl pity party. And worse, what if I hadn't survived? Then Henry would have been forced to mourn my death for, like, fourteen months as the sad, dutiful boyfriend of three and a half days? Not on my watch. "I liked him before ... you know ... and I'll probably like him again. I'm just, I don't know, I met Levi and—"

"Sparks?"

Sparks, an inferno, take your pick. I sigh. "It's complicated." I tap the glass and for a second Elsie pauses in her quest to beat the cotton stuffing out of her penguin's head.

"It's not a fucking mathematical equation," Brynn says.

Elsie stares up at me. Her tiny lower lip is starting to get wet and slimy, the way it does right before a good, solid cry. I've only got a minute before the real screaming starts. This wouldn't be half as difficult if I didn't want to shove my tongue in Levi's mouth every time I laid eyes on him.

"Fine, I'll cancel my date with Levi, okay?"

Brynn pinches my cheeks. "Look at you, heart of gold."

I think of Levi's throaty baritone voice, the sound the tips of his shoelaces made on the pavement, and the way I wanted to reach up and smooth his rumpled collar. My chest seizes with something almost like anger at the idea of not seeing him on Friday. I don't know about my old heart, but this one is anything but gold.

chapter nine
117 BPM

"Turns out I can't go Friday."

This is officially my third out-of-body experience this month. What's wrong with me?

The corners of his mouth turn down and he manages to look perfectly adorable. My heart twists painfully, like it might be wrenched free of its arteries. I hadn't known I'd feel this guilty.

"You're canceling? Why?" There's a quick twitch that wrinkles his forehead near the brow bone. A glance down to his lap and then back up to me.

"No!" I jump in. "I mean yes, but not because I want to. To cancel on you, I mean." I take a deep breath. "I don't want to cancel on you, but I am canceling on you, so yes. Sorry, these plans were made before, so yeah, that's what I'm doing." Cool, desperate, cool, desperate. Get a grip, Stella.

"It's okay," he says, in a way that makes it seem like I've

made plans to drown kittens on Friday instead. He swirls one French fry around in a puddle of ketchup and meets my eyes again. This time he holds my gaze. "Stella, you could have just said no, you know. I'm a big boy."

"It's not like that," I protest, leaning forward, my hand on his knee. I glance down, wondering how I had the guts to pull that off. It was instinct, and now that I'm touching him, I only want to move closer. Tentatively, I inch my chair toward his. He looks down at the hand and his Adam's apple spikes. "I—it's not like that, Levi." My face is hot. Electricity courses through me.

"Then what is it like, Stella?" Levi slips his hand under the table and plays with my fingers. Parts of me wake up, like he's touching the keys on a piano.

I sigh, glancing at Henry, who's dabbing mustard off his chin. "It's just that my friend Henry got us tickets to see Action Hero Disco that night."

"Damn," he says under his breath. "He's got good taste at least."

"Henry doesn't really like them but he knew I loved them and somebody had tickets or something. *You* like Action Hero Disco?"

He drops his chin as if to say, Duh. Levi leans over to get a better look at Henry. "Your friend, huh?"

It takes me a moment to process that upward lilt in his voice at the end. The skeptical *huh*.

"No! Seriously. Friend. I've known him for ages." It's only once the words are out that I realize how much I've made up my mind. I want Levi.

I squirm against the cold plastic. Inside, I feel my heart wrenching again toward Levi, and a small part of me mourns the loss of what Henry and I might have been—no, still could be—if I wasn't here trying to convince the boy in front of me that I'm totally and completely unattached. But it's too late. I already left the old Stella standing on top of that pier.

I want Levi so badly to like me. And I barely know him.

"Just friends," I repeat.

He nods and then slides, without a word, out of his seat. I watch him—my mouth hanging open like a saltwater trout—as he crosses the short distance to my usual lunch table. Henry's got his earbuds in and he's bobbing his head along to some music while jotting down notes in the margin of his textbook.

Levi sits down in an empty seat next to him and gently taps his shoulder. Henry's shoulders jolt up toward his ears and he yanks the headphones down.

The cafeteria's in full lunchtime roar and I can't hear what they're saying. Brynn looks over at me and I shrug. *No idea,* I say to her telepathically.

Levi's gesticulating and Henry nods along, a blank expression on his face. I look on, contorted in my seat, elbow hiked over the back of my chair, unsure of what I'm watching, but dying to know the outcome.

After a couple of minutes have passed, Levi reaches into his back pocket and digs out a black leather wallet. He thumps Henry on the back, shakes his hand, and makes his way back to where I'm sitting, a huge grin on his face that makes me want to hold my arms open wide to welcome him back. My throat feels tight and there's an unexpected aching in my chest, the way a patient might feel sore after a particularly invasive surgery. I bury the idea, and besides, it starts to disintegrate with every step closer that Levi takes.

"You look pleased with yourself," I say, eyeing him curiously.

The sleeves of his polo get tighter around his biceps as he leans forward to rest his elbows on his knees. "Stella Cross." His head tilts. "Would you like to go to Action Hero Disco with me?"

"But..." I try to pluck the right words from the dozens rattling around inside my skull and finally settle on "But what about Henry?"

"You're friends. Can't you just hang out another night?" His voice prods and pokes at me. I want to go with Levi. I want to. I want to. I want to. The way I feel about him is so different from the way I feel about Henry.

"Yeah," I say, timid as a rabbit. I try to avoid the other lunch table, but I can't help but notice Henry hunched over, more focused than usual on a textbook.

"Well"—he leans back and crosses his arms over his chest—"proper dates happen on proper date nights, Cross. And, here's the thing..." He whispers this, and I feel myself leaning closer. "I didn't think I could wait any longer than Friday to take you out. Is that okay with you?"

My heart feels so full it might explode. A dozen helium balloons float up in my chest. "Of course it's okay," I respond. "I just—"

Levi jumps in before I can finish. "Besides, Henry was totally cool with it when he heard that I'm a huge fan too. You're right. They're not his favorite. He just wanted to make sure you got to go. Great guy, by the way. I'll pick you up at eight."

He couldn't wait any longer to take me out? He paid Henry just to be able to take me? Until now, I'd thought swooning was something only chicks in Jane Austen novels did when their corsets were laced too tight. At least I hope that's the reason I'm having trouble breathing. Because it's either that or the fact that I just betrayed Henry.

I check my watch. One thirty-three.

Brynn texted me in class: *Meet me in the bathroom at 1:35.* I'd tried to slide out of my seat unnoticed so that I could quietly excuse myself to use the restroom, but on my way out, my eyes locked with Levi's. As soon as the door shut, my heart began to throb and hasn't stopped. My standard meeting place with Brynn is the bathroom behind the portables, the ones that nobody uses. Even the potheads gave up on it, since the school-assigned detective started doing random checks. It's been a while since we had a class-time rendezvous, come to think of it. Definitely pre-surgery.

I take quick strides across the soggy lawn over to the brown, freestanding buildings on the east side of campus and slip into the girls' bathroom. I'm already eager to return to Levi. At least to have eyes on him. Crazy, I know.

Brynn's not here and the restroom's filled with the kind of silence that buzzes in your ears. The air smells sickly sweet, like that of a well-kept Port-a-Potty with those little blue discs that dissolve in the water and look perpetually slimy.

I lean over the sink to wash my hands, one of the many things I'm supposed to do countless times a day to keep my heart in working order. I pump the soap and lather when, without warning, the lights flip off. A spark and then total darkness. Instinctively, I feel my eyes grow wider.

I turn off the faucet. "Hello?"

No answer. I hold one hand in front of my face and wave it around. Can't see it in the mirror. Damn.

I hate the dark. I've always hated the dark. Even at seventeen, I sleep with a night-light. Embarrassing, but true.

Here, not even a sliver of outside light penetrates. Something about the inability to see makes me want to stay still. And so I do. Frozen in place, I listen to the sound of my own breathing.

That's when the scratching starts. It starts out small. As if a raccoon's raking its claws against one of the corner floorboards. Quick, short scrapes, one after another.

I strain to listen. My eyeballs turn in the direction of the noise without the rest of my body moving. The sound grows. Only a little at first. Like another set of claws has joined the first.

I feel a pinprick tingle slide from the small of my back clear up to the base of my skull.

More scratching. Clawing takes over an entire wall now. Long scores of nails against wood. A chorus.

I plug my ears.

Unmistakably, I can sense someone else in the space, as if the air in the bathroom has shrunk. Only I didn't hear the door open.

More grazing, tearing, scrabbling.

Could someone have already been in here? I didn't check but didn't think so.

Amidst the scratching, a shuffle—faint.

Or I think I hear one.

The hairs on my arms defy gravity. My heart flops around, whacking my insides.

Another shuffle across the tile. Can't tell from where.

"Who's there?" My voice rasps.

I can't get myself to turn around. To move. The scraping only escalates. From the floor up to the ceiling all around me. And I can feel someone there with me.

Unshakable.

The nerves in my legs beg me to run. Instead my feet are planted to the floor as if fear is a glue that has seeped into the very soles of my shoes. My heart beats faster and faster, the pace hammering so that I think whoever's out there must hear it knocking.

On three, I'll run, I tell myself. My legs shake. I shut my eyes.

One. Breath rattles. Two.

All at once, the clawing stops. My eyelids fly open. Lights snap on. Eyelashes flutter to adjust.

Blood rushes against my eardrums. I catch myself in the mirror and scream. There's a figure at my right shoulder, hovering behind me.

I whirl around, and it's gone. Vanished.

Without a word, the door to the bathroom opens and closes. A whoosh and I wait, heaving.

Inhale, exhale, inhale.

Next there's a loud bang that forces a squeal out of me and I spring to my feet.

"Stel?" I hear.

My muscles go rigid. *"Brynn?"*

Thoughts swirl in my mind—what did I see? What was I doing? I wipe my hands on my jeans and spin to watch my best friend, hair in a messy bun, tuck her cell phone into her back pocket. Never have I wanted to hug a person as badly as I do when I see her. She bends toward the mirror, picking at her eyebrows.

The scene's so normal, I can hardly process it.

"Jesus, Stel." She stops plucking and turns to look at me. "You look like you've seen a fucking ghost." She's right. I catch my reflection in the mirror. I'm a tearstained mess. Streaks of mascara smudge my cheeks and my nose is bright red, as if I've just taken a short stroll through the Arctic.

I rub at my face with the sides of my fists. "I saw a rat—a huge one," I offer. I'm losing it. The realization crashes over me and I'm worried that I might crack in two. I'm losing it and no one can know. No one. I'd sooner throw myself off the Fremont Bridge than wind up back in the hospital. Paper gowns, IV tubes, nurses checking in at twenty-minute intervals—I'm not doing it at any cost.

"Okay . . . well, get ahold of yourself, will you?"

"Yeah, sorry. I . . . I don't know what got into me." Truer words have never been spoken.

Brynn scoffs. "I'll say." There's something hanging in the air between us. Something that she wants to say but doesn't. "This place is a dump anyway."

I smile. Or at least my mouth does.

"Okay, so," she continues, "what was *that*?"

"What was what?" I ask, seeking support for my wobbly legs by leaning up against the wall. "I already told you. It was a rat."

"Don't play dumb. The knight-in-shining-armor routine at lunch?"

"Oh, that." Levi. Henry. The incident in the lunchroom feels worlds away.

Brynn's eyebrows arch.

"I tried to cancel."

She rolls her eyes. "Okay, well, then what happened?"

Pressing my wrists against the cool tile of the bathroom wall, I allow it to relax me and continue talking to Brynn. "He asked if Henry and I were dating. I said no. Next thing I knew, he was over talking to Henry."

Brynn frowns. "Wow. That kid must really like you. Those tickets were, like, three hundred bucks."

"They were *what*?" Most of the fear I'd felt moments ago evaporates. "No way. But why would Henry—?"

"Stella."

I shrink. "Has he said something?" It's been a couple weeks since I've been back in school and even longer since Henry asked me out the first time. Truthfully, I hadn't known how I felt. Not really, anyway. And since then, I hadn't exactly had time to figure it out. Until now, that is. Until Levi. I always thought Henry and I would have time to sort out whatever we were supposed to be.

But things change. And what I feel for Levi is different from what I feel for Henry. Ten times bigger and nothing has even *happened* yet. It's a bonfire compared with a candle flame.

Brynn twists her mouth to the side. "No, but..."

My eyes flit up to the ceiling. "Then you're just speculating. I've known Henry for a long time. He doesn't, like, expect anything, I don't think. Not really anyway." The words leave a sour taste in my mouth, a copper-plated tinge the second they're off my tongue.

I know Brynn's protecting Henry, but I'm her friend, too.

"He bought the tickets before your surgery, Stella. To

celebrate with you. He's been planning this thing for a while I think."

"Before my surgery!" I throw my hands up. "Are you kidding me? He could have jinxed me!" But secretly, I know this the nicest thing anyone's ever done for me.

Brynn rolls her eyes. "Well, he didn't. I just feel bad, okay?"

"Look," I say. "I know. I just I need this right now. I—I can't explain it. Besides, it was done before I even knew what was happening. And Levi's right. Henry's not, like, a huge Action Hero Disco fan, and Levi loves them. It's not like I left Henry high and dry." I'm shocked that I can say that statement without breaking into hives.

Brynn thumbs at the tattooed script that reads *Breathe* inked into the underside of her wrist. "I want you to be happy, Stel. You know that. You deserve to be happy after . . . well, you know. But . . ." She trails off.

I cross my arms, my nervous energy channeling itself into anger. "Do you have something else you want to say?" I ask pointedly.

She drops her wrist to her side. "Is he?"

"Is he what?"

"A huge Action Hero Disco fan, Stella? Is he?"

I all but choke on a gob of spit as I sputter at her. "What, so you think he's lying now? You don't even know him." I catch a glimpse of myself in the mirror, and my face has contorted into something ugly.

She studies me. "Guys have done way more to get in a girl's pants, dumbass."

"Guys have done way less to get in yours."

I hold my breath. I can't believe I said that.

Brynn narrows her eyes to a squint. Only she's not mad. I've known Brynn long enough to know that if she were mad, she'd probably slap me square in the face. Now pink shows through her freckles and rims her eyes. "You know," she says without emotion, "I'm not sure I like this new heart of yours." We stare at each other. "Stop scratching yourself."

My hands clamp into fists. The long scrape burns on my forearm. I hate that she knows my nervous habit. I hate it even more that I actually listen to her.

She shudders as if trying to shake off an unpleasant thought. "I'm sorry," she says. "You're right. It's up to you. I just—"

"Just what?"

A squiggly line forms on her forehead and she looks at me for several beats like she's trying hard to make out letters on an eye exam. Whatever she was going to say, she doesn't, because instead, a faint ghost of a smile catches the corners of her lips and she simply says, "Nothing. You're fine. I've got to get back to class."

And then her footsteps are echoing against the bathroom walls and before the door closes behind her I get out, "Just what, Brynn?" She either doesn't hear or chooses not to respond.

I splash cold water on my face. The circles under my eyes are darker than concealer can mask. The whites of my eyes are bloodshot. Pale and sickly, I look like a girl haunted.

chapter ten
112 BPM

The first thing I see is his chest. That little V shape of tanned skin peeking out, where the muscles and collarbone converge to form a keyhole right at the bottom of his throat. He's wearing a black button-down with the sleeves rolled up and dark jeans that sit low on his hips. At the sight of him standing there, the strange, hollow ache in my chest vanishes, replaced by pure longing. As if I've been missing him all these years and still can't quite reach him. I wonder if it's the same feeling that Eve had as she watched that juicy red piece of forbidden fruit dangling right in front of her on the Tree of Knowledge.

"Hey, we match," I hear him say, all bright teeth and perfect lips, forearm resting on the doorframe to my house. His voice startles me out of my reverie, and it takes me a second to register what he means.

I look down at my outfit, selected with painstaking care yesterday afternoon. A fitted black cashmere sweater, skinny jeans, and a pair of black Tory Burch flats. My heart sinks. "Shoot, we do." I look up at him nervously. "We look kinda dorky, don't we?" My fingers tug at the bottom of my sweater.

Levi laughs. "Impossible. I prefer to believe we both have impeccable taste." I notice the bottom of his jeans are soaked and I wonder briefly if he traipsed through our lawn instead of coming up the walkway. "Shall we?"

I begged my parents not to come to the door to meet Levi. Not this time. I'd imagined the whole disaster in my head. My dad would be chummy and try to pretend he actually cared about sports. My mom would fuss with my hair. And then Elsie—Elsie would of course bawl and snot while we all tried to yell over her. They said no, but in the end, Elsie had the sniffles and so they both rushed off to the twenty-four-seven clinic, leaving me to greet Levi solo. I guess I should thank my little sister for once.

Levi steps to the side and gestures toward the Tahoe idling with its headlights on in my driveway and I duck out after him, barely remembering to grab my clutch off the entry table.

He holds the door open for me, just like I knew he would, and there's an Action Hero Disco song blasting through the speakers.

"Sorry about that." He jumps in and twists the knob to turn the volume down. "Just getting in the mood." *See,* I knew he really was a fan. I make a mental note to tell Brynn that I told her so. Maturity, thy name is Stella.

I glance over at him while fumbling with my seat belt.

Although I'd totally never admit this in a million years, I'm loving the way our matching outfits make us look like we fit together. Stella + Levi. Levi + Stella. God, I'm practically doodling my first name next to his last in my notebook. Pull it together, Stella.

He twists around in the driver's seat, putting the car in reverse, and I take a deep breath, determined for this first date to go well.

"Where are you from?" I ask. "I mean, originally."

"Originally? Here." He points down. "Seattle."

"A native?"

"Can't beat the weather." He grins. "Rain with a side of rain."

The back of my jeans squeak against the seat. We can't talk about the weather. Any discussions that involve temperature, the relative moisture in the air, or the seven-day forecast have to be early warning signs of a date about to go belly-up. My mouth suddenly feels dry. The silence goes on for an extra beat.

"I—"

"Where—"

We both speak at once.

I look down at my hands. Both of our laughs seem to balance on a nervous edge, like a gymnast fighting to stay on the balance beam.

"Go ahead," I murmur.

He clears his throat. "How about you? Native or transplant?" *Transplant*. That word will only ever mean one thing to me. I swallow it down. Not tonight. Tonight I'm normal.

I pick at a loose stitch on my jeans. "My family moved from Eugene, Oregon, when I was five," I say. "I don't remember much about it. Except this one time when my dad took me riding around Hendricks Park in this little sidecar that he rented. He attached it to his bike." More tight lips and I'm now thoroughly uncomfortable. "I don't know what made me think of that. I guess for a five-year-old it was pretty cool," I say.

Levi navigates the twists and turns through my neighborhood. "And what about now? What's your thing?"

"My thing?"

"Sure. Miniature Stella apparently most enjoyed being pedaled around in sidecars. The Current Stella's thing...?" He glances at me sidelong. "Or is it still sidecars? Because if it is, no judgment here." The shadow of his sly grin plays at the corners of his mouth.

I frown. "I—" *Swimming* sits at the tip of my tongue, but it's not true anymore. "I don't really have a thing."

"I reject that out of hand, Cross," he says, thumping the steering wheel. "Everyone has a thing."

I shrug. "Not everyone, apparently. I guess I'm in the market."

He lifts his eyebrows. "Is that a challenge?"

"Okay, fine, what *are* you into then?" I fold my arms across my chest.

"Music." He turns serious, his eyes trained out the front windshield. "Music is my thing." The roads are slick, reflecting the pale, yellow glow of the streetlamps. The muscles on his forearm ripple as he twists his grip on the wheel.

"All right, what's your favorite AHD song?" I ask, resting my elbow on the console. Music's at least one thing we have in common.

"'Made-Up Moniker,'" he responds without hesitating.

I nod slowly as if considering his choice on its merits. "Interesting. That's . . . interesting."

"What?" He chuckles. "What's wrong with 'Made-Up Moniker'?"

"Nothing." I'm not impressed and I make no effort to hide it. "It's just that, well, no one's favorite song is 'Made-Up Moniker,' that's all."

"Not true. Didn't I just tell you that it's mine?"

I watch my green eyes in the side-view mirror. "Sure. That's what you told me."

"Okay, then, smarty-pants, what's yours?"

"Easy," I say, folding my arms. "'Pragmatic.'"

He guffaws. "What? No. That's so cliché. That's everyone's favorite."

"It's everyone's favorite because it's the best," I point out. "I'm not going to change what I like just because a lot of other people like it, too. That's way too arbitrary, and besides, if I picked something different, then what I'd really be telling you is my second favorite." I pause. "So what's your *real* favorite?"

I'm not just messing with him. Something I've never understood is why people stop liking something just because it gets popular. I mean, if everyone on the planet started liking Action Hero Disco, would I stop liking them? No. Why? Because they're good. It's simple logic, really.

"Fine," he grumbles. "'Pragmatic.' You're right. But don't count that against my otherwise mysterious and dangerously moody persona."

He winks, clicking a button on his steering wheel twice, and 'Pragmatic' starts playing. He opens the window and I turn the volume up and we're both singing out loud now, at the top of our lungs, and I'm holding my hair back against the cold wind and we're screaming, *"If you're such a pragmatist, then what the hell you want with this? Oh, oh, oh, oh."*

Stoplights flash red and car headlights whiz by. The Tahoe speeds toward the backdrop of tall buildings downtown where the Space Needle looms, an alien green, hovering over the city like a real UFO.

Beside me, Levi's voice layers beneath mine. *"My behavior's not erratic, you're just being melodramatic. Stop trying, trying, trying, to be so pragmatic. Oh, oh, oh, oh."* The me who's afraid of karaoke, the me who barely lets out a *woot-woot* at high school football games, the me who's questioning and rational and methodical sloughs off and blows away like a silk scarf out the window.

I raise my voice, tilting my head back and clamping my eyes shut to try to outdo Levi in our loud, off-key competition. *"Baby, if you're such a pragmatist, then let me be your catalyst."* As the last word slips out, I realize that I'm the only one singing. My hand slaps over my mouth and I peek over at Levi, who's staring at me intently, skin crinkled at the corners of his eyes.

"Sorry," I say, my voice muffled through my fingers. "Got carried away."

The light turns green and Levi pushes down on the accelerator, eyes returning to the road.

I'm blushing. I know that I am, but inside the dark cabin of Levi's car, our faces are streaked with shadows and I pray he can't see the way my skin gets blotchy when I'm mortified.

"Okay. You're killing me. What are you thinking? I couldn't have been that bad, could I?" His eyes stay focused on the road, and I find myself wishing he'd look at me.

"I'm thinking about melodies."

"Melodies?"

"Yep. And how one wrong note in a good melody can make you feel off, but the right one, once you find it, can make you feel complete again."

Why do I get the sense he's not just talking about music? My insides glow, lighting up until I swear my skin must be translucent.

We ride the rest of the way mostly in silence, with Levi occasionally asking me questions about my family and about Brynn and Henry, and me finding myself surprised that I want to answer him with complete honesty. Levi hums snippets of AHD songs and eventually his hand crosses the center console and finds its way onto my thigh, where I watch it, not sure whether to hold it or let it be. Instead I do nothing and fold mine in my lap, breathing in the night air until I'm filled to the brim with it.

The parking lot's crammed with cars that navigate around each other, backing up and lurching forward and honking until the space between me and Levi is eaten up by one, long, blaring horn. Stuffing my fingers in my ears, I jut my chin to the left in the direction where I think I see a spot a half-dozen rows back. The dirt lot crumbles beneath the tires as he threads us between the other cars, searching for spots until we find one big enough to fit.

"Ticket, please?" I hold my hand out and Levi digs a perforated ticket out of his jean pocket.

A tiny thrill gurgles up in the back of my throat. Two months ago, I was on my deathbed—literally—and now here I am, a regular teenager going to the best concert in the world with the hottest guy ever.

Levi takes my hand as we walk to the front entrance, and it's so natural that I hardly even notice until we're halfway there. Our fingers are intertwined, his thumb brushing gently against mine. He doesn't let go even when we hand our tickets over to the bouncer and he stamps our hands with an inky blotch of UNDER 21.

"We're in!" I squeal. The concert venue is an old aluminum-roofed warehouse, floors slick with dust. Levi's hand is still cold against mine, and he cranes his neck around.

"First thing's first—we stake out our spot. Then I'll grab drinks." Blue, pink, and green strobe lights flash across his face from the stage. The opening act has begun to warm up the audience—not that I require any warming.

We snake through the crowd, with Levi leading me through spilled beer and sweaty T-shirts so that I don't get left behind. People have already started dancing, bumping into my shoulders and sending me stumbling. More than a couple times, I'm saved from falling by Levi's firm grip. Eventually he tows me to the side of the crowd, tucked back from the stage where there's a short rail.

"Look, you can sit on it to see better," he says into my ear.

I smile and he gives me a boost up onto the rail so that my feet dangle over the concrete floor.

"Lick your hand."

"Huh?"

Levi wraps his fingers around my wrist, flattens his tongue over the back of my hand, and then rubs at the stamp until the ink disappears. "There." He grins.

"Hey!" I wipe off the saliva, but I'm giggling. "Did you seriously just lick me?"

Levi licks his own hand and erases the underage stamp

from his skin. "Trust me. It'll be worth it." For my part, I try not to look nervous. "Guard our spot with your life, Cross." He nudges me. "I'm going in search of sustenance."

"Aye, aye, Captain." I salute as he leaves and notice him laughing as he melts into the crowd. Almost at once, the ache starts up again. I have to clutch my chest it's so real. A gnawing in the hollow underneath my ribs, it burrows into my back and starts running up against my spine.

I knead the spot closest to the pain with the nubs of my fingers and wonder if I'm imagining it. But then, of course I'm imagining it. What else is pain but convincing fiction? A bunch of nerves snapping and zapping at each other, telling your brain there's something there when, in reality, there's not. It's Sick Kid 101.

I settle onto my rail to watch the stage. The band opener consists of a boy and a girl, both equally gaunt, with matching black hair that parts down the middle and slides down to their chins. They look at each other while they shout into their microphones and pick noisy melodies out of their guitar strings. The panic eases and is replaced by excitement. Maybe I'd just been scared Levi would get lost in here and I wouldn't be able to find him for the rest of the night. That's silly, though, since I'm staying in one spot. I drum my fingers on the cold metal rail, thankful to be perched a head above the ruckus below. A few screeches come from a microphone and then there's a tug at the bottom of my jeans. I look down and there's a guy in a blue baseball cap. For a split second, I think that it's Henry, but of course, it's not, since I ditched Henry to come here with Levi. With a pinch of guilt, I lean down so that I can hear what he's saying.

"What's your name?" he yells.

I scrunch up my nose. "My name?"

He's a tall string bean of a boy with a baggy shirt and a tuft of brown hair growing out of his chin.

When he nods I can just make out his eyes, glazed over, like those of a taxidermied fox.

"Stella," I shout back. I should have lied.

The boy's grin is soupy on his angular face. "Joshhhh," he slurs. He wobbles to the side before grabbing the railing to right himself.

"Great. Nice to meet you, Josh," I say curtly. I press my lips together into a tight line and try sitting back up, but Josh pulls on my pant leg again and I'm forced to lean forward, my eyes scouting the throngs of people, looking for Levi.

"Wanna dance?" asks my new friend, his breath rotten and sweet all at once, stinking of beer. I don't want to dance. Considering he can barely stand up straight, he shouldn't want to dance either.

"Not this time," I say, scooting an inch down the rail. I clutch my purse in my lap, tucking it close to my torso. He follows.

"Come on," he insists. Tug, tug, tug on my jeans. I don't like the sensation of his fingers pawing at my leg. They feel clumsy. "Just one . . . dance."

"Maybe you should go find a glass of water." I trust this guy as much I would a thin sheet of ice over a lake. I pull back my shoulders and try to look grown-up, self-assured. Only I know that he must have chosen to pursue me the same way a lion chooses to pick off an injured gazelle from the herd. "Okay, seriously, dude. I'm good."

"You're really pretty." His words feel grimy and mucus-coated. I slide out from underneath him, but he catches my wrist. "Come dance," he repeats, tugging at my sweater. "It'll be fun."

I shake my head, rigid, wishing he wouldn't touch me.

"Come on," Josh whines, but this time he yanks down on my hand and a rush of wind flies up in my face right before I hit the ground.

Pain drives up through my right knee like an iron rod. Blinding white pain. His lumpish fingers—fingers that could not be counted on to successfully drunk dial at this point—clasp at my sweater and as he pulls at me, I crawl to a standing position. "Stop," I yell, hoarse.

At this, other people around me finally take notice. I wedge my elbows between my torso and his. Onlookers crowd in on us. I'm surrounded. The crowd crushes in on me. My heartbeat skyrockets and I start to gulp in air as if through a straw. People are shouting. The noise tickles my ears.

Somebody pushes me from behind and I lunge back into Josh, whose sour smell overwhelms me even more.

"What do you think you're doing?" There's a break in the mass of bodies. Levi shoves two cups into the hands of a stranger. He's not talking to me. He's talking to Josh, who now appears to have the mobility of a slug.

"I didn't do nothing, man," Josh replies, all tongue.

"Bullshit, I saw you."

I squirm backward, away from him. There's a sickening *thwap* of skin on skin. Josh stumbles, clutching his jaw and crossing his feet one over the other in a wobbly grapevine.

"Dude!" Josh yells, bringing his fingertips away from his lip to reveal a bright patch of fresh, shiny blood. For a tense second, I think Josh is going to take a swing. Levi edges around toward me and as he does, Josh apparently thinks better of it.

By the time Levi's hand has found its way around my waist, Josh is already stumbling away.

Levi pulls me close to his side and guides us to a clear spot on the floor. He looks at me hungrily. "You okay?"

I swipe at my bottom lashes, praying I don't have smudged eyeliner. "I'm fine." My voice is high and squeaky and Levi chuckles. "Freak," I mutter as anger wells up inside me.

The ache in my chest subsides and my heart rate slows to a steady beat the longer Levi stays with his thumb latched onto my belt loop.

He stares over his shoulder in the direction that Josh went, hovering protectively over me before a visible quiver runs through him and he seems to shake something off. He returns his attention to me.

"Do we need to go home?" Levi searches my face.

His concern wraps around me and I feel cared for, like something that's precious and rare. An ostrich egg or Swarovski crystal. And my anger dissipates.

"No way," I insist, though I can already feel the soreness creeping into my kneecap. "We're here to see Action Hero Disco. Hello!" I put extra pep into my voice. I don't want to be the wimp who forced him to waste his money.

He gives me a long look but says nothing and instead smiles and helps me back to my perch. He grabs another two beers to make up for the ones we lost, and when he returns Action Hero Disco is onstage and I can't believe I'm breathing the same air. I don't know how else to describe the fact that they are right there. I could walk up to the front and touch Jordan Montegro's shin. Sure, I might get tackled by security, but still, it could happen.

I try hard not to feel self-conscious. There's the urge to hold this tiny space in time, to keep it for myself. And I can sense the hot flush of pleasure rising in my cheeks. I want to pull back because it feels private.

For these moments, it's as if the transplant never happened. I feel nothing but the vibration of the speakers that mixes with the beer, which is followed promptly by two more beers. Together, they form a subtle buzz in the center of my skull. Without concentrating too hard, I can convince myself that I'm not sick. Never have been.

By the time they play "Pragmatic," Levi and I are singing every word. My throat becomes woolen and stick-scratchy. I take swigs from my beer to soothe the burn. I don't mention to Levi that they're my first. By the end of the night my insides are as warm and gooey as freshly baked cookies and my mind is tingling and I think that if this is my life now, it should never have to end.

chapter eleven

113 BPM

"I should probably go inside." My arms are freezing, with puckered skin and little hairs that won't lie down. The first hint that October will transition us into the cool months of winter and summer has passed. We're both sticky with sweat from the concert. I lean my head against the rest. The car engine's off and there's darkness surrounding us, cut with shards of light from streetlamps. We're both that kind of happy-exhausted that comes when every limb hangs loose from the socket and your entire body could melt into whatever surface on which it's currently located.

I smile deliriously up at the ceiling, so delightfully tired I feel silly. "That was by far the best concert I've ever been to." I rub my throat. "I think I lost my voice, though."

"High praise," Levi says. "What other concerts were we up against?"

I lower the direction of my gaze and nuzzle into the

headrest. "Okay, so, that was my first. But don't let that detract from the significance of my statement." Before I got sick, my parents would never have let me go out alone. I savor the leftover hum. The music had been so loud that it sent every particle in me vibrating in unison with a thousand other bodies.

Levi laughs. "Well you did say by far."

"Does it crack your top five?" I ask.

He leans back. "By far the best. Of course the company may have given it a competitive edge."

I look down at my lap, the corners of my mouth creeping up. Another moment passes. "I really should go inside."

I let my head loll to the side. It's then that I notice Levi's eyes. I mean *really* notice them, because when I do, when I glance up to make eye contact, to say my best prim and polite first-date good-byes, they glue me to my seat. They're like two swirling planets and I'm a speck of dust pulled into their orbit. I feel myself leaning, being sucked into the vortex.

We're two magnets. I feel the instant pull at that moment we decide we're going to kiss. And then Levi's thumb is tracing the soft skin on my throat and sending a tickle down through the arches of my feet and I'm squirming against the upholstery. And there is no nose bumping or teeth colliding. It's the kind of kiss that I've seen in the movies. The ones where music plays and credits scroll. He smells like salt water and tastes cold like the ocean spray.

Our lips still move together. The thumb at my throat slides down to my collarbone and rests over the thin skin that covers it. My heart pumps fistfuls of blood, which I can hear whooshing through my ears as it makes its way to my fingers and toes and the backs of my knees. My whole body tingles.

The fingers on my collarbone flatten into a hand on my chest and slip an inch. Then another. My pulse quickens.

The urgency in Levi's kisses increases, but all I can feel is the hand. It's as if my entire consciousness is focused on that one particular spot on my body. He must catch the pounding of my heart. How could he not?

Then, like his hand has a mind of its own, the fingertips steal into the V-neck of my sweater and I jerk back, alarmed. The connection snaps in half.

Levi's eyes go wide. "Stella, I'm sorry, I just—" he stammers.

Oh my God. Ohmygodohmygodohmygod. What did I just do? He thinks I'm pissed about the—about the—about the thing. I'm such a spaz. Worse. He must think I'm acting like a twelve-year-old.

"No!" I blurt out. "I mean, no, it's not that. It's—" I take a deep breath. If I tell him, will he see me as a sick girl too? I don't want him to like me because he feels sorry for me. But if I don't tell him, what will he think then? "It's my scar."

Levi cocks his head and I tug down the neck of my sweater. It's the first time I've shown anyone but my mom and dad. The thick scar tissue—tight, shiny, and ruler straight—runs from the middle of my belly up the length of my chest. It's the sort of scar to cause a stranger in the supermarket to stare. And one of the first things I thought about when I first saw it: how could anyone ever be attracted to *this*?

Levi stares at the point on my chest while I try to force myself to sit still.

"I had a heart transplant," I explain, my words spilling out too fast. "I was going to die, see, but I got off the waiting list. I got a heart and it saved my life, but . . . now . . . now I'm stuck with this."

His brown eyes lift up to mine and I see them gleaming in the dark. There's a slight wrinkle in his forehead. "Seems like a small price to pay then . . . for your life?"

A lump rises in my throat. "Sure, I guess." The strength of my words is slighter than a sheet of paper.

Gently, he touches the angry welt. I try not to wonder too hard what he's thinking, whether he thinks I'm a freak or disfigured or just plain unsexy. I'd never thought of myself as sexy before, but the scar, it has definitely made me think of myself as *un*.

"I know it's not, um . . . the prettiest thing in the world."

His thumb runs over the hump of scar tissue and my skin erupts with a shudder of electricity, every atom in me connecting and exploding in my chest.

"It's . . ." he starts then trails off and I hold my breath. "It's not ugly, Stella." I experience a small dip of disappointment when he doesn't call me by my last name.

Sometimes I see the scar when I'm getting out of the shower or pulling on my polo for school and I think I look like a murder victim, a corpse on a cold, metal table. I imagine myself, purple lips and pale white cheeks, black hair that's as brittle as straw.

He retrieves his hand slowly and returns it to his lap.

I give a dismissive roll of my eyes. "It is and it's fine. Like you said, it's a small price to pay or whatever."

A corner of his mouth turns up. "Seriously. It's unique," he says. "Some people get tattoos to remind themselves of what they've been through. You"—he shrugs—"have this."

I'd never thought of it that way. I try it on, this new point of view. It feels nice. Even if it is a lie.

"I thought I was going to die," I tell him, surprising myself.

Strange as it seems, I've never talked about this before. I'm not sure why I suddenly want to, except for maybe the beers or the fact that someone else has seen my scar. The confession just spills out of me, as though Levi had pulled at the tip of a buried object and in doing so had managed unwittingly to unearth the whole thing.

Our faces are so close I can sense the coolness of his skin. "How does it feel?" he asks.

"How does what feel?" The trees rustle in the quiet driveway, mimicking the sound of our whispers.

"Thinking that you're going to die." His dark skin is dewy in the soft light. This, I realize, is how it feels to share secrets.

"It's . . . terrifying. Like time is working against you. Like there's a literal hourglass that contains the minutes of your life." How funny that I've never said that out loud even though I've thought it a million times. That feeling, of the ticking countdown, still clings to me. I haven't been able to shake it. Not yet, not completely, at least. I can't comprehend the vast expanse of time that's in front of me now. Years upon years upon years that stack up in short, time-capsuled columns stretching farther than I can see.

"Why, though? Why was it terrifying?"

"Because I hadn't lived long enough. What if I missed something? What if I missed everything? What about my parents?"

"Sometimes," he says, glancing down at the space between

us and then up at me, "I think about dying." Almost like a declaration of guilt.

My breath hitches. "Why?" Before my illness, I'd never once thought about dying. I drove around on highways, got on planes, ate questionably cooked chicken served by my mother, but never once did I think about what it might be like to die.

But things are different now. Death follows me around like a shadow.

"I think about what holds me here." He sits back in his seat now, chin tilted up, staring at the car ceiling. "There was this philosopher, Eckhart, who said he saw hell and that the only thing that burns there is the part of you that won't let go of life. You know, like your memories and attachments and stuff. Hell burns them all away, but it's not punishing you. It's, like, freeing your soul. So if you're afraid of dying, Eckhart would say, you're holding on, and you'll see devils tearing your life away. But if you've made your peace," Levi shrugs, "then the devils are really angels, freeing you from Earth."

I sit in silence for a minute, remembering the feel of Levi's lips on mine and contemplating his words, morbid but strangely beautiful. An invisible thread links us, knowledge of our own mortality, and I feel inextricably bonded.

"What holds you here?" I finally ask, almost too low to hear.

"Right now?" His head rolls to the side and he stares at me as if he can see all the way through me to the other side. He says simply: "I guess it's you."

chapter twelve
101 BPM

As a teenager with a terminal illness, I got used to low expectations. So when my phone buzzes on Saturday at a quarter to three with the name Levi hovering over the message, I'm surprised and more than a little skeptical.

I've spent the entire day suffering. The space between my ribs feels like someone took a metal trowel and raked it between my bones. I'm getting to the point when I have to debate telling my parents and risk going back to Dr. Belkin.

Mom makes excuses to check on me by carrying the world's smallest stacks of folded laundry so that she can come and go as she pleases. I think she's weighing whether I'm sick or hungover. The answer is neither.

I don't know much about booze, but I'm fairly confident a hangover doesn't set up shop between your lungs. And I'm not sick, unless I've been that way since the day after surgery.

I'm in pain. There's a difference, however minuscule. I

rub at the sore spot over my heart. The tenderness makes my limbs heavy, but when I sit up and read the message, I smile despite all this.

I once read in a *Teen Vogue* magazine that there are three ways to know a boy likes you. I'm looking at number three. Cue the victory dance.

"Mom, I'm going out," I say, next time she swoops the vacuum into my bedroom. I'll wait another day to tell them. At least. Things are going well and I have to protect them. I have to protect my new life.

"Stella Cross, you've been moping in bed all day and now you're well enough to go out?"

"Uh-huh." I slip on a fleece jacket and a pair of fluffy boots. "Pretty much."

She unplugs the vacuum. "And what about your Stanford application? Your dad said he was going to take a look at your essay but that you hadn't sent it to him yet."

"I will," I say, grabbing my keys. And maybe I will, but right now Stanford University is the farthest thing from my mind.

"Stella—" It's the last thing I hear before I slam the door. I can't believe I just did that. I smile stupidly, pulse pounding in my eardrums.

Once in the car, I punch the address into my phone's GPS. It's a spot on Ballard Street, one I'm not familiar with, and on the drive over, I have to force my foot off the gas pedal. My nerves, frayed from the hours of monotonous throbbing, are eager for a distraction. For the span of a breath I worry that my quick acceptance of his invitation reads "too available." Another sliver of wisdom gleaned from the glossy pages of back-of-the toilet literature. But then again, he asked me first, I reason. I take a deep breath. Those magazines really ought to be more specific.

After a short drive, the female robot voice tells me I've arrived at my final destination, and when I determine I'll have to squeeze my compact car into a tiny parallel-parking space, it's all I can do not to leave it in the middle of the road with its hazards blinking.

For me, Levi Zin appears to have his own gravitational pull.

I pay the meter and stroll along a tree-lined stretch of sidewalk, searching for an address. It doesn't take long before I locate the right numbers on a shabby storefront. The sign marking the entrance depicts a cartoonish red fox wearing a blue suit and carrying a saxophone. The letters spell out BOP STREET RECORDS.

A cowbell chimes when I walk through the door. A kid with curly hair that covers his ears welcomes me without looking up from a comic book. His style walks a thin line between punk rock and homeless.

Vinyl records fill shelves upon shelves from one end of the small, musty shop to the other. The bell clangs again and in walks Levi. A worn hoodie hangs open over a gray tee. He spots me and grins. Almost at once, my chest quiets. It's like burning your finger on a curling iron. First the sting grows and you want to shake it in the air to force it to stop, but then you remember to stick the burned skin under cold water, and it's magic. The finger doesn't burn anymore. And that's how it is with Levi—he's the cold water.

As he walks over I'm suddenly self-conscious of how, I don't know, *dorky* I look in comparison. With my cable-knit sweater, skinny jeans, and flats, I could be swapped with a suburban housewife, while Levi could pass as an off-duty rock star.

"What are we doing here?" I ask.

"I heard you were in the market for a Thing," he says. I hear him capitalize the *T* with his voice. I think at this point I should explain to him that I'm not completely milquetoast, that I had a Thing, but that thing was taken away from me. The bite of ice-cold water in the morning when it's still dark outside, the red sting of chlorine, the strain of lungs filling to the point of near combustion, these were details that required a deep and pure love, the way a mother loves her child even though everyone else can see he's mean and nasty and always has dirt underneath his fingernails. I miss swimming like I'd miss a person. This, though, is too much to explain and, besides, what does it matter, really?

"I am, but—" I protest while he takes my hand and pulls me into the heart of the stacks.

"Then I thought maybe you could borrow mine." He turns to walk backward through aisle. "At least for now," he adds.

"I've never even heard of this place." All around me I'm surrounded by large, square sleeves filled with vinyl records. I don't have a clue where to start.

"Blasphemy." He stares greedily at the overcrowded rows as if he's a dog eyeing a juicy piece of steak. "This," he mutters, "was worth coming back for." I'm about to ask when he was last here when he pulls out a record, decorated in collage and newspaper scrap art. He holds it out for me and I take it gently because, at least to him, the flimsy sleeve with torn-up corners seems valuable.

"'Mother Love Bone,'" I read aloud. "What kind of name is that?"

"They started from . . . hold on." He holds up a finger and then skips further down the row, rifling through a pile of records until he finds what he's looking for. "These guys. Green River."

"Look." He turns to the back of the Mother Love Bone album, where there's a black-and-white photograph of five long-haired boys. "Three of these guys started out in Green River, which was sort of this grunge rock band. They didn't get much airtime, but they're, like, the great-grandfathers of the real scene. This one in the middle—he's Andrew Wood. He was from a different band. Malfunkshun. Completely insane. Would have been an icon, too, but he overdosed when he was only twenty-four." Levi grows solemn, as though this might have been a close personal friend.

He rebounds quickly, though, and we're off on a whirlwind tour of Seattle's music history. Every so often, he passes me a record with an explanation, like "These guys were influenced by Hendrix" or "This band shared the same label as Kurt Cobain." I teeter under an armful of vinyl that feels like a musical graveyard of singers that, according to Levi, died too young.

When my record load threatens to topple over, Levi leads me to one of the sound booths. I've begun to think of this record store as Levi's version of a temple and the music as his religion. The way his eyes dance as we put on Nirvana's first album I can see that he practically worships them.

I slide a clunky pair of headphones over my ears. A snare hit ricochets through percussion. Kurt Cobain—I know only because Levi tells me—starts singing quietly and then carefully, gradually, the music builds to the chorus until it's loud and angry. Before I know it, my foot is tapping along to the furious beat. The music is unlike anything I've heard on the radio. I've always enjoyed music and I love Action Hero Disco, but this is different. It reminds me of unfair things like the random injustice of my illness and the fact that I'll never swim again and about the moments I've missed that I'll never ever get back. The song makes me mad, but what's weird is that I like it. It's as if someone finally gets me. The heated voice inside, the little bit of rage that feels like a rush.

Like standing on top of the pier looking down.

I don't know how long it's been when I realize that my eyes are closed. I peel them open to peek at Levi. His teeth dig into his lower lip. His nose scrunches. He uses his fist to drum on his thigh. At the instant I open my eyes, our stares meet, and we're caught in a split-second flash. I imagine the expressions on our faces as mirror images and I know that somewhere, at some time, he's experienced the same anger and that it's reflected here between the notes and words blaring through the headphones.

At the end of the track, he lifts the pin and places it on another rib of the record. I don't know how he selects the songs, exactly, since there are no titles or search functions the way there are on a smartphone or computer, but the fact that he can seems sophisticated: it's something no other boy at Duwamish High would know how to do.

As the static breaks to mark the beginning of the next song, my phone buzzes. I slide it out of my back pocket.

We on tonight?

Henry.

I'd forgotten all about the new episode of *Lunatic Outpost* tonight. Earlier this week, they'd aired a repeat of the twice-weekly show. In fact, I'd forgotten it so completely that even after reading the text, it takes me a few blinking seconds to recall what he means. That's how narrow my focus is when sharing a room with Levi.

I glance at Levi. In the tight booth, our knees touch. Occasionally he leans over and drums on my thigh, a gesture that sends my heart into the same frenzy as a June bug in a jar. I'm not ready to leave yet.

And so I pocket the phone unanswered. It's easier to ditch Henry the second time, I realize. If I'm not careful, it's bound to become a habit.

"What do you think?" he asks, lifting the headphone from his right ear. "This was the first song I learned on guitar." He bites his lip and mimics riffing on an electric guitar. His fingers fly in midair, so precise that I get the sense that if a real instrument were in his hands, he'd hit the notes exactly.

"I didn't know you played guitar." I shrink when I realize that I've been yelling to compensate for the music, which is only playing in my headphones.

"Used to. Hendrix was my idol until I got introduced to Stone Gossard." He finishes the air guitar, but even when he rests his hands back on his lap, his fingers continue twitching like he's dying to play. "All of the good ones die early, you know. Blaze out like comets. When I was younger I'd get all sad about Cobain. I'd, like, mourn the loss of all the music he could have made if he hadn't killed himself. But now I get it." Levi leans over and switches the track again. "If you live that hard you run out of wick fast. Cobain said in his suicide note that he hadn't felt the excitement of listening to music in years. Can you believe that?"

I shake my head. But I think Levi and I can both understand it, even if just a little.

I don't keep track of how long Levi and I spend in Bop Street Records. The clerk at the front never bothers us or asks if we're going to buy anything. We wander around the store and I pick out records for Levi to try while he picks out ones for me.

Most of the albums I select are terrible. A noisy racket of screaming, yelling, and thrashing that makes little sense. But even those are worthwhile, since they serve to increase our appreciation of what I've come to mentally call "the good stuff."

Levi's mania for the music is like the flu—contagious. By the time we leave—cowbell clanging behind us—we're bleary-eyed and staggering. The sky is a deep shade of navy, pricked with pinpoints of light. I should have noticed this first. Instead, I notice the cold numbness in my fingertips and Levi must notice it, too, because he pulls me tight into his chest and my heart beats happily against his stomach.

"Thank you," he says into my hair.

"Thank *you*," I return, nearly overwhelmed with the feeling of completeness.

Reluctantly, we part. Our hands drop away and I tear my eyes from him, worried that I'll go to sleep and this will all disappear.

When I get back in the car, I know two things. First, that unmistakable pain is already busy crawling back into the cavity of my chest.

Second, it's past five oh eight.

chapter thirteen
121 BPM

A sculptor. Tall, wiry, craggy-faced. Shards of limestone crumble to the floor. His hammer strikes at the toothed chisel.

Tap-tap. Tap-tap.

I watch the falling stone break into powder and dust as pointed metal bites into rock.

Tap-tap. Tap-tap.

The ra–ta–tapping is coming from inside my skull, which is eggshell thin. Petrified calcium. The metal spike tries to break through to the other side. I watch and feel, waiting for the stone to morph into . . . into something.

Tap-tap. Tap-tap.

Louder now. My eyelashes are moth wings fluttering toward the light until my eyelids snap apart and darkness burrows into my pupils. I search the room, confused. It comes into focus, slowly at first, outlines of a desk, the foot

of my bed, a chair and a nightstand blurred by the moonlight. My chest is raw and achey.

Tap-tap.

My heart skips. I sit up in bed, pulling the covers up to
my chin. At the window is a face with hooded eyes and skin
that shines an eerie silver. Shadows criss-cross my bed and I
sit still underneath them.

"*Stella?*" The voice is muffled through the thick pane of
glass between us. "Stella, are you awake?"

"Levi?"

"Yeah. Who'd you think it was?"

I swing my legs out of bed and land barefoot on the plush
carpet. "I don't know, an axe murderer? That was my first
guess." I'm wearing plaid pajama bottoms and a thin white
T-shirt. No bra. I pad over to the window, unlatch the top,
and slide up the bottom half to create a space large enough
to crawl through.

"Sorry to disappoint." He smiles wickedly, teeth gleaming. "Can I come in?"

I peer down through the open window. He's wearing
the same dark jeans and black V-neck he wore a few hours
ago. I nod and, with hardly a sound, he hoists himself into
my room, where we stand together, my nose inches from
his chest.

"What are you doing here?" I whisper, feeling small as
he looks down at me.

And then his hands are cold and damp against my neck.
His thumbs skim my jawline, pulling me in. "I missed you,"
he breathes into my lips. The ache in my chest is a memory.
I let his fingers skim the length of my spine, finding their
way to my hips as he guides me. I follow his lead, mouth

pressed into his, as if caught in a dance. And then I'm falling backward. His arm curls around to catch me and I land with a light thud on the mattress, caught in a cocoon of down comforter and twisted bedsheets.

"I missed you, too," I venture, pressing my nose into his shoulder. I look up and our mouths find each other. His tongue is soft at first. Twirling. Testing. He tastes cool and salty, like the sea.

Gradually, his kisses grow stronger, more purposeful, and I work to keep up. The bones of his hips lock against mine. I feel heady, the fabric between us a formality. He hovers over me, and before I can resist, my shirt is over my head, the air cold and exhilarating against my bare skin. He covers my entire length without even touching me. My body hums as his kisses wander lower. Icy lips caress my throat. I arch in anticipation. I can't stop myself—or him. I'm powerless.

He lightly touches the bone between my breasts, causing me to gasp. He plays my flesh like notes on a scale. Rising, rising, I get higher and higher.

"Yes." The word flows out of me in a slow murmur as his fingertips graze my rib cage, tracing each ridge until he reaches my belly button. Underneath his weight, I squirm closer. "Please," I whisper, so softly I'm not sure he can hear. But in response, his hand slips from my stomach to the groove of my spine.

He kisses the underside of my chin. I tilt my head back further, anticipating the next touch.

There's a nip at my neck. My breath hitches. The next time, nails sink in. I cry out but can't get up. My arms are pinned. I try to kick, but the weight of him is too much. The nails pick at the top of my scar and it breaks open, tearing me apart where I've been stitched together. Only they are nails no longer. There's the glint of moonlight on metal and I see the scalpel in Levi's hand, wielded like a knife as it shreds at my skin, too deep to feel.

I watch as Levi raises the nasty, surgical point, red eyes glowing in the darkness. It's aimed at my heart like a scorpion ready to strike. I shriek as it plunges in and—

My chest convulses, and I lurch off the bed, then slam back down on the ground. It convulses again and my body is tossed as if I'm possessed by demons, but then, once I fall for the last time, I also fall still. The first thing I realize is that I'm awake. The second: I'm alone. My pajamas are soaked through and I'm lying in a pool of sweat. I sit up, heart thumping.

My shirt's been tossed to the floor. I flip on the nightstand lamp to see scratch marks etched across my chest in angry lines like stigmata. A rabid cat could have gotten to me. If only I didn't know better.

I hold my shaking hands up in front of my face and turn them over. My breath rattles, catching in my lungs. Underneath my own nails are thin traces of pink.

chapter fourteen
133 BPM

"Come outside." The flat surface of my iPhone is cool pressed against my face. It's early for a Monday morning. Any morning, I guess, but especially a Monday. The air's dark and chilly. Daylight has already begun to shorten on both ends.

"Am I under arrest?" asks a husky voice over the line.

"No, your chariot awaits—you know you want a ride to school."

"It's early." A whine, but a good-natured one.

"I'm told the driver's stunningly attractive, so you better get moving." I click the phone off and drop it in the center console.

Steam billows off my car, swirling in the headlights and out into the fresh morning air. From inside the two-story brick house, I see a pair of fingers poke through the blinds and then disappear. Seconds later, Henry stumbles out, his backpack looped over one arm while he tries to button his uniform over a white undershirt. Henry lives in a Betsy Ross–style home with a white-and-blue awning that embellishes its bay window and a Washington Huskies flag flapping alongside the front door.

A crisp breeze rushes in as he slides onto the passenger seat. Neither of us is dressed for the drop in temperature. He blows hot air into his hands, removes his cap, and tousles his damp hair with long fingers. Droplets nip at my cheeks and I try to shield myself from the rest. Being with Henry is a lot like having a standard poodle puppy in the car. Curly head and gangly limbs, neither of which he can seem to control.

"Where's this stunningly attractive driver I heard about?" He stuffs his backpack between his knees.

"Okay, that part was a ruse, but I did bring coffee, which in my opinion is better anyway." I point to the second cup holder with a travel mug.

"This is why you are not a dude."

"I'd always thought that was one of my better qualities."

Henry jiggles his mug from the holder and takes a sip, jerking away with a wince when apparently the contents are too hot. He touches his fingers to his lip and looks at the cup with a frown. "Okay then, to what do I owe this pleasure at"—Henry glances at the clock on the dash and returns the mug to its original spot—"seven oh five A.M.?"

I'd spent all of Sunday feeling anxious. I couldn't sit still for any period of time. I'd grab a book and quickly decide I'd prefer to watch TV. I'd flip the channels and not be able to find a single thing to watch. I offered to give Elsie a bath. I hovered around my mom in the kitchen. I attempted homework well before dinner. But the dream continued to color my mood for the entire day. I had to remind myself that none of it was real. Of course, I knew this, but that didn't stop me from sneaking looks underneath my shirt to check that it hadn't been clawed open, or from recalling the dream as though it weren't a dream at all, but instead a memory. Thin pink scratches crisscrossed the skin. Where my nails had dug deeper, there were orange-yellow scabs, rimmed in red. They'd now started to itch.

A quick Internet search about the meaning of dreams and I'd come across an article that I thought at least came close. The category "horrified dreams" described a nightmare in which the dreamer is typically murdered or torn apart by wild animals. It's a stretch, but it's caused by an onslaught of negative emotion, usually guilt, which fits the bill. Granted, the horrified-dream effect is one most often seen in psychological evaluations of serial killers, which I'm most definitely not, but I *am* guilty of killing a potential relationship.

"I . . ." My eyes search his and I lose the words I'd intended to say. His eyes are so perfectly sweet. A little droopy, like he might have just woken up. That would be just like him. Sleepwalks to the shower, throws on a shirt from the pile of clothes lying at the bottom of his closet, and stuffs an uncooked Pop-Tart in his mouth while he drives to school. From bed to school in fifteen minutes flat. There are dashes of pink on his cheekbones and the fresh smell of soap on him—such Henry-ism. "I just wanted to say sorry for not making *Lunatic Outpost* on Saturday," I say. "What'd I miss?"

I have to tell him, I think, grimly. Unless I want to take up insomnia, the guilt will tear me apart. It's clear that I won't be able to see where things go with Levi if I'm not honest with Henry.

But when his face lights up I think it might break me in

two. "Oh, it was awesome," he says, clearly gearing up to tell me every detail.

Putting the car in reverse, I let it roll back out of his driveway. Henry and I used to carpool to school more often. His house is on the way home to mine, but we'd gotten out of the pattern. The upheaval caused by my illness made keeping any routine next to impossible.

The worst part is, he doesn't even seem mad. In the past few days I've ditched him twice and there's not so much as a slam of the door to let me know what a bitch I've been. I mean, that's what I would do.

"It was about body snatchers," he begins.

"Like the book?"

"No. Well, kind of. Quentin took all these calls from people claiming that their real bodies had been invaded by aliens or whatever. They didn't call them aliens, but that was the gist."

"If their bodies were snatched, then what bodies were they calling from?"

"That was the weird part. Each had a different story. Most said they were now cohabitating in the body of their girlfriend or brother's best friend or something. Just quietly taking up residence."

"Aside from taking the time out to call into podcasts, of course."

"Of course." He turns toward me. "Okay, serious question: if your body got snatched, whose would you take?"

I squint one eye shut, thinking, while Henry hums the tune to *Jeopardy*. "That's easy. Harry Potter's," I say. Years ago, Henry and I had concocted our most-epically-awesome-graduation-slash-never-grow-up-slash-off-to-college dream trip. We would go to Universal Studios to visit the Wizarding World of Harry Potter and afterward we'd walk through the House of Horrors maze thirteen times in a row or until the park kicked us out—whichever came first.

"Harry Potter? That's not even a real person!"

"We're talking about a world where aliens-but-not-aliens invade people's bodies. I think I'm entitled to take liberties with the Wizarding World."

"Fine. Then I'm going with the Wolf Man."

"Circa 1940s or the remake?" I ask in earnest. *The Wolf Man* is a cult favorite among regular *Lunatic Outpost* listeners. It's regularly cited as actual evidence by people calling into the show. Example: *"I know there's a werewolf living in the woods behind my house, because I hear the same type of howling as in the final scene of* The Wolf Man." Case closed.

"Remake. Way scarier."

I roll my eyes. We have a fundamental difference of opinion when it comes to remakes versus originals. The only thing we agree on is that if someone tried to reboot *The Twilight Zone* again, we'd both puke.

We fall into a relaxed silence. Comfortable, like a pair of old fluffy socks. If I wanted to be the type of girl who still loved staying home in her pair of old fluffy socks, this would be great. But I'm not. There's been plenty of time for fuzzy socks, drawstring pants, and other articles of clothing that should never be worn outside the home.

"Henry, I kissed him," I blurt.

He looks at me heavy-lidded for a moment. "Oh."

"It just happened and—look, it's not like I planned this. Any of this." My voice pleads with him. Henry stares out the front windshield now speckled with raindrops, motionless. "I wanted to at least talk to you first. You know... before."

A ten-pound weight settles itself somewhere between my belly button and rib cage, pressing into my gut until I can hardly breathe. "Please don't be mad."

Henry's ears are red. He moves to put his cap back on, covering his mess of curls in one practiced motion. "Not mad."

We listen to the engine hum and the vents blast hot air. I stay twisted in my seat, scrutinizing Henry's profile for the slightest hint of what he might be thinking. The straight line of his nose. The dark freckle that sits underneath the corner of his left eye. Not knowing what to do, I start to drive faster in the direction of school, past aluminum mailboxes with their red flags standing at attention, past overflowing trash cans lined up on the curb and past strangers walking their dogs on leashes, plastic baggies swinging in sync.

I sneak glances at Henry every few minutes, but each time his posture, his expression, they're the same. A couple blocks from school, I can't stand it anymore. The silence is maddening.

"Henry, say something."

Henry's cheeks puff out. "What do you want me to say, Stella?" His voice is calm, which might be the worst part. I wish he'd yell at me. Tell me what a selfish bitch I am or what a shitty friend I've turned out to be. Anything would be better than this: disappointment.

"I don't know. Anything."

"Okay." He swipes his hands over his khakis. "Look, Stel, I know what happens on dates. I've gone on a few. I'm not an idiot." The rain picks up and I flip on my windshield wipers. "There. I said something."

"I never thought you were an idiot." A line of cars jams the dirt path leading into the student parking lot. I have to cut off a sophomore driving a silver Beamer to get in. "But I don't want you to hate me."

At that, his lips press together and a dimple forms at the top of his cheek. It strikes me that most girls would think it's adorable, but not me. I can't. I'm not allowed to. Not anymore. He says nothing, but he doesn't have to. I don't need someone to tell me that what I've just said might be the most self-involved thing imaginable. Never mind how Henry feels. Let's make sure that everyone still likes Stella.

I resist the urge to beat my head against the steering wheel and instead wedge the Jetta into a tight parking space between a truck and a red minivan. A cheerful chime comes from my phone in the cupholder. I slip it out to sneak a peek at the screen. Levi and I have been texting nonstop since Saturday.

"Is that him?"

"Sorry." I say, shifting the gear and refusing to look Henry in the eye. "It's just that I never—"

Henry's hand is on the latch and he yanks it open. "You did, Stella," he says, one foot planted on the asphalt outside. There are splotches on his neck. He waits several breaths before driving in the last spike. "You gave me my answer. Just now."

"Hey, stranger," Levi greets me, sliding to the side of my locker door. The feeling left over from my confrontation with Henry melts. I'm free. Or at least I think I am. A rip of electricity runs down the length of my scar. I shudder as the memory of Levi shredding through me at the seams bubbles to the surface. *Not* a memory, I silently scold. A *dream.* I force a timid smile and shake off the vestiges of what was no more than a nightmare. A scary, pain-in-the-butt nightmare. Next thing I know, I'll be asking my dad to check under my bed for monsters. "What'd you do yesterday?"

"Um, nothing much. Hung out with my family." I immediately wish I'd done something noteworthy. "You?"

"Not much. I went out to the cemetery for a bit." He shrugs.

"Cemetery?" I ask, turning the dial to my lock and popping open the door. "Did, you, er, did you lose someone?" I ask, trying to sound casual and not as if I'd already suspected as much. I've never been to a cemetery. Not even when my grandmother died. My parents had decided it wasn't the sort of place I needed to be. Strangely enough, I agreed.

"Yeah." His lips press together.

I remember the moment at Pike Place and his unreadable expression. *Not everything or everyone lasts.* I feel like this is something I should know even if whatever-we-are is new. But when he doesn't volunteer more, I satisfy myself with a curt nod. This isn't the time to play detective. Dead people are strictly off limits, even for me.

He shoulder-bumps me playfully. "And played basketball," he adds, clearly trying to lighten the mood.

I can't help it, though. I'm intrigued.

I grab my books and Levi takes them from me, cradling them as we walk together. Rain thunders against the windows and the musky smell of a storm percolates through the walls. Levi cuts across my path and leans against the door to the quad. Droplets explode on the glass and dribble down in zigzag lines. The picnic tables and red brick of the courtyard are soaking as though they've been set under one big faucet turned all the way left.

He grins. "Shortcut?"

I lift an eyebrow, craning around him for a view of the torrential downpour that has built to a crescendo from its trickle not fifteen minutes earlier. For an instant, I worry about my curls, about the time I spent this morning arranging them perfectly. Then suddenly I couldn't care less, because Levi's tugging at my hand and we're making our way directly across the quadrangle, water flipping up on our pants.

"You're crazy," I yell up at him, because he's a few steps ahead. I realize that if it weren't for him escorting me to my class, he probably wouldn't have had to get wet at all.

On the other side of the quad, once under the cover of the east building, Levi rumples his hair with his hand, sending droplets flying everywhere. I squint against them while trying to run fingers through my own tangled mane.

We both laugh and out of the corner of my eye, I see Tess standing there staring at us, *her* hair freshly coifed and slicked back in her signature Burberry headband. She probably has the umbrella to match. Levi hands me my books and tells me he'll see me at lunch; then, when I'm not expecting it, he leans down and plants a kiss on my lips for everyone to see.

I die.

I mean, almost.

When our lips part, I can feel my face flush with embarrassment and pride, two things I never knew went together until this instant. There's a brief fraction of a moment when I try to feel a pinch of guilt—over Henry—but I can't. I'm too happy. I wander into class, soaked, and by lunchtime, we're a couple. Everybody's talking about it. That's what Brynn tells me, anyhow, as we walk to lunch. And it's as if my transformation is nearly complete. *Nearly.*

"I've never seen a guy without any commitment issues," Brynn remarks. "He's like an endangered species or something." The rain's stopped but our hair's still wet. In true Brynn fashion, she'd volunteered to ignore our previous argument in exchange for the details of my date with Levi. I considered this more than fair.

"I know." I hug my textbook to my chest. It's throbbing again and I'm wondering at this point if I should call Dr. Belkin. "Something has to be wrong with him, right?"

"Maybe he's older than we are. He looks mature. Have you asked him?" We pass the portables and I skip my usual bathroom trip at the math building.

"No, but he hasn't said he was held back or anything. I'm thinking maybe he's just more evolved?"

"Evolved, huh?" Brynn twists the metal barb in her eyebrow. "How very Darwinian of you."

"He said he was at the cemetery this weekend, Brynn." I've been waiting to confide in her about this particular tidbit.

Brynn's face screws up like she's just mixed toothpaste with orange juice. "The cemetery? Who died?"

"Don't know that part yet." I frown. "Maybe that's why he's in school here, though."

Brynn grabs my arm. "Oh! What if he, like, lost his girlfriend or something? How tragic would that be?"

"Brynn!" My heart sinks. "I hadn't thought of that. How the hell would I ever live up to a dead girlfriend?"

Brynn opens the door to the cafeteria for me since my hands are full. "Don't worry. It's probably his mom."

I crack a smile and pray that I'm not risking eternal damnation for preferring a dead mother over a dead girlfriend. Our table comes into view and at it is a new addition. There, at the spot usually next to mine, Levi sits chatting with Lydia, who's busy belly-laughing, apparently at something he said.

"I guess it doesn't matter either way." My pace quickens as I hurry to close the distance between me and Levi. Is he flirting? I shake the thought from my head, writing it off at once as either pathetic or paranoid. Most likely both.

"Not when you look like that it doesn't," Brynn finishes.

I shoot a look at my best friend, who's ogling my boyfriend. "Amen," I say, because you can't blame a girl for good taste.

I slide in next to Levi, who pats my leg. When he's not looking, Lydia gives me a thumbs-up, her eyes crinkled and glistening at the corners with tears of laughter. I can't help it: I beam.

"Hey, man," Levi says, mouth full of pizza. I glance up to see Henry, holding his tray, frozen midstride.

He blinks twice in rapid succession and then seems to reanimate, striding quickly the rest of the way. Brynn and I share a look.

"Hey," he responds, setting down his food.

"Thanks again for those tickets." Levi reaches across the table and holds out his hand, which Henry stares at a moment before shaking. "Concert was awesome. Really appreciate it. We had a great time." Levi's arm wraps around my shoulder and he pulls me into him. Like magic, the aching in my chest vanishes.

Henry stabs his fork into a Tater Tot. "I heard."

"What'd you end up doing?" I ask tentatively. We hadn't gotten to that in the car and I'm determined to make this whole thing *normal*.

Henry pops the tot into his mouth and looks me square in the eyes. "Got drunk with Ty."

I shouldn't care, but the statement jabs at me like a screwdriver. "Okay..." I roll my eyes. "Good for you."

He lifts his eyebrows and stabs his fork into another Tater Tot. Two points for my evolution theory, I guess. Levi's chowing down on a soggy hamburger, oblivious.

"Awkward," Brynn sings, as she fiddles with a piercing at the top of her ear. The tension only increases. "Anyway... who's going to Mitchell's next week?" she asks, ignoring the ticking atomic bomb that's set to go off at our table.

"Me!" Lydia pipes up. "His parents haven't gone out of town in ages."

"Henry...?" Brynn pokes his shoulder as if poking a bear.

He pulls his hat down lower. "I'll be there."

"Great! It'll be like Stella's official-official debut. And I guess Levi's, too. Are you in?"

"I assume we're talking about a party?"

"No shit, Sherlock," says Henry.

Stunned, I feel my mouth clamp shut. I've never seen Henry act this way. He's the resident nice guy, good student, teachers love having him in class. He asks girls on proper dates and I've never once heard of him kissing and telling, and, let's face it, I'm positive he's had things to kiss and tell about.

For his part, Levi lets the comment go. Instead, he pulls me closer with the arm that's already draped around my shoulders. Henry's eyes disappear under the shadow of his cap.

Levi must know the choice I've made. I only hope it's worth the cost.

chapter fifteen
102 BPM

It's both comforting and unnerving to learn that the most important person in your life may be someone you haven't met yet. That alone can make you feel not nearly as balanced or grown-up as you'd previously thought. At seventeen, I've already had to learn this twice. The first time was when I received a heart transplant from a stranger. The second was when I met Levi.

As a girl who loves rules and turning homework in on time, I've always reserved special contempt for those old married couples who met and got married five days later, like that's a reasonable life plan. Since middle school, I've had a planner filled with reminders of twice-daily swim practices and school somewhere in between. Then, once I reached high school, I included AP tests, SAT prep, and application deadlines that reached far into the future. There would have been no way I'd fit in a whirlwind romance. Until Levi.

Ever since the day we met, we've stuck together like Bonnie and Clyde. I find an endless number of things to be fascinated by. Like how Levi once rented a van and followed Pearl Jam on tour all the way to the East Coast. Or how he worked at Pike Place one summer and ate fresh fish on the docks as if it were sushi. Or the time he hijacked the microphone and sang onstage at Blacksmith Lounge.

The guys at Duwamish are into fishing and polo shirts and making varsity lacrosse, all things Levi couldn't care less about, which is good, because neither do I anymore.

In our first week of dating, we go to three concerts and I stay out as late as my parents will allow. Levi takes in music as if each note could be the last he hears. It's the same way he looks at me. In fact, that's how he does pretty much everything and this, I realize, is a feeling I understand.

After the last show, we hang around in his car. He takes out a pack of cigarettes and asks if I've tried one. I haven't, so he shows me how to hold the paper tube in the gummy part of my lips while I cup my hand around the flame to light it. The first time I take a drag, the smoke gets in my lungs and I wind up hunched over, coughing in the front seat. Levi laughs. My eyes sting. I catch a glimpse of them in the side-view mirror, pink and watery. The next time, Levi tells me to suck in my cheeks but not to let the smoke go past the back of my mouth.

I do. A small rib of embers and ash sinks into the paper at the other end. I pull it a little deeper with the next inhale. It's satisfying to hear the crinkle of the burning cigarette. I blow out a puff of gray and we talk about heavy things like guilt and dying and what we'd want people to say at our funerals. He's the only one who's ever asked, even though it's something I've thought about a lot.

When we have to separate that night, I get the sense that I'm wrenching something loose, liking pulling an arm out of its socket, and as soon as I do, the pain floods back into what's left.

It's four o'clock on a Tuesday. Reluctantly, I agree to meet Brynn on the stadium bleachers, where she's basking in the remnants of today's unexpected sun. Nightfall has been creeping up earlier and earlier, but there's still a spot in each day where, if the clouds have burned away and the temperature holds steady, you can laze in the sun without a jacket. In the fall, the light takes on a more orange-gold tinge, like the yellow foil on the inside of a candy-bar wrapper. Soon, the foggy winter will take even this away.

Brynn skipped cross-country practice, claiming she had one of her chronic sore throats. Translation: She wants to work on her tan lines. I don't get this. When I was a swimmer, I wouldn't miss practice if you paid me.

"Um, hi, who are you and what did you do with my friend?" Brynn props herself up on her elbows. Streaks of sunscreen cover her nose and cheeks.

I run my fingers through my hair, still surprised at how quickly they reach the end. I feel for my long locks as for the ghost of a missing appendage.

"What do you think?" I get a small charge from her reaction. In all our years of friendship, this is the first time I've shocked her rather than the other way around.

Yesterday, my dad got off work early. A few weeks ago

I would have been thrilled, the way a little girl is when her father brings home a present from an out-of-town trip. But this time my parents insisted I stay home for family dinner. For the first time in several days, I watched in horror as the clock turned slowly to 5:08, at which point my brain split open like a coconut and my chest turned into a black box of torture. Levi was the only one who could comfort me, who could keep the pain at bay.

When my mind cleared, I'd taken a pair of scissors from my desk drawer. I'd worked from one shoulder to the other, hacking it off in one blunt line at first and then retracing my steps to angle the scissors. The blades made the satisfying sound of sharpened metal as I sliced at random to turn the ends jagged. My hair now hung from a center parting and swung even with my chin. By the end, I looked like one of the punk rock chicks Levi and I watched onstage. The moment he saw me he touched the ends delicately, sending my heart into wild thumping as he wrapped the frayed ends around his fingers and pulled me closer.

Brynn gives me a long look. "I think an alien invaded your body." The reference reminds me of Henry. I push the thought aside. A small metal stud now adorns the left side of my nose.

"Well, that's supportive." I recline on the bleacher.

She sighs. "Well, a hot alien." I roll my eyes. "I'm sorry, I'm sorry. I'm supportive, I swear." She makes a motion of zipping her lips. I cock my head and wait, knowing Brynn can't possibly keep quiet about anything. A moment passes before she makes a dramatic gesture of unzipping her lips.

"I'm sorry it's just I'm not used to—what I mean is, it just doesn't look like *you*."

"Well, it *is* me, okay?"

Brynn's polo is pulled up to her bra and she's unzipped the top of her khakis and shimmied the waistline to meet her underwear. From this angle, I can just make out the gothic angel wings that are tattooed on the side of her hip.

Even with my new haircut and piercing, I'm not quite as ballsy, but Brynn wouldn't be either if she had a scar the length of a yardstick running up her abdomen. I wear my clothes in the way they were designed, taking in the UV rays like a lizard on a rock.

Brynn turns on her side and peers down at me from one bleacher up. "Yeah, okay, I get it," she says.

I stare up at the sky and watch clouds drift by in slow motion. With nothing to obstruct my view, the space above me stretches out into oblivion. I laze back against the warm metal, comforted by the world's vastness and the feeling of being just another living human being within it.

The day of my diagnosis, I had passed out at a swim meet. I was soaking wet. My hair was matted with chlorine and all I could think about was how I needed to get back in time for my relay. I was swimming the first leg, the youngest in the lineup. It was a big deal. I'd been poised on the diving block just before the starting beep, when all of a sudden my vision went blurry. I couldn't tell which way was up or down and the next thing I knew I'd fallen forward into the swimming pool. I remember staring up at the mottled surface like I was in a dream. I couldn't move.

Once I'd been fished from the bottom of the pool, I sat

in a doctor's office with my arms folded and legs crossed, huffing about how long it was taking and could we *puh-lease* get out of there already. It was nothing. I was fine. This was all a colossal waste of time.

That was the first time I met Dr. Belkin, sitting in the middle chair between my mom and dad in a square office that ought to have belonged to an accountant, not an MD.

That was the moment when he told me I'd swum my last lap. No more swimming—not now, not ever. I remember he started with that. As if he could ease me in before delivering the kicker. (Oh yeah and you might *die*, too.) It didn't help. Instead it was like two tidal waves crashing over me, first the tsunami, then the second groundswell to finish the job. I left the office numb.

Over the next few months, things got worse. First, I didn't make The List. Then I did. They issued my Life-pager, only it never beeped. I watched it, stared at it through the night, but still no match. The numbness encased me, becoming a permanent condition. I wouldn't survive. I would die at sixteen years old. There would be an obituary with nothing to say except how my smile lit up the room or some bullshit like that. Honestly, I'd rather not have one at all.

But then came the spark of curiosity. What if I was right? What if the pager *didn't* ever beep? What if I *was* never matched with a donor? *Then* what?

What happens . . . when you die?

The thought mesmerized as much as it terrified me. I started doing research. Near-death experiences—what were they and who had them?

I read stories of tunnel experiences, of the sensation of traveling through a passageway or up a staircase. Others felt a sudden immersion in a powerful light or even an ability to communicate with the light. As for me, I could never imagine a scenario in which I would find myself conversing with a beam of light, but, hey, what did I know?

In real time, a person experiences near-death in a span of thirty seconds to three minutes. A whole life review can take place in a time shorter than a commercial break. I wondered if I'd see angels or heaven or the members of a boy band singing me into the sky. The one thing I knew was that mine wouldn't be *near*-death. It'd be the real deal.

"Are you dead, Cross?" I spring upright when I feel a pinch on my leg. I'm blinking back the sunlight and trying to shade my face. I rub the spot where my skin is stinging.

"What the hell, Brynn!" I pinch her back.

"Guess not." She shrugs and frowns, closing her eyes again.

I try to smooth my hair. "You couldn't have just asked?"

"Well, I wanted to be sure." She flashes a grin without opening her eyes. "Plus, I'm bored. And I think you might be mad at me."

"What time is it?" I ask, digging my phone out of my pocket.

"What? You got a hot date?" This time she crunches her shoulders off the bleacher. But I don't have a date today. Levi said he was busy this afternoon but didn't give a reason. He doesn't know he's the only one who saves me. The mere thought of another afternoon without him leaves me nervy. And why wouldn't he tell me what he's doing? My mind has done several tailspins imagining the possibility of other girls. As though I weren't crazy enough. "God, I hate you," she says, misreading my silence. "You know that? Henry and Levi? I mean, Christ, Stel, leave some for the rest of us. Preferably Levi."

I hold out my middle finger. "Pretty sure Henry hates me."

The clock on my cell reads four thirty. I can't waste too much time, but I haven't made Brynn privy to my daily routine. Nor do I plan to.

"Yeah, right." Brynn pulls down her shirt and sits up. "That boy would lick your sweaty socks if you let him."

"Okay, thanks for the visual."

"He'd be better off if he did hate you, though. You *do* know that."

"You don't get me and Henry. It's complicated."

"Except that it's not. You want to keep him on the hook. You can't let him go. Just admit it." When I don't say anything she continues, "Now *why* is that, do you think?" She purses her lips as if to say, *Hm?*

"It's not that salacious, Detective McDaniel," I say, getting to my feet. "I'm perfectly happy with my choice, but I did forget to bring my meds, so I need to get home." The buckles on my backpack clang against the bleachers as I sling it over my shoulder.

Brynn stares at me a beat longer than usual. I know that she'd prefer to forget that I was sick, that a part of me still *is* sick. I need medicines and regimens and checkups to keep me running. Huff, puff, and you could literally blow this house down. And Brynn's not exactly the type to treat anyone with kid gloves.

"Fine." Brynn tugs on the hair tie holding up her bun and auburn curls tumble out. She threads her hand through the elastic and tousles her hair, creating a wild but sexy look—like she's fresh off a steamy make-out session. "Your vampire complexion is looking a little rosy anyway."

I touch my cheeks. "Great," I say. My phone buzzes in my hand and my breath hitches with excitement. Maybe Levi changed his mind. I turn it over. It's a text from my mom.

Brynn slaps my butt. "Okay, lovebird. Stop making me want to vom and don't forget to use protection."

I glare back at her. "You need a hobby."

The sun has burned a complete hole through the clouds, so that now when I look up, it's at a fiery yolk surrounded by cornflower blue. Wispy gray clouds still hover at the periphery. I slide into the driver's seat and twist on the AC for the first time in weeks.

I click on my blinker and wait for a car to pass before I edge onto the main road that runs alongside campus.

My wheels hit a puddle and I bounce in the seat. I hear mud splatter the exterior. Whoever thought having a black car in Seattle would be a good idea was an idiot.

Oh, right, that's me.

I tap the lever for the wipers to clear off the droplets still clinging to the glass and they smear mud across the windshield, tainting the blueness of the sky. Meanwhile, the clock on the dash reads *4:51*. I shouldn't have stayed so late with Brynn. I was supposed to take my meds fifteen minutes ago. At this point, Mom has probably perfected her lecture and is now pacing the entryway, waiting for her audience to arrive.

I press a little harder on the gas pedal. My commute to and from school isn't long, but my prescriptions don't exactly work like Tylenol either. It's not a take-every-eight-hours (give or take a few) situation. The medications are synched with my body down to the minute.

At a red light, I slam on the brakes.

What happens when I miss my meds is a mystery to me, but my imagination has a way of filling in the blanks.

I blink and the light turns green. I race onto Flora Avenue. What had I been thinking? *That* is the question. My car speeds down the narrow, two-lane road and I search the side streets for cops. It would be my luck. Par for the course.

For an instant, there's a sick mental picture forming behind my eyes. Arteries and veins snap and my heart plummets into my stomach. I shake it away like a crude drawing on an Etch A Sketch. I focus on the road. My street is coming up. Two more stop signs. I roll through both of them.

My tires screech on the concrete as I veer onto my street. Familiar addresses. Familiar houses. I try to wrestle my heart into submission. It's going to be fine.

My phone buzzes in the cupholder. A goofy picture of my mom from her third-grade yearbook flashes on the screen. I fumble for the button to silence it. I'm almost there. When I look up, there's a reflection up ahead like the glint of a mirage on a hot day. I keep driving, but as I do, I see that the mirage at the end of the lane is moving, and not in the way that mirages typically do—disappearing in one place before reappearing at a point further out. Instead, it seems to be spreading closer, morphing into a long sheet of water.

I lean forward to try to get a better view. As the wheels edge closer, I can make out white ripples pushing forward like gentle waves crashing onto shore. Is the street flooding?

The sun still gleams overhead. Not a drop of rain in sight. Where's it coming from?

There's a roar as loud as the Pacific Ocean and then, from the gutter openings on the side of the street, water gushes out onto the concrete. The first spray slams my car door. I tighten my grip on the steering wheel and press on the gas pedal toward the shrinking spot of open asphalt.

Droplets splatter the windshield. I squeeze my eyelids shut and then open them, but nothing changes.

The water sweeps in from all sides.

The next wave crashes into the passenger side and slams me the other way. My temple knocks against the glass, smashing it.

I can't tell if the crack I hear is my skull or the window. A trail of blood begins sliding down toward my chin just as the wheels lift from the ground and the car tilts over onto its side.

The car lands with a metal thud; I hear the back window shatter. A Coke can falls out the passenger-side window. I lean into the steering wheel, screaming.

Then, the water starts to seep into the cracks. First in the door and then through the rifts in the window. It's rising all around and it smells of seaweed and cold and salted fish.

I push at the water with my hands. Slapping it away. Flailing.

Through the boom of the water I hear blaring horns, insistent and shrill. I fight through the water, look back through the broken back windshield. Only it's not broken at all.

Two angry drivers lay on their horns behind me. I swivel back and find myself stopped dead in the middle of the street.

The sun shines impossibly bright and I squint to see that everything's exactly as it should be.

I wipe my cheek. No blood. The windows? Unbroken. And my clothes are bone dry.

Another car joins the chorus. The air fills with the noise of honking horns. Shaking, I lift my foot from the brake.

More cautiously this time, I let the Jetta creep forward. My mind feels soggy and my hands tremble like autumn leaves. It's 5:05 by the time I pull into my driveway. Inside, Mom's holding out the pills in her fist, measured for me and warm from her grip. She doesn't say anything when I tear by her, but she doesn't have to. I know by the lines around her mouth that she's not only worried, but angry at me for treating my gift, the one that cost them ten college educations, with the same level of care as a sweatshirt from Goodwill.

But she doesn't stop me. By the time I get the pills down and chase them with a couple mouthfuls of water, it's time. And then—

chapter sixteen
107 BPM

The next day at school, my chest feels as though it's recovering from an infected bullet wound. Three more days, I bargain with myself. If it doesn't stop I'll go see Dr. Belkin. The thought of hoisting myself up onto another examination table, of being issued another hospital bracelet, makes my stomach turn sour. Weak and feverish, I wouldn't have come to school at all but for Levi. I don't care that it's only first period. I need to see him.

The lecture begins with a stuffy drone on the assassination of Archduke Franz Ferdinand. History used to be my favorite subject. I did extra credit for it. Now it feels useless and like I'm being confined in a pen with twenty other students for no reason.

I count the minutes, then the seconds, until I can't stand it any longer. I slide my phone under my desk, keeping it out of view, and text Levi. The whole point in coming is to see him, so what am I doing here? I sigh too loudly. Our teacher's eyes snap to me, but she doesn't stop talking. It's as if she's applying a cheese grater to my ears. I'm antsy. Agitated. Can't sit still. I quietly slide my elbows off my desk. My eyes meet Henry's. Our gazes lock together like magnets. My lips part, but he cuts his glance away with the sharpness of what may as well be a knife.

I hesitate for a split second before reanimating and excuse myself to use the restroom. But when I slip out of the classroom, I head straight for the glowing red EXIT sign at the end of the hallway. I take one look over my shoulder before pushing through into the open air.

Whenever I leave the school building, I get the briefest sensation that I'm entering another world. The effect is double when I leave at a time that I should be in class.

The space behind the school building has the feeling of lawless abandonment while at the same time being peppered with signs that somebody's been here. Aluminum cans and discarded chip bags litter the grass, which is dead, permanently blocked from the sun by the colossal brick mass of Duwamish High. Even the air holds onto the shadowy cold.

I cross through the darkest patch into the woods.

When I step into the tree line, the trunks are actually plentiful, but within several paces, I can see that the forest is shallow and that the number of trees quickly thins out within less than a quarter mile.

My footsteps are soft on the floor of matted pine needles. I've never set foot back here. A good girl wouldn't.

I breathe the smell of tree sap and rain. There's a snap of a twig. I whirl around to see Levi, picking his way down an overgrown path.

"You made it," I say, my insides bubbling like soda water. His grin is wolfish and it takes self-restraint not to throw myself into his arms. The second he's close, my rib cage unclamps, and I take what feels like my first full breath in two days.

"In the flesh," he says, erasing the distance between us. I feel my heart rate spike. A mixture of Levi's sudden closeness and the fact that I'm cutting class to see him.

"What did you need?" he asks. Only Levi could make our school uniforms look cutting-edge. He wears his shirt and his pants too tight. A ropy bracelet twists around his wrist and a guitar pick hangs on a piece of hemp close to this throat. I shiver as he tucks a strand of hair behind my ear. Maybe it's this electric charge that gives me courage, but before I can stop myself—

"I needed you." I stand up on my tippy-toes and press my lips gently against his. And it's as if a knot in my stomach untangles loop by loop. He tenses. Breath hitches. I feel the tightness reach his mouth and I pull away, lowering back onto my heels, worried I may have done something wrong.

His eyebrows draw together. I catch the strain in his face. He needs this as much as I do. I try to speak, but his arm wraps around my lower back and he yanks me into him. He holds me roughly against his chest while he runs his hands down my sides, pulling at the fabric of my shirt.

His tongue forces my lips apart. He mumbles something unintelligible. The hand at my back slides up to the space between my shoulder blades, where he grabs a fistful of my polo. I gasp. His mouth pushes harder into mine. Hot and salty.

For once there's nothing but pleasure. Outside in the

broad daylight, we kiss. The pain and sickness that drag at me like cement blocks are less than a memory. I want more. He gropes at my arms, my neck, my waist. Each touch sends my heart pounding so hard I'm sure it'll burst through my chest.

I kiss him harder and he returns it voraciously. I run my hand over his stomach. His abs tighten. We both pant. Quick breaths. Shallow.

His teeth softly bite my lip. I rock my hips into his. He murmurs. I don't want this to end. The breeze blows through the trees. Goose bumps erupt over my skin. *This.* More of *this*, is all I can think, my thoughts muddled and heady. I slide my hands over his hips. He runs his fingers through my short hair, playing with the strands. He holds me to him. And there's this moment again, the feeling of standing above-water with toes hanging off the pier, of doing the one thing that no one expects of me. And I wonder what else I will do and how much further I will go to chase this rush.

If I keep pushing for the next high, will I eventually fall?

chapter seventeen
131 BPM

It's Thursday. The throbbing in my chest is raw as I pace the living room floor with Elsie on my hip. My parents have a dinner thing tonight. They're sucking up to me since I agreed I'd go see Dr. Belkin. After giving me a twenty-minute lecture on the dangers of underage sex, they said I could have Levi over while I watched Elsie. Naturally, Elsie's chosen this moment to be fussy. Her tiny face is pinched into a raisin. I know this face. It's the one that comes right before the screaming.

"Come on, Elsie." I tickle her tummy. "Just this once, please?" I beg, and in response she balls her hands into fists.

"No! No! No!" She tosses her head into my shoulder.

"Elsieeee," I whine. "I'm your big sister. Trust me, when you're in high school, you'll understand." My tone is singsongy.

A new whimper escapes and I pace faster, bobbing her

up and down, up and down. I glance at the door. He should be here.

As if knowing, Elsie grabs at my breast and together we stare at her tiny hand, pressed into my bra. "'Ella." Spit bubbles crop up on her lips, but, for the moment, she's quiet. I try not to move, my heart thumping against her, when the doorbell rings.

Elsie breaks out screaming like I'm ripping out her toenails. "Christ, Elsie!" My blood pressure spikes as I hurry to the door. The last thing I need is for Levi to think I make a habit of torturing small children.

I jiggle the doorknob and Levi's standing there looking painfully beautiful. "Whatcha doing in there?" he asks, stepping over the threshold.

Elsie wails.

"God, I know, right?" I try pressing Elsie's head to my chest and rocking her. "And to think we hadn't even started the Chinese waterboarding."

Levi laughs. Our eyes catch. I blush and look away. I rub the back of my neck, prickling from the memory of the two of us in the woods. "What, um..." The words stick in my throat. "What'd you bring?"

He flashes a DVD. "*Live at Reading*. Your education continues," he says, looking quite pleased with himself.

"Live at who?" I battle Elsie to be heard. Her flimsy baby nails scratch at my arms.

"The 'who' is Nirvana. The 'where' is Reading. Full concert feature. Get with the program, Cross." He nudges me.

"*Whyyyyy?*" Elsie howls, her face now tomato red. "*Whyyyy?*" Tears slide down her cheeks and into her mouth.

"Want me to try?" Levi asks, holding out his arms for Elsie.

"Seriously?"

His fingers twitch, gesturing me to hand her over. I bite my lip and do what he says. As soon as he scoops Elsie up, she stops crying. It's as if someone's flipped a switch. On, then off. Me, then Levi. He smiles at her, white teeth gleaming, and she grins back with her fingers hanging half out of her mouth.

"That's better," Levi whispers. "I'm Levi." He points to himself. "Levi." He bops her nose. "Elsie."

She giggles. "Eevi," she repeats. I can't help but giggle right along with her.

"Okay, how did you do that?" I fold my arms over my chest. No way is that the same kid I was holding two seconds earlier.

Levi winks and starts walking Elsie around the room, gently bouncing her as she watches him like he's a slice of chocolate cake. It must run in the family.

"Is that your sister?" Levi asks in his best baby talk, pointing to a photograph of me with my parents pre-Elsie. "Yeah? It is?" he answers for her and continues down the line. "Who's that? Is that you?" She hides her face in his shoulder. "But you look so pretty, Miss Elsie. Why are you hiding?"

Elsie peeks again, sniffling, and, mimicking Levi, finally points at the framed picture.

"Hey, you guys have a hot tub." Levi peers through the blinds, looking out at our backyard.

I stand at a distance from Levi, on the other side of the

room, watching him with Elsie, who shakes her brown curls and sneezes. "Well, it's certainly not our bathtub."

Levi looks at the window a second longer. "Shall we?" He waggles his eyebrows.

"Shall we what?"

"Go in the Jacuzzi. It works, doesn't it?" His grin is devilish.

My mouth goes dry. I asked a boy to my house while my parents aren't home. What did I expect? And besides, it's not that I don't want to, but the thought of putting on a bathing suit in front of Levi makes my throat practically close up.

"We've got Elsie, though. We can't just leave her in here by herself." My parents would kill me.

Elsie clutches one of Levi's fingers. Her bright green eyes are the exact same color as mine. "Jeez, I'm not that irresponsible." His eyes cover the length of me. "Not that I wouldn't like to be." He pauses for that to sink in. "I meant that she'd come with us. We can hold her. It'll be fun and Elsie will love it, won't you, Elsie?"

"Yeah!" Her curls fly in agreement.

"I haven't been in a pool in, like, forever," Levi says.

"Me neither, actually," I say. "I'm more of an ocean girl."

Levi's lip curls up. "I hate the ocean."

"You hate the ocean?" I laugh. "How can anybody hate a massive body of water?"

He turns pensive. "That's the problem. It's too big. It'll swallow you up. Plus, you can't see what's underneath your feet."

Through the kitchen window I can see the moon, suspended like a lopsided orb over our backyard. The night's been clear since it stopped drizzling about an hour ago, and the sky's spotted with a few low-hanging clouds, turned gray and shadowy by the murky backdrop.

A dip in the Jacuzzi *would* help tire Elsie out, I reason. Plus, if I can get her to bed early, that will leave more time alone for me and Levi. And he's right. She'd love it. Much more than watching something that doesn't involve a talking panda.

"Fine, fine. Hot tub would be nice. And warm," I concede. "Can you watch Elsie? I've got to change and order the pizza."

"Hooray!" Levi lifts one of Elsie's pudgy arms and waves it around as they celebrate together. It's impossible not to smile.

"I'll turn it on," he says, and with one last glance back, I leave to dig for my bikini.

Partway up the stairs, I realize I have no idea what Levi's planning to wear, and the thought makes me heady. What if he wears nothing? As soon as it crosses my mind, I shake the thought away. Your little sister's out there, Stella! I rub at the back of my neck. I have to give the guy credit. He has some effect on the Cross girls.

In my room, I rifle through my dresser drawers. I can't remember the last time I had to wear a bathing suit. Who knows if my boobs will even fit in the ones I have anymore?

Finally, I dig a stringy two-piece out of the bottom of the third drawer from the top. It's bright blue with red strawberries on it. I cringe at the juvenile fabric, wishing I had one of those white numbers that make guys hope the bathing suit's see-through.

Since it's all I have, I slip it on, examining myself in the full-length mirror that hangs on the back of my bedroom door. At the sight of my reflection, I tense. The scar cuts through me in a single, long slash, looking violent and new. I take a deep breath, staring down at my disfigured torso and letting my fingertips graze the raised skin. Levi's seen it, I remind myself. A small part, but still. He didn't freak out. I force myself to look again. I can't spend the rest of my life wearing muumuus, can I? I tilt my head the way Levi had when he looked at it. See, not so bad.

Grabbing a towel, I wrap it around me and cross the room to peer down at the hot tub. Levi sits on the edge, the water steaming up to meet him and making his T-shirt cling to his body. On his lap, Elsie reaches up to touch his face.

Watching the two of them, it's easy to forget that Elsie drives me insane. Her chubby arms flap happily, and I wish this was the only version of her I could see, the Precious Moments angel baby that my parents fawn over.

I'm about to turn away from the window when there's a blur out of the corner of my eye. Followed by a splash. At least I think there's a splash. The night is black, with curly white tendrils of steam obscuring everything below like a veil. I peer hard through the thick mist.

The soft glow of the pool lights is hardly enough to see by. Darkness seeps in at the corners, nearly snuffing out the scene altogether.

Then a tiny, peach hand breaks the surface. Elsie flails in the water. I watch motionless, waiting for Levi to grab her. The windowpane blocks the sound, trapping me like a glass cage.

Her head bobs up for a split second. Sinks back under.

I push at the bottom of the window, knocking against it with the heel of my hand. Useless. It's stuck. My hands fall futilely to my sides and for a moment, I can't move.

Every muscle in my body locks up. Stiff. The water in the Jacuzzi glitters below. Fake blue and inviting. Levi cocks his head. He watches her as if she's an experiment.

Do something, I plead silently.

Bubbles crop up at the pool's surface. This isn't happening.

As if finally coming to life, Levi reaches into the water. He submerges his arm up to his shoulder.

Out pops Elsie's head. Her mouth is open. I still can't hear anything. A silent movie.

A sob racks my lungs. Oh, thank God. He must have freaked.

She's okay. She's okay.

But before I can steady myself, Levi palms the top of my baby sister's skull like it's a basketball—and plunges her back down.

A scream lodges in my throat.

"No!"

A whisper.

Levi looks up at the window where I'm standing, a glint in his shadowed eyes as he holds her underwater. My knees jerk. A sick feeling wells up.

Not Elsie. Not Elsie.

My joints unlock. I spring into motion, racing down the stairs. I skip stairs as I go. Not Elsie.

My legs pump. I yank open the back door. "What are you *doing*?" My voice is a shriek.

Levi jerks back, startled. "Stella?" He's sitting on the side of the hot tub, Elsie in his lap. She scrunches her hand to wave at me, her wispy curls dry as tumbleweeds.

I blink, stopping in the doorway. "What's going on?" The words stick to my tongue and I have to scrape them off.

"What do you mean? Did you order the pizza?"

"I . . ." My vision starts to tunnel and I feel faint. "Is Elsie okay?" I ask weakly. My heart thwacks at the inside of my chest like a mallet on a crab's shell.

"Yeah." Levi swings his feet out of the hot tub, holding tight to Elsie. "Are *you* okay?" I can't look him in the eye. "You look a little—"

"I know." My hands are shaking. "I actually don't think I'm feeling well. Do you mind if maybe we just watch the movie?"

"Sure, yeah, okay." He hops off the ledge and strides over to hand me Elsie. Never before have I wanted her so much. I clasp her to my body, smelling her hair and baby-powdered skin and clenching her like someone might try and take her from me.

I find a towel for Levi, who dries off his legs and feet. My face is hot with shame that I thought Levi would try to hurt Elsie, but still, I won't let her go. My ears keep buzzing and my breaths are shallow. Even when Elsie starts to cry, even when our pizza arrives and Levi scoots in close to watch the Hitchcock movie, I hold her, letting her sit on my knees and hugging her until our breaths match and she's an extension of me. I look down at my sleeping sister and can see through the wisps of baby hair that cover her fuzzy head and smell the sweet skin underneath, both fresh and familiar. There's a flat stretch at the crown of her head that's the same as mine, and when I notice, it's as if I'm seeing her with new eyes. It's as though I can finally see her. I pull Elsie into me. This miniature human bundle is made up of the same ingredients as I am. No longer the Replacement Child, but she could have replaced me, maybe, if she'd needed to.

chapter eighteen
122 BPM

What are u doing?

I'm w Brynn.

Why?

It's just for an hour or so. My thumbs work furiously across my phone's keypad. *I need fashion help.*

Don't get it from her. I chew on my cheek and contemplate ditching my friend.

Play nice, I type instead.

I need you. Upon reading this, I feel my throat constrict. The pain in my chest roars.

"Hello!" Brynn butts in. She has a pile of clothes strung over her arms and shifts the weight from one elbow crook to the other. "It's me. The perfectly acceptable human specimen perusing the mall with you. Can you see me? Am I invisible?" She looks down at her forearm and makes a big show of examining it. "I don't *appear* to be invisible. Maybe

I'm only invisible to certain people. Like, say, ones with boyfriends?"

I roll my eyes. "Invisibility would be completely wasted on you. You can't sneak up on people if you can't keep your mouth shut."

She heaves an exaggerated sigh. "You've been glued to that stupid phone since we got here."

"That's not true."

"Um, except that it is. You're obsessed, Stel. And you're kind of giving me a case of the icks."

"Someone can't stand not being the center of attention," I mutter.

She throws the potential costumes we'd pulled over a clothing rack and stretches out her arms. "No. What I can't stand is going shopping with my best friend—or at least the girl formerly known as my best friend minus all the garbage-punk-rock-goth-eyeliner stuff—to do her a favor and being ignored. I did not come to Creepy Costumes 'R' Us for my own health." She eyeballs the place. It's the only store in the mall that's not open the whole year round. The place is stuffed with limp masks, displays of face paint, and demon baby figurines whose eyes flicker red whenever someone passes by.

"If you don't like my haircut you might as well cut the passive-aggressive routine and just say so."

"Excuse you. When have you ever known me to be passive-aggressive? I'm aggressive-aggressive. I don't care what you do with your hair. I care why you do it." Brynn bats away an orange streamer hanging from the ceiling.

"What's that supposed to mean?"

"It means I don't think you should have to be Stella two point oh just to make some guy like you."

"He liked me before," I point out.

"You know what I mean."

"No. I don't." I cross my arms.

Brynn picks a mask off the rack. She turns it over in her hands, sees that it's an insane clown face, and shudders, stuffing it back behind the others. "Henry liked the old you. Just saying."

"That's the point. I don't like the old me. And either way, I'm *not* the old me. I can't be. I can't swim, I have to take horse tranquilizer pills every five seconds, and I'm constantly on the verge of a mechanical breakdown. No offense, but you have no idea what you're talking about."

Brynn frowns. A little kid wanders too close to our conversation, swinging a pumpkin candy holder and humming "The Monster Mash." Brynn makes faces at him and he scrambles over to an adjacent aisle. "Okay, I get the whole desire-to-reinvent-yourself thing or whatever. It's very Madonna. But..."

"There has to be a 'but.'"

"Only because you're kind of acting like one."

"Mature, Brynn, real mature." I smirk.

"*But*," she continues, "just make sure you're doing it for you and not some dark, brooding dude with a record collection."

I laugh uneasily.

She relaxes her shoulders, grabs a witch's hat off a nearby rack, and pulls it over her head. "Okay, the public-service-announcement portion of this afternoon is over. Now put the phone away and let's find you a costume."

"Right." I nod. Halloween is in two days and I have nothing to wear. Brynn made her costume, but I have neither the time nor the creativity, so that meant I had to settle for the big-box store, which is why we're braving a mob of sticky children and their trailing mothers who look worn at the edges and wary of what a pound of sugar will to do their little hellions. Three times this trip miniature ghouls and goblins have jumped out from behind corners and yelled, "Boo!" kicking my heartbeat into warp speed.

"You're so lucky." Brynn retrieves the stack of costumes she's picked out for me. We've wandered back into the "adult section" of the Halloween store, trying to act as if we belong.

"I don't think *lucky* has ever been a word used in the same sentence as my name, but thanks." I stare at a scantily clad model posing on the package for an angel costume. There is nothing angelic about her.

I find a salesperson—a gothic girl with a bored expression, chewing on the twine of her pentagram necklace—and ask her for a fitting room. Brynn throws her costume stockpile on the floor and I barely have room to stand on both feet. She steps out of the stall and draws the curtain shut behind me.

"Previous notes aside, you have a boyfriend for Halloween."

"Why? It's not like it's Valentine's Day." I pull a long black dress over my head and fasten the nun's habit over my hair.

"It's better than Valentine's. It's the one day you get to dress like a slut and no one can say a word about it. Levi's going to flip."

I slide open the curtain to model my nun costume.

"Oh God." Brynn slaps her hand over her eyes. "Unless you wear that. That was not in my stack of approved costumes."

"I thought it might be funny," I whine, but I'm laughing already. "Like ironically funny?"

"Nobody cares about your irony, Stella. Irony does not get you lai—" I shoot her a glare. "—lucky."

I turn away to hide the fact that I'm blushing. I haven't told her about our rendezvous in the woods, which, okay, might not quite have been newsworthy in the Brynn McDaniel universe, but it was approaching the perimeter.

"Fine." I disappear back into the fitting room. I stuff the outfit back on the rack. "No matter what the context, I'm still not sure *lucky* is the right word to describe me."

"Have you *seen* Levi?"

I dig through the costume choices and select a blue-and-white number that's supposed to make me look like Cinderella. "Yes." The fabric feels rough and cheap on my skin.

"Okay, then. I rest my case."

"I . . ." I reappear from the dressing room and twirl. Brynn immediately shakes her head, nixing the outfit. I forge on anyway. "Look, this is an embarrassing question, but how do you know if you're, like, in love?"

Brynn stands up straighter. "You're in *love?* Stel, you didn't tell me you were in love, for Christ's sake."

My eyebrows lift and I hold up a finger. "I didn't say that. I asked how would I *know.*" I'm in the process of ruling out possibilities—the same way Dr. Belkin does with my tests. *No signs of organ rejection,* that's what he told me. After I relented and agreed to a half day of testing at the hands of Dr. B., I wasn't sure whether to be relieved or disappointed when the results came back showing a big fat nothing.

So maybe it's not medical. I know it's *something*. And there's the distinct possibility that I don't know what love is. I hate being away from him. I'm uneasy around him. I want to touch him so badly it hurts, but could all these things added together equal the *L* word?

People are always talking about butterflies and longing and lust, but maybe these are only euphemisms and the truth about love is that it's highly uncomfortable.

"I knew it." Brynn's cheeks turn into those of a chipmunk as she swallows a smile. "Well, I guess that makes sense. You have to be either in love or insane." Maybe a little of both, I want to say, remembering Levi's hand forcing Elsie's tiny head underwater.

Only I'm not remembering exactly. I can't remember something that never happened. To avoid Brynn, I delve back into the overstuffed dressing room. If it's not a memory and it's not a dream, then what?

I chew the inside of my lip and stare absentmindedly into the mirror. Every sick girl worth her weight in IV tubes knows that physical illness can cause psychological manifestations and vice versa. But I'm not sure whether a hallucination is physical defect causing something psychological, which seems less likely given Dr. Belkin's test, or an emotional response causing the physical manifestation of seeing something that isn't there.

At that second, a queasy pit begins to open just below my belly button. Because, I think, the emotional trigger would have to be Levi.

"Did you decide to take a nap in there?"

I blink, coming to and catching my reflection. The

too-bright satin and silly ruffled sleeves—what was I thinking? Levi would hate this.

I rummage through the pile, landing on a packaged costume that reads ADULT DARK DOLLIE on the label. I tug off the Cinderella getup and change into the costume. Before opening the curtain, I step into the pair of purple-and-black-striped stockings, sliding them up over my knees and midway up my thighs. I look down, wiggling my toes, before showing Brynn.

"Well?" I put my hands on my hips. I'm wearing a tight and very short dress that fans out at the waist. A gothic-inspired black crinoline petticoat peeks out underneath, while my fingers stick out of cropped lace gloves. The neckline is a low-cut sweetheart design, the sleeves of which hang slightly off the side of each shoulder.

"Creepy," Brynn says, but with a sly grin. "And sexy. If you're into that sort of thing."

"I am." And I'm hoping Levi is too.

Brynn cocks her head as if she can see the outfit better sideways. "You'll need black lipstick. And boots. And definitely a push-up bra."

"Hey!" I cup my chest protectively.

"You do have a push-up bra, right?"

I shift my weight. "Yes, I have one." It was an impulse buy at the mall. I never thought I'd actually use it. Besides there's hardly anything there to push.

"Good." She puts her hands on my shoulders. "Because nothing spells true love like two extra cup sizes."

"Did anyone ever tell you that you should write greeting cards?"

"What can I say? I'm a hopeless romantic." She pushes me back into the dressing room to change into my real clothes and as the curtain seals me back inside, I'm left wondering: Is that it, am I a romantic?

Or maybe I'm just hopeless.

chapter nineteen
131 BPM

"Trick or treat!" Brynn's voice rises above the rest as our pack of seniors crowds onto a sparsely decorated porch. In the night air, fall has sprung up all around us. The smell of wet leaves infuses the dark sky along with the smoky scent of a neighbor's fire.

"Aren't you all a little old for trick-or-treating?" says the middle-aged woman who answers the door. Funny, my parents had said the exact same thing.

She sizes us up. Brynn's dressed as Zombie Barbie—blond wig and ghostly white makeup covered in purple and red splotches—while Lydia has donned a denim skirt, cowboy boots, and a ten-gallon hat. Brandon's toilet-paper mummy costume is already starting to fray, and Henry's skeleton bodysuit only vaguely glows in the dark, but he's skinny enough to pull it off anyway. It's Levi's costume that's truly succulent, no pun intended. A black, high-necked cape drapes around his shoulders, and his Count Dracula fangs look almost too convincing.

"Come on," Brandon whines. "Give us a break. We're seniors!" She wouldn't be the first to have turned us away tonight. Turns out playing dress-up is cuter on seven- than seventeen-year-olds.

Brynn shoves her pillowcase out at the lady. "Consider it a Peter Pan thing. One last chance before we're all grown-up." She juts out her lower lip for good measure. Despite her obvious lack of adult appeal, Brynn could sell potatoes to a potato farmer.

The woman softens and reaches into her pumpkin bowl. "Fine, but you kids behave now, okay?" We all squeal at once and shuffle around so that she can dole out handfuls to each of us. "And I better not see you pulling this same routine next year."

"You won't." Lydia promises.

We file off onto the lamplit street with hardly any intention of behaving at all. The neighborhood we gravitated to butts up to Lydia's. Its homes have pool houses that could eat my entire home for breakfast. We pass a bunch of little kids triumphantly waving king-size candy bars. The sound of branches scraping the side of a house makes me feel as if I'm reliving a scene from *Hocus Pocus*.

"Where to next?" I skip ahead to Levi, purposefully bypassing Henry in the process. The black asphalt sparkles with a fresh rain and a thin layer of clouds has turned the moon blood orange.

"Damn it." Brandon twists to check out the back of his costume. "I'm already starting to unravel."

"Maybe you shouldn't have used generic," I call back.

Levi laces his fingers in mine. "How about that one?" He points to a sprawling mansion with iron gates adorned with fake spiderwebs. The collar of his cape casts dark shadows across his cheekbones.

It wouldn't take much for someone to convince me he's a real vampire, not when he looks at me like I'm a candied apple he'd like to take a bite out of....

A shudder, equal parts pleasure and nerves, runs through me. I let it.

It's Halloween.

"On it." I walk over to the house, push open the gate, and, in minutes, return grinning with half a pillowcase full of Starburst and Twizzlers. "They weren't home." Levi's shoulders slump. I hold the bag out for his review. "But I might share if you're nice."

A smile playing under the shadows on his face, Levi leans in to kiss me on the cheek, but nearly head-butts Brynn instead. "Excuse *you*," I tell her.

"Thanks." She plunges two hands into the stash of candy, wedging herself between me and Levi. "I love Twizzlers."

Levi pulls away before his lips can brush my skin and I'm left with a craving for his touch. I get a slight twinge of the ache in my heart when he's gone, but it passes as quickly as a gust of wind.

"Please, Brynn." I snap the ends of the pillowcase closed. "Help yourself."

She waggles her eyebrows and takes a bite out of a red licorice stick. "Don't mind if I do." She turns to Levi and points at me. "You should have seen this one in middle school. Weirdest costumes ever. But cute." She pinches my cheek. "In seventh grade she was a 'little green man' and in eighth—what were you again?"

"Stop!" I cover my face. "It's so embarrassing."

Henry clears his throat. He's been so quiet I almost forgot he was standing right beside me. "She was the Loch Ness Monster, and she called herself Nessie." His efforts to keep a straight face fail and he crumples into snorting laughter. "Only—only she didn't look anything like a sea monster. Like at all. What'd you wear again?"

I stare openmouthed at him—so glad that he's finally talking to me, I can't believe it. "I did too!" I get out before launching into a fit of giggles myself. "I wore seaweed on my clothes." I shove him playfully in the arm.

"Seaweed? That's what that was?"

"Yes, I got it from the aquarium aisle at PetSmart!"

At this he rolls his head back and laughs up into the sky. A huge weight lifts from my shoulders. It's been weeks since Henry and I have found anything funny together. It's been almost that long since we've said more than two words.

"Okay, fine, but remember what *you* were? Freddie Krueger, only your mom said you couldn't take her nice steak knives!"

He wraps the crook of his arm around my neck and pulls me in to a headlock to ruffle my hair. I stumble, laughing. "I was—"

Before Henry can answer, there's a tug at my hand and I'm ripped away. I'm pulled up against Levi's side and staring from a short distance at Henry, who goes quiet. I nervously flatten my hair. Levi wraps his arm tightly around my waist. "Hey, Cross, do you think we should be heading home soon?" he whispers in my ear.

My eyes flit away from Henry, but I notice him straighten his skeleton shirt and take a few careful steps back.

"I..." I begin, but I'm not sure what to say. I keep my voice quiet, hoping no one else can hear. "I'm having a good time. Let's stay out a little while longer."

Levi's breath comes in short puffs against my earlobe. "You do seem to be having a nice time, but with Henry."

I allow our pace to lag so that we can fall back from the pack. Nobody seems to notice except for Henry. "He's just my friend, Levi."

Levi's fingers clutch hard at my side. "Maybe I should go home, then, and you two can hang out." He says these words in this tone that's supposed to be kind but sends a shiver up my arms. A brief flash of pain erupts underneath my ribs. I picture myself being ripped away from him, and it's like a hole is being torn through my gut.

"No." I gasp. "I just..." I peer up at him. "I'm sorry. I wasn't—"

"Flirting?" He interrupts. He stares down at me hard and I squirm.

"I wasn't," I say.

Then he kisses my forehead. "It's okay, Cross. Just... be good."

I close my eyes, trying to focus on the feeling Levi's lips leave on my skin. Meanwhile, my stomach is brewing with a strange mix of emotions. Tiny hair follicles rise on the back of my neck, like the pressure in the air has dropped just before a storm and I can feel the first ghostlike fingers of its icy breeze pass through me.

I know that if I look over, Henry will still be watching.

Instead, I lift my chin and look into Levi's eyes. I'm not sure what I expected—or rather, I am: I thought they'd be cold, hard, mean—but they're not. He's Levi once again. My Levi. I reach down for his hand and squeeze it. Now's not the time to start a fight. We can talk about this later.

I plant a long kiss on his lips before catching up to the group. Holding hands, we rejoin them at the spot where everyone else is stopped. I nuzzle into Levi's neck, content to be free from any pain or discomfort. *Later*, I assure myself, we'll talk about the thing with Henry. Just not now.

Henry and I don't acknowledge each other, and I realize that I've never felt further from him. There may as well be an ocean between us, and it'd be easy to stare longingly across it, but I try not to, because the pang I feel for Henry is nothing compared to what it'd be like if I lost Levi.

"What are we doing?" I ask. The group is huddled at the end of the street, where Halloween spirit has apparently come to die. The rest of the avenue is buzzing with trick-or-treaters and whoops and hollers and candy highs, but a single house on the corner is a vacuum for light. Darkness bathes the tall, skinny house with the pointy roof. A wire fence hems in the overgrown yard. Weeds spill out through the chain link. Across the front gate, a sign warns that the house's occupants will call the police on all trespassers.

Brynn separates from the group and walks up to the fence, lifting the bottom of the sign up for closer inspection. "What jerks," she says, peering up at the blacked-out windows. "There's not even a bowl of candy left out. Do you think they tell kids that Santa Claus isn't real, too?" She turns, a familiar glint in her eye. "Guys, I think it's time to add a little trick to our treat."

Kids come close to the end of the street, before parents quickly steer them clear. Past the last lamppost, this side of the road feels abandoned and unused.

"What did you have in mind?" Lydia asks with a nervous giggle.

"Just a little good clean fun." Her blond wig has fallen a bit cockeyed and she looks more Creepy Cabbage Patch Doll than Zombie Barbie. "The dare is to take a lap around the house, knock on the door, then meet back here."

"Brynn!" Lydia yelps. "We *can't*."

"Says who?"

Lydia tugs her cowgirl hat down lower over her eyes. "Fine. I can't, then. My mom would kill me if someone called the cops."

"Okay, Lydia's out. Everyone else? Who's first?"

"How do we even know they're home?" Brandon asks, edging farther down the street to crane for a look around the side.

I squirm in my knee-high laced boots. I take a deep breath and remember the moment I stood on the pier looking down at the water. I know what Old Stella would do. She'd back out. Levi squeezes my hand as if reading my mind.

"We'll do it," he says. The corners of his mouth curl up like a snake into a wicked smile. My heart thumps. I eye the size of the house, judge the distance around it.

"We've got a live one here, folks," says Brynn. "You in, Stel?"

Levi watches me expectantly. I crack my neck. "I'm in."
I try to ignore Henry, who's making a show of rubbing the back of his neck and shifting his weight.

Levi pokes me in the side, prodding me forward. "We've got this, Cross." His grin charges me with energy. A familiar rush runs through my body. My heartbeat accelerates. Palms sweat. I wish Levi had supplied me with a sound track for the moment, something to propel me forward.

"You owe me for this," I tease. Gingerly, I tug at the base of my push-up bra, which feels as though it's cutting off my oxygen supply. I couldn't help but notice Levi appreciating my enhanced bustline, but next time I go out for an evening of childish antics, I'm totally dressing as something other than a deranged dolly. With fabric that doesn't make me sweat rivulets.

My heeled boots click against the rain-soaked pavement and I force myself not to glance back. Levi's hand is hot against mine.

The metal fence creaks open. I hike my shoulders up, afraid someone will hear. I slip in through the gate.

"Shhhhh." I hold my finger up to my lips. Both of our eyes are dancing in the dark. The sidewalk leading up to the porch is cracked and uneven. There's a rush of static electricity between us.

Leaves rustle overhead. I tug him after me. *Let's get this over with,* I think. We make our way around the side of the house. The tall grass itches my ankles. It's a short distance to the back, but even spookier. The yard is nearly pitch-black here. The roof blocks the moon and power lines sway ominously overhead.

Levi meanders, taking his sweet time. My heart, on the other hand, won't relax. "Hurry up," I tell him, then jump at the sound of a rustling bush. We edge around to the opposite side of the house. The wood siding is peeling off in layers, the paint completely eaten away in places. When we reach the front again, I see our friends silently goading us on from outside the fence. I shoot them the thumbs-up and peer sideways at the porch.

"Are you ready?" Levi asks in my ear.

I nod. "As I'll ever be."

"One . . . two . . ." On three, we trample up the short flight of stairs to the porch. Levi and I both knock three times on the door. A jolt of energy. The feeling of being seventeen. Truly seventeen. I feel myself smiling stupidly. And then Levi's pulling me in. He kisses me there on the porch in front of everyone and there's a cheer from the street. Levi's fist shoots up and we're smiling into each other. My insides buzz.

Then there are voices behind us screaming my name. Louder and louder. It's only when I notice that the front door has cracked open and I hear the guttural rip of a dog's growl that something inside me jars awake. Shit.

"Hey!" an angry voice yells. I don't see the face or size of the dog. I only hear the snarl and feel the puff of hot breath on my calves. I've already turned. I'm sprinting in the opposite direction, barreling after Levi, out the gate, slamming it shut behind us, trailing a cheap blond wig, a man-size wad of toilet paper, and a billowing vampire cape.

"Oh God, oh God, oh God," I mutter. My feet fly across the road, leaping curbs and a fire hydrant. I catch up to the group and we veer right, winding our way around a sweeping corner past little fairy princesses, Batmans, and goblins.

There's a clicking in my chest. A dying carburetor that turns over and over and over again. *Click-click-click.* I try to keep up, but that's when I start coughing.

My lungs are begging for air. It's only when we're on the next street that we let our pace lag. A few feet more and we come to a dead stop.

Brynn doubles over. "Oh my God, Stel! You should have seen your face."

I clutch my side and walk in circles, breathing in and out. In and out. Henry looks hard at me. "You okay?"

I nod. Not ready for words. And also not really okay. Levi's laugh sounds hollow in my ears.

"I thought you weren't supposed to run," Henry says.

"Helpful," I gasp. I make a final effort to sound normal. Like everything is fine. Completely routine. "Who's next?" I say, which elicits a couple laughs.

I place one hand on each knee. My hair cascades over my shoulders, covering my face like curtains. Every nerve teeters on a knife's edge. In fact, my entire body shakes like I'm a junkie in need of a hit.

"Stella." It sounds as if someone is saying my name through a long tube. "Stella."

Black spots creep into my vision. First my hands hit the ground. Followed by my side. I crumple, all the while choking as if someone's shoving a length of drainpipe down my throat.

A blond wig hangs down over me. "Stella? Stella?" A cool hand is pressed to my cheek. Brynn's pulling out her cell phone. She's dialing.

"No!" My words are strangled by gags. I don't want an ambulance. I don't want the hospital. "No, please," I groan.

The vision of my life as normal cracks over me, shattering like crystals on the concrete. I sob and gasp for air while directly overhead, the moon closes in on me, a giant hanging orb. The coppery smell of blood taints every lungful of air.

If I should die before I wake . . .

My eyelids grow heavy and then . . . and then, the light's gone.

chapter twenty
92 BPM

The back of my throat is raw. My nose is dry. A cold compress clings to my forehead and there's a tug from inside my skin when I try to move my arm. I can hardly move my limbs anyway, let alone speak. I'm surrounded by a heavy, warm darkness that feels stuffy and difficult to breathe in without wheezing. I let my head loll to the side and fall still. When opening my eyes is too hard, I give that up, too.

The next time I wake, I can just peek through my eyelashes. My breaths are cooler and full. I wonder if anyone's here, but when I notice movement, I'm too tired to investigate. I seal my eyelids shut and doze off instead.

"Stella? Hello? Stella?" I wake up abruptly to a hand holding mine. It's Mom's. She's here, smiling.

I nod, groggy. "Where's Levi?"

Her smile falters. "Levi?" I nod. "He's not here. Your doctors aren't letting in any visitors." She moves her hand to my shoulder. I don't find this comforting.

"But you're here," I say.

Ropy lines strain in her throat as she swallows. "Yes, but I'm your mother, Stella."

Through whatever pain meds they have me on, an aching starts to radiate from my back through to my sternum. I recognize the pain instantly and feel my eyes widen. I stare around the room, unseeing. The anxiety only heightens the agony. My fingers claw at the hospital bedsheets. "Where's Levi?" I repeat, my voice unrecognizable even to me.

"Stella, stop it." My mother hushes me.

"Where is he?" Pain trumpets out of me. I kick my legs. "Where *is* he?" I'm yelling now. I thrash my back against the mattress. My paper gown tears.

Mom jumps to her feet. "What's gotten into you? What is the matter?"

I pound my fists into the bed and the machines attached to my veins crash toward me. "I need Levi. I *need* him. Where is he?" Tears slide down my nose. "I'm not joking." This time it comes out as a scream. White pain goes off inside me like flashing bulbs.

My teeth rattle, clacking against each other. With effort, I lever my weight up in bed. But Mom pushes me back down, this time not so gently. I glare at her. An open wound howls in my chest. I snarl for Levi again. My mother freezes, and then I start to scream.

The shrill pitch of my shriek reaches the nurses' station first, and three women rush in. Hands force me down. Hands brace my legs. A white coat appears with a syringe. I flail against them. My mom's fingers are pressed against her lips. She diverts her eyes, staring at the far wall. I don't stop screaming until the needle plunges into my thigh and the sound withers in my mouth.

It's time to go home, Mom says in that flower-petal voice reserved for patients. It makes me want to break things. "They have you sedated." That's not what she says, but it's something like that and I understand her meaning even though my head is filled with cotton balls. I don't mention Levi or the cramping between my rib bones. I want to go home. Anywhere but here, where it smells of burned coffee and disinfectant.

I find myself wrapped in clean sheets and a lavender down comforter, but the pain is already busy driving up through me. How long has it been? Either way, it's managed to catch me off guard again, which makes me angry. Like my body forgot to play fair.

Blurry numbers on the alarm clock read *5:08*. No one's around. Definitely not Levi. There's no point in even saying his name. I pull the covers over my head and breathe in short sips. My arms are weak as I clutch the blanket around me like a fort. One by one, each bony knob of my back pushes pain through to my stomach. The aching rips a hole through the fog of medicine and my eyes spring open. A thick sweat springs from my upper lip. When I can't sit still any longer I screech and when I do I sound like something wild. An animal. No one approaches my room, and as the hurt unhooks its raking claws from my body, I begin to slip back under the fog of unconsciousness.

*　*　*

Eventually, I'm able to sit upright in bed. There's an inky speck on the white underbelly of my forearm that someone might mistake for a freckle. The skin around it is a yellowing bruise where the nurse inserted the IV. Inside my room, I notice that the box of swim trophies stashed in the corner is gone. I guess even my parents realized I won't be needing those anymore. Better to forget.

chapter twenty-one
107 BPM

12:25. I stare at the glowing red numbers of my alarm clock until they smear.

If I fall asleep now, I can still get at least six hours of sleep. I flip onto my back and push the comforter down to my waist. I've been playing this game for an hour and a half and I'm no closer to nodding off than I was at eleven.

Three days I've been a prisoner in my room. My legs are limp and my arms feel wilted, like cooked spaghetti. My entire body's dwindling. Pretty soon, I think, I'll be a pile of skin sagging off the bone. I can feel pain and sickness hanging around me like a phantom and yet somehow, in the span of these few days spent completely sedentary, marinating in my own overused bed sheets, my mind has sharpened. My thoughts ring clearer than they have in months. A side effect of this is that I can't sleep. Another is embarrassment. I am suddenly all too aware that I was screaming my boyfriend's name in a public space. While there are about a dozen signs that I'm not healthy, this is one of them.

I sigh into the dark. Giving in at last, I prop myself up with two pillows and fumble for my phone on the night-stand. The screen casts a ghostly pallor over my blankets as I navigate to my various social media forums and then to my e-mail account. The Internet's quiet at this hour. Levi isn't on Facebook, Twitter, or Instagram, a fact that I'd found cool, mature, and a tad edgy, but now, while I'm bored and, despite myself, wanting to poke around, it's just aggravating.

Updates are both scarce and boring and I have no new messages save from the numerous shopping sites to which I've been unwittingly subscribed. So I scroll through my texts. Six from Levi. Mom and Dad are convinced that my schoolgirl crush has gone stalker-level serious. I make a promise to them—and a little to myself, too—that I'll be better now.

For some reason, though, I keep scrolling. What I need tonight is something different. Next on the list are texts from my mom asking if I need more notebooks and what, if anything, I want for dinner. Lydia wants to know the homework assignment on Monday. Brynn asks if she can borrow a dress for her cousin's wedding. Below that are text messages from various numbers, most of which I don't even have saved in my phone: neighbors, my dad's secretary, a few nosy do-gooders from school I don't really know, all wishing me well and hoping I feel better soon. When I got my phone back after surgery, it was flooded with them, and I'd given up on reading them all in favor of taking frequent naps. I scroll through now, trying to feel warmed by the notes of encouragement. I notice a message that looks longer than the others. It doesn't appear as a complete thought in my window until I click on it

My breath hitches. I recognize the conversation right away. The words I'd so stealthily typed out in a hurry before I'd been whisked away. A sort of confession and then the response that I'd missed—

It's ok to be scared Stel. It only means you value life. I was starting to worry that The Great Stella Cross didn't get scared. But maybe you do that for everyone else. I don't know. If we're being honest here, I'm scared too. Bc *I* value your life.

How had I not seen this? I scroll up and see more recent texts from Henry, but they're from his new phone number. I'd changed the contact details. My chest pulses with a fresh ache, completely different than the one I feel for Levi. This one doesn't hurt. This ache swells inside me like the rising tide.

I've been telling myself he's too safe, that he's not what I want right now. But reading this, I begin to think that perhaps what I want and what I need are different. It's funny, I never knew what bittersweet meant.

I check the clock. It's twelve fifty-one.

It's late and my eyelids are just now starting to feel heavy with exhaustion, but I slip out of bed and pull a pair of sweatpants and purple Ugg boots on over my striped socks. My Duwamish High hoodie is hanging over the back of my desk chair and I tug it down over messy hair. Grabbing my keys, I jiggle the window until I can slide it open without making a sound.

The night outside my window is cold and damp, a rude awakening from my room, which was toasty and warm, especially when I was burrowed beneath mountains of blankets. I don't turn my headlights on until I get to the stop sign at the end of our street.

I drive with the radio off. My sweatshirt sleeves cover my hands so that I can barely feel the cold leather of the steering wheel. When I see Henry's house, I turn off the lights and park several mailboxes down.

What if I get caught? What if Henry doesn't wake up? I think ten minutes too late. I'm already here.

I hunch over as I creep along the thick row of hedges that line the Joneses' yard. Henry's room is located at the rear of the house on its right side, free from the Betsy Ross–style awning that adorns the front. When I reach it, I cup my hands on the glass and try to peer through, but the room's pitch-black and the reflection of my eyes combined with the shadow from my hands prevents me from seeing anything other than shrouded blobs looming within. The one thing I can make out is a green light flickering a few feet above the ground that must be his laptop.

I shouldn't be here, I realize, my breath fogging the window. What was I thinking, showing up at Henry's in the middle of the freaking night? This is creepy. I feel like I should be in some classic '80s movie, holding a radio over my head while I belt out "In Your Eyes."

I start to turn away to return to my car when I hear . . .

"Stella?" Henry whispers. "What the hell are you doing here?"

I mentally weigh whether he said, *What the hell are you doing here?* or *What the hell are you doing here?* When I can't decide, I unfurl my arms and tilt my chin up toward the window. "Trespassing?" I venture. This is not how I saw this going.

Henry sighs and leans further out the window. The outline of his curly hair sticks out against the navy sky. "Obviously," he says, "but why?"

"Ugh, look." I pull myself into a more dignified position. "I know this is really lame of me. But... I wanted to see you."

I try not to think too hard about what I'm saying. After all, it's a little too late for that. It's like recently, when I'm around Henry, I think I might be spewing selfishness faster than the Hoover Dam.

"Are you sure your *boyfriend* would want you here?" He says *boyfriend* the way other people might say *barf.*

"I read your text. The one right before my surgery. They took my phone away before I got it and... I don't know, I think my parents must have opened it or something, because I didn't see it." I'm jogging in place now and rubbing my hands together. "Until now."

The silhouette of Henry's head droops for a moment before he says, "Come in." But he says it warily, like he's not sure it's a good idea.

"Thanks," I say in a soft voice as Henry helps hoist me over the sill. It's hard to believe I used to swim for miles and now climbing through a first-floor window leaves me winded. I try not to remember the Before. This is who I am now. Why does anything else matter?

I take a few moments to catch my breath, my back to the drywall, while Henry stands eyeing me.

"What?" I ask finally, pinching my side, which is cramping. "What's with the head shake?"

He pushes his finger into his mess of curls. "You're, like, the most complicated girl I know, Stella."

A year ago, I'd have thought he was crazy, but now I don't bother to disagree.

Once I'm inside, my eyes adjust to the darkness of the room. The moon provides just enough light to see by. In the corner is a bookcase overflowing with novels by H. P. Lovecraft and Ray Bradbury and Peter Straub that jut out from the shelves and spill over into stacks of paperbacks at the bottom. The bed's a twin, pressed up against the wall, sheets hanging halfway off. I'm still freezing, so without asking, I kick off my Uggs, plop down on the mattress, and wrap myself up in the quilt bunched at the foot of the bed.

"Stella . . ." Henry's voice is cautious, low. "What do you think you're doing?" I wish I knew. I'm not exactly clear on all the rules of relationships, but I have a sneaking suspicion I might be breaking one or two.

I pat the spot next to me and Henry dutifully trudges over to the bed. He's wearing plaid pajama bottoms and a gray long-sleeved T-shirt. His weight on the mattress dips me in closer.

We sit there, breathing together, while I wait for my toes to thaw.

I'm not stupid, though. I know what this looks like, even if it's not what I intend.

"Well, this is a surprise." Henry leans back, arms folded behind his head on the pillow.

"A good one?"

"Just a surprise."

On the nightstand I spot a familiar book, facedown, lying open. I reach over him to grab it, using my thumb to hold his spot. "Are you reading *Carrie* again?" I ask.

He snatches it from my hands. "Maybe. So?"

I push my hands in my lap. "Nothing." I guess I wasn't the only one feeling nostalgic.

I lie back next to him and stare up at the ceiling. A few glow-in-the-dark stars still cling to the popcorn plaster, barely emitting the faintest hint of light. I can imagine a miniature Henry directing his dad regarding the exact placement of each one. I bet he was cute.

"Do you ever think about what would have happened if I'd died?" I ask, letting my cheek fall against the soft fabric of his T-shirt. It occurs to me that I haven't been this relaxed in months.

My head rests on his shoulder and I hear a strangled grunt when he responds, "No," that makes me think he means yes. He clears his throat. "What do you mean?"

"I mean, like, okay, we're always hearing people call in to *Lunatic Outpost*, right? And they're going on about how the ghost of their cousin's dead uncle's great-aunt Bessie won't leave them alone. Do you think any of that's, I don't know, real?"

I feel his chin pinch down and I could swear he takes a whiff of my freshly shampooed hair. "Do I think you would have been a ghost?"

"Come on. *Ghost* is never the word they use. That sounds lame. A poltergeist, an apparition, a shade. Or do you think after you die you're just another blip on history's radar? Nothing." My voice is low and gurgles from lying on my back. I listen to the sound of the overhead fan click.

He sucks in a deep breath. "I have a hard time believing you could ever be nothing."

"So a ghost then." We're talking low so that his parents won't hear, but we're both giggling.

Henry's body tilts into me and I breathe in the smell of fabric softener and guys' deodorant. "Would you come back and haunt me, you think?"

"I don't see why not." I poke him in the ribs. "You feel as much like home as anywhere else." I hear the crackle of Henry's smile.

His hand's resting just next to my thigh, not on it, and I can feel his pinky grazing my knee.

"Why'd it take you six years to decide you like me?" I ask.

"It didn't take me six years to decide. It took me six years to *tell* you. There's a difference."

I scoff. "Okay, yeah, whatever."

"Shut up, Stel. You know that's true." He's turned serious. I don't know what I was thinking, taking the conversation in this direction.

"What I know," I say, "is that you turned me down when I told you I thought I might have feelings for you." The truth was that ever since that day we started reading *Carrie* together, I'd had a crush on Henry Jones. Only *he* didn't know it. He was cute and sweet, the most considerate boy in our grade by far. He never snapped bra straps or tried to steal girls' thongs from the locker room or drew penises on other people's notebooks. Back then, that's about all it took to brew true love.

Henry sighs. "We were in ninth grade. I was dating Tess then." *Tess.* Henry's big betrayal. "I didn't know what I was supposed to do. And then, after that, you got sick and it . . . it just didn't seem like the right time to bring that stuff up. It felt almost selfish. I don't know."

First I was too late. Then he was. I guess that's the way the world works sometimes.

I sit up straight in bed. (I still can't get over the fact that I'm *in* Henry's bed, but whatever.) "Let's go do something exciting. Let's take a swim in the ocean. *Something.*" Already, I'm imagining the feeling of my hair trailing in the water behind me. The weightlessness of water.

Henry grunts and rolls over onto his side. "It's the middle of the night."

"So?" I poke his back and then when that doesn't work I tug at his hand, trying to pull him up out of bed. He doesn't budge. "Please?" I beg. "We haven't done anything normal together in ages."

"Whose fault is that?" he asks.

I want this small part of my life back. I want things with Henry and me to be okay so badly I'm willing to make a fool out of myself by showing up in the middle of the night.

"Come on. You're going to wake up my parents." The corner of his mouth is pulled into a grin, which only serves to encourage me.

"You know you want to," I lean down and say this in his ear.

"Stel..." He swats me away. I know Henry. I know he can't stay upset with me, no matter what we are.

"You're turning into a lug." I push with both hands, trying to force him off the bed. It has to be past two. "Don't you like me anymore?" I ask without thinking. I know it's like prodding the underbelly of a cow, and right away I feel bad for saying it.

Henry flips onto his back and stares at me. His eyes shine

through the dark. "Stel, *you* can't." My arms go limp as I deflate in an instant.

He's right.

I can never swim again—or at least that's what the doctors told me. But it's only when I hear somebody say it out loud that I feel the limitations crushing in on me all over again. *Swimming* is practically a curse word in my household, the mere mention of which would cause my parents to send me straight to my room for another three capsules of Paxil just to be safe. And even I understand it could be a death sentence. But how can my parents keep bringing up Stanford without knowing that they're making me think about swimming? The two go hand in hand for me. Without swimming, Stanford is just a school—worse, it's their school. Their dream. I have no idea what I'm doing anymore.

My voice is small. "I just miss you. I miss us," I mutter.

He rubs at his eyes. We're both getting tired. I can feel it. Even the glow-in-the-dark stars have lost their charge.

Gently, cautiously, he tucks a loose strand of hair behind my ear. His hand lingers. The warmth of his skin hovers close by. "Did I ever tell you I liked your new hair?" His fingers thread through my slept-on tresses, snagging on the knotted rats' nests. He gently lifts my face to his, and then he kisses me.

His lips are thinner than Levi's and taste like cherry Chap Stick. Kissing Levi is more like taking a long sip of water straight out of the Atlantic Ocean—ice-cold and outdoorsy.

Henry's kiss is tentative. He cradles the back of my head but gives me my space. It's only when a sigh escapes me that I realize what I'm doing.

I find his chest and push against it. "Stop, Henry." Our mouths part. "I can't," I mutter, folding my hands back in my lap, where I can stare at them. "You know I can't."

He licks his lip. "You can." I can see by the way his fingers twitch that there's an internal war going on inside his head as he decides whether or not to reach out and touch me. Easy. I make the decision for him.

Grabbing my fluffy sheepskin boots, I shove my bare feet inside and toss the quilt back onto the naked twin bed. "I miss you. I do, but—"

Henry's nails dig into the leg of his pajama bottoms and he chews hard on his lip. "But for all the wrong reasons, Stel."

Transplant NTE   CROSS, STELLA M.

Final Report

Document type: Transplant NTE
Document status: Auth (Verified)
Document title: Post–Heart Transplant Note
Performed by: Belkin, Robert H.
Verified by: Belkin, Robert H.

Final Report

Post–Heart Transplant Note

Patient: Stella Cross
Age: 17 years
Sex: Female
Associated diagnosis: Acute cardiomyopathy
Author: Belkin, Robert H.

Basic Information

Reason for visit: Patient admitted after losing consciousness
Transplant diagnosis: measurable deterioration of the function of the
    myocardium; dilated left ventricle
Transplant type: Deceased donor heart transplant
Transplant info: Last biopsy: N/A
Cardio allograft, needle biopsy:
            —Negative immunoperoxidase staining
            —No vasculitis identified
Acute dehydration; immunosuppressants caused shutdown of circulatory
    system, exacerbated when patient moved from state of rest to intense
    physical exertion without warm-up; will instruct patient again on the
    dangers of physical exercise on current medication and at this stage

History of Present Illness

The patient previously returned for an unscheduled checkup related to chest
    pains; no signs of organ rejection

chapter twenty-two
122 BPM

I notice the pain more now in its absence than I did in its presence. It has, I realize, become a source of background noise, and the moment I see Levi, it's as if someone switched it off completely. My body unwinds, adjusting to its new normal. The immediate wash of relief.

Take it slowly, I remind myself, as I lace my fingers with his.

We walk hand in hand down the hallway. Other students stream past us. Levi hands me an earbud and together we listen to Mudhoney, a band I've recently discovered through him. They're part of my education, he says, a musical romp through Seattle's rock history, which I soak in effortlessly.

I like to sneak glances at Levi while he's listening to music. Even when we're walking, he'll shut his eyes for several beats too long, and I have to steer him clear of any oncoming traffic. I like the way there are two lines that form a triangle between his eyebrows when he's listening to a complicated guitar solo. I like how his teeth bite his lip and he rocks his head to the music. I think about what Levi told me about Kurt Cobain, about how one day he stopped feeling the excitement of listening to music, and I wonder if that will happen to Levi. I hope not, because this is what I like most about him. My favorite part.

I must look up at Levi one too many times, because something catches my ankle and I fly forward into the back of a lowerclassman walking several feet in front of me.

I push into her backpack. The earbud is yanked from my ear and I'm thrown from the happy bubble Levi and I have been occupying, and we both tumble to the ground.

"Hey, watch it!" The petite blond girl glares at me. Scooting myself off of her and feeling like a giant in comparison, I reach down to help her up, but she pushes my hand away. "I'm fine." She brushes off her khakis and collects her books from the hallway floor.

Behind me there's a loud cackle. I turn to see Tess slapping her thighs. Levi sees her the same moment I do. I push past him, hiking my book bag up on my shoulder. "What was that?" I demand when I'm close enough that I could spit in her face.

"What?" She looks to Brandon and Connor with this can-you-believe-this-girl face I wish I could smack right off.

"You tripped me."

"Hardly." She drops her fake smile. "Honestly, I think everyone's growing a bit tired of the victim card."

"Liar." People are watching, whispering. "You tripped me."

"Then maybe"—she cocks her head—"you should look where you're going."

I take a step forward. "What's your problem with me, Tess?" People are all around now, pushing and shoving like wolves. Closing in on me. A ring.

"Ooh. Tough girl. You know your little punk-rock-princess act isn't fooling anyone, right? Under all that eyeliner you're still the girl people are only nice to because they feel sorry for you." Several sharp intakes of breath from the crowd. My pulse drums wildly out of control. Humming in my ears.

"Shut up." I don't know what makes me do it, but without thinking, I shove Tess. At first I think I've shoved just hard enough to give her a jolt, but her head whips back and she loses her footing. She rocks back on her heels. Her hands reach for me but grab thin air before her head clangs into the rusted metal edge of an open locker. In that instant, when her body makes impact, my vision shifts.

Her eyelashes flutter against her cheeks. She doesn't say a word. Her back slams against the bottom row of lockers and her knees buckle. The whites of her eyes take over the pupils and it's only in the fraction of time before she crumples that I know something's wrong.

Her torso makes an anticlimactic slump to the floor, her cheek pressed against dirtied linoleum, speckled with the shadows of footprints and the gray sweeps of a janitor's mop.

"Oh God," I whisper.

She lies on her side, and if this weren't the middle of the hallway in the middle of a school day, she might be sleeping. A single drop of blood plops onto the white tile. The crown of her hair is already matted dark red.

Her wrists, turned up to the ceiling, suddenly look to me to be unnaturally thin, with bones as fragile as a bird's.

There's a ringing in my ears. I can't remember why I pushed her. I shake my head slowly at first and then frantically.

More drops stand out, bright as poppies. I'm mesmerized by the pool of blood. And something deeper, more visceral, rises out of the horror in my gut—satisfaction. I swallow it down, frightened of my own fascination. Her eyes go still first. Her mouth hangs open.

"What the hell?" My vision shifts again. I gulp back a wad of spit and the ringing stops. Tess is there, screaming at me, flattening her pleated skirt. "She pushed me!" she shrieks to anyone who will listen. "She pushed me!"

I gape at her, dumbstruck.

"Students, students." I hear the voice of old Mrs. Truitt. I see her gnarled hands trying to part the crowd.

I back away. Slowly. Slowly. No, I think. Not happening. No. I try to disappear in the mess of people. Where's Levi? I lost him. I can't wait for him.

"She pushed me? Did anyone see that?" I turn. And I go.

When someone catches my arm I think immediately that it's him. I spin into his chest, grateful that he's found me. The breath I've been holding is already on its way out.

"Stella. What happened back there? Why is Tess saying that you pushed her?"

It was Henry. I glance over his shoulder at the dissipating crowd and tug at the sleeves of my school-issued sweater to pull them down over my knuckles.

"Don't worry, your little designer doll is fine," I mutter. "It was stupid."

"I don't care about her. I care about you." He ducks to look me straight in the eyes. "What's going on?"

I'm shaking. Tremors shoot through my hands. Henry grabs them and holds them together in a strong grip. I find this oddly comforting. "Talk to me," he says. "What's wrong?"

I swallow down the ache in my chest. "I don't know." We've resumed a certain degree of normalcy since my midnight visit, not comfortable, but something. "I thought I saw—"

"Thought you saw what?" Henry's eyes search mine. He holds my hands close to his body. His chest is warm. "What did she do to you?"

I look down. His hands clasped around mine. "Nothing," I mumble. "I don't know." Tess. Dead. My fault. The thoughts are disjointed. More so when I keep having to come to the same revelation that none of it is true. "I was with Levi and—"

"Where is he?" There's a growl to Henry's question and I can tell he's latched on to Levi as some crucial part of the story.

"I don't know." I clench my teeth to keep tears from forming. If I could only get the trembling to stop. It had seemed so real.

"This isn't you, Stella." He glances over both shoulders. "I know you. You're not yourself when he's around."

"I—" My eyes snap up to his. My mouth falls open. "I thought you were...I don't know...being *supportive*, not looking for an excuse to bring up your one-sided grudge match with Levi."

"I am being supportive, but..." He sighs. "Stel, there's something creepy about that guy. And since you met him you've been acting—" He squeezes my hands and I snatch them away.

"Creepy, huh? You think my boyfriend's creepy? God, Henry, I should have known this whole be-a-good-friend bit was just that. A bit."

"Okay. I don't know what you're talking about." He drags out the words. Henry tugs his hat down over his eyes. I swear, I can tell the ten degrees of Henry's discomfort just based on how he maneuvers that damn baseball cap. "I mean, he follows you, Stella. Like, I don't know, like a stalker. That's kind of creepy. I've seen him just, you know, trailing behind you, watching you. There were times *you* didn't know he was there."

I drop my chin and glare at him. I feel my lower jaw go stiff. "Did it ever occur to you that maybe Levi and I go to the same school? There are only so many places to go."

"Yes." Henry glances in both directions again and lowers his voice. "Of course it did. At first I thought it was just a coincidence or something, too. But then . . . Look, this is going to sound weird, but I was at the mall the other day." I narrow my eyes. "My mom asked me to pick up her alterations. Anyway. I was walking by the costume store and saw Levi hovering outside and only realized later it was the exact same time you were in the store with Brynn."

Anger opens up in me like a pit. "It sounds like you're the one who's stalking me, Henry. *Now* who's creepy?"

"For Christ's sake, I'm not stalking you

"So let me get this straight. You saw Levi quote-unquote following me. So in order to check that he was quote-unquote up to no good, you checked up with Brynn about me. And Levi's the stalker?"

"Okay, it's not just the stalking thing. What about Halloween? Did you not think it was weird how he jumped on you just for talking to me? I know you noticed it too. We've been friends for years and—"

"Maybe Levi thinks you want more than just friendship. Shocking, I know, since you have quite obviously headed up the welcoming committee."

I start to leave, but Henry catches my wrist to stop me. "Stella, I'm worried about you. And about him. I'm telling you, there's something wrong with that guy."

"Enough, Henry. Drop the act. I made it perfectly clear that I wasn't available."

"Made it perfectly clear in my bedroom, in the middle of the night. I'd call that murky at best," he says, but I can tell he wishes he didn't as soon as it's out.

I inhale deeply. "My boyfriend's not evil, Henry, and this isn't *Lunatic Outpost*. If you've begun to think that everything and everyone is conspiring against you, then clearly you've been taking that stuff way more seriously than I have." Suddenly all the hours we spent laughing over our crazy theories about Roswell and the Kennedy assassination don't seem so funny. I twist my arm out of his grip.

"But—"

"But nothing. This is my life. And I'm done with having other people decide what's safe for me and what's not. Find another job." He opens his mouth, but I cut him off before he can speak. "And I'd have thought we were good enough friends that you'd have gotten over the whole jealousy thing by now." I lift my eyebrows. It's mean. I know it's mean. Too mean. Henry's face crumples. I might as well have kicked him in the groin. But for some reason I can't stop. "I'm sorry I didn't go to the stupid concert with you, Henry. But he didn't ruin things between us. If I'd wanted to be with you, I would have. Quite frankly, you remind me of a past life I'd rather forget, okay?" Kick, kick, kick. "Why'd you agree to sell him the tickets if you were going to act this way?"

"I didn't sell him the tickets."

"Oh, really? Yeah, that makes perfect sense."

Henry's brow line lowers until it's cloaking the top half of his eyes. He looks away and then back at me. "I gave them to him." He pauses for that to sink in. "I wanted you to be happy. Stupid me."

The revelation plunges into me like a javelin and I snap, a caged animal. "Good news. It worked." This doesn't change anything. "I'm with Levi now, whether you like it or not. So you can stop trying to convince me I'm dating a psychopath." Henry's Adam's apple bobs. "Seriously, Henry. It's pathetic."

I pivot on my heel and storm off in the direction of the math building, tears cropping up in my eyes that I pray nobody will notice.

I spend the first half of Calc cursing Henry in my head, telling him he's stupid and ugly and a world-class asshole. He doesn't know what he's talking about. That much is true, at least. He doesn't know Levi. He hasn't tried to know Levi.

For Christ's sake, I put up with him when he dated Tess Collars. And, what, he can't handle the fact that now I have someone? That I'm not the fallback prom date he thought

I was? He asked me out a few days before he thought I might die. And that qualifies as some grand romantic gesture? Please. What's more, who asked Henry to martyr himself? Certainly not me. Surprise, I'm not as desperate as he thought I'd be. I didn't fall headlong in to the arms of the first person who stood by me.

I pinch my leg hard to keep from tearing up in class. By the second half, I'm still pissed, but regret is seeping in, too, and I wish I hadn't said what I'd said quite the way I'd said it. Henry was still wrong, though. I'm not backing down from that.

The bell for class rings and I realize I haven't listened to a single word. Were we talking about functions of derivatives or derivatives of functions or limits of properties or continuity of a function? It's always something of something, and I know nothing of nothing.

I have a flash of the Stanford application stuffed in a drawer in my room. The essay I told my parents I'd write, but haven't started.

I squeeze through the door with the crush of other students trying to steal a spare minute or two of a social life between classes. My mood is foul, rancid, and putrid to the point I think students passing by must smell it decaying around me as I storm across campus, head down, hands shoved in my pockets.

As I walk, though, I feel a shudder slink up the back of my neck. The odd, uncomfortable feeling that somebody's eyes are on me unfurls over my shoulders and, without wanting to, I quicken my pace. What am I thinking? Nobody's watching me. Henry put this in my head. Out of principle,

I refuse to look back. I mean, I know I could look back and it would be fine. But I won't, because that'd be giving his stupid theory power over me. So I won't.

This is so Henry's fault.

chapter twenty-three
153 BPM

I haven't been to a lot of parties. At least not lately, but here's what I remember:

The best part of any party happens before you even get there. It's the getting ready. The listening to loud dance music with your friends while curling your eyelashes and mixing lip glosses into the perfect shade. Attempting that smoky eye tutorial you saw online. The taking an hour to choose an outfit. It's the driving to so-and-so's house singing at the top of your lungs in your best friend's car with the windows rolled down, but here's what it's not:

It's not the actual party.

I've been lucky so far. And I use that term extremely loosely. My partygoing has been, up to this point, pretty much devoid of the typical pitfalls that bring the average party experience down (or so I've heard). For instance, I've never had to lie to my parents about where I'm going. I've never gotten in trouble for going to a party. My parents have never once checked my breath for booze. These are sick-kid perks. The benefits of the fact that (a) when you're measuring your life in months, things can't really get worse and (b) the sick kid in question (me) apparently deserves some semblance of normalcy, and parties, apparently, qualify. (Thankfully, my parents are still operating under the tenets of [b].) That said, it was still never the party—the loud, booming speakers, the hot-potato game of trying not to get stuck standing alone, the sloshing liquids on new clothes—that was fun. That stuff was all pretend, straining-to-look-like-I'm-having-fun fun.

This time's different, though. This time I have Levi.

I'm still curling my lashes. I've chosen a bright, berry lip gloss and a tight T-shirt with skinny jeans and riding boots, but now it all has a point, an audience. Levi.

"He's here!" my mom calls upstairs. I peek through the curtain and see the Tahoe's headlights sweeping into the driveway. The ache in my chest opens up again, making me hurry faster.

"One second!" I yell back, swiping the flatiron over my hair one last time. Grabbing my pink cell phone case and debit card from the nightstand, I stuff them both in my back pocket and gallop down the stairs.

"So can I finally meet this young man?" My dad appears in the foyer. His shirt's unbuttoned, tie strung over his neck and hanging at loose ends. There's another pinch of guilt. He's been working late again. For me.

I pause at the bottom of the flight of stairs. "Dad," I whine. My head tilts and my arms hang limply at my sides. "Please? We're running late and—"

He waves one of his pawlike hands. "Fine. Fine. I get it. Too cool for your old man. Can I trust you?" At this he drops his chin and gives me the dad look. The one he's been giving me since I was two. "Because I know I can't trust him."

"Yes, you can trust me . . . and him," I add.

Mom pops out from the hallway bathroom. The ends of her hair are soaked and she's holding a naked, slick-skinned Elsie. "Back by two," she says.

"Definitely," I call over my shoulder as I bolt out the front door. I'm down the path cutting across our front lawn before they can consider changing their minds.

And it's worth it. Levi's leaned up against the Tahoe waiting for me, legs crossed one in front of the other. I catch a moment of abstracted fatigue on his face as if the day has worn him out, but he straightens as soon as he sees me, right before I run headlong into him and throw my arms around his neck. Relief washes over me as the throbbing in my chest dulls. I wish I could stay pressed up against him like this forever, but I can't. Instead, I let Levi take my hand and help me into the car.

"You look pretty," he says, grinning and staring. Sometimes I like the way he seems to feel me up without even touching me. Like I'm his prize.

"You saw me only a couple hours ago." I smile back at him. "You don't clean up bad yourself."

Levi rubs his eyes and traps a yawn behind his hand. "Sorry." He squints and tilts his head. My face goes momentarily slack. "Didn't sleep well. I'm ready, though." He grins. "Swear."

"Okay," I say. "But you're going to have to shape up, Zin. I'm watching you." On second glance, I see that the creases around his mouth are deeper and his expression more drawn. Not that this does anything to detract from his appeal.

Levi's in a soft gray T-shirt that hugs his biceps and chest. His hair's still soaked and he smells like a river on a hot summer day. There are even a few beads of water streaming down his neck. I breathe him in, wishing I could bury my face in the fabric of his T-shirt and kiss away every last drop. Maybe later. If everything goes well, there could be plenty for later.

Already, I can tell I'm right. Tonight's going to be different. A million times better than any night before it.

Outside, mist covers the windshield as we drive. It's not raining, but the tiny droplets hit the front of the car like someone has spritzed it with a giant bottle of Windex. I imagine it'll wreak havoc on my hair before the night's over.

"So," I start, slapping my palms to my thighs. "Your first Duwamish High party. Are you ready?"

Levi smirks, but behind it there are shadows forming underneath his eyes. "Can't be that different than other high school parties, can it?"

"Probably not. Red cups, sticky floors, ill-advised attempts at keg stands. You get the gist. What was your old high school like, anyway?"

Levi drums his fingers on the steering wheel. "You know, it's weird. I can barely remember. It was…" His face scrunches up and he gazes off down the road.

"Levi." I laugh. "It's been, like, five seconds since you left."

He huffs quietly. "I know. I guess. I mean, I didn't come straight here. Straight to Duwamish, you know. There was a little…break."

"There was?"

He nods. "Yeah, but before that, I don't know. I mostly hung out with my best friend, Dan, I guess. I'd play guitar and he'd play the drums. We used to jam in his garage and drink beers from his dad's icebox."

"Will you play guitar for me sometime?" I clasp my hands together, begging.

"If you're good. I'll warn you, though, that I sing better than I play guitar. But I love guitar more."

"Why don't you play anymore?"

"Maybe I will. One day. One last time at least. I don't know." One thing about Levi is he has a tendency toward the melodramatic. One moment he's all sparkly eyed and flirtatious, then the next he's spinning off into the philosophical, going on about firsts and lasts and the end of the world as we know it. It's all very exciting when each conversation seems to take on a meaningful weight that I don't experience with any of my other friends, but sometimes it can be hard to keep up.

"Will you sing for me then?" I brighten.

He rolls his chin toward me and peers up through his eyelashes. "I *have* sung for you, Cross."

I think back to the Action Hero Disco concert and the first restless flutters in my chest before he put his hand on my leg. "Yeah, but that didn't count.

"Well, the night is young. And maybe"—he reaches over to take my hand and I swear I could melt into the seat right there—"we'll get a moment *alone* later." There's a warmth in his ordinarily cool eyes, and I feel the heat in my cheeks return it tenfold as I smile.

I try to look unfazed, but I had already searched whether

it's safe for a recent transplant patient like me to engage in sexual intercourse. Oh God, I sound like my mother. *Engage in sexual intercourse. Sex, Stella. It's called sex.*

I comb my hair with my fingers, flipping down the overhead mirror, so as to look busy and *not* preoccupied with the previously mentioned alone time.

It's as if my life has been divided into two halves. Before and after. Darkness and light. No Levi and Levi. Simple as that. I sink into the seat, relishing the quiet in my heart. For a girl for whom pain is a constant, the lack of it comes with its own distinct feeling—relief.

When we pull up to Mitchell Boerne's house, I know we've timed our arrival right. The bass is thumping in the air outside of the house and I can see a whole mess of kids through the window. A beer-pong table is set up next to the garage below a rusted basketball hoop, and a few of the guys from the swim team are tossing Ping-Pong balls and guzzling booze.

Mitchell's house is in a big subdivision where each home is spread out a half acre from the next one. The two-story mansion backs up to a field full of Douglas firs and a man-made lake that I can just make out from the car, where the crescent moon glints off the water. His parents had to be either totally oblivious or clinically insane to leave him home alone here for a weekend. Have they never seen a teen movie before?

Now that we're here, my knee bounces involuntarily and my palms sweat. I forgot about the pre-party jitters. It's not that I'm nervous. Not exactly. But the truth is, I don't know a ton of people. At least not well. Since I've been in and out of school for a couple years, I'm not past the small-talk stage with many people other than Henry, Brynn, and now Lydia. And one of those people isn't even speaking to me.

Not that I can unravel whose fault that is anymore, mine or his.

I pull out my phone and text Brynn. *U here?*

Brynn knows everyone from cross-country and so does Lydia. I'd never admit it, but it bothers me that Brynn has other friends besides our small group, and I don't. God, that sounds selfish.

My phone buzzes. "Brynn's in the kitchen," I relay to Levi.

The muscles in my shoulders relax and I climb out of the car, boots sinking into the soft ground. Mist clings to my hair as I wait for Levi to come around the other side.

We find Brynn sitting on a marble kitchen counter, taking sips of something clear out of a shot glass.

"I think you're supposed to take that all at once," I say, poking her in the arm.

"Stella!" Brynn squeals. "You made it!" Her eyelids are droopy and her nose is red. "And you brought Levi!" She reaches her arms out wide and Levi hesitantly leans in for a hug.

"Wouldn't miss it."

"You're drunk," I tell her.

"So?"

I crack my knuckles, not wanting to look her in the eye. Why should I care if she's been drinking without me?

"Stella." Her face is blank for a moment before a lopsided grin stretches over it. "I'm only a little drunk. Swear." She holds her pinky out for me to take and I do, hooking my finger around hers like we'd done so many times before.

Meanwhile, I try to shove down the hurt of being left out of her life and of life in general once more.

As if sensing my mood, Levi's at my elbow with a red cup full of beer. "Here you go. Cheers." He holds up a plastic cup for me as he takes a swig.

I stare at it. "I'd rather have what *she's* having." I point at Brynn's shot glass. He lifts his eyebrows but doesn't object and instead pulls a University of Washington shot glass off the counter.

I down the vodka in one gulp. It scorches my throat on the way down and I start to choke.

"Stella Cross, ladies and gentlemen!" Brynn whoops and cheers for me.

I smile, wiping my mouth. Take that, Old Stella. Levi slaps me on the back until my eyes quit watering. I take the beer back from him and take a long sip to hide my embarrassment.

"Soo. Are you two going to..." She smacks the heels of her hands together. "You know—is tonight the night?"

"Brynn!" I yell, nearly dropping my own cup. "Don't be such a bitch!"

As if in slow motion, Brynn covers her mouth with her hand. "My bad." She slurs. "I just thought—"

I can't look Levi in the eye.

"Where's *your* boyfriend?" he asks Brynn smoothly.

Brynn's nose wrinkles and she cocks her head at Levi. "Boyfriend?" We share a look. I'm still mortified by what she said, but I'm also confused now. I have no idea what Levi's talking about. Last time I checked, Brynn had almost had sex with Davis Briggs after Homecoming, but she'd stopped short because she said Davis kissed like a gorilla and she didn't want her first time to be someone who reminded her of an ape. I'm pretty sure Brynn just chickened out, but the gorilla-kissing thing stuck with poor Davis and I don't think he's had a date since. In any event, that hardly qualifies as boyfriend material. I can't imagine Brynn having the patience for one.

"Yeah, what's his name?" Levi snaps his fingers. "Henry, is it?"

I playfully shove Levi's shoulder. "Come on, you know who Henry is." And, I add silently, you know he's not Brynn's boyfriend.

"Henry?" Brynn hesitates. "Trust me, he's not *my* boyfriend." She gives me a meaningful look, because he was supposed to be mine.

I tug at the sleeve of Levi's T-shirt until he bends down so I can whisper in his ear. "What was that?" I ask, annoyed.

Levi winks at me. "Just thought maybe I could plant a seed, that's all. You don't mind. Do you?" He ruffles the hair on top of my head. I look off to the side to hide how much I mind. He pinches my chin between his thumb and forefinger and brings his face closer to mine. "Do you?" he asks again.

"No." I pull away. "Of course not." I know then that this isn't Levi playing the clueless boyfriend. This thing about Henry . . . He's testing me.

He kisses my cheek. "Good girl," he says, squeezing me to his side. A test I've passed apparently, at least according to his rules.

Lydia comes over and gives me a hug. She's dressed up in a jean skirt and a long-sleeved red shirt. Her hair's been pressed into a bun to reveal gold chandelier earrings and, unlike Brynn's, her eyes are bright and clear. "Have you ever been out here?"

"First time," Levi and I say at once.

Lydia lifts an eyebrow. "Have you all seen Henry? He said he'd be here by eleven."

"Weird. We were just talking about him." Levi nudges me again.

I ignore him, wishing he would just drop it. "No." I shrug. "We just got here."

She looks over her shoulder at the front door and flips her hair.

"Hey." I turn to Levi. His eyes are sparkling at the mention of Henry's name again. It's like he thinks we're in on a joke together, only I don't think it's funny. "I've, uh, got to run to the restroom. Can you wait here for a sec?" I feel bad leaving him unattended at a party where he barely knows anyone, but I need to regroup.

I know, I know, people are always saying communication is the key to any good relationship, but when it's an hour before a guy is supposed to see you au naturel for the first time ever, there has to be some sort of exception.

"I think I can manage." He looks adorable, as usual, and it's easy to forget, without even trying, that he had just been poking at me about Henry two seconds earlier.

"I'm sure you can," I say.

"Thanks." He kisses me on the cheek. "I'll be right here."

I take an educated guess that the closest, least occupied bathroom will be upstairs and start threading my way through the throng of people. There are a handful of unfamiliar faces—kids from other schools, I guess.

Someone sloshes beer on me, leaving a big wet spot on my pant leg. Fantastic. I'm close to the speakers now, which are situated by the couch in the living room. A new song starts up. Loud. A rap song I've never heard, and it vibrates through my chest.

There's a line that reaches partway down the top of the stairs and I climb to meet the back of it. So much for thinking I was two steps ahead of everyone else. I tap my foot while I wait impatiently. I knew I should have gone before.

It takes at least fifteen minutes until it's my turn. Rachel Cami opens up the door and I dart inside, where I find a hair dryer and manage to shrink the spot on my pants to the point it doesn't look like I had an accident.

When I'm finished, I examine my reflection, wishing I'd stuffed a tube of Chap Stick in my back pocket. "You're fine," I tell myself. "You and Levi are fine."

I use the tips of my fingers to tousle my hair, then flip it upside down and back over to give it some volume. "Better."

There's pounding on the door. "Are two people in there? Because some of us have to go!" I shrink, having forgotten that people may be able to hear me.

"Coming!" I finish up and hurry downstairs. I'm almost in the kitchen when there's a tap on my shoulder. Whirling around, I'm met with a skinny frame and a baby-blue polo. My eyes travel up to meet Henry's.

"Hey." He shifts his weight on his feet. We haven't spoken since our fight. I'm not sure if I'm mad or if I feel sorry or what. It's complicated. There's too much left unsaid.

"Hey," I repeat, avoiding his eyes. Craning my neck, I look into the kitchen, but there's no sign of Levi.

Henry sighs. "Okay then." His hands get shoved in his

pockets. "Look, I, uh...I don't want things to be weird. You know, between us."

"They're not." I cross my arms.

"Right."

I can't help it. I look for Levi again and spot him through the back door talking to Tess. An involuntary quiver passes through me. The rational part of me knows that whatever I saw or didn't see was nothing more than my brain playing tricks, but I can't look at her without imagining that spot at the top of her head crowned in blood. And even still, the fact that he's talking to her after she'd been such an asshole to me feels suspiciously like betrayal.

But he's right there, I tell myself, returning my attention to Henry. Don't jump to conclusions.

I see Henry take note. He takes a deep breath, shutting his eyes for a moment longer than a blink. "I know you're mad at me, Stella, and I can't stand it, okay? Seriously, it's eating at me. So can we just forget I said anything? I'm sorry. You're right. It's none of my business." He rubs at his forehead with the back of his hand.

I soften. I wasn't expecting an apology. I'm not even sure I deserve one. "Fine. I'm sorry, too. About—"

Henry shakes his head. "No need to relive that. Thanks, though. Anyway, I thought you and—"

"Levi," I supply.

"Right. I thought you guys would have been officially stitched together by now."

"Hilarious. I was actually going to head back to him right now." A piece of me feels guilty for being in such a hurry. Henry's right. The two of us *are* practically joined at the hip. "I, um, I think Lydia was looking for you, though," I say.

Only a brief flash of disappointment registers on Henry's face when I drop him off at the kitchen and step out onto the deck, but there's no sign of Levi or Tess. A dozen or so of my classmates are standing outside, drinking and smoking cigarettes. I ask a girl if she's seen Levi and she tells me he was here a minute ago.

The throb in my chest suddenly radiates pain. I duck back inside and ask Lydia if she's seen Levi.

"Not in a bit. He went to get something to drink, I think. I don't know, sorry." She goes back to talking to Henry, who only offers me one more fleeting glance, but he's shut back down at the mention of Levi.

Trying to stay calm, I walk through the house, checking every face, looking for Levi. The living room, the basement, outside where the guys are playing beer pong. He's nowhere.

With leaden steps, I trudge up the stairs to the second story, past the line of girls waiting for the restroom. *Don't freak out, Stella,* I tell myself, but it doesn't do much good. My mind races ahead of me and the raw spot in my chest has opened up into a roaring cavern of pain. Huffing, I make it to the top of the staircase and turn left down a dark hallway.

The carpet mutes the sound of my footsteps. I pass an open room and poke my head inside. A ray of moonlight slices through the empty study, casting a silvery glow over a heavy, claw-footed desk and towering bookshelves. A rocking chair teeters unoccupied in the corner next to the window.

With no Levi in sight, I move on. Mitchell would probably kill me if he caught me up here. As I pad down the hallway, I stop at the sound of a giggle escaping from behind a closed door.

I step back a few paces and stare at the door. Another squeal. Eyes wide, I press my ear to the door and listen. There's the sound of muffled rustling. A few grunts. The creak of a bed. My nails dig into my palm. There's a guy's voice. I can't make out the words. They're soft, dampened by the wood between us.

The pieces fall into place, tearing into me like plummeting shards of glass. It's him. It has to be him. Where else would he have gone? Without thinking any further, I shove open the door.

One shadowy figure lurches out of bed, pulling the comforter as he goes, while the other sits up pin straight. "Stella?"

My eyes adjust as what little light the hallway contains floods into the bedroom. "Brynn?" Her eyes shine in the darkness. Her hair is ratted and her arms are wrapped protectively over her exposed top.

"What are *you* doing here?"

My mouth works, struggling to produce words. "I was looking—I thought—"

There's a rustling of fabric and then Brynn crawls out of the bed wrapped in a sheet. Another figure moves in the background. "Stay there, Connor," she snaps.

Brynn shuffles toward me. She gives me a quick once-over and seems to assess me as the crazy one, even though she's standing there undressed. "What's wrong? What's going on?"

"I can't find him. I can't find him anywhere."

"Who? Levi?"

I try to leave, eager to return to my search, but she catches my elbow. "Stella," she says seriously, "get a grip. You're going overboard."

"What's that supposed to mean?"

"Don't you think you're being a little obsessive?"

"Shut up, Brynn."

"No, Stel. Look at you. You're crying." I hadn't even noticed. "You think this is normal?"

"Shut *up*," I repeat.

"I'm sorry, but I—"

"You're jealous. Excuse me for having something that doesn't involve you." I say this without thinking. Like my mouth has a mind of its own and I'm only along for the ride. I push every inch of pain out and try to inflict it on anybody else but me. "Admit it. You can't handle it."

"*I* can't handle it?" she hisses. "Do I look like the one not handling things?"

"Let go of me." I wrench my arm free. She stares at me, openmouthed.

"Stel, stop. This isn't you." She hikes up the sheets and follows me. "He's not worth this."

At the stairs, she stops trailing me, peering down at the partygoers with still nothing on but the Boernes' bedding. I turn back to her. The pain in my chest flares. "How would you know? If you're such a relationship expert, how come you've never been in one?" My stomach begins to ferment in a sticky, swampy consistency that makes me feel as if I'm about to hurl.

Brynn and I storm off in opposite directions. A door slams upstairs. I pound my fist to my forehead. My chest radiates pain to the point that my breathing is now shallow. Oxygen flows into my lungs in tiny swigs. Where is he? I pull out my phone and call Levi. No answer. I don't even know why I'm so panicked, but my armpits are sweating and I'm starting to get dizzy, so that must be what it is. Panic.

I just saw him on the deck talking to Tess. That must have been when he went to get a drink, but where'd he go from there? He wasn't hooking up with anyone upstairs. That much I've ruled out, at least.

I stagger downstairs and outside through the growing crowd of people. The cold air hits me and I gulp it in, as if I've only just now realized how cramped it'd been in there. My legs are as wobbly as if I'd spent a month bedridden, only I haven't. Not this time. I make my way across the yard to where Levi parked. The Tahoe's still there, not that he's in it. But it's there and I'm comforted, if only a little.

Why wouldn't he be there waiting for me when I got back? Or if he stepped away, why wouldn't he come looking for me? He's supposed to be my boyfriend.

My heart thrums inside my chest and I press my fingertips to my throat, counting the beats. As I mutter numbers under my breath, the words run together. My pulse is fast. Too fast. I try to calm down. Blackness eats at the edges of my vision.

Towering pines twist around the property like a veil. The sound of their rustling leaves swarms the sky. Wind picks at my hair, lifting it off my shoulders.

My feet tread gently across pine needles and cones. I skirt the edge of Mitchell's house in search of Levi. The sound of the party is muffled by the pitter-patter of rain falling loose from branches, stirring treetops, and the occasional hollowed out howl of the wind. I hug myself against the chill. Even as I search, I know that Brynn's right. I'm acting crazy.

But I forge on anyway.

Retrieving my cell phone, I aim it at the ground to mark my steps. The deck juts out from the back of the house. I blink. An image butts in uninvited. Levi and Tess talk— no, *flirt*. I haven't seen her since I left for the bathroom either. I don't know if it's real or my imagination, but I can smell beer, hear the sound of clanking glasses from inside the house. The bass is thump-thump-thumping and it tickles my insides. Henry is saying something near me. I catch him smiling, but cut my glance away before I can return it. Tess and Levi. The names smash together in my head, setting off alarm bells. Why her? Why is he talking to *her*?

A twig snaps behind me and I jump back to the present. "Who's there?" I hiss. No one answers. More sticks crack. There's rustling. I ready myself to run even if it kills me. Because it might. The doctors have made that much clear. Out of the underbrush, a raccoon trundles along the dampened ground.

Who did I think it was going to be, Charles Manson?

"Levi?" I call, following the outline of the deck. It forms a large rectangle, at the end of which is a set of wooden stairs. I stand at the foot and stare out. There's a barely visible path leading into the woods, where the floor of needles has been stepped on and, in places, brushed away. This is the last place I haven't looked.

Moonlight trickles through the trees, casting an eerie sheen on the woodland path. When I was little, I would have loved exploring the forest. I would have imagined all of the types of animals I might see, the places I could hide.

My boots sink into the soft ground. I push past thin branches and bushes that block the path. Pretty soon I'm so deeply entrenched in the woods that I can no longer see the lights from Mitchell's house. Everything is as dark and opaque as crushed velvet beyond the subtle glow from my cell phone.

I push down the fear that's threatening to explode my lungs and press into the darkness. With each step, the air becomes more damp and cold. "Levi?" I cup my hands around my mouth and call as loudly as I dare.

The first time I hear a branch break, a few invisible feet to my right, I force myself to ignore it. It's another raccoon. They're everywhere in Washington. Then another limb cracks. Still nothing, I tell myself. They're more scared of you than you are of them. I remember when my dad used to tell me that about spiders.

I rub my palms on the front of my jeans for warmth. Only a little farther. If I don't find them, I'll turn back. There's a break in the canopy up ahead where the moonlight pours in and paints a silvery window on the nettled floor. I aim for that point, comforted by the interruption from blackness. My nose is running. It coats my upper lip. I wipe it away, continuing to punch and kick my way through the bramble.

Is Brynn right? Have I lost it?

The next snap of a bough is so close to my ear I jump back. "Who's there?" Unlike the previous noises, this one wasn't from an animal foraging on the ground. It was higher. I aim the screen of my phone outward and try to use it as a flashlight. The soft, electronic blue illuminates only a foot or so in front of my outstretched hand. A maze of tree trunks surround me. Between each is nothing but empty space.

I take tiny steps, rotating a full three hundred and sixty

degrees. Breath drains out of me in a slow, belabored rattle. "I have a weapon," I call. I wish I had a weapon—a knife, a screwdriver, anything. Branches and twigs splinter in rapid fire, surrounding me like a circle of dominoes falling one after the other.

A swoosh of leaves, like a rake sweeping the ground. I whip to my left.

Watched.

Watched.

Watched.

You are being watched. My skin feels like it's being over-taken by scuttling beetles. My joints are suddenly stiff, and when I try to move my cement-block feet, the motion is robotic and clumsy. *Move, feet,* I demand, but they fight to stay on the ground. I tear each one from the dirt like my shoes have grown roots.

I twirl back the way I came, away from the mirror of light shining through the trees. The leaves ripple around me. I'm being chased. I break into a run. Any second, Mitchell's house should be visible.

The toe of my boot catches on a root and my stomach goes flying into my throat. My hands and chin skid into moist dirt. Scrambling, I push my knees and elbows into the mud. Wet leaves and undergrowth coat the entire front of me. My phone skids, faceup, out of reach.

On all fours, I crawl toward the phone. Just as I curl my fingers around the cold, hard glass, my eye catches what looks like a bloody handprint on one of the tree trunks. Steamy white breath puffs from my flaring nostrils.

I squeeze my eyes shut. Lightning pain shoots through the back of my head and, after, my vision is tinted in red.

I do a crab-scuttle back, and before I can see any more, I've clambered to my feet. In a ring around me, every trunk is splattered in blood, dribbling through the cracks between the bark. Faint sounds of laughter and music trickle through the leaves. I hobble toward them, knees stinging, thorns and branches tearing my clothes, scratching my face.

I stagger all the way back to the house without looking back. *It's not real. It's not real.* I say the words over and over again until they lose meaning. The dissection, the handprints, Elsie's drowning—none of these had been real.

I push my knuckles into my temples. Why's he letting this happen to me? It's his fault. He's the one who left me. Swallowing hard against tears, I slump onto a couch and wait. White and blue spots flare up like fireworks each time I blink. The clock on my phone says *12:00.* Then *12:20.* The people in front of me are swirling and I feel as if I'm just watching a scene. It's twelve forty now. I check my phone to make sure I have service. I do. But there are no calls or texts from Levi.

My insides have twisted themselves into a fistful of angry knots, and I will myself to hold down the bile that's burning the back of my throat. If he were here, none of this would have happened. Everything would have been fine.

We're supposed to be at this party together, me and Levi. I bite back tears thinking about how I'd imagined taking him upstairs. How it should have been me instead of Brynn. I've never done anything like that and it was supposed to be tonight.

Instead, I wait on the couch, embarrassed by how angry I am, embarrassed that I'm not enjoying the party without him. I should go get wasted and dance on the kitchen counter. That's what I *should* do. But that's not what I *would* do and it turns out that's a tougher thing to change than I thought

It's twelve fifty-three. I look up from my phone, my vision blurry. People are dancing. The bass has become as much a part of me as my own heartbeat. This isn't normal. Brynn is right. My parents are right. Henry's right. Everyone's right but me.

A hand's on my shoulder. All of the pain that I've been feeling for the last hour seeps out of me. I've been staring into space, completely blank, and when I look up, there's Levi.

"Stella?" he asks.

"Yeah." I don't get up. My insides are churning, but my chest is calm. I can actually think. "Where have you been?" I wish I didn't say it with so much venom, but it's out there.

Levi looks affronted. His chin snaps back. "I was hanging out with some of the guys."

My eyes narrow to a squint. "Which guys?"

One side of Levi's mouth snags upward into a snarl. "God, what are you? The police?"

The comment hits me in the gut. I've always had trouble trusting people. I even believe my parents have ulterior motives.

"I went looking for you and I didn't see you with any of the guys here." I'm still doing it. I can't help it. Something's wrong with me.

"You went looking for me?" Levi says, like I'd done something vile.

"Well, you said you'd be there waiting for me and then . . ."

I sniffle without meaning to. "And then you weren't." I can't bring myself to tell him about the woods.

Slowly, calmly, he folds his arms across his chest. "I suppose the concept of personal space is lost on you then?" Something about him looks radiant. Like he's just gotten back from a workout and all his blood is pumping life into him. He looks high.

My lower lip starts to tremble. I'm going to cry. I'm going to cry right here in the middle of Mitchell Boerne's living room, surrounded by drunk people and the smell of booze sweat. So I do the only thing I can think of. I leave.

Grabbing my cell off my lap, I shove it in my back pocket and make a beeline for the front door.

I'm sick with shame. As soon as I'm outside, I round the house and crouch down next to a bush, my face already slick with tears and snot. Salt pours onto my lips and into my mouth, which I'm breathing through now, since I can't possibly take a breath through my nose. The more I tell myself not to cry, the more I sob, the more I feel like I'm suffocating. We are, it turns out, completely and utterly screwed up.

"You're acting insane."

"Only because you're making me that way."

"What did you say?" Lightning fast, he snatches my wrist and twists. The force crushes my bones.

"Stop, you're hurting me." This should be the moment that I collapse into a fit of renewed sobbing, but strangely, my tears dry up as if they've been vacuumed. I'm met, for the first time, with the hardness in Levi's eyes. Cold and unforgiving as marble. He glares at me and a chill races down my back.

"Don't tell me about hurt," he says.

"Let me go." I smooth my voice into a pitch that doesn't waver. And when he finally does, I feel a swell of fear and relief, because I know what it is I'm really telling him; my heart is already aching in protest.

It's over.

chapter twenty-four
126 BPM

"Are you watching?" Brynn asks before I can say hello.

I bury my face in the pillow. "What time is it?" I groan and peel open my eyelids, which are puffy and crusted

"Almost after twelve. A time when civilized people are out of bed, Stella."

My temples throb and I press my thumbs into my skull. "Screw civilization. Totally overrated." I'd given up early rising when I had to give up swim practices.

"Says the girl who once lived off Doritos. Turn on the TV." This isn't what I thought she was going to say. After all, I basically called her a slut last night. My best friend. What is *wrong* with me? Throwing the comforter off, I swing my legs over the bed and gingerly stand up, feeling like somebody punched me in the eye sockets.

Clicking on the television, I'm about to ask which channel, when the face of a pretty, dark-haired girl appears.

"Is that Tess?" I ask, forgetting all concerns over the awkwardness of last night. A newscaster is saying something that I can't hear, and in a box at the top of the frame is a school picture of Tess. Her hair's down and she's smiling against the muted blue-sea background that school photographers always seem to favor.

"Yep."

I turn up the volume and listen to the newscaster as I piece together the meaning of the words. *Missing* and *Friday* and *If you have any information . . .*

"She never came home after the party."

"They *know* about the party?"

"Yeah." Brynn sighs. "Mitchell came clean pretty quickly this morning after he got a couple calls. I think his parents are okay. Just glad he was honest. But they're on their way home from their trip. Early."

"Jesus." I pull myself up so that I'm kneeling in bed. "My parents are going to flip. What happened?" The image of Levi and Tess standing together on the deck flashes like a camera in my mind. Followed by something worse.

"They don't know. Somebody said she had a fight with her mom earlier. Maybe she ran away."

"Right." I nod, even though Brynn can't see me. "That makes sense. It's kind of early, isn't it? I mean, to call out the bloodhounds and whatnot. It's been less than twenty-four hours."

There are still shots of our school flashing across the screen now and a caption below saying that our principal will be interviewed in an hour.

"Apparently there were signs of foul play. Whatever that means. No one's saying a thing, but Mitchell told

Connor, who told me that there were drops of blood on his deck."

"Really?" My voice is hoarse. The image of blood splattered across the tree trunks springs to mind and then vanishes.

"I know, right?"

We sit quietly for a few moments, listening to each other breathe. I watch a few new photographs scroll on-screen. Tess in her cheerleading uniform. Tess in a goofy Christmas sweater. Tess holding her scruffy shih tzu dog.

"You think she's okay, don't you?" I ask. This time it's the impact of her head against a sharp corner that I see. A slow, controlled folding inward of the body, like human origami. I push my head into the crook of my elbow.

"I don't know. I wouldn't wish this on anyone, not even her. Anyway, it's probably too early to start thinking about that stuff."

"Yeah, you're right." I wait a few more seconds. Part of me wants to say something, to tell Brynn about how I'd seen Levi talking to her outside. And about how I'd looked but couldn't find him. To have her say back, *Oh, isn't that strange?* But in a lighthearted, what-a-coincidence sort of way. I want to tell her because it should be a small detail, a nothing. Why should I think it is anything else? But I don't.

Like Brynn had said, Tess was drunk. She had a fight with her mom. She could have run away or wandered off or anything. I think back to my vision, but what would I say to the police? I'm not even sure what I saw. Trees? Wet trees? It's Seattle. That will go over well. And besides, they could think I'm involved.

Then comes a more chilling thought. What if I *am* involved? What did I do during my vision? I have no idea.

"Brynn, about last night——" I say instead.

"Let's not," she cuts me off, and I can tell that she means it.

I sit quietly, not knowing how to continue until, to my surprise, I say, "I broke up with him. You were right."

"I know," she says, but for once she leaves out the I-told-you-so tone.

After a while, I tell Brynn I have to finish my homework but that I'll see her tomorrow and then there's a *click* and the line's dead. The phone bounces on the mattress and I stare blankly at the TV without blinking. Finally, when my eyes are dry and itching, I lie back down on my pillow and close them, the image of Levi and Tess burned like a brand into the back of my lids.

That afternoon, I refuse to eat or get dressed or shower. Levi calls. My finger hovers over the buttons until I summon the willpower to hit ignore. As soon as I do, the space underneath my breastbone swells with an agony so deep it nearly buckles my knees.

Then, at five oh eight, I crawl into bed and accept that there's no way out from the pain. I slip in and let it engulf my body from head to toe like I'm drowning, and afterward, I don't bother getting up until morning.

The next day, they find her body. Even though I'm not there, the scene plays vividly in my imagination. A man with a forest-green uniform and a holster that swivels on his hips leans back on the leashes of two black-and-tan German shepherds whose noses churn up the dirt and undergrowth. They find her beneath a thorny shrub. A torn piece of fabric hangs from one of the branches. Twigs and leaves accessorize her knotted hair as though she were a fairy wood nymph waiting to awaken.

The dogs howl, long and forlorn. They paw at the ground as if they're trying to dig a grave with their short claws. Yellow tape wraps around tree trunks. Sirens. A boxy ambulance. An unzipped plastic bag. And when they lift her, the weight of her middle sags low.

But there's one thing I can't picture. No matter how many times the reporters insist in their zappy, sensationalized-headline way that it's true.

Tess Collars was found Sunday morning with a single, gaping hole and nothing inside the cabinet of her chest.

Her heart, they said, was missing.

Transplant NTE	CROSS, STELLA M.

Final Report

Document type:	Transplant NTE
Document status:	Auth (Verified)
Document title:	Post–Heart Transplant Note
Performed by:	Belkin, Robert H.
Verified by:	Belkin, Robert H.

Final Report

Post–Heart Transplant Note

Patient:	Stella Cross
Age:	17 years
Sex:	Female
Associated diagnosis:	Acute cardiomyopathy
Author:	Belkin, Robert H.

Basic Information

Reason for visit: Biopsy, echocardiography, electrocardiography
Transplant diagnosis: measurable deterioration of the function of the
    myocardium; dilated
Transplant type: Deceased donor heart transplant
Transplant info: Last biopsy: N/A
Cardio allograft, needle biopsy:
       —30% obsolescence
       —Acute tubular injury
       —Diffuse inerstitial fibrosis
       —Negative immunoperoxidase staining
       —Vasculitis identified

History of Present Illness

The patient voices concerns over nausea, migraine pain, and dizziness.

chapter twenty-five
142 BPM

"You look terrible," Brynn says as I squeeze past her along the bleachers. I find a spot in the basketball gymnasium between her and Lydia, a few rows down from the top, just high enough to be dizzying.

A recorded violin plays through the loudspeakers. Students shuffle to their seats, voices held lower than usual. I shed my jacket and fold it in my lap.

"Please, be more honest." I say in a voice no louder than a croak. "Don't spare my feelings."

She levels her chin. "Serious question: Have you seen yourself in the mirror? Follow-up: Are you doing all right? Because—"

"Yes, I know." I let out a tired one-note laugh and even that hurts. "I've seen myself. And I have no idea, it's pretty touch-and-go at this point."

"I'm sorry about Levi," Lydia says quietly.

I give her a grim smile that I have no intention of making reach my eyes.

"It'll get easier," I say, unconvincingly.

She squeezes my hand. "Yeah, it will."

A normal girl would eat a pint of rocky road, watch *The Notebook*, and spend an entire weekend wallowing in her PJs, but I'm finally coming to terms with the fact that I'm not a normal girl. In the past seventy-two hours, I've deteriorated significantly. Brynn and Lydia pass worried looks between each other and quickly shuffle apart to make more room for me.

My doctors would call it something fancy, like "regression of pulmonary arteriovenous malformations." I would call it something simpler. Withdrawal.

From Levi.

My legs are brittle and quiver even when I'm sitting. Plus, it hurts too much to eat, so I've given that up, too. When I left the house, there were rings underneath my eyes—yellowish-blue, the color of three-day-old bruises.

"Don't you have, like, a million doctors you could talk to?" asks Brynn. Considering she generally refuses to acknowledge the fact that I'm sick, this is a huge step for her.

"I'm fine," I insist. But this isn't true. Last night I'd dreamed of Tess. Or at least I thought it was Tess. There was a girl and she had a hole in her chest, hollowed out like somebody had taken a serrated cookie cutter to it.

The edges were toothed and flayed, shiny with thick, gelatinous blood. Sticky, if you touched it with your fingers. When I looked over, I could see all the way down, like I was staring into a pit of molten lava. It gurgled when she tried to breathe.

I woke up from my dream drenched in sweat, and I could have sworn I saw a figure in the window, staring in. Dark hair, hooded eyes. But when I sat up, it was gone and I wasn't sure anymore whether I'd been fully awake or not. Either way, I hadn't been able to get back to sleep.

By then, the pain was raging. If I asked to skip school I knew Mom would make me visit Dr. Belkin and I didn't want that. I could make it through this. I could be normal.

"At least you're better off than her." Lydia nods to the gym floor down below. At the center, an easel holds a blown-up picture of Tess Collars. Flowers and teddy bears litter the mascot emblem.

My stomach turns like a screw.

The microphone screeches. Our guidance counselor, a thin man named Dr. Yang, calls for us to quiet down. Lydia and Brynn straighten beside me. I relax, thankful for the privacy that comes with the new distraction.

I hug my jacket to my chest, trying to stanch the aching with pressure, but no luck. I settle in for the long, tedious business of memorializing Tess while suffering the sensation of my torso being rammed through with a saw-toothed blade.

As soon as Dr. Yang begins, saying words like *a positive force*, *encouraging*, and *big-hearted*, I know this whole eulogy will be a work of fiction. Tess wasn't that nice and she definitely wasn't encouraging. And if I were him, I might have stayed away from the mention of hearts altogether.

I look around, though, and the audience is nodding. Pairs of girls lean together, hugging, and we're only a few sentences in. I've thought about my own eulogy often. Wondering what, if anything, anyone would have to say. I flinch at the idea that it would have been anything like Tess's, bland and dishonest.

Among a sea of peers, I feel a single shiver sneak its way up the back of my neck. Goose bumps pop up on my arms, puckered at the hairs. My throat tightens, fingers tense on my legs.

It's the same sense that woke me from my dream last night. The feeling of being watched.

As casually as I can, I glance around the cavernous room. Everyone is listening attentively to Dr. Yang. Sniffles, quiet coughing and rustling clothes fill the surrounding air. But the tingling intensifies.

I keep my breath steady. Slowly, I turn my head to one side. I search the bleachers. Nothing out of the ordinary. My knees start to jiggle. I want to shake off the sensation, but it sticks to me. Gradually, deliberately, I pivot the other direction.

Just two rows up and catty-corner, Levi is fixing me with an unwavering stare. I nearly jump. When I catch his eye, he doesn't smile or try to look away. He watches me, motionless.

My heart pounds. I realize in that moment that I'm scared of him. Terrified. How did I let it go on so long?

A single droplet lands with a plop on my lap. Breaking our eye contact, I look up to the ceiling, searching for a spot that's leaky. Another drop lands.

It's then that I see the two bloodstains on my pant legs. Three more fall with a satisfying pitter-patter. I rub at one of the spots. It smells like a penny.

One drips onto the back of my hand. Another on my cheek. My breathing grows shaky. Blood rains down on me. I whip my head back to Levi and he's still staring, this time with a smirk and I realize, with a start, that somehow he knows.

Meanwhile, Dr. Yang is telling us something about how Tess wouldn't want us to feel sad forever. In fact, what she would want is for us to go on with our school year and live life to the fullest. Or at least that's what Yang's takeaway must be. I can hardly hear, my ears are so full with a metallic buzz, and I sit very still, letting the scarlet soak my khaki pants.

At the end of the memorial, Lydia insists I have to go to the nurse's office. Dazed and catatonic, I allow her to gingerly hold my hand so that she can help me pick my way over the bleachers. She keeps up a steady stream of chatter, which should be the first sign that something about me appears seriously off. But it hardly registers, because I'm not listening.

When I look down, what I see is a bloody mess, clothes coated in crimson, but nobody else seems to notice. People pass me by without a second glance.

I trail Lydia until we reach the nurse's. She wants to stay, but I tell her I'm fine. The nurse will send me home with a note anyway, which she does.

Only, when I get home, I realize I'm not alone. A black Tahoe idles a short distance down the street and an icy ripple of fear follows me like a ghost into the house.

chapter twenty-six
105 BPM

I bang through the front door.

"Stella?" Mom calls from the kitchen.

"I'm home," I shout. I palm my forehead and try to take deep, normal breaths. What's happening to me?

Mom appears in yoga pants and an apron. "Quiet, Elsie's down for her nap." Of course. I'm on the verge of losing my mind, but let's all make sure I do it quietly, because my little sister's very busy napping. "What are you doing here?" Her eyes grow wider as if she's only now registering the fact that it's the middle of the day and I'm home. "Stella, what's wrong? Do I need to start the car? I'll call your father."

"No." I pinch my forehead. In normal life, I'd have any number of perfectly non-alarming excuses. I have a cold. I have the flu. I have food poisoning. But if I say any of these, it'll be an instant red flag. The symptoms are a match for basically every sign of transplant rejection. Doesn't high school come with enough rejection that I shouldn't need to worry about my immune system rejecting my organs, too? "It's nothing. Just . . . cramps," I say, pulling out the oldest trick in the book. "I was feeling exhausted, so I figured I should come home anyway."

Mom relaxes. "Smart, Stella," she says, becoming once again businesslike. "You're finally learning to take care of your body first." Tess's murder had really freaked out the Duwamish parents. Mine were no exception. I felt the heightened worry. The need to check in, text every hour. For my parents, any change in the status quo was an excuse to go into military-operation helicopter parenting.

"That's me. A model patient." I wander over to the dining room and separate the slats on the blind over the front window.

"Still raining out there?" she asks.

The street outside is slick, damp in a way you can smell just by looking at it. It's still out there—the black Tahoe, its windshield wipers shuddering menacingly across the glass. Fumes snort up from its mouthy muffler and swirl between the drops of rain, where they blend and disappear.

I drop the blind with a snap. "Yeah, it's a real nightmare."

I can't get to my room quickly enough. Mom, usually eagle-eyed when it comes to my symptoms, completely misses the amped-up, paranoid energy that makes my hands shake and leads me to crack all my knuckles to the point that it sounds like rapid machine-gun fire.

I close the door behind me and lock it. Retrieving my computer, I start it up and nervously chew the inside of my lip until there's a painful sore bitten into the gum. Who, I wonder, is Levi Zin? I should have a better answer for this. Immediate. Apparent. None comes.

I had known that he wasn't on any social media, and at the time, it felt like an edgy choice—avant-garde, even. Akin to liking a band before it was popular. But now, this single fact has taken on a more onerous hue. Who is this person that I've been spending all my time with? The fact that I don't know is unsettling. I think of the way his fingers crushed into my wrist, threatening to snap it.

Sure, my parents' generation loves to poke fun about our reliance on all sorts of Internet outlets, but in some respects these collections of profiles serve as an anchor, a way to keep personalities from becoming too slippery.

While my browser loads I try to summon a list of people who have no virtual footprint, but the only ones I can think of are members of the Mob and of the CIA, both groups that seem far too "establishment" for my Levi.

My heart contracts. *My* Levi? He's not *my* anything anymore.

When the search window pops up, my fingers—brittle as hollow bones—tap furiously at the keys. First, I check all the major social media outlets for good measure. I find one locked account, but without a picture or any other information, it's impossible to tell if this is the same Levi Zin.

Next, I cast a wider net, punching his name into the search engines for the Internet at large. This turns up a flood of useless information. I scroll through it, skimming the underlined headers, hoping for a stray word to catch my eye.

It'd help to have an inkling of what I'm looking for. A title in all caps: YOUR EX-BOYFRIEND, LEVI, IS A CREEP? Not likely.

When I'm starting to realize the task has taken on a distinctly needle-in-a-haystack feel, I narrow the search words to "Levi Zin" "Seattle." In the moment it takes for the computer to process, I have a moment of clarity—that may not even be his real name—but in the next...

Bull's-eye.

"'Boating excursion turns tragic for local teen,'" I read aloud. Breathless, I double-click the link. The header leads me to the Web site for the *Seattle Times*. This alone feels almost too official for my wild-goose chase. The article's dated only a few months back. I bite the corner of my thumb as my eyes scan the page.

Boating Excursion Turns Tragic for Local Teen

By: Edward Bulletin

The U.S. Coast Guard has closed the Stacy Street Dock on the Duwamish Waterway where a pleasure boat ran into a power line Saturday afternoon killing one local teenager.

The coast guard sent out a radio message at 2:30 p.m. closing a section of the river and warning of the hazard, but Levi Zin, Daniel James, and Stefan Ashbury of Crown Hill did not have a marine radio onboard.

Zin, 17, was killed when the friends' small boat ran into a transmission line the Seattle Port Authority was lifting out of the water for repairs.

Two SPA boats were allegedly patrolling the area and tried to signal to Zin, James, and Ashbury to slow down.

Zin was airlifted to Harborview Medical Center in Seattle, where he was removed from short-term life support and declared dead from blunt-force trauma to the head and neck. Toxicology reports revealed a high level of alcohol in the teenager's system, and it is likely that Zin was driving the boat at the time of the accident. The two other boys sustained minor injuries.

My mouth goes dry. It takes me three full read-throughs to digest the contents of the article and even then I feel full paragraphs—letters and punctuation—stewing half-chewed in the pit of my stomach.

This, I remind myself, could be any Levi Zin. Not one in particular. But even as I practice self-soothing by repeating these thoughts, I know that they have a ring of falseness. It's not as if Levi Zin is a particularly common name. The probability shrinks more when narrowed to the number of Levi Zins in Seattle. Not impossible, but the chances are minimal that there's no connection at all.

I pull out a tattered notebook from my school bag and jot down the names Daniel James and Stefan Ashbury. These feel important, like a trail of bread crumbs. No photograph accompanies the article. I also copy the name of the hospital, Harborview Medical Center. Because of my transplant, I'm familiar with most of the surgical facilities around Seattle, and this one I recognize as the hospital where Henry's father works.

My work takes on a more purposeful air, but I'm still not able to ignore the consistent throbbing in my chest. One thing's clear: the boy who entered Duwamish High isn't the one who died. The boy at my high school must have assumed the identity of the deceased Levi, but why would anyone do that?

As I see it, there are two options: witness protection—or worse. And since the witness-protection program provides people with new identities—not old, stolen ones—this leaves me with only one real possibility.

And it's much, much worse.

chapter twenty-seven
136 BPM

When I wake, my room is dark with shadows tinted sepia by a yellowing moon. It's the middle of the night, hours before my alarm clock will go off. Everything is still but for the pounding of my heart. Right away, I'm as alert as if I'd had two cups of coffee.

My sixth sense buzzes in my ears. I lie stock-still. Afraid to move. The sensation of another human presence nearby settles over me and I remember being very small and too scared to check inside my closet at night.

I slide the covers off my chin and peer down my nose at the window on the other side of the room. But no one's there. My pulse skips. Slowly, I push myself up, back to the pillows, and draw my knees to my chest. The space outside is empty, but the acrid scent of fresh cigarette smoke seeps through the cracks in the sill.

Without looking away, I fumble for my phone on the nightstand and slide it into my lap.

Henry, I type into the keypad, *I need to come over tomorrow.* There's no response until morning, and all I can do is sleep with one eye open.

"Hi, Dr. Jones," I say, stepping over the threshold into Henry's home. Henry's father, dressed in baby-blue hospital scrubs, is a grown-up replica of Henry. His boyish, curly hair gives him a vaguely hyperactive appearance, and it's occurred to me more than once that I rarely see adult men with curls you could loop your finger through. His demeanor is unfailingly earnest and sincere. He has a way of making me feel as if he cares deeply about the answers I give to any offhand question.

"How are you?" he asks, ushering me in with a hand placed gently between my shoulder blades.

"I'm..." I contemplate this for a moment, since answering Dr. Jones always seems to warrant a bit of reflection. "I'm okay."

He raises his eyebrows. "'Okay'?"

"Well..." I push nervously at the spot over my heart where it aches.

"Have you had any complications?" When I'd first been diagnosed, I'd wanted Dr. Jones to perform my surgery. Especially after I'd met cold, hard Dr. Belkin. I didn't know at the time that not just any surgeon could perform a transplant. Dr. Jones covers more general emergency-room trauma.

But he'd taken pains to talk my parents through the selection of a doctor and a surgery center. It was he who'd gotten me in with Dr. Belkin, who, despite his chilling bedside manner, is still one of the best doctors in the country.

"Not exactly," I say. Though my life has gotten complicated, that's for sure. "It's just a transition." This is my canned response, the one I give to any adult who asks. A *transition*. A transition to what? Into insanity?

He nods, shifting his feet out to shoulder-width. "That's what I tell all my patients. People think you can have a major surgery and—poof!—they'll be shooting baskets the next day. But that's not realistic. The body has its own timeline and its own matters to attend to. You just need time to heal." I don't argue with him on that front. My heart certainly does seem to have a mind of its own.

"Is Henry here?" I ask after an awkward pause.

"Ah, right. Sorry to keep you. It's just such a pleasant surprise." I blush. "Henry's downstairs in the basement. You know the way."

I usher myself down the carpeted hallway. Henry's mother has never met a scented candle she doesn't enjoy, and the house usually smells fragrant with spiced pumpkin or apple cider. Today I detect something candied and appetizing.

The door to the basement is closed and I knock lightly before opening it. At the bottom of the stairs, I find Henry sprawled out on the couch. He straightens, pushing a pillow back into place, when he sees me.

"Don't look so alarmed," I say, plopping down next to him. A flood of memories rushes to meet me. I've spent hours on this couch devouring grainy episodes of *The Twilight Zone* or tuning the AM radio dial to just the right frequency to catch *Lunatic Outpost*. But it's been months and the basement's been cleared of all of our strewn-about books and posters and empty popcorn containers.

"I'm not. I just thought under cover of darkness in the middle of the night was more your style."

It's been a while since I smiled, and my lips feel tight and chapped when I try. "I'm sorry, Henry."

"For what?"

"For not believing you about Levi." He glances away, suddenly interested in the large projection screen where nothing is playing. "Something's not right about him."

He huffs. "No, really?"

I roll my eyes and scoot closer. I dig my phone out of my pocket. "I found this." I hand him the cell, with the article pulled up on-screen.

He looks at me and then at the phone. Carefully, he takes it. I watch as he silently forms the words. I can read his lips and know when he reaches the end, but he returns to the beginning, just like I did. When he's finished, he taps the screen off and hands it back to me.

"Christ, Stella. When did you find this?"

"Yesterday. You're right, though. He's following me. Watching me like I'm a mouse and he's waiting for his moment to pounce. I swear he was outside my window last night." When I say this to Henry, it comes across as nonchalant, easy to talk about when someone else is in the room with me...but when I'm alone, the thought makes my insides shake.

Henry rakes a hand through his hair and lets out a deep breath he's been holding. "Jesus. We have to tell someone."

"Tell them what? That a guy who goes to my school is

following me? What proof do I have?" I'm not sure how much to tell him about Tess.

"You're a pretty seventeen-year-old girl, Stella. He's your ex-boyfriend. People will believe you."

I brush aside his compliment. "I don't know if you've noticed, Henry, but I don't exactly have the best track record for, you know, stability." In the past few weeks alone I've had screaming fits, fainted, and chopped off all my hair. Inventing a stalker would be the cherry on top.

"Still—"

I hold up one finger. "Wait. That's not all." I gulp. "But if I tell you, I need to tell you everything. And you have to promise not to have me committed on the spot. Swear?" I hold out my pinky finger. He stares down his nose at it.

"I know you sometimes *conveniently* forget, but I'm a guy. Guys don't pinky-swear, Stel."

"Swear," I insist, shoving my pinky in his direction.

He sighs and loops his finger into mine. "You better not be messing with me."

"I wish I were." I hesitate on the brink, knowing that once it's said, it can't be unsaid. "You know how I've had a few episodes recently?" I curl my fingers into air quotes. He tilts inward, listening. "Well, they've been a little more than just passing out, headaches, routine medical stuff. . . ."

Henry plays with the brim of his hat while I talk. He doesn't interrupt me. Not when I tell him about the anatomy-class hallucination or the splitting pain every day at five oh eight or the fact that I saw Tess dead at school only days before she died. I come clean and tell him that I saw Tess with Levi just before she disappeared and that I looked for them in the woods behind Mitchell's house and worse, that I have absolutely no alibi. Plus, who knows what incriminating evidence I may have left in the forest? I have to hope that Henry will trust me, despite all the heaping mounds of proof edging him to the contrary. He has the same ability as his father to make me feel as if what I have to say is vitally important, so I find myself going on longer than I'd intended, telling him details that I wish I'd forgotten.

When I stop, he just stares at the opposite wall. "Why didn't you tell me sooner?" His voice is broken, hurt.

"Because I've had everything they could think of tested and there's nothing *physically* wrong with me. It's in my head, Henry. All of it. In my head." I take a moment to let that sink in. "I can't go back to the hospital. You don't get it. I'm so sick of being sick. I just thought if I could convince everyone else that things were normal, then maybe they would be. Now, if I tell people about Levi, who knows what they'll think? I'll need a psych evaluation or treatment or, I don't know, some other type of poking around."

He slides one of his big hands down his face. "Okay, so if we don't go to the police, then what do we do?"

"Those two other boys. Daniel James and Stefan Ashbury. I think we need to track them down. The Levi we know must have stolen the identity of their dead friend. But I have no idea why. I don't even have a solid guess. Did our Levi know the other one? The problem is, I can't get in touch with either of them. I tried friending them, but neither of them will accept."

"From your regular profile?" Henry asks.

"Yeah."

Henry holds out his palms to me like stop signs. "As soon as I say this, you're totally going to take it the wrong way, but I think we need to go—how do I say this—hotter."

My eyes bug out. "Henry!" I chuck a sofa cushion at his head. My face burns up at his comment. It's not like I've ever thought of myself as supermodel material—especially with the scar—but hearing it from Henry puts a puncture hole in my self-esteem.

"Wait, Stella. Ugh, I knew you were going to take this personally."

"Is there another way to take it?"

"You're beautiful, Stel. *Beautiful*." There's the dimple again, just below the freckle under his left eye. I soften. "But I think we need someone a bit more obvious as bait. You know what I mean?"

I fold my arms over my chest and slump down, unsure if I want to be considered beautiful by Henry if I'm not also hot.

His mouth twists into a half smile. "You're hot. Just... hold on, you'll see."

I wait while Henry runs upstairs to get his laptop. When he returns he sits next to me. Our hips butt up against each other and I catch the comfortable whiff of Dove soap. He navigates through several Web pages in quick succession and then suddenly a series of images are on-screen.

Henry clears his throat. "One of these," he says. Each picture is a variation of the same look: Fake tan, highlighted streaks, bare midriff, copious cleavage, and a sexy pose in front of the mirror with the camera held out.

"This"—I touch the screen—"is what you want me to look like?" I defensively think of my scar and the way it looks, pink and bulbous in the mirror.

He snaps the computer shut. "No!" His cheeks turn red. "I want you to look like you."

I stare hard at him. "But—"

"But do you have a better plan?"

"No," I mumble, miserable. "You pick."

He shakes his head, opens the computer back up, turns the screen slightly away from me, and—not that I'm counting the seconds or anything—spends way too long selecting our lure. When he's finished, I check out the beginning of the profile he's created. I swallow a smile when I notice that, if I tilt my head just right, the girl looks like a sexed-up Russian version of me.

"Name?" he asks, hands hovering over the keyboard.

I stare up at the ceiling, thinking. "Tatiana," I say. "Name one Tatiana who's not triple-T hottt."

"Name one Tatiana, period," he says, typing.

I crane my neck to see the screen. "What are you doing over there *now*?"

"Searching for Russian last names."

I lean back into the cushions. "There's an equal chance they'll think this girl is either irresistible or a Soviet spy."

The tap-tap-tapping pauses. "Hopefully both." I shove him playfully. "And . . . voilà." He spins the computer around to show me Tatiana Petrov, hottie extraordinaire.

"Let me guess, she likes yoga, singing in the rain, and long walks on the beach."

He smirks. "Close. She enjoys football, heavy metal, and raunchy comedians."

I toss my head back. "That girl doesn't exist!"

He turns the screen back to face him. "Yeah. That's kind of the point." More typing. "Just a few finishing touches and . . ." He punches the return key with a flourish. "Done!"

"And what, exactly, makes you think this will work?"

He looks up at the ceiling and then crosses himself from his forehead to his chest and across both shoulders like he's saying a Hail Mary. "Nothing, except for a hope and a prayer and a little bit of testosterone."

We pass the time comfortably enough. I'm grateful for the distraction. Henry snags us soft drinks and a container of packaged cookies. We listen to a recording of an old episode of *Lunatic Outpost*.

The host, Quentin, lectures emphatically about the existence of the Babylonian Brotherhood. One of my and Henry's favorite conspiracy theories, it claims that the world is run by a collection of lizard people who manifest themselves here on Earth as politicians and other famous, influential people. We thought this was a joke Quentin made up until we researched and found that the contingency of people who believe in the brotherhood is actually quite large. Callers dial in to posit their guesses about which famous people are lizard people in disguise.

"Howard Stern," says one woman with a raspy, smoker's voice.

"Kim Kardashian," says another.

Henry and I make our own list that consists primarily of legendary boy-banders.

I'm conscious as an hour slips into two. There are diversions from my ailing chest, but the feeling never goes away. It remains a constant, throbbing force pulsating for attention at the back of my mind.

As it gets closer to five o'clock, I consider leaving. My

palms are already soaked. My muscles are as tense as bow-strings. But for the first time I recognize that I don't have to hide it. He knows and, again, I feel a small burden lift.

Henry senses it, too, though. The ticking of the clock. I see him check his watch every minute. I'm embarrassed to stay, but I don't want to be alone either.

At five oh eight I half expect Henry to have the same effect as Levi and for the pain to evaporate before it can touch me. But the moment the clock changes it's as if an iron spear stabs me through the back and comes out my chest. I gasp. Desperate. I try to stay upright. I can't see Henry, but I feel his presence there. He moves closer.

I curl into the fetal position, tears beginning to pour down over my knees. I wipe the snot on my pant leg. My brain ruptures. I go blind with agony. The smallest twitch hurts, but I can hardly sit still as the pain moves in waves from the top of my head through my spine. I rock back and forth, teeth dug into my hand.

Distantly, I feel Henry's arms wrap around me. He hums and rocks with me, hugging tightly so that the scent of soap breaks through my haze. This is the thing I cling to as the pain crashes around me, beating against me like a stormy ocean pounds against the seawall.

In increments so tiny they are almost immeasurable, the anguish slips, replaced by the sense of being hollowed out and bone-tired, filled with elusive tears that, despite my being shattered, can't find the space or the effort to leak through.

I burrow my face into Henry's T-shirt as he strokes the ridges of my back, and I'm just drifting off to sleep when we hear the hopeful ding of a message on his computer.

chapter twenty-eight
135 BPM

Henry looks out of place as we clomp down the concrete stairs into the crowd of brassy punk rockers. His long-sleeved polo and pressed jeans are at odds with the sea of greasy hair and ripped, acid-washed denim. I have the guilty unease of wanting to distance myself from him in this place, like a kid embarrassed of her parents. *Who, that guy? No, I'm not with him. Never met him before in my life.*

With my choppy hair, thick eyeliner, and fishnet stockings, I slip into the swarm of people. A heavy clubgoer with bearded jowls scowls at us as we pass.

I glance back at Henry. "Put that away!" I snatch the flyer from his hands:

SATURDAY NIGHT AT THE CROCODILE! LIVE UNDERGROUND! DRINK SPECIALS ALL NIGHT!

"Why do you care so much what other people think?" He frowns, gazing around at the unpainted walls plastered with posters and graffiti. "Especially what *these* people think. This place is kind of a dump, huh?"

"It's not a dump, it's a dive. And I don't care what people think, I just don't want you to get your face bashed in. Fair?" The truth is, I like this place already.

Henry shrugs. "Sure, whatever."

I lead him farther into the mess of people. The band onstage, who had paused to take swigs of liquor out of shot glasses, pick their instruments back up and strum a few noisy notes.

Red lights flash over the audience. Disorienting and surreal. Henry and I reach an impasse near the center of the teeming club, where the sweaty bodies become so thick and pressed together it's impossible to shove through without getting separated.

"I don't know about you," Henry shouts into my ear, "but this is exactly how I imagine the apocalypse."

Elbows and shoulders ram into us. We're jostled several steps to the left and then back to the right. It's like trying to walk in a fun house. I clutch Henry's arm for balance. The lights flash faster between redness and dark. Henry's face flickers in and out of focus.

"So what now?" he asks.

Henry, of course, had been right. It'd been Daniel James who responded to the elusive Tatiana's request and it was through his profile that we'd been led here, to the Crocodile club.

This wasn't one of the venues I'd frequented with Levi, but it felt significant that the friends of the dead boy Levi is impersonating share the same interests as the one that I know.

I stare up at the stage. I'm surprised to find that alone, without Levi's encouragement, I still find that the blaring music and throbbing energy turns my heart punchy with excitement. The lead singer is a pointy-faced girl with a confrontational chin, and for a moment I'm mesmerized by the way she throws the microphone stand between her hands and stomps her foot on the ground like she's gunning to incite a riot.

It's only when someone steps hard on my own toe that I'm able to cut my gaze away. "Gosh darnit!" I yell, hopping on one foot.

Henry catches me by the shoulders. "'Gosh darnit'? Wow, a rebel on the outside and in." He clucks his tongue, clearly teasing me.

I scowl. "I figure at this point there's got to be somewhere in between."

We both find ourselves looking over our shoulders, trying to make sense out of the throng of hardcore fans.

"We should split up," I say decisively. Henry starts to open his mouth. "I'll be fine. We'll both be in here. It's no big deal. Otherwise, it's a madhouse. We may miss him."

Henry digs his teeth into his lip. "Fine. But meet back at the front door in twenty minutes if you haven't found him." With a smug look, he extends his pinky finger. "Okay?"

I take it. "Okay." With one final glance, I start to slip into the crowd. The drumbeat bounces around inside my lungs. Bodies slam into me. I can just make out Henry watching me go. He holds his hand up to his ear, hooked into the universal sign of a telephone—*Call me*. I nod, and then I'm swallowed whole.

By now the band has found its momentum. At the front

of the stage the guitarist thrashes his long, unkempt mane. Nimble fingers perform complicated riffs. The thrum of the guitar and the wild beat of the drums vibrate through my hollow pit of a chest, mixing with the persistent ache to form a musical cacophony both stimulating and unsettling, like abstract art.

Each time the red lights flash overhead, a different face is illuminated, revealing expressions frozen in time. The strobe effect throws me off-kilter and I stop and start. Several times I stumble and grab onto the nearest limb for balance.

"Sorry, sorry," I mutter. I check the faces in the crowd, sometimes squinting to try and make out the features of Daniel James. "Do you know a guy named Daniel James?" I ask at intervals, but invariably the people questioned shake their heads, and I can't decipher whether they didn't hear me or they actually don't know the boy I'm asking about.

I press through the heart of the crowd, where the bodies are densest. On the other side, the flailing mob begins to thin and I find concertgoers nursing their drinks or leaning in for conversation.

I ask a couple with matching dreadlocks if they've seen Daniel. They've never heard of him. My shoulders sag. What if he didn't come after all? A change of plans. He got sick.

In the spot where I'm standing, I revolve slowly in place, taking in a panoramic view. It's then that I spot a face, some-one I can't place, whom I'm sure I don't know, but the fea-tures are familiar.

I move closer to the spot where he's leaned up against a wall, talking to a heavyset girl whose bulbous rear end hikes a short black skirt up to the very top of her thighs. The closer I get, the more certain I become.

As I approach, staring blatantly, the pair stop their conversation and stare back. The girl screws up her mouth into a sneer. Her look is punk rock meets 1940s pinup. Dark eyeliner fans out into cat eyes, and her heart-shaped lips are painted a shocking hue of cherry red.

"Can I help you?" she asks in a way that suggests she has no interest whatsoever in helping me.

"Daniel? Daniel James?" I say, ignoring her.

He straightens. In person, he's a shadow of the boy I saw in the photograph. He has none of the brightness, eye twinkle, or toothy grin I'd seen there. Instead, he's as colorless as watered-down milk. If it weren't for the haircut, I might not have been able to piece the features together to spot him, but his white hair, shaved on one side and plastered down over his left eye on the other, is distinctive in its irregularity.

"That's me. Dan," he says in a voice that's deeper than I'd expect given his skeletal frame and pale blue eyes.

"I'm..." I hesitate. "Veronica Leeds." I cringe at the use of this fake identity again. It hasn't exactly worked in my favor in the past.

The girl beside him curls in closer like a cat kneading her way into a beloved owner's lap.

"This is Raven," he says, nodding in her direction, as though I'd asked. I wish Raven would get lost, but I get the sense that she's staked her claim for the night and that extracting her would take jaws of steel and a tranquilizer gun.

"I was hoping I could ask you a few questions, Dan."

"Depends who you are. You a cop?"

I roll my eyes. "Do I look like a cop? I'm seventeen."

"Whatever.

"Right, yeah, whatever." I consider taking out my phone and calling Henry, but worry that Dan and his goth girl are set to dart like frightened animals.

I take a deep breath. "Do you know a guy named Levi Zin?"

A slick-looking tongue slides over Dan's lips. "Why should I tell you?"

"You don't exactly look like you're busy." He shrugs. I exhale hard. "Fine." I pull my wallet out of my purse and hand him twenty dollars.

He grins. "Yeah, I *knew* him. Why?" There's an uproar from the crowd. I glance back to see that the female lead singer dove offstage and is now crowd-surfing.

Returning my attention to Dan, I make a decision not to volunteer any more information than necessary. "So he, um, passed away?" I ask, trying to keep my voice light, as if I'm merely curious. For his part, Dan doesn't seem to be the brightest specimen, or maybe he's just too drugged out to process beyond surface level.

Two pale eyebrows crawl inward at the top of his nose. "You really don't know? Levi kicked the can. He's six feet under. Worm food." He takes a sip from his plastic cup, eyes already heading from glassy to totally vacant.

"You have a gift for imagery," I say curtly. "Okay, so he's dead. Did anyone take a particular interest in him either before or after his death?"

"What does *that* mean?" Raven takes a break from swirling her finger around Dan's ear to interject.

I raise my eyebrows.

"I'm not sure," Dan says. "Not really. I was friends with

him. We played in a band together sometimes, but I wouldn't say many people were super close to Levi. Nobody was even that shocked."

"Why not?"

"I don't know—I guess he was in trouble a lot."

"What kind of trouble?"

Dan slouches against the wall. "I'm not so sure I should keep telling you unless . . ." He nods at my purse.

I narrow my eyes at him, but in a war between who can be more patient, Dan would most certainly win. I look in the crevices of my wallet and hold up a ten.

He scratches his eyebrow. "It's not as much."

"It's all I have." I hold it close. "Take it or leave it."

He tries to make a grab for it. "Take it."

"Not so fast." I hold it tightly in my grip. "After."

He glares at me but continues. "Like typical stuff. Skipping school. Drinking. I don't know. He thought he was destined to be some kind of rock god. Kurt Cobain. Andrew Wood. Layne Staley. Live fast, die hard, only-the-good-die-young type of thing. You know what I'm saying?"

Unfortunately, I know exactly what he's saying. My veins feel icy. Dan's friend sounds exactly like the Levi I know. Where's Henry? I do a quick sweep to see if I can spot him. No such luck. "But you were with him when he died?"

Raven glares at me. "You don't have to answer her question, you know."

I wave the ten and he shrugs her off. Clearly, Raven's not meant to become a permanent fixture. He continues, stroking the gelled strand of hair over his eye. "Yeah. I've already told all this to the police, though."

"But I'm not the police."

"Right...Yeah, sorry...I don't know, it was like..."
He squeezes his eyelids over pinpoint pupils and shakes his
head before reopening them. "It was terrible. Even for someone like Levi, who...I don't know how to say this, but
just seemed sort of destined for bad things. Levi was drunk
and wasn't paying attention, but still, that wire came out of
nowhere. We were going so fast. When the boat crashed it
sounded like an explosion. Like, I don't know, like something out of Abu Dhabi. The wire just grazed my arm, but
even still, it nearly cut it off." Dan rolls up the sleeve of his
shirt and holds out his forearm for me to examine. A fresh
scar runs from the knobby bone of his wrist to his elbow.
He shudders visibly, then replaces the sleeve. "Levi must
have gotten knocked out and drowned, because when they
fished him out of the waterway and pushed on his chest—"
As human brains are inclined to do, mine is filling in the
blanks, illustrating this story with the Levi I knew, my Levi.
"You know the way they do in movies—seawater shot out
of him like a fountain." I swallow. This wasn't my Levi, I
remind myself. This was someone else, someone I've never
met. The flashing red of the lights and the persistent thump
of the bass feel trippy and wrong. Disorienting.

I can't help asking. "What did he look like?"

Dan trains his insipid, waterlogged eyes on me more
intently. "Who did you say you were again?"

Onstage, the lead singer belts a violent scream that sends
the crowd into another roar. Light flashes across Dan's face.
I smell sweat and skunked beer.

"I'm a friend of the family."

For a split second, Dan's eyes become unfocused, glazed
over. He clears his throat. "Black hair like hers." He points

to Raven, who purrs at being noticed. "Tall. I think I have a picture of him on my phone." Something thick and sticky globs at the back of my throat. Daniel fishes in his pocket and clicks through a few screens before turning the phone toward me.

I take the phone in my hands and hold it close to my face to study. Suddenly, my chest cramps. I feel my heart being smashed into a box too small for it. Strangling. Wheezing. Sputtering for blood.

The phone slips from my hands and cracks on the concrete floor.

"What the hell!" Dan yells, diving to retrieve it.

I clutch my chest, world spinning rapidly out of control like a kaleidoscope. Red lights flashing. Music pounding. I catch Raven's arm to keep from plummeting to the ground. The pain in my heart threatens to buckle my knees.

"Get off of me. What's wrong with you, you freak?"

Heart still crushed to the point I can't breathe, I find the wall and prop myself against it. I shut my eyes, listening to the frantic notes of an electric guitar, which sound tinny and distant. The image of Levi's beautiful, unforgettable face feels like it's been tattooed under my eyelids.

It's him.

chapter twenty-nine
143 BPM

My alarm goes off at too-early o'clock. Thoughts bubble to
the surface, sleepy and muddled. Black hair. Tan skin. Shattered glass. *Him.*

But at the same time . . . not him. Dozy eyes, unfocused.
A look that I'm not used to. Smile directed away from the
camera. What had he been looking at? I don't know. I don't
know anything, I realize. My alarm chirps again. Repeti-
tive. Irritating. I roll over and slap my hand over all of the
buttons until it shuts up. My mouth tastes foul.

Henry had to see it to believe it himself and for this, he
had to wrestle the phone free from my new friend Dan and
pay up another twenty. But once he laid eyes on the photograph, I watched as a curtain like an oncoming storm spread
over his features. *Him.*

Painful knots still fill my chest. *There's got to be a logical
explanation,* he said. *We'll figure this out.* Will we? It hurts to

move; hurts to breathe. I'm beginning to the think the well of logical explanations has run dry.

There's knocking at the door. "Stella! Are you up?"

The effort it'd take to lift my head feels insurmountable. "Define up," I yell back to Mom.

"Stella Cross! We cannot be late!" Even through the door I can tell she has a serious case of the *I-mean-it*'s.

I groan loud enough for Mom to hear it through the door. We never go to church and I have no idea why Elsie should need to be christened anyhow. I'm sure her soul will be perfectly safe, holy water or no.

"I can't hear movement!" Mom jiggles the locked door.

"Okay, okay." I shove the blankets down to my ankles and crawl out of bed like a zombie from its grave. "I'm up."

One day. Just get through this one day. I say this as a promise to myself. Besides, I have no other plan at the moment, so I'm not sure there's another choice.

On the other side of the door, I find Mom busy fastening a pair of earrings, her entire head of hair rolled up in hot curlers. "I ironed a dress for you. It's hanging in the laundry room. And can you do something with that hair?"

I scrunch the stringy black mop in between my fingers. To my mom's credit, she hadn't made a big deal when I'd chopped it off. I'm sure she wrote it in her Stella files. Probably under the heading POST-SURGERY REBELLION, but she let it go. So I'll try for her because I can tell that she's entered the crazy zone, the mode usually reserved for cleaning the house before we have company. When we used to have company, that is.

"Stephen!" she yells, padding off barefoot down the hall.

My dad, clean-shaven and dressed in a suit and paisley

tie, whooshes past her. "I can't find the camera battery. Have you seen it? Morning, Stel." He lifts his chin and nods before jogging over to look under the living room sofa. I follow him with my eyes, feeling weird and adrift. Thoughts, theories, and opinions are mixing wildly in my brain, half-formed, the cogs of steampunk machinery turning over and over, clicking in and out of place. And yet neither of my parents can see through me to this place of palpable turbulence.

Inside the laundry room, I slip into a knee-length navy-blue dress. I realize with a pang that it's the one Mom bought me for my Stanford admissions interview. I haven't told them yet that I missed the application deadline. I don't know when I will. I zip the dress. How can any of that matter when I've just found out that my ex-boyfriend's face matches the face of a dead boy? Which means what, exactly? That my ex-boyfriend is, in fact, dead?

At least the dress covers up my scar nicely.

I'm pinning my hair into something less shaggy and more coifed when I hear a scream from the kitchen. "Mom!" I rush out. "Are you okay?"

"Shoot, shoot, shoot." She blots at a dribble of coffee on her cream pencil skirt. "It's not coming out."

"Here, let me try." I hurry to wet a dish towel.

"No, no." She shoos me away. "I'm an idiot." She smacks her forehead so hard I expect it to bruise like an overripe apple. She shakes her head, chin dimpled and lips pressed together. "Can you go put Elsie in her christening gown? I need to change. It's ruined." The look on her face is pained.

"Of course, Mom. Are you sure?" Tears have started to pool in her eyes, so I throw the dish towel down on the cabinet and scurry off to Elsie's room. I shut the door behind me to seal off the chaos. Elsie peers at me through the bars of her crib.

"'Ella?" She removes her thumb from her mouth and scrunches her tiny sausage fingers. "'El-la."

I rest my back on the door and take a deep breath. The room smells like vanilla and baby powder. "Yes, hi, Elsie," I say patiently. "Our family has gone loony tunes, Elsie. Did you know that?"

I have gone loony tunes, that's for sure. I'm finding it impossible to come up with a non-crazy explanation for the fact that I've been seeing a dead man walking.

Elsie pats her hands together before depositing her favorite thumb back between goopy lips. Soft baby curls practically float off the top of her head, and I watch her balance on a base of two chunky toddler thighs.

A frilly white gown six inches too long hangs from the edge of a changing table. Folded on top of the table are a pair of petite lace gloves and a matching bonnet.

I cringe at the bonnet. "Don't blame me for this," I say, fingering the abundance of white ruffles.

Elsie will be baptized at the Church of the Sacred Heart, the same church my parents and I have been attending every couple years for Christmas since I was born. The church's symbol consists of a traditional heart shape, adorned with a crown of thorns and bursting with flames. Mounted on top of the burning heart is a cross and below that a lance puncturing the bleeding organ. Since my diagnosis, I've never liked attending. The image unsettles me, and I'm approaching Elsie's baptism with dread.

What's so sacred about a heart anyway? Mine's gone,

replaced by somebody else's. The doctors switched it for a better model and I've been suffering ever since. Suffering like that supposedly sacred heart of Jesus.

Gently, I lift Elsie from the crib and set her baby bottom down on the plush carpet. She giggles as I unbutton her onesie. "That's right. Be good for Stella," I coo. Her tiny body shivers under the light draft from the air-conditioning vent.

Elsie reaches for me, fingers splayed, in that way babies do, back arched—stretched—striving like she's trying to grab a star. I slide the christening gown off the hanger and hold it to my chest, looking down at her squirming. "Once all this white goes on, Else, all bodily functions must cease, *capisce?*"

Elsie cooperates when I sit her up and pull the frock over her head. Once I'm finished, it's hard not to laugh. There's more ruffle than there is Elsie. Sometimes it pays not to be the Replacement Child, after all.

"Right. The final touches." I'm crawling to my feet and turning to the changing table for the lace gloves and bonnet when I hear a voice say my name in an urgent tone.

Stella.

A shiver brushes my neck. I turn, expecting to see my mother having entered the room in search of help scrubbing her skirt or pinning on a brooch. The words that are half-way past my lips stumble and flutter helplessly into silence.

A streak of darkness blurs across the room and my blood freezes at the sight of a shadowed silhouette lurking in the corner behind the crib.

Tingles scuttle like insects over my scalp. I'm unable to move.

The figure looms, motionless, human in form but not in substance. Without taking my eyes off the dim outline, I inch closer to Elsie.

Its darkness sucks the light out of everything around it. Even the damp sunlight trickling in from the window is extracted from the air and sunk into shadow.

"Who . . . who are you?"

The figure cocks its head. Eyes on me. Watching.

Elsie babbles words that are intelligible only to her. She's not close enough to touch. A needle of fear pins me like a butterfly to a display board. Heart flapping.

"Elsie, come here," I whisper. The smell of baby powder and vanilla has been pulled out of the air and replaced by that of mothballs and urine.

I take a step closer to my sister, but as I do the figure dissolves, reappearing in a thick but foggy mass just behind her.

I scream.

Black fingers reach for her. The figure crouches. A head tilts hungrily and Elsie cries out, wails for "'Ella."

I watch in horror as a shadowy hand plunges through the back of her tiny skull. A gray talon pokes out her mouth. She gags. Chokes.

I spring to life, unsure of what to do. I try to beat back the shade. Fists punch at the air. I fight to pull it off of Elsie and the thing screeches in protest.

Her strangled wails spur me to fight harder. Another shadowy, clawlike hand pushes through my sister's small chest. Grabbing. Grabbing.

The stink of sour breath stings my nostrils. Whimpering, I nearly gag.

My vision is swimming. It hitches, giving the sense of a shift to double vision. I blink. Blink again. Wrenching my eyes to focus on the spot where my hands are gripping, I see only Elsie and my fingers wrapping themselves around her neck as though they belong to someone else. I freeze. My rear end drops to my heels and I sit back slowly. My hands are rigid as they draw away from my baby sister's throat.

There's nothing here. Nothing in the room with me. Her wails pierce the silence, grounding me. It wasn't real. None of it was real. A trick. A lie. My stupid, stupid brain.

I scoop Elsie off the floor and hold her to my chest. Her chin rests on my shoulder and her screams bounce directly off my eardrums. It doesn't bother me. She could scream all through the night and I'd gladly listen.

I rub her tiny back and bounce her up and down the way she likes me to do.

There's a click behind me. Footsteps. "Stella!" I twist around. My mom is standing above me. Air whooshes out of her and she pushes her bangs off her forehead. "You guys scared me. Is everything okay?" At this point, Elsie's wet sobs are beginning to dry up. I can't see her face, but I'm sure the entire lower half is plastered in snot.

Dad follows closely behind Mom. Is it surprise that I see in both my parents' eyes? And if so, surprise at what? That I'm here nicely cooing to my sister? I realize how far their opinion of me must have fallen since my surgery.

Dad plants his hands over his belt and shakes his head. "Jesus, it sounded like an axe murderer was in here."

Dad's arm wraps around Mom's waist and he pulls her near. I swish Elsie back and forth, wondering if when she's ten years older she'll look at me and this moment will come to her in a weird flash of memory and she'll wonder whether it's true or just her imagination. She'll wonder whether her sister really once tried to kill her.

"No," I say, without smiling. "Just me."

chapter thirty
105 BPM

"You want to steal?" Henry says incredulously. "From my *father?*" I waited until we were in the parking lot of Harborview Medical Center before unleashing my plan on Henry. "I thought you had a medical-something-or-other here?"

I stare flatly at him. Grim. If I'm going to figure out how Levi—whichever Levi he is—is walking around and why he's particularly walking around *me*, it seems like the best place to start is here, researching the details of his death. Sometimes sick-girl logic comes in handy.

"I lied," I say.

"Well, that's comforting."

"But who said anything about stealing?" I say, staring up at the building. An ambulance siren blasts through the adjoining driveway as it races up to the emergency room entrance. For as long as I live, I will hate hospitals.

Henry twists the bill of his cap. "I'm sorry. Did you have another word you'd prefer I use? I'd hate to muck this up over semantics."

"Taking a peek? Poking around? Anything that doesn't make it seem like we're committing a crime." A technician in bright, polka-dotted scrubs wheels a patient past us.

Henry throws his hands up and they fall with a clap onto his pant legs. "But we *are*! That's the whole point."

"We're accessing your dad's files, Henry." I have to admit, rifling through Dr. Jones's things does feel a bit icky, but I can't think of another way and I don't have time to try.

"Files my dad has privileges to," he corrects. The sliding glass doors to the hospital swoosh open and shut. Balloons disappear inside. Haggard-looking people stagger out from the waiting room for a smoke.

"Same thing. *Relax*." I try to sound like this is no big deal, but my palms are already slick with sweat. I have no idea what I'm going to find in those records, and after hearing the short version from Daniel, I'm not sure I want to. "Other girls have malls, I have hospitals. Trust me, if there's one thing I know, it's this."

He sighs. "I just wish it *weren't* my dad. At least I'd feel like less of a jerk."

"So you'd prefer a stranger catch us thumbing through hospital records?" I quirk an eyebrow. "Now it's starting to sound like a crime."

"You'd make a scary lawyer, you know." He shudders.

"It's in my genes."

Together, we enter the bustling lobby of Harborview Medical Center. The antiseptic scent of plastic gloves and freshly mopped floors bowls me over. Nausea pushes at my throat. I take a step back and Henry reaches for my hand. I wave him off. "Just a reflex," I say, swallowing hard. I can't wait until the last time I have to set foot in one of these buildings.

The hospital is a labyrinth of corridors and double doors that seal shut the second anyone walks through. "Do you know where your dad keeps his office around here?" The atmosphere of Harborview is more frantic than at St. David's, and I have a strong urge to wash my hands as soon as possible.

"Sort of. I think so. It's been a while." Henry turns on the spot, looking at each of the signs. He pauses when he lands on one hallway, thinking, then . . . "This way."

He leads me down a long passage lined with small waiting areas. People slumped in chairs. Coughing. Sour stench of sickness and apple juice.

I stick close to Henry. We wind up in an elevator. He punches the button for the fourth floor first, then thinks better of it and decides that it's actually the sixth.

Although the elevator is empty, instinctively, we huddle close together. Coconspirators on our way to a heist. I inhale deeply the eau d'Henry, letting it calm me, since it smells nothing like a hospital.

My chest emits a few painful pulses and I wonder how much effort it would take to steal a bottle of morphine from the pharmacy. Then I wonder more whether morphine would even work. I consider it doubtful.

The elevator dings. We step off onto the sixth floor. Around here there are none of the sunny decorations that try so hard to be upbeat in the lower floors, but instead come off as looking too bold and too impersonal, always primary colors. This floor is cool, quiet, like an office building. Our steps echo and so would our voices if we didn't fall into a hushed silence. We're stopped at a reception desk by a bubbly voice.

"Hello there," says a bottle blonde from behind a desk. "May I help you?"

Henry turns and puts on his church smile. I'd hoped we'd be able to march through unimpeded. "Hi, we're looking for Dr. Jones?"

"His dad," I add.

The blonde with the name tag that reads, in bold letters, CASSANDRA tilts her head and taps her fake-tanned chin with a French-manicured nail. *"Henry?"*

"Yeah?" Henry shoots me a sidelong glance.

"Well, look at you," she squeals. "Your father has photographs in the office, but you're . . . well, you look so grown-up." Eyelashes flutter.

I scoot an imperceptible inch closer to him. Back off, Blondie.

I clear my throat, since Henry appears to have lost the use of his vocal cords. "We're meeting Dr. Jones in his office in a few minutes"

She rests her palm on the phone. "Sure you don't want me to page him?"

"That's okay," Henry says quickly. I elbow him in the ribs. "Yeah, we're, uh, we're going to go wait for Dr.—I mean Dad—in his office, okay?"

"Sure, I don't see why not," she says, grinning at us. Then, to Henry: "Can I bring you anything? Water? A juice box from downstairs?"

I've already started to drag Henry down the hall, away

from Cassandra and her white dental-assistant teeth and perky hair flips. "No. We're fine. Thanks," I answer for him.

"Did you see how she looked at me?" he asks, craning to look over his shoulder.

I search the nameplates for the office that belongs to Henry's dad. "Slow down, Romeo. The woman offered you a juice box."

At the end of the corridor, I spot the familiar name: JOSHUA H. JONES, M.D. We slip into his office and close the door behind us. I take a deep breath, the doorknob poking into my lower back.

"How long do you think we have?"

Henry crosses a white rug and sits down on a stiff leather sofa.

"Not sure. Should be a while. He only comes back here to do paperwork."

I exhale and crack my knuckles. "Okay, then. In that case, I'm going in." I slide into the massive rolling chair and do a quick spin to face Dr. Jones's computer.

I remember the first time I saw the records Dr. Belkin kept about me. You could scroll and scroll and keep on scrolling and still you'd never reach the end.

I see at once that this hospital doesn't use the same record system as St. David's, but it's similar enough.

"Are you sure you know what you're doing?" asks Henry, breathing over my shoulder.

The screen is dark, but I rattle the mouse and it brightens. Dr. Jones has already logged in for the day. A stroke of luck.

"Shhhh." I hold up a finger. "I told you. I've got this." I'm clicking the top right-hand side of the screen and typing in the words *Levi Zin*. A short list of documents appears in the drop-down box. "This is it," I whisper. "Should I click on it?" I look up at Henry, who's inches from my cheek.

"Are you kidding me? Open it." He pokes my shoulder. "What are you waiting for?"

We both go rigid at the sound of approaching footsteps. "Thanks, Cassie." We hear the unmistakable voice of Dr. Jones. "Tell Margo I'll call her back in an hour. Back-to-back appointments until then."

"Henry," I squawk. A turn of the knob.

"Shit, shit, shit." Henry slaps the back of the chair and then springs to the door.

Stepping outside, he must run headlong into his dad because I hear, "What are you doing here, Henry?" Followed by a pause and then, "Whoa there, oh shoot. Oh, darn."

I mentally groan

"Dad, I'm so sorry." I can envision renewed hair-tugging. "Can I get you a cloth? A napkin?"

I cringe. The door is only open a crack. I'm not sure what to do or how much time I have to do it. Any? No time to second-guess. I click on the file.

A warning for the Health Insurance Portability and Accountability Act flashes on-screen. I click through it with the mouse. I tap my foot on the floor. "Come on, come on, come on. Load." A glance over my shoulder. I can just make out a sliver of Henry.

"You really got me," says Dr. Jones. A rustle of clothing. "Was I expecting you? I didn't see anything on the schedule." He pauses. "Not that you have to schedule anything with your dad. Sorry." He sounds flustered. "I didn't mean it that way."

"No, um—" *Think, Henry, think,* I will him. "Just a spur-of-the-moment decision. Sorry about your coat."

"No worries. I have a stain-remover pen inside. Your mother insists."

I jump from the chair. Should I duck? Dive?

The door swings open another two inches. "Wait! Dad!" I'm paralyzed. "Stella's, uh, in there."

"Stella?"

"Yeah. We were in the area and she wasn't feeling well, so I said maybe we could go to your office and she could lie down on your couch for a while." I can count out the seconds by the pounding of my heart. "I hope that's okay. I know we didn't ask first."

A hand appears on the knob. It closes another couple inches.

I sigh, sinking back into the chair and wiping my brow. I don't have time to read the file. I glance around. A printer is perched on a desk stand beside the filing cabinet.

I have no spare time to think. I punch a couple keys and, to my relief, the ink-jet starts coughing up pages.

"Then I should go in to see her. Is she okay? Henry, this stuff is serious. Stella—"

Only a couple more pages. The printer is a dinosaur.

"Actually, would you mind feeling my glands?" I hear Henry closest to the door now, as if he's physically blockading it. "I'm worried I'm coming down with something too." I bend down and peek into the bowels of the printer. Why is its speed glacial?

Henry's getting desperate.

"If you're coming down with something, then you

shouldn't be around Stella. And you definitely shouldn't be kissing her."

"Dad! Please!"

My eyes bug and I'm a thousand times grateful that Henry isn't here to witness my reddening face.

Last page. It chug-chug-chugs, lurching out of the machine all maddening stop-and-go. The door is opening again. And from Henry's strangled warning, I gather that there's no stopping Dr. Jones this time. Henry's used all the tricks in his bag. I lean down and grab the page from the printer. Just as I'm preparing to fold it in with the rest of the stack, a familiar number catches my eye, one that I have branded onto the back of my eyelids, one that I will forever associate with the deepest, purest form of pain and that, even now, in its immobile black typeface, read at a time that can't possibly harm me, makes me want to faint.

chapter thirty-one
147 BPM

When Dr. Jones opens the door, he's facing Henry, who I see is still making a big show of pointing at his glands. This gives me a split second to make it from the desk to a position reasonably close to the sofa where I was supposed to be resting. "Dr. Jones!" I say in a voice that's far too cheery for someone who only moments earlier was napping. My cheeks warm. *Napping?* I can't imagine what Henry's dad must think of me if I'm the type of girl to make myself at home in someone's office. Fantastic. I take the enthusiasm down three notches and try again. "Nice to see you again." I fake a more feeble smile.

"Nice to see you too, Stella." His white coat flutters behind him as he whooshes through the room, dropping a stack of files on his desk. His smile could melt butter and I feel a surge of guilt for snooping through his things. "Henry tells me you're feeling out of sorts?"

"I, uh . . ." Henry gives me a subtle shrug. Right. Improvise. "Yeah, I'm sorry. Just a faint spell, I think."

Dr. Jones starts to open his mouth.

"But just for a minute," I interject. "I'm feeling much better now. Strange how it can just pass like that, but hey, count your good days, right? That's what the nurses are always telling me." I'm rambling. "Anyway, thanks for letting me use your office. Sorry to barge in like that." Behind my back I point to the bulge of paper tucked into my jacket. Henry squints. Then his eyes widen. Meanwhile, his dad takes turns looking between us like we've both come down with some rare avian flu. "So," Henry says, trying and failing to sound natural, "you seem really busy."

"Really busy," I agree with a serious crinkling of my brow.

"And we didn't mean to disturb you." Henry retreats one small step toward the door.

"Yeah, that's the last thing that we want to do."

"You two aren't disturbing—"

"Sure, sure, I know, Dad, but we should get going and besides, Stella's feeling better."

"So much better," I agree.

"Right." Henry rubs his palms together, backpedaling farther toward the door. "Anyway, thanks for letting us pop in, and I'll see you for dinner." He waves.

Trailing Henry, I back out of the door so that Dr. Jones won't see I'm hiding something in my jacket.

Henry tugs at my arm and we both break off in the opposite direction, toward the elevator, giggling in spite of ourselves. He hardly even acknowledges Cassandra when she tries to make parting conversation.

We stampede into the elevator, which lurches to a stop on the next floor, where a young, pregnant woman gets on. I take this as our cue. "Come on." I look both ways, and together we tumble out into a hallway.

"What are we doing here?" Henry asks. Both of our shoes squeak loudly across the floor.

I spot a supply closet. The coast is clear. I swing open the door and we duck in. I have to know what the report says. If what I thought I saw is real.

We're now standing toe-to-toe. I fumble for a light and switch it on. My nose is an inch from Henry's chest. The shelves surrounding us are stocked with jugs of cleaning fluid and cartons of gauze. Beside our feet is a mop bucket. I scoot it sideways.

"Are you crazy?" Henry asks in a hushed tone.

I retrieve the papers and spread them out flat. "I'm pretty sure that's already been established. Here." I turn the pages horizontally, so that we can both read them.

Medical jargon fills the first page. Blood type. Echocardiogram numbers. White-cell count. I'm used to the language and understand most of it. I scan the small print, not sure on which page I'd seen the number. When nothing on a page catches my attention, I hand it to Henry, who folds it up and sticks it in his pocket.

"Look." I point to a spot halfway down the second page. "A description of his injury." I underline the words with my nail. "Doctors observed severe head trauma as well as blunt force to the neck and spine. Residual water in lungs.

Severe laceration on the throat. Heartbeat low at thirty-six beats per minute."

I flip quickly to the next page. Henry's breath is hot and tickles my scalp.

"His family signed to take him off life support," Henry says about the fast, looping signature scrawled at the bottom of the sheet. I'd worried about the same moment for my parents. The one where they had to admit that I wasn't coming back. Pull the plug. The idea had the finality of a period, not at the end of a sentence or a paragraph, but at the end of a weighty Russian novel.

We're to the final page now. A sharp intake of breath. I can scarcely focus on any of the words. The ink runs together in dark blobs that appear to pool on the white paper. My hands tremble because I know what will be on this page. The number.

I lick my lips and read on, through the medical report of the cause of death. The combination of Levi Zin's injuries paints a violent picture of an end not peacefully met. Even with the physicians' sterile terminology, it's as if I'm looking through a projector lens and playing on the screen is a reel highlighting each cut and blow. In my mind's eye, I see as the life force is beaten and slashed from Levi Zin's fragile teenage body.

And right there on the still-warm leaf of paper is the time that it all ended.

"Five oh eight." I lift my eyes to meet Henry's. "That's the time that he died." There's a click in my chest, as of a piece of a puzzle snapping into place. "That's our connection." I stare at the numbers in disbelief. "This is it. The time I—"

"The time you feel the pain," Henry says without taking his eyes off me.

I nod. The moment teeters on the edge of reality. It has the shimmery quality of something out of a dream. Currents hum in the air. "Henry, I'm scared." I don't mean to say this, but I do and it's out. He shifts protectively toward me, and I raise up on my tippy-toes and I'm thinking that maybe, just maybe, if our lips touch in just the right way, my pain will slip away, but just as I'm committing, a blast of light blinds me.

Henry raises his arm to shield his eyes, but in doing so he jabs one of mine.

"Ouch!" I stumble back, knocking boxes off the shelf behind me with a loud clatter.

"What are you kids doing?" a man in a blue janitorial jumpsuit demands. "Get out of here! Does this look like the back of a movie theater to you?" He grabs Henry by the collar and yanks him away from me. "Show some respect."

I scramble out after Henry and we do exactly what the man says. We get out of there. Fast.

chapter thirty-two
154 BPM

I lie on my bed, staring up at the ceiling, scatterbrained with sickness. Unable to form complete thoughts.

At five oh eight on the dot, the splitting pain had once again racked my body with seizures. Knives and needles and fire all wrapped up into one. This time I didn't even attempt to wash myself of the sweat when my heart rate slowed. My weak limbs lie limply on the mattress, begging for a reprieve. But even with the worst of it gone, what's left is still devastating. It's like trying to be relieved that the bombing has stopped, when the city is in smoking ruins.

How many days since my surgery have I been suffering? I start to count on one hand and then two and then I have to add in my toes. The torture is so complete that I wonder if I'd have chosen to die if I'd known.

Deliriums, nightmares, visions that haunt me in broad daylight—I want nothing more than a moment of relief.

Every so often, as the seconds tick by, I'll summon all of my focus. I'll close my eyes, concentrating, until I can imagine for the span of one breath the sensation of anguish lifting out of my body and away. It's beautiful. Freeing. Like running my hands through a cloud. But I can only hold the illusion for a single instant before it wobbles and fades like a mirage.

After that I crash back into my own body, filled with its nails and saws and sharp things that scrape my soul and it's then that I always realize what it is I'd been thinking about to give me such a small break from reality.

Levi.

Dark thoughts swarm me. My mind is a cobweb for the gloomiest of ideas. Sticky, it nabs and cocoons them so that my conscience has time to toy with them before gobbling them up. Several times I contemplate whether it's worth it to live at all. If this is the quality of life I can expect—and so far I've seen no evidence to the contrary—then why should I fight so hard to stay? But then again, how could I ever overcome the guilt of wasting the gift of someone else's heart?

When I can no longer stand the clawing, hollowed-out sense of my torso and limbs, and when my brain is so fuzzy and disenchanted that nobody could convince me there is an ounce of good in the universe, I make a decision. I need to know. I need to understand why.

I type the words into my phone and hit send. There. It's done. It's reckless and stupid and ill-advised, but I don't care. My heart has made me into someone who can't care.

I've spent two years, I realize, waiting for the other shoe to drop. Ever since my diagnosis, my days have been filled with the possibility of more bad things to come. The bad things have never failed to come. And I've never failed to wait for them. But I'm bone-tired from the waiting. I can't take the suspense. This time, I'll make the first move.

It's an hour before I get a response. I walk a trench through the carpet in front of my windowsill, the tempo of the rain picking up. I push my fingers into the base of my jaw and rub hard.

At last there's a tap on the window. I listen for my parents or for Elsie. When I hear nothing in return, I jostle open the glass and Levi shimmies through, a gust of cold air and rain following him. Here he is, my moment of weakness.

"I didn't realize it was raining *that* hard," I say to the boy who is now dripping onto my carpet. As if on cue there's a rumble of thunder. The downpour sprays me in the face as I wrestle the window back shut.

He shakes his hair out. Droplets fly in all directions. "Just a shower." He winks. Not all guys can pull off a wink. Levi Zin can.

A flash of lightning brightens my room for a split second. Five seconds pass and then another crash of thunder.

I hover, unsure of what to do now that I'm deep into the process of doing it.

He blots his face and arms. "Someone's had a change of heart."

"Or lack thereof." I stiffen. He has the type of chest I'd like to bury my face in and breathe in for life. Just being near him makes me feel equal parts better and worse. Better because his presence eases my discomfort, worse because the craving to touch him is so strong it's unbearable.

I should be afraid. I should be terrified. But I only feel ready.

He continues brushing rain droplets from the shoulders of a black overcoat and I continue watching him more greedily than I should. The torrential downpour volleys against the window. I take a deep breath. He raises his eyebrows as if to say, *Oh?*

"Who are you, Levi?" It's a rush to ask him.

He crosses his arms and leans against the far wall. "Levi Zin." Lightning illuminates half of his face.

I take a step closer. "Levi Zin's dead."

I can't read his eyes behind the shadows. "I'm clearly not dead."

"There's nothing clear about it." I jump as thunder rattles my shelves. "You look like him. I saw. You look exactly like him."

It's his turn to take a step closer to me. "You're being ridiculous."

"I know things."

His glare cuts like stone. "Haven't you had blackouts, what, like four times now? And those are the ones that we know of."

"What are you?" I say it as much to myself as to Levi.

"You're as crazy as they say you are." Our toes are nearly touching. I watch his chest rise and fall. Real breaths. Don't listen to him, I will myself. It's not real.

I close my eyes, try with everything I have to shut his words out. Lies. What he's saying, it's all lies.

I squeeze my fists closed and press them tight to my sides. "No," I say at last. "I saw that you died. I saw how you died."

His lips tighten into thin lines.

"Tell me what you are, Levi." The shake won't come out of my voice now. I think that I'm standing at the point of no return, that we have nowhere to go from here but down. And yet my heart still claws for him, storming the prison made from nothing but the bones of my rib cage. It beats so hard that I know it's trying to fracture my skeleton. I wait for the first shard to puncture my skin or lung.

Levi tilts his head a small segment of an inch and I swear he's listening to my heartbeat clamoring for him. He takes a step closer to me, the fabric of our clothes brushing together. I stand my ground, knees trembling underneath a body they are too weak too hold up. Every particle inside me screams along with my heart.

"Does it matter?" Levi asks, moving his thumb under the tip of my chin and pulling my jaw up so that I'll look at him.

A crack of lightning strikes and then the blue light of the television turns black. The hum of the heater stops. The power is dead.

I let him run strong hands through my hair, then down my neck. My skin lights up wherever he touches. The pain in my chest vanishes.

He doesn't say anything, but scoops me up and repositions us on the side of my bed.

Relief washes through me as his hands travel up the outside of my legs until they loop around the small of my back. He rests his head on my chest. Just one moment longer, I promise silently.

He lifts his chin from my breast and stares up at me. In one swift motion, he's up and twirling me around. He pulls me onto the bed and slips off my shirt.

The pain feels farther and farther away as he kisses me. Our hips push together and we're so entangled in one another it's hard to tell where one of us begins and the other ends. The only coherent thought I can formulate is, Don't leave.

Our foreheads press into each other; I'm tugging at the edge of his shirt, pulling it up and over his head.

All at once this moment feels strangely familiar—it's how I imagined things would go the night of the party, before everything came crashing down. And that's when I know: I can't lose myself to this, to him. Not again. Not ever. I dig my fingers into the comforter before looking up at him and saying a single word: "Tess."

It's not a question. I'm not even sure that it's what I meant to say, but the moment I do, something predatory flashes in his eyes and I know without a doubt that he is responsible for her murder.

Lightning goes off like a flare and it's only then that I see it.

An angry scar, thick as a rope, nearly identical to mine, cuts down the middle of his chest. His muscles go rigid. I dart to the other side of the mattress. Scramble off the side of the bed, trying to put space between us. It can't be.

But all I have to do is look down and study my own chest to know that he has the unmistakable mark of a transplant. *Five oh eight.*

"You." I grasp instinctively at my own mark. The reporter's words ring in my ears. *Her heart,* they said, *was missing.* My mouth goes dry. "You—you took—"

He reaches for me, but not gently. "Come here, Stella."

I leap backward. "Why? Why should I come to you? Why would I ever come to you?"

He edges off the bed, one foot planted and then the other.

I'm conscious of the wall behind me. "Oh, come on. Don't act like you don't feel it too."

I shake my head. Hair flies over my face.

"We're both stronger"—I notice his shoulders curved inward, his head lowered: the posture of a killer—"when we're near, Cross."

"No." The realization crashes over me. The constant ache in my chest. The relief only when he's near. My heart. *His* heart.

He lunges for me. I jerk to the side. He smacks into a bookcase. I have one more instinct. And it's to scream.

I fill my lungs and let out a bloodcurdling bellow sure to wake everyone within a five-mile radius.

Levi narrows his eyes, swipes at a row of books on a shelf and knocks them to the floor, breaking a framed picture of Brynn and me in the process. I can hear my parents yelling. "Stella! Stella?" I don't stop screaming.

Wordlessly, he glares at me. He snatches his shirt and I only catch one more brief flash of his scar before I avert my eyes.

"Go," I say, in the spare moments just before the door bangs wide open and Levi has slipped through the window.

chapter thirty-three
157 BPM

"And you just stayed there? He could have come back, Stella." Henry's pacing his bedroom. He throws his hat on the ground. "And, what, you think he took Tess's heart then?" He shakes his head. "What would he have done with it? That sick bastard."

"I have a few ideas." I sit cross-legged on Henry's bed, watching him walk off his nervous energy like a windup toy. He picks a Rubik's Cube up off his desk, a three-dimensional puzzle made of smaller cubes. The smaller cubes are all covered in different-colored stickers on every side. The goal of the game is to rearrange the puzzle until each side has stickers of a single, uniform color. Henry fiddles with it, twisting the small cubes over and over.

"None of which I like to dwell on in particular detail," I say.

It's not even seven yet. I'd been too scared to leave the living room until closer to daylight, and after my "nightmare" Dad had agreed to stay with me, drinking hot cocoa and playing a board game until he nodded off in his old recliner. As soon as I dared, I came to Henry's, where he insisted on excusing himself to brush his teeth. I stay at a safe distance so that he doesn't catch on that I forgot to do the same.

"I have his heart, Henry. And he wants it back. That's why he's still here."

Henry stops pacing and stares hard at me. "How did you see the scar anyway?" The question hangs between us. I'd skated over that part, hoping that we'd both agree to leave it at that. But as the crease leaves his forehead, I watch as he grasps the full picture on his own.

"Henry, it was one moment, I swear. That's it. I—"

He holds his hand up to stop me. My mouth snaps shut. I can see his pulse beating at the base of his jaw. He cuts his gaze away and stares at the carpet.

"So what do we do now?" he asks, voice low.

"You believe me then?" I'm not sure if this is the appropriate time to ask, but my sanity—already thin and threadbare—depends on it.

He halts midway to scooping up his ball cap. The remnants of sleep have faded from him. "Why wouldn't I?"

I lower my eyes, a lump forming in my throat. "I don't know."

He slumps down, back to his unmade bed, and folds the brim of his cap in his hand. "One too many Stephen King novels for us," he says darkly.

I half laugh and half cry. It comes out as a hiccup.

He shakes his head. "*Bag of Bones*. This has *Bag of Bones* written all over it."

"Great. My life isn't even one of his good books."

"We need a plan." He replaces the hat on top of his head and mashes down the curls.

"We have a plan. Step one: *You're* going to go to school," I say.

"Like hell I am."

I pick at a thread on his comforter, trying to decide whether it's worth it to argue. "It's senior year," I say.

"Stella, stop it. For someone who's smart, you can be a real idiot."

"Gee, thanks."

He leans his head back on the mattress and stares up at the pale, unlit stars on the ceiling. "How many years have we spent laughing at all those callers on *Lunatic Outpost*?"

"Serves us right. Now we're them." In the quietness of Henry's room, I listen to the typical sounds of morning. Sputtering sprinklers. Barking dogs. The slamming of car doors. All so utterly normal and suburban that our conversation feels like that between two kids playing pretend.

And that's exactly what I would think it was if it weren't for the swelling ache in the cavity of my chest. If I didn't feel the pressure of my lungs pushing in on my bleeding heart.

I crawl to my feet. The fetid taste in my mouth and the never-ending throb have produced in me another wave of nausea. "Do you have a spare toothbrush?" I ask, because brushing my teeth will give me something to do.

"You can use mine." Henry blushes. "It's on the sink."

I seal my lips together to repress a smile. I've never borrowed a boy's toothbrush before, and the idea feels adult.

Not something that high school couples typically do. Not that Henry and I are a couple.

I wave the blue toothbrush under the water and try not to chew on the bristles like I do with my own. I'm totally swapping spit with Henry. I want to laugh, but when I stare into the mirror, what I see is a girl haunted.

Literally.

And not by my past or my illness or the choices I've made, but by a spirit with a vendetta.

If I repeat it enough times, maybe it will stop sounding so ridiculous.

When I return, minty fresh, Henry has his backpack straps over his shoulders and his laces tied.

"I thought you weren't going to school," I say, unable to hide my disappointment.

"I'm not, but we can't stay here," he says. "My parents need to think we're going to school."

"Do you think he knows where I am?"

"We'll figure it out." He tosses me my book bag. "Together. In the meantime, where to?"

I pause, looking around the room filled with books and DVD sets, that smells like Henry and feels safe and known and secure, and I know that I won't have this feeling again until I win, but if I'm taking bets, let's face it, I wouldn't put the odds in my favor.

A wave of sadness moves through me. "I need to see it for myself," I say. "I want to go to the cemetery."

chapter thirty-four
151 BPM

It may be naive, but I've always believed the carvings on headstones. Anything etched in stone has the ring of both finality and truth and there's something particularly comforting about those three short words *rest in peace*.

A sort of send-off, a fond farewell, like people waving from the shore to a departing ship.

But who knows if any of that is true? With so little peace in the world, why do we suddenly expect to stop on a dime at the threshold to death's door?

I don't. Not anymore.

It's as if I've been walking around beneath the cover of a veil for my entire life and now that it's been lifted I can see the circus of sideshow freaks lurking in all of the world's nooks and crannies.

In the silence, I wonder if Henry now feels the same way.

I follow him out of the car. Our slamming doors ring

out with a loud aluminum echo in the open air. Together we stand, shoulders touching, and stare up at Sacred Heart with its steeple that tickles the clouds in the sky and stately graveyard that stretches for a mile back.

"Church twice in one month?" I say, thinking back to the day of Elsie's christening, where I'd slinked into the back pew, scared to go anywhere near my sister for fear I'd try to hurt her again. I thought that I'd hit rock bottom. Little had I known I was still on the fifth floor. "I ought to be sainted." I slide my hands into my back pockets.

Henry starts off toward the side of the church. "Somehow I doubt that."

"Oh, right." I trot after him. "I'm sorry, that's you, Saint Henry of Seattle. Patron saint of sick girls everywhere."

He smirks. "Not everywhere. Just one. Just here."

At that, my heart skips like a stone. "Okay, then, Saint Henry of Stella. It has a lovely ring to it."

I lead Henry around to the back of the chapel, over a path made of misshapen stepping-stones. A bell in the steeple tower tolls ten times over. I look up at it. The large brass bell swings like a pendulum. My dad took me up there once when I was a kid so that I could see the whole city on one side and the water on the other. There's a small lookout with a railing, and he held onto the back of my shirt while I gripped the railing and looked down at the tiny figure of my mother waving up to us.

When the last bell chimes, I find myself in a garden looking out over the church cemetery. I love that Henry didn't ask why I needed to come here or how it would help anything to see a rock with a few words carved into it. He just came.

Gray headstones stretch away for a mile. I stare out at the field, decorated with the physical remnants of death—some arched, some rectangular, others flat squares planted in the ground—all lined up, an army of graves. I push my side into Henry's to soak in his warmth. He slides his hand up to the back of my neck and gives it a comforting squeeze.

"Jesus," he says. "How will we ever find it?"

I cup one hand over my eyes. "Fan out, I guess. Check every one . . ." There's no need to finish. We both understand the task at hand.

Henry lets his hand fall from my neck. The cold seeps in, wrapping around me like a scarf. I watch as he trots down the short flight of stairs to the graveyard before following.

The soil is soft from last night's storm, but not muddy, on account of the lush grass that must be meticulously cared for. A few branches and bits of leaves and other debris have blown into the cemetery and are scattered around like Easter eggs.

Henry cuts left, so I make my way to the right side, past the gravelly aisle that runs down the center to meet with a marble statue of the Virgin Mary.

As suspected, the first couple rows yield nothing. I linger at a few of the headstones, whose dates span particularly short lengths of time.

April Linley Hayes lived only six years, but her tombstone towers over the others. A wreath of roses and ferns loops over the top like a halo. On the other end of the spectrum, a certain Matthew James McDougal lived for just three days. His grave marker is one of those plaques dug into the dirt with grass growing over the edges, which probably means no one's bothered to visit in years.

I sneak a glance over at Henry. He's stooped down,

brushing his hand across the ground. My breath catches before he quickly moves onto the next.

I experience the same effect each time I come across a name that starts with an *L*. The *Z* last names are much less common, but I do happen upon a Zucker and a Zimmerman, both of whom died well into old age.

Maybe it's because my neck hurts and my eyes have glazed over. I suppose that'll happen after intense peering at etched words, which tend to lose all meaning after around one hundred or so, but when I'm nearly even with the Virgin Mary, in her frozen head scarf and robe with a look of utter grief preserved in the lines of her forehead, I stop. I trace my steps back two headstones. I squint, understanding now why I'd stopped.

In careful block letters, carved into a pearly white stone that measures just south of my knees, I read the following inscription:

REST IN PEACE
LEVI MICHAEL ZIN
TURN, MORTAL, TURN, THY DANGERS KNOW,
WHER'ER THY FOOT CAN TREAD;
THE EARTH RINGS HOLLOW FROM BELOW,
AND WARNS THEE BY HER DEAD.

"Henry," I croak. He doesn't turn. He's several rows ahead of me on the other side of the cemetery. But if I leave my post, I risk losing the placement of the headstone. I take a deep breath. Something in the cemetery's atmosphere begs me to stay quiet, maybe in solidarity with the dead. I hold my hands around my mouth like a megaphone and yell. "Henry!"

A small flock of pigeons launch into the air nearby. They chirrup and flap, knocking into each other as they rise to the level of the trees. Henry's head snaps up. I exaggerate my gesture of waving him over. He cocks his head. I point at the grave in front of me, afraid to shout again.

Finally, Henry must understand. He bows his head and jogs toward me, zigzagging through the gravestones.

"I found it," I say when he arrives. Now that he's here, though, the whole thing feels a bit anticlimactic. We stare down at the rock, which seems cold, dead, and as lifeless as the corpse buried underneath.

Henry circles the headstone like he's in search of a trapdoor. "All this time and his body's been right here." He trails off into silence and then: "Now what? Should we whip out the Ouija board? Hire an exorcist?"

"Call Ghostbusters?" I add. "I'm glad my eternal damnation is a joke to you."

My legs have taken on the consistency of jelly. Rustling leaves fill the air with white noise, and pretty soon the same wind picks our cheeks raw, and Henry and I are left cold and shivering. Who knows how long we've been standing at the grave of Levi Zin lost in thought? Long enough for Henry's nose to turn reindeer red.

Without thinking, I move toward him and burrow my nose into the soft spot below his throat. He cups my head and I think I feel him smell my hair again. I let him. I'm exhausted and he's Henry, and I'd been wrong about us all along.

"At least one person doesn't think I'm crazy," I say, fracturing our silent vigil.

"Oh yeah? Who's that?"

I pull away. Henry raises his eyebrows, but the crinkling at the corners gives him away.

I shove him and he stumbles back a step and I return my attention to the gravesite. *Thy dangers know, wher'er thy foot can tread,* I read once more with a shiver.

Scoping the surrounding tombstones, I spot a large bouquet of long-stemmed roses nestled in the grass nearby. I stoop down and from the flowers, I shimmy one rose free, careful not to prick myself on the thorns.

Standing at the foot of Levi's grave, I cross myself from my forehead to my chest to my shoulders. Here lies the boy who has given me his heart. This is why I wanted to come here, I realize. To pay my respects to the person who has given me the greatest gift I could ever ask for.

"Thank you," I whisper. Crouching down, I lay the rose gingerly on the spot where he's buried. "But you forgot the most basic rule," I say, standing up and brushing my hands free of dirt. "No take-backs."

chapter thirty-five
149 BPM

And just like that, I declare war. There will be no going back, no surrender, no chance for diplomacy. We play for keeps.

"Busy signal," I tell Henry when he ducks out of the car, carrying two cans of Coke that he picked up from the Quickie Mart. I'm sitting on the hood, hands tucked into the sleeves of his Duwamish sweatshirt, which is so big I can tuck my knees inside it. The moon is a fingernail sliver hanging above. The sun, sunk below the horizon, has left a bright smear across the lower half of the sky that now lingers noncommittally between silver and navy blue. "Are you sure you've got it on the right station?" I ask. We're parked at an access point somewhere between two rickety piers. Unseen below, the Duwamish Waterway splashes and churns. Wisps of sea breeze still reach us up here, where we can taste the salt that clings to our cheeks and tangles our hair so sharply that we may as well be sitting on the beach. The car sinks under his weight.

"This isn't my first *Lunatic Outpost* rodeo." Henry pops the top and hands me one of the cans. I slurp bubbles off the rim.

"Busy signal still," I say. I check my messages. None from my parents, which means they still believe the cover story that I'm sleeping over at Brynn's.

"Try again in a few minutes," he says.

I twist to peer through the windshield. The doors to Henry's car are open, the windows down. Static buzzes through the stereo system.

"What if he's not taking calls tonight?" My arms feel too tired to move. At some point, I'd fallen asleep in Henry's car while he researched how to become Henry the Spirit Slayer on his phone or something. This, I've learned, is my standard defense mechanism. If life begins to overwhelm me, no matter where I am or what I'm doing, I will inevitably choose to take a nap. After the five-oh-eight pain, it's like a hole has been punched through my chest.

"He is. Relax." He grabs my arm and shakes me playfully.

"I'm trying." I play with the drawstrings of the sweatshirt and put my nose to the sleeve. The scent of Henry mixed with fabric softener helps, if only a little.

A few minutes later the static breaks. An eerie melody takes its place. Then Quentin, per his usual routine, welcomes all the Earthlings and non-Earthlings to tune into the show.

"Call now." Henry nudges me. "Before all the lines fill up."

I hurry to punch in the numbers and, with effort, hold the

cell phone up to my ear again. In the background, I can hear Quentin introducing the show's topics and inviting callers to contribute. The phone rings and rings. My foot jiggles. At least it's not busy. "He's not picking up," I tell Henry, but as soon as I say it, there's a crackle on the other end of the line. I sit up straight.

"Caller number one." Quentin's nasally voice breaks through. "What's the signal?" My eyes widen. I grab Henry's shirt and point to the phone. *It's him,* I mouth, then motion to Henry to turn down the car radio.

I clear my throat and, despite myself, grin. No good conspiracy theory show would operate without a proper password, especially with the number of prank calls Quentin receives. "The lunatics," I say, enunciating, "are running the asylum."

I've tried a thousand times to draw a mental picture around Quentin's voice. In my head, he exists in a corner of his mother's basement. A scrawny man-boy wearing a tinfoil hat and sporting thick glasses that magnify his eyeballs to resemble those of a goldfish. The reality is probably far more mundane. I'd hate to be disappointed. I switch the phone to speaker and turn up the volume.

"Very well. Welcome to *Lunatic Outpost.* Are you a first-time caller?"

"I—I am," I say, and realize I've been chewing a hangnail on my thumb.

"Question, comment, report of extraterrestrial life or out-of-body experience?"

I look to Henry. He shrugs. "The first two, I guess," I say.

"I'm listening, caller."

I hesitate. I can already tell that I'm going to sound like

either an idiot or a loon. Probably both. "Um, right," I hedge, trying to work up the nerve. "You know how you're always telling the audience that the world chooses to be blind? That people will concoct the most improbable, illogical scenarios just to make sure the world keeps operating within this little box that works according to their rules, even when the simplest, most logical explanation is that the world itself doesn't run on rules at all?" I bite the inside of my cheek instead of my thumb. "Well, I think my friend and I have been guilty of that."

"The universe is not a Rubik's Cube," says Quentin, more good-naturedly than I'd expected. "But some people need to fiddle with it longer than others." Quentin's favorite quip.

For years, I've thought of Quentin as an absent friend. An invisible part of a trio made up of me, Henry, and our beloved host. While I always thought the subject matter of *Lunatic Outpost* was eccentric, Quentin himself is brilliant. Possessed of a detailed mind. Sharp. Neurotic. Quick-witted. Under any other circumstances, I'd probably be melting into a puddle of fan girl.

"I, well, I don't know how to say it, I guess, but I—or we—think my *friend* is being haunted." Just saying it out loud gives me the shivers. The sun stain has been wiped clean and the atmosphere is now teetering toward nightfall. I pull the hood of Henry's old sweatshirt up over my ears.

"What exactly makes you think your friend is being haunted?" He says this in the same tone as a doctor examining a patient.

"It's been going on for a few months now only I—she— didn't realize the person wasn't a person until recently." I tell

Quentin about the transplant and about the medical records and our theories about the boy doing the haunting, whose name I change to Lucifer. "I guess our question is, how do we get rid of it?"

I touch the scar line underneath my shirt.

"You should know," Quentin pauses, "that once you go searching for answers you can't unfind them."

"We know," I add quickly.

There's another pause, and I think I hear him take a sip of water. "There've been reports," he begins. "In Qingdao, China, there was a shark attack over a decade ago. Very bloody, very violent, witnesses say. The victim died. The body was recovered, but without an arm. Since then, six children have drowned during family beach vacations on calm days. Loyal listeners may remember that I was called to investigate." This rings a small bell somewhere in a darker stretch of my memory, but I come up short. Henry and I both suck in our breath. "Are you sure you want me to go on?"

"We're sure." This time it's Henry. He's leaning forward, chin resting on his bent knee.

"A few years later, there was a car bombing outside of Baghdad. Four people were killed, one of whom lost a leg, which was never recovered. Dozens of people report having been robbed of precious articles by him in the months following, along the same stretch of road." I wonder if Henry can hear my heart pounding. "A similar story surrounds the 'donor' of an illegal transplant in Mumbai. The victim of a lobotomy in Shanghai. I've been called to complete substantial research on each of these, for lack of a better word, incidents. You'll notice none of these reports issue from the

United States, which is undoubtedly the worst when it comes to its desire to fit the world into its box."

"So what?" I ask, not sure I can bear another gory secondhand account. "They're each missing something?"

"I'm sure there are many reasons why souls might not find rest. I'm sure you've heard the bit about unfinished business? Or particularly violent deaths?"

"From you," I say.

"According to some cultures, a body is to be buried with all of its limbs and organs, too, or else the godly soul which it was housing can't return to its natural state. You know that spirits are strongest near the place that's most important to them. That's why some spirits haunt their old houses or the side of the highway where they were killed or the place of their murder. You've already told me that the cemetery where his body has been laid to rest is close—too close, if you ask me—and this in itself is bad."

"So, what, you think his grave is the most important place to him?" Henry interrupts. "He wouldn't have even known where his grave would be before he died."

"No, I don't think it's his grave, although that's certainly adding to the mix. It's his body. There's an old tradition dating back to tribal witchcraft: to destroy the curse, you must destroy the bones."

I straighten. "The bones? We dig the bones up and destroy them and then, what, poof, no Le—I mean, Lucifer?" The idea is risky. In fact, it's a crime, but already I'm concocting ways to rob the grave of Levi Zin.

"We have many more accounts pre–Industrial Revolution," Quentin continues, ignoring me. "When tribal witchcraft wasn't relegated to whack jobs and quacks, we knew that the success rate was high for this method of expulsion. *Bones*, of course, was used as a catchall term for *remains*, but still, the formula was simple. Modern technology has changed that. The cobbling-together of one body from the parts of another has obfuscated, at least in some cases, the ability to destroy the bones in one fell swoop." There's the nebulous feeling of a situation sliding from bad to worse. "You can imagine why the narrative accounts are few, then. The technology for transplanting one organ into a body is relatively new. That and the fact that most organ donors are cremated, not buried. For obvious reasons, I think."

"I'm not sure I'm following," I say.

"A transplanted heart is kept beating even when separated from the body, until it's placed inside its new host. I mentioned the illegal transplant in Mumbai. There was another in Mexico. But there was one big difference between the two. In Mumbai, Hinduism dictates cremation. The donor's body was burned to ash as soon as the transplant was complete. The result was a powerful, malevolent spirit that wreaked havoc on the recipient's family until one day, the patient was found hanging from the Mahalakshmi Temple. In Mexico, though, where most are Catholic, cremation is considered sacrilege. The donor's family insisted the body be buried. Of course, we've all heard of poltergeists moving furniture or leaving bruises on human skin and in occasional instances even killing unsuspecting victims, so we know that it's possible for the spirit world to affect the living one. Normal horror-movie stuff, based in reality, naturally. The Mexican incident went one step further. Although the reports are very few and the set of circumstances so rare and unique, in this instance, especially given that the heart is the strongest and most important of the organs, the spirit had the combined power of its one living organ along with the proximity of its bones and returned to haunt in corporeal form." Quentin lets this sink in. "He existed in the world physically."

"Like Lucifer." I will myself not to flinch.

"Like Lucifer," Quentin echoes.

I'd been so mesmerized by Quentin that I'm surprised when a gust of air comes through and blows off my hood. A shiver races the length of my spine, pooling in the hollow at the base of my neck. "But if we destroy the body, we should still be able to destroy him," I say. I close my eyes and listen. His words come double, through the phone and softly repeating through the stereo speakers.

"Yes and no," he says. "You have to destroy all of the remains. To destroy Lucifer, you must destroy the heart."

My hand goes limp. The phone slips from it and lands in the dirt. I can hear barely hear Quentin's voice in the background. "Caller one? Caller one? Lunatics, looks like we lost her. Time to open back up the phone lines."

I fold over. My chest falls against my thighs. My hands cover my ears and I rock back and forth. Pretty soon, I'm on all fours taking in panicked gasps, sucking in my belly until I'm light-headed from the lack of oxygen and worried I'll pass out.

Henry lunges for the phone and presses the off button. "It's not true, Stel." He shakes his head furiously, standing in front of the low beams of the car's headlights. "It's just not true. That guy doesn't know what he's talking about." He goes around to the driver's side and flips the station.

I push my fists into my forehead, my heart going haywire in my chest. It knows, I think.

Henry paces from one end of the car to the other. "He's the lunatic. Jesus."

"He asked if we wanted to know."

Henry quits pacing and climbs back onto the hood of the car. We sit, staring out over the invisible water, our shoulders and hips touching. City lights have begun to sparkle, making the bottom of the sky look like it's hemmed in glitter.

Henry laces his fingers between mine and squeezes. "We'll figure this out, Stel."

He pulls me to rest in the crook of his arm. Staring straight up, I feel as if I have blinders to the rest of the world. I can see nothing but stars. "It's a little bit better than the stickers in my room, I guess." His mouth is close to my ear.

My pulse slows. I feel the weight of my entire being. I feel the warmth of Henry. I feel the spray of the ocean when it carries on the wind. I feel it all and I don't want it to stop. But the universe isn't a Rubik's Cube for me to solve and maybe it's possible that I'm the one square that doesn't fit. "Did you know," I say, "that the name Stella actually means 'star'?"

Millions of shimmering pinpricks poke through the blanket of midnight blue above.

I hear the crackle of Henry's smile more than I see it. The deep hum of his voice reverberates through his chest. "Why do you think I'm seventeen and still have stickers in my room?"

"I thought it was because you were a dork."

His chest shakes with silent laughter. "That, too." Then, he turns into me, only slightly, but enough to make me feel cocooned and protected from the breeze. "There are a million, trillion stars," he murmurs. "But there's only one Stella. You have to promise me that we'll figure this out. You have to promise."

"Okay. I promise." Because I will try. For Henry. But I'm both very sore and very tired, and the fight in me is slipping.

chapter thirty-six
160 BPM

The lingering taste of pepperoni sticks to the roof of my mouth. Nobody could fight the forces of evil on an empty stomach, Henry insisted, but I strongly suspect that he was just trying to cheer me up. Unfortunately, I've made the recent discovery that no amount of deep-dish pizza is capable of staving off one's sense of impending doom. Judging by the continuous sidelong glances, I think he's worried I might spontaneously combust.

I push my plate away. Henry takes a final bite of crust, then stands to throw away our trash. "I told you we needed brain food," he says, sliding into the booth across from me.

I stare glassy-eyed and miserable at nothing in particular. Imagine going to the dentist's office and being numb everywhere except for the spot where the dentist is drilling. This is my current state: anesthetized save for the spot of blinding pain. "No, you didn't." This is the most I've said since sitting down for dinner. The effort feels useless and too much. I think I need another nap.

"Well, I should have, because I have an idea." He says this like he's just invented the Post-it.

"Super. Does it involve curling up into a ball and losing consciousness?"

"Even better." He reaches for my hand and drags me out of the booth. "Quentin may be an expert, but he's not the only expert." Henry pushes the door to the pizza joint open and a cowbell clangs. I follow him out to the car. "I'm under the age of, like, forty-five, so I've been scouring the Internet for information." He goes around to the opposite side of the car. We both slump into our respective seats. The dash dings twice when he inserts the key into the ignition. "But Quentin said himself that most reports on this stuff are old," he continues. "Before the Internet, what did people use for research?" Henry doesn't wait for an answer. "Books!"

"Oh, so that's what those rectangular things are with the pages in between them."

"Buckle your seat belt," he says, pulling out of the parking lot. "We're going to the library."

I check the clock. "Not to be a downer—or correction: to be even more of a downer—but the library's closed."

"Stella." He flips on his blinker and then presses his foot onto the accelerator. "I don't know if you've heard, but the world doesn't follow rules. And neither do we."

I want to convince Henry that breaking and entering isn't the answer, but he looks so hopeful, and besides, I promised him I'd try. The public library is a utilitarian concrete building. It's spooky, all bathed in shadow and completely deserted.

"Henry, we could get in serious trouble for this." I stare up at the building while he digs around in his trunk.

"You're already in serious trouble. And besides, it's not like we're going to vandalize anything. We're going to read books."

He surfaces with a crowbar-looking tool.

"Why do you have that?" I ask, slightly alarmed.

He turns the bar over in his hands. "Don't you have a tool kit in your trunk?" I shake my head. "All right, after all this is finished, we're fixing that. First thing on the list. You're like a walking disaster, Stella Cross."

"One thing at a time," I say, but I lower my head and smile at the pavement.

It takes us a few laps around the building to locate the best window. The surrounding trees cast spooky shadows that move and transform on the ground below. Henry and I resort to whispering and hand signals in the dark. At last, Henry settles on a low window. He drops to his knees and places the bar between the sill and the bottom pane of glass. I turn my back and stand watch.

"Car," I warn, and we both drop to our stomachs while a swish of headlights scans the building then rounds a corner and disappears.

My heart thumps wildly out of control. I dust grass off the front of my clothes and Henry resumes fumbling with the window. I hear a seal break, followed by the sound of sliding glass.

"You got it?"

"After you."

A blast of artificial air. The musty smell of old books. I crawl inside, then offer my hand to help guide Henry in after me. Maybe this isn't such a bad plan after all, I think, looking around and taking in the stacks and stacks of books arranged in categories from Spirituality to Self-Help to Eastern Asian Religion & Meditation.

To avoid detection, Henry and I keep the lights off. We explore together in silence. For a moment, it feels as if we're the last two humans on earth. I move silently through the rows. Near the entrance, Henry finds a directory and drags his finger down the list of topics. Then I follow him to the darkest corner of the library. He shines the screen of his cell phone over the spines. We stick close together. Instinctively. Alert.

Henry begins to pull titles and hands them to me. I cradle a stack of them in my arms. When they grow too heavy I tell him that I'm going to drop them on a table near the children's section.

"Be there in a few," he whispers. Without making a noise, I pad over to the kids' tables. This corner of the library looks even more creepy and abandoned, with its furniture made for small people and too-bright posters muted in the ambient gloom of nightfall.

I rap my fingers on a book and, even though I know it's him, I startle the moment Henry appears.

"Just me," he says, and I relax.

Together, we settle in on opposite sides of a polished-veneer table and each select a book from the stack. A few pages in, I sigh. I'm getting a distinctly needle-in-a-haystack vibe. I flip through another forty pages, scanning them as carefully as I can. For authors writing about the supernatural, they have managed to make the subject extraordinarily dry.

I rub my eyes. Henry is bent over a book, nose inches from the page, mouthing the words as he goes.

Another hour goes by and I push aside an old hardback. *Banishing the Dead* by Milton Bradshaw. A lot of pages, none of them useful.

Henry yawns.

"Anything?" I ask.

"Maybe," he says, dog-earing one of the pages to mark it.

"That doesn't sound promising."

He rocks back in his chair until the front legs come off the ground. His frustration over Quentin's prognosis has hardened into a steely resolve while mine remains gelatinous at best.

"This is useless." I idly thumb through the pages of *The Real Ghost Story* and stare at the black-and-white illustrations between the covers. The whole library has begun to smell like sweaty socks.

"No, it's not." Henry beats his knuckles against his skull. "There's got to be something."

"For example?" I ask.

I check my phone. We're closing in on midnight.

"An exorcism, holy water, I don't know. Something. We just need to keep looking."

I take another book off my collected stack. *Clearings: Everything You Need to Know About Clearing Ghosts, Demons & Other Entitities* by Jane Stewart. I studiously bury my nose in the pages of the book, reading the introduction and the first chapter, but in a few short pages it's crystal clear that Ms. Stewart has never seen a spirit—at least one like Levi— in her life.

I snap the book shut. "Henry, I've got to use the restroom."

He looks up. "Need me to come with you?"

I tilt my head and give him a *really?* look.

He hikes his shoulders up. "Sorry, sorry."

I leave the small work space we'd fashioned together.

Hundreds, maybe thousands of hardbacks line the shelves, each covered with a thick cloak of plastic, like dead scales on a snake. I walk through the rows as if strolling through forgotten crypts. The piss-colored carpeting muffles my footsteps and there's no noise but for the swishing of my pants.

I wander farther, letting the bookshelves lead me from Self-Help to Religion and Spirituality to Mystery.

At one shelf, I pause to look at a thick volume with curling script decorating the spine, intriguing, but difficult to read. I slide the book into my arms. In the gap created by the missing tome an eye is staring at me from the other side.

I jerk back before observing the freckled cheek and auburn eyelashes. The eye blinks. Then the hazel irises disappear. I look to either side of the row. Empty. I peek through the shelf to the other side. Empty too.

Quickly, I replace the book and hurry over to the next row, where I'd seen her. I arrive just in time to see a mess of curly, reddish-brown hair disappear around the bend.

"Brynn?" I say in a soft voice.

Glancing both ways, I follow. Among the next set of shelves, there she is again, toward the end. "Brynn," I rasp. She doesn't turn. I catch a glimpse of her profile as she vanishes down another aisle.

I furrow my brow. Why doesn't she hear me? I have a deep, niggling feeling that I should know the answer to this, but it sits tantalizingly out of reach, like a word on the tip of my tongue. I shuffle along, trying to catch sight of her between the books. I see flashes of motion. Her pinkish skin as she passes in the shadows. But each time I try to catch up to her, she withdraws into the next row of books.

Finally, I stop following. Heart pounding, I wait at the foot of one of the rows. I can hear nothing of her approach. I hold my breath, waiting, sensing. Sure enough, she appears, having wound her way from one end of the aisle and into the next.

We're near the end of the rows, the place that backs up to a dark, abandoned wall of the library. She doesn't acknowledge me as she passes. She doesn't even seem to register me. Instead, she rounds the corner and strides toward a push-through into the women's restroom.

Before the door swings shut, I take off after her. "Brynn," I say again. I check over my shoulder and barge in behind her.

Right away, I know something's off. Pitch-black. Cold. There's a snap behind me. The door locks.

I fumble along the wall for the light switch and flick it up. Nothing happens. Still empty, hollow black. A tingly feeling races through me like a rat crawling up my back. I shudder as though it's something I can literally shake off, and then, all at once, I become very still.

"Brynn?"

The sensation of being watched pushes at me from all sides, begs me to acknowledge it.

This is just the crazies talking, I tell myself. Be reasonable.

The crazies are getting louder by the minute and multiplying like bunnies.

Another shudder. I'm hardly breathing.

The pitter-patter of footsteps is unmistakable. My chest

caves in on itself as a whoosh of air falls out. I push my hands against the door. It doesn't give. Trapped. Deep breaths. I venture farther into the darkness. The footsteps skitter to the other side of the bathroom. Close.

Breathe. In. Out. In. Out.

Brynn, this isn't funny.

Think. Whispers in the walls. I cup my hand over my mouth, stifling a scream.

This isn't happening.

But even as panic sinks its claws into me, the lights suddenly blink on.

Eyes wide, I glance around an ordinary bathroom. Yellowing porcelain sinks. Peach tile. My reflection in the mirror as anemic as a poltergeist.

"Brynn, are you in here?" Underneath the door of the first stall, there's the fuzzy outline of a shadow.

A low hum fills my ears. It only pauses when I swallow. My legs want to disobey. *Bend down,* I command. They do. Knees crackle like Rice Krispies.

My hands touch the tile floor. Lemon Lysol. Mothballs. I turn my head to peek under the stall. A body sprawls on the floor. The hair's dark and soaked. Blue chipped nail polish reaches out toward me.

Scrambling to my feet, I shove open the stall.

Blood seeps out from underneath Brynn's neck and shoulders. Her chipped nails scrape against tile as I roll her over onto her back with a thump. Her head still hangs limply to the side. I grip her chin between my pointer finger and thumb to straighten her face.

From the center of her chest, a hole bubbles up with more blood. Frayed, chewed-on edges of flesh peel back to reveal a line of broken ribs, pointy and jagged where they've been cracked.

I want to look away, but I can't move. There's a deep twisting around my insides. Spit floods my mouth. I hold my hemorrhaging best friend in my arms, unable to tear myself away. I'm staring into the abyss. An oozing, scarlet gorge with no bottom.

Because of her missing heart.

chapter thirty-seven
171 BPM

"We have to go." I grab Henry by the arm and pull him upright.

"What? What do you mean? Why?" He starts sweeping books into stacks and scooping them off the table. He reaches for a ragged old paperback and sets it on top.

"We have to go now."

He grabs his keys and shoves them in his pocket, following me over to the jacked-open window.

"What happened?" he asks.

"Everything's *happened*." I'd seen a vision of Tess dying a day before the event occurred in real life. I know a pattern when I see it.

The things I see, they aren't random. Something or someone is driving them.

I can't help sneaking a glance over my shoulder. "Brynn." I force open the glass pane and hike my knee over the windowsill. "He's after Brynn next."

"What do you mean he's after Brynn?" He hands me the books and climbs out after me. He grabs the bar off the ground and we hightail it toward his car.

"My heart," I say, "is fucking with me." I take several fast gulps of air. "I saw her. It was just like Tess." I turn my head, looking away and squeezing my chin to my shoulder. "It's like my heart knows what he wants." This was the worst part. There was terror when I'd seen Tess and Brynn, but there was also a deep, grinding satisfaction.

"Stella." He moves to hug me, but I push him away. "We have to get to her."

"But how can you be sure?"

"I'm sure. He can't find her first. It has to be me."

I pull out my cell and choose her name from my list of favorites. Ringing. Ringing. I tap my foot on the ground. "Answer."

The ringing stops. I hold my breath. "You've reached Brynn McDaniel. Leave me a message and I'll call you back sooner or later, depending on my mood. Hasta la vista."

"Brynn, call me back . . . soon." *Click.* I drop into the car and look helplessly to Henry. I'm drained. At this point I've been up for well over twenty-four hours and I'm approaching shutdown.

"What should we do?" Henry asks.

"Find Brynn."

Finding Brynn proves to be harder than expected. A tangle of nerves, I won't let Henry speak, turn on the radio, or even hum until we're pulling up to the McDaniels' home.

Brynn lives in a red, wood-sided home with a pointy farmhouse roof. When I see that her car isn't in the driveway,

I feel my stomach drop out of my butt and onto the seat. It's after midnight now. None of the lights in the house are on. I open the door and step onto the curb.

"What are you doing?" Henry leans over the center console. "Her car's not even in the driveway."

I duck so that I can see him. "It could be around back."

"Hold on, hold on." I hear the click of a seat belt. "I'm coming, too."

He catches up. I hike the sweatshirt hood over my head again, tuck my hands into the front pockets, and trudge across the lawn toward the side of the house.

How many hours after I envisioned Tess in the forest before he got to her? Impossible to say, but within twelve, she was gone.

A floodlight clicks to life. I jump back. "Motion detected," Henry mutters beside me. We continue skirting the outer edge of the lot.

On more than one occasion I'd heard Mrs. McDaniel use the words *positive influence* and *one of the good kids* attached to my name. I wonder what she'd think now.

We check the back, near the garage. No sign. It could be parked inside, I tell myself, but there's an unmistakable sick feeling pushing up the back of my throat.

Our shoes swish in the mowed grass. We slink through the space between the McDaniels' and their neighbors' as I count the windows back to the third. Brynn's.

I cup my hands and peer through the glass.

"Anything?" Henry's breath is hot against my ear.

"Nope." My palms leave smudges on the window. I tap my nail. "Brynn," I say as loudly as I dare. "Brynn!" Henry uses his knuckles to knock.

We wait, but after a tense minute, there's no answer. I curl my fingers into my hair and tug. I kick the side of the house. "Where is she?"

Henry wraps his arm around my shoulder and begins guiding me back to the car. "Don't freak out. She's probably with Connor."

"Connor?" My mind flashes back to the night of the party. Connor rustling around in the bedsheets. "What makes you say that?"

He shrugs. "They've been dating for a few weeks." I can't believe what a monumental idiot I've been. My best friend has been dating someone and I've been too self-involved to notice. "You've been a little preoccupied," Henry adds, reading my mind.

Back in his Volvo, I sink my head into my hands. I hardly notice when the car rolls forward or when it comes to a stop a short distance down the block.

If anything happens to Brynn, I won't be able to forgive myself. She's not going to die because of me.

"Stella?" Henry taps my shoulder. I jump. I'd almost forgotten he was in the car. "I think I have something."

From the backseat, Henry pulls out a book. There's no plastic slip over the cover. This one is a paperback. It's thick with torn edges from library patrons thumbing through it. It has the weight of a book you would buy in the grocery-store checkout line, but the cover is plain and tan, the color of a fancy envelope. Red block letters adorn the front. Biting his tongue between his front teeth, Henry flips to a dog-eared page a quarter of the way in and begins to read:

"'Under certain circumstances, a malignant spirit may be banished through the process of binding, a technique whereby a living person places the apparition in a secure, confined area such as a bottle or a black box. There, the incapacitated spirit will linger, safe from human interaction so long as the container remains locked.'" Henry thumps the book with his pointer finger. "This. We can do this."

I frown. "Levi isn't an apparition. He's real. And he won't fit into a bottle."

"No." Henry's eyes gleam. "But he'll fit into a coffin."

chapter thirty-eight
191 BPM

I leave these items to the people I love:

To my parents—my complete collection of Stephen King novels; a lifetime of scares that have nothing to do with your daughter for once.

To Elsie—my room; it has a better closet and is farther from Mom and Dad, so they won't hear you sneak out when you get older.

To Brynn—my yearbooks and photo albums; thanks for never letting me fall too far behind. All my craziest memories are with you.

To Henry—the past week to remember me by.

While Henry digs in the garage for supplies, I sign the sheet of paper and tuck it in his glove compartment. In the event that I need to resort to plan B, I have to hope that someday somebody will find it.

The crunch of shoes in the dark. Henry appears, white teeth glinting in the night. He's smiling. In the past hour, his mood has buoyed upward into the stratosphere. "You ready to do this?" he says like we're a team readying ourselves to make a push for the playoffs. I shrug back into his old zip-up hoodie.

My intestines shrivel. I force my lips into a smile. I push my hands through the sleeves and am swathed again in the innocent smell of him. Sweet Henry. I told him I would try and I will, but I have a secret, and he would never let me go with him now if he knew.

When the church comes into sight, I hold my breath, just like I did when I was little and we drove past a graveyard— breath held, feet up. I have to remind myself to breathe again, but even as oxygen returns to my lungs, it feels as if I'm still holding it. Heart thumping. Pulse pounding in my wrists.

The deep, velvety night acts as our cover as we unload the trunk for part one of The Plan. According to Henry's book, Levi can be bound to the spot where his body was laid to rest.

Starting between a massive stone cross and a square tombstone the color of dusty red dirt, we tread between the makeshift aisle, through row upon row of the consecrated dead. Everything is quiet except for the dragging of metal along soil that comes from the two shovels in tow.

I count the rows back from the church steps until we reach the fourteenth. Levi's row. From there, it doesn't take long to locate the thick white headstone that seems to match the color of the moon. LEVI MICHAEL ZIN. The letters carved into stone look angular and confrontational. We tiptoe around the edge of the area leading out from the stone, tracing the line where his body must lie beneath the grass.

If anyone were to ask what events led me to this present moment, there'd be no explanation that would make me sound anything but crazy. And not crazy like a girl who calls a guy fifteen times without leaving a voice mail. Like full-on, straitjacket crazy. Even with a shovel pointed at the ground, I wonder if maybe I really am insane and have only convinced Henry to carry out a delusion that started manifesting itself way back in anatomy class that day.

I balance the weight of the handle and drive the metal tip into the hollow earth. I try to stay focused, energy trained on churning up the ground, but I sneak glances at Henry. A curl falls over his forehead every time he buries the blade in the dirt.

A lump rises in my throat. I wonder if they'll bury me in this cemetery if I don't return.

The shovel slides in, making the sound of a pail through wet sand. The next thrust buries the shovel up to the shaft. I jerk my elbows to yank it out. It takes some maneuvering to tear out the first divot of mud and cast it off to the side. The earth wants to slurp the shovel up and not let go, as if hands are holding the shovelhead from underneath. It's only when I can wrestle it away that I'm able to widen the hole.

Before long, my triceps and shoulders are heavy and sore. I have only a small crater about as deep as the distance between my foot and my ankle to show for it. A fraction of Henry's progress. I've never known whether it's true that bodies are buried six feet under, but God, I hope not. I wipe the first drop of sweat from behind my ear.

Over and over, I plunge the shovel down, and each time another prickle works its way up the back of my neck. The breeze picks up, rustling the leaves on the trees above and changing the dappled shadows below. As another clump of dirt slides off the point of my shovel, some of the drier bits are carried off in a thin tail of dust.

It takes over an hour to retrieve the bones of Levi Zin. Both of us have to use all of our weight to pry open the coffin lid. Across his skeleton, mummy skin stretches with gaping tears like wet toilet paper. But I can still make out the threads of dark hair on his scalp and a fully intact Nirvana T-shirt draped over his carcass.

"Send it," Henry says. And with that, the cogs that push us into part two of the plan are set in motion. *Rest in Peace, Levi,* I think dryly.

I turn away as Henry loads the remains into a large fertilizer bag.

Soon the momentum will build. Neither of us will be able to stop it. And what Henry doesn't know is the one thing that would kill him if he did.

I'm capable of ending this on my own.

chapter thirty-nine
206 BPM

I wish I could talk to Brynn one last time. I wish I could know that she's safe and that she's okay, but of course I can't know any of those things. Sweating, breath shallow, I punch in the letters on my keypad to type out the ransom note. In this case, though, what's being ransomed is me.

"It'll be okay." Henry squeezes my shoulder. "It'll be over soon." He hadn't liked the idea of me acting as bait, but unless we're willing to serve up someone else's heart on a silver platter, neither of us can think of anything else.

He's right, of course. It'll be over soon. It'll all be over. I take a deep breath.

Leave her alone, I write, *or neither of us will have what we want.* Enter. I give the time. I give the place. A different time and a different place than I've told Henry, but still. I hit enter again. And for good measure, I include a final threat—*I'll destroy it.*

Now we wait.

"It's done." I look to Henry. He nods at me, suddenly solemn. "We should have an hour." I can't look him in the eye. I make a mental note. The last thing I say to him shouldn't be a lie.

Dirt stacks up on either side of Levi's grave. A sleek mahogany coffin lies open underneath. If Henry's plan is successful, the physical manifestation of Levi's soul will be confined to his casket for eternity. Except I know that it won't work, because I still have part of it beating inside me.

"Come on." Henry reaches for my hand. I take it, warm and damp and unmistakably living. I crane my neck and stare up at the stars. When did I become too old to make wishes?

I pick the brightest and send a positive thought up to the universe, hoping that I will leave my mark in some way on the world, even if it's just a feeling, an invisible imprint.

Henry and I cross the remainder of the cemetery with its scraping branches that cast shadow puppets on the ground and the plush grass beneath our feet rendered colorless in the night. Henry loads the remains into the trunk.

As we drive to the drop-off point, I'm reminded of a Bible story I learned in kindergarten. There once were two women who lived in the same house and who both had infant sons. One had accidentally smothered her own son and so had swapped the child with the other mother's living one to make it look as though the second woman possessed the dead child. When the second woman denied that the dead child was her own, the pair went to King Solomon for a judgment. After thinking on the problem, King Solomon called for a sword to be brought before him. He decreed that the baby would be split in two and each woman would receive her half of the child. Upon hearing the judgment, the true mother threw herself at the king's mercy and begged him to let the imposter have the child, but to please not kill him. On the other hand, the pretender, bitter with jealousy, screamed that it should be neither hers nor the other woman's—"Divide it!" she said.

The tires crunch along gravel and an old railroad bridge comes into view. I'm ready to play the imposter. If I can't have the heart to myself, then neither of us should have it.

This is the secret I've kept from Henry. I'll still destroy Levi. I just may happen to destroy myself, too.

Henry presses the brakes and pushes the gear into park. His headlights create a halo of light in the clearing. The bridge, copper and rusted, is decked in graffiti. Abandoned and fallen into disrepair. The Duwamish Waterway, which coils around the east side of Seattle, crashes into the canal walls below. Neither of us says a word. We just sit there for a moment in silence. Nearing the end.

Although I never wanted seventeen to be the period on the end of my very short life sentence, I'm practically giddy at the thought of the last moments of my pain. The big finale. Soon it will be gone and I'll feel nothing, and the idea of it is almost sweet enough to make my teeth ache.

"Henry, I want to do this part alone," I say. "This is between me and him. I just need a second, okay?" He starts to open his mouth, but I talk over him. I have to talk fast before I lose my nerve. Or worse, before I cry. "You can see me. I'll be right there," I insist. "Let me do this. Please?"

He nods. "Okay. Fine. If you have to."

My smile is weak, but I try to make it reassuring.

I unload the bag of remains from the trunk. The bag is

unexpectedly light in my grip. My knees tremble. The smell of damp earth and falling leaves is pungent, but as soon as I step out onto the bridge, the sea overwhelms it. The echoing roar of water is heavy in the air.

I walk all the way to the center of the bridge and peer over the edge: the drop is enough to kill me. The bridge is lined only in short rail ties that emit heady waves of gasoline. I gulp air, suddenly terrified. Shaking, I lift the bag to the ledge and let go. The remains of Levi Zin tumble down and disappear into the black water below. I watch, speechless, as the bag sinks below the surface.

I catch the scent of cigarette smoke just before I hear the strong baritone of his voice.

"If you do this, you'll lose everything."

I spin around, and as I do, I feel my heel catch the lip of the bridge. I lean forward for balance. "Stay right there." I hold out a trembling finger.

He obeys. In the time since I've seen him, Levi has changed. The beauty in his face has shifted and turned into something lean and hungry. The second he appears, the swollen, tender ache in my chest subsides to a dull pinprick, and I still wonder how I've resisted him for so long. His hair shines with moisture and so does his skin, both hinting of the ocean at twilight.

A cruel smile spreads across his face. He has always been the predator toying with his prey, waiting for the moment to pounce. He's been there every second. Every moment. Waiting.

Chills raise goose pimples over every spare inch of me.

"Is she safe?" I ask, shifting both heels back to the brink.

Levi's jaw is taut. He nods. This, though, this moment

of defiance, he wasn't expecting, I realize with a rush of satisfaction.

I back up a centimeter, conscious of the boggling heights. Starlight shines off his sodden hair, slicked sideways across his forehead.

"You donated it," I tell him. "It's mine now." I'm not sure whether I think he needs to hear it or I do.

"It was taken from me." He snarls.

The water thunders below us. One step. That's all it would take.

"If you've wanted my heart all along, what were you waiting for?" I'm surprised by the sudden steadiness of my own voice.

He lets out a cheerless, one-note laugh. He watches me, hawk-eyed. Hands shoved in his pockets, his posture is relaxed, but I notice the flex in his muscles and my own stomach clenches into a fist.

"Doesn't everyone deserve a final spin around the block? Once my heart's been returned to me, I'll be banished forever." Levi strolls toward me. He takes another pull from his cigarette and the end glows orange. "Besides, Stella, give yourself some credit. You're not a total bore." My cheeks burn. It seems as if he's about to reach out to touch me.

This is it. I've run out of time. I put one foot over the rail tie and balance my toe on the narrow outer ledge. Levi freezes, watching me. Testing.

"You're not thinking." His lips curl over his teeth in an ugly grimace.

"You're not real."

For a moment, we're both stalled at an impasse. Then the silence shatters. Footsteps pound the bridge. A metallic echo. A figure barreling toward us. *No, Henry.* It's too late. He's sprinting toward us. Face contorted into a battle cry. He closes the distance in no time.

Levi spins deftly and catches Henry in the chest with a swift kick. He clasps Henry's ribs, pushing him up off of his toes so that his feet dangle. Henry's face contorts, and for an instant, I see the tormenting chest ache that I've been suffering reflected on someone else's face.

"Tell me," Levi says. "Is this real enough for you?" I see torn edges of skin and bloody holes that gurgle for air. I don't need a vision. I know what comes next.

"Stop or I'll jump." I don't have to say it loudly for Levi to hear. Henry's face is white and lolls to the side. Not Henry. Please, not Henry.

Levi aims his stare at me. Hooded eyes, dark and devilish. "You were a coward when I met you and you're a coward still."

He's wrong. I was a coward when we met, but his heart changed me. I'm not scared to live anymore. And I'm not scared to die.

I turn and place both feet on the outer ledge. I stretch out my arms. I imagine myself on the starting block, preparing to dive. *Are the swimmers ready?*

On your mark. Get set. Behind me, a dull thud. My right foot moves to take a step. I lean forward, heart over my center of gravity. I feel the pull of the ground. A flit of breeze.

And then a hand takes a fistful of my shirt and I'm thrown sideways away from the ledge. Steel railroad tracks scrape the skin from my elbows. Henry's figure is crumpled a few feet away.

I scramble to my feet and run.

I run without thinking about in what direction. As long as it's away from Henry. The clanging of the bridge vanishes. My feet find soft ground, slippery underneath them. The road is lined with spindly trees. Downhill, curving right. Panic blocks my throat. I'm fast. But not fast enough. I can't outrun Levi. Not forever.

I hammer my legs, propelling myself toward the first signs of civilization I see. A cluster of sleepy houses nestled between road and water. I wonder if I should scream. Would anyone help me if I did? Would anyone believe me?

The street's deathly quiet, as if Levi and I are the last people left in this town. What I need now is options. The only option I can think of is to stay away from him.

My rib cage expands and contracts painfully. Three years ago I could have run ten times as far without feeling my lungs knot. I reach a stop sign at the end of the main road and turn left. Rows of the neighborhood's wooden fences begin to wedge me in.

"Don't worry, Cross," Levi hurls the words at me. "I'm patient."

My legs already prick and burn like they've been stuck by a nest of a million hornets. There's a chance I won't make it much farther. A good chance. There's adrenaline, but even that can't keep my legs moving as fast as they need to. My instincts are screaming, Fight or flight. Fight or flight. I screw my chin over my shoulder and see Levi walking toward me, slowly, like Vlad the Impaler.

When I turn back I notice the reflection at the end of the lane ahead. As my head bounces up and down in time with my steps, the horizon bobs with it, and every so often I catch a twinkle of light or the frothy crest of a whitecap.

An option.

I don't have time to wonder or confirm my theory. I use the last bit of resolve to pump power into my legs. My shoes slap the pavement, doubled by the sound of Levi's.

I start counting back from ten. The numbers run through my head like a ritual prayer. Anything to distract. I have to keep going.

I cut through a lawn, trampling a well-tended crop of hydrangeas in the process. At the end of the street, I slip between two brick houses and am choked by the smell of garbage spilling out of the bins. The solid wall between Levi and me makes me feel safe for an instant, before I hear the crunch of Levi's feet in the gravel alley. And it's in that heartbeat that the toe of my sneaker catches the ground wrong and I sprawl forward. Rocks scrape my hands. I bite my lip against the sting and work to scramble to my knees, but it's too late. Levi's hand has latched onto the hood of Henry's baggy sweatshirt.

His breathing is a snorting snarl that tears at the space around me. I can't breathe. He's pulling me up by the hood and the neck of the sweatshirt strangles me. I gasp and search for air that won't come. Tossing my head, I fight to get my fingers inside the collar, but it's too tight. I arch back. My eyeballs roll in their sockets.

The zipper is in between my fingers. My head fills with cotton and my legs go numb. I slide the zipper down and muster my last bit of strength to wriggle my arms out of the jacket.

Levi falls back bellowing. I rise to my feet and again I run.

The sound of the tide crashes into the shore. Gusts of mist land on my face and I emerge from between the houses, mist land on my face and I emerge from between the houses, staggering. On either side of me, expensive canal mansions loom like monsters, with their lavish balconies and extravagant outdoor living rooms. Every one as indifferent to me as the ocean.

The salt-laced wind kicks up spray. My run has deteriorated into a lopsided limp. One long stride, one short. I cross the stately backyard of one of the channel homes with its hollow windows, sleepy and oblivious. A stepping-stone path leads out to an empty boat dock.

The wood creaks underneath my weight. The boards of the dock vibrate. I feel Levi reach the small pier before I hear him. But I'm near the end of the runway. With my toes hanging off the ledge I take one final look back. His bottom teeth jut forward. He stares at me hard, daring me to jump, and I know that I'm right. He won't follow me to the place where he met his watery end.

I step off the ledge. And I fall.

chapter forty
212 BPM

A mix of gravity and momentum plunge me far below the surface, where the water stabs at me with icy needles. I scream and the last of my air explodes into a thousand bubbles that I watch float up.

My heart begins to pound and I roll over, belly down. I sweep my arms and kick my legs in large strokes. The ocean pours through my outstretched fingers.

I fight the current to avoid being pulled into shore. All the while, I imagine Levi, waiting for me. Watching.

My mind goes back to counting to ten. How long can I stay under? The farther I go, the more protected I'll be by the night. Another push, I tell myself. Just one more.

I keep lying to myself until my chest feels so tight and full I'm sure it'll burst. I can't swim anymore. I need air. I stare up. The moon is a round orb, wrinkled and dangling above. I kick my feet. The image of lane ropes. Chlorinated water. Gold medals.

The surface shimmers and fractures light like glass. Clicks and sputters fill my body and I know, at once, that I've made a fatal mistake.

Wet cement seeps into my arms and legs. I'm no longer kicking or flailing or moving. I'm only falling. Away from the air, sinking and watching the world fade away in slow motion. The moon grows smaller and fainter and soon, it's blotted out.

chapter forty-one
FLATLINE

The first time, it's like getting kicked in the chest by a horse.

The second, like being struck by a stray firework.

By the third, I swear I've been shot with a bullet.

"Clear." A voice I don't recognize. My back twists off the rough surface. I slam back against it. "Clear." Liquid squelches from my lungs. Coughing. Spluttering. Gasping for air.

Someone pushes my shoulder and rolls me onto my side. More water spews out. Toward the end, I'm puking it in stringy ropes that stick to my chin. A hand strikes my back, thumping me over and over until I vomit whatever dregs are at the bottom of my stomach.

My eyelids flutter open. Sirens. Flickering red lights that turn the waves scarlet. Salt burns my nose and throat and coats my lashes.

"She's conscious," says another adult voice. Shadows swirl around me. So much movement and activity, I can't keep up. At last I'm allowed to recline on my back again. Stars blanket the sky.

"Can you state your name?" A woman in a navy-blue uniform enters my line of vision.

"Stella Cross." My voice comes out as no more than a murmur, but the effort feels as if it strips my throat of its pinkish tissue.

She's kneeling. One hand rests on my shoulder. "How old are you, Stella?"

"Seventeen." The salt water stings.

"Do you know what happened?" The woman's hair is pulled taut into a bun that stretches the skin near her temples. But her face is friendly and I have the urge to reach out and grasp the hand on my shoulder.

Instead, I save my vocal cords and shake my head.

"Stella, I don't know what you were doing in the water, but you're lucky your friend over there called when he did." I have a brief flash of terror that I'll look over and see Levi standing guard, but when I turn my chin, it's Henry who's lingering beside an ambulance and a police cruiser.

Curly-haired, rail-thin Henry. My fingers fly to my lips and I let out a sob.

"Your heart stopped," she continues. "I understand that you've recently had a transplant. Your doctors should have told you that at least for the foreseeable future, strenuous activity of any kind is off limits. That includes swimming. Especially in water that has currents like that." She looks out over the ocean. The world to me smells like seagulls and fish.

"Wait, my heart stopped?" I return my gaze to her.

"Yes. These"—she picks up two large paddles connected to a machine—"were able to bring you back, but that's not always the case. Next time, you may not be so fortunate."

"So I was dead?"

Her cool palm moves from my shoulder to my forehead.

"Yes, Stella. But you're not anymore."

Tears slide straight down to my ears and I begin to sob, and as I cry, it dawns on me that I've lost something in the water.

The pain.

I've been carrying it for so long, I feel like a person who's lost fifty pounds and doesn't know what to do with her new body. A wound inside me closes, stitched tight at the seams.

"Can I see Henry now?" I point.

The paramedic lifts her chin and she nods to Henry, standing at the sidelines. He doesn't jog, he runs, and, thankfully, the woman pats my arm and gives us our space.

I'm so overjoyed to see him. I have a thousand things to say but can't seem to choose one.

"Where...did it work?" My smile crackles over my teeth.

A damp lock of hair falls over his forehead. Behind him, the first hint of sunlight is smudging silver along the horizon.

"He's gone." He takes my cheeks in both hands and we're both grinning like we drank too much champagne. "I saw it happen. He just crumbled into the ocean. You did it."

For the first time in a long time, I know that even if I let myself feel all the emotions the universe has to offer, I won't break. My heart will keep on beating.

"I thought you were dead," he says.

I reach up. I touch the dark freckle on the side of his face and beam until the corners of my mouth tire and I can't hold it anymore. "Nope," I say. "Definitely alive."

chapter forty-two
101 BPM

The heart, I learned, no matter what we're told in fairy tales, doesn't work off love or affection or fondness or devotion. It essentially works off of electricity. When an electrical shock was sent through my heart six months earlier, it was as though it was given a jump start, just like someone would a car, and now here I am, up and running—only not literally.

My feet are planted firmly on the ground, right where they belong.

A black tank top sticks to my ribs. The sun beats down on the Walmart parking lot where we're making our final run for supplies.

The entire city of Seattle has become one big steam room in what's being called the hottest summer ever, and I'm looking forward to spending most of it holed up on an air-conditioned bus.

I carry two armfuls of plastic bags and stash them in the

compartments underneath the bus. Batteries, potato chips, liters of soda—I check each item off of the list on my clipboard. The last thing I need is to forget someone's favorite brand of cereal or whatever. I lift a heavy crate of bottled water and shove it into the underbelly of the bus, too.

"You need a hand with that?"

I spin around to see Henry cutting across the parking lot, still in slacks and a tie and sporting his graduation robe.

"You made it!" I squeal, closing the distance between us. He picks me up and spins me around. I can't believe I had to miss everyone's graduation. When he sets me down, he takes off his tasseled cap and puts in on my head.

"Not so fast," I say, sliding it off and replacing it over his curls. "Next year. I'll do it on my own. Promise."

I hadn't graduated with my class after all. My parents, as much as I hated to admit it, were right. I needed more time off to let my body catch up and recover. Years of stress had eaten away at me and it was time for a real break. I'd go back to Duwamish in the fall and finish then, graduating with the lowly juniors below me, just like I'd vowed not to do.

But life has a way of changing plans on you.

I move Henry's tassel over to the left side. "You make a very handsome graduate, you know." I rise to my tippy-toes and kiss the freckle underneath his left eye. "Will you still remember me when you're a big shot at UDub?"

He absentmindedly touches the spot where my lips had been. "It's right here in Seattle." He rolls his eyes. "I'll be here all the time. You on the other hand . . ." He pinches my nose playfully.

With my hands on my hips, I turn back to admire the bus. It's not big, but it feels like a big adventure. "I know, right?

I can't believe my parents are letting me go." I twirl around to model my tank top with the words TOUR CREW written in bold white letters. "How do I look? Official?" It's not as if I'll be doing anything fancy, unless it's considered fancy to be doing glorified gofer work and selling merchandise, but it still feels grown up.

He catches me by the waist of my jean shorts. "Just don't go off and become a groupie," he says, eyeing Danny Marino, the band's drummer, as he climbs the steps onto the bus.

"Please, that's so seventies."

Just then an SUV pulls up. A car door slams. Out of the backseat jumps another swirling gown, sprinting at me so that it flutters in her wake. My parents trail behind Brynn at a more reasonable pace, but I can barely see them, because Brynn's hair is currently suffocating me.

"You brat." She pulls away. "You were going to leave without saying good-bye."

I pull a clump of auburn curls out of my mouth. "The tour manager set the time. Nothing I can do about it. I'm just a lowly peon here to cart around boxes and equipment and stuff."

"I hate you. I hate you. I hate you. I hate you." She stomps her foot, but she's smiling.

I wave to Mom, Dad, and Elsie, who's half-asleep with her thumb in her mouth.

"Well, will this make it up to you?" I ask, pulling out three tickets to Action Hero Disco's show from my pocket. "It's for Portland. Can you guys meet me there? The band's in town for a couple days and I thought maybe we could at least get a sliver of our last summer together. One's for Lydia."

Brynn snatches them from my hand. *"Backstage?"* She dances around. "I am totally going to make out with a rock star. You know that, right?"

My dad clears his throat. Brynn, on the other hand, doesn't seem the slightest bit embarrassed. "We have a little going-away gift for you," he says. He steps forward and presents me with a black guitar case.

I look at him in disbelief. "Seriously?" I take it in my arms and kneel down, unhooking the clasps of the lid. Inside is a brand new Epiphone Les Paul edition. I run my hands over the cherry-red wood.

I scoop it into my lap, cradling it on one thigh. My fingers find the strings at the neck of the guitar and I strum the opening notes to "Lithium" without a sheet of music in front of me.

"How do you do that?" Brynn shakes her head.

Grinning, I replace the guitar in its case. I shrug. "Don't know." Which is the truth, kind of. "Thank you." I wrap my parents and Elsie in a group hug. A lump forms in my throat.

Maybe I'll go to Stanford one day, or maybe I won't. Maybe I'll figure it out on the road this summer, when there's nothing but miles of time to plan my next dive into the deep end.

"Stella, the train's rolling out." Joe, the tour manager stands tapping his watch.

My stomach tightens and I press my lips together to keep from tearing up. "I'll call you." I hug my parents again and then Brynn.

Last there's Henry. My cheeks get hot when he plants a kiss on my lips right in full view of my parents, but I get over it and wrap my arms around his neck and kiss him back, drinking in the scent of Dove soap and Ralph Lauren cologne until I hope I have enough to hold me over for the next month. He tousles my hair, which has grown out to shoulder length.

When I turn to leave, there's no raging pain that scrapes through my chest, but a pleasant ballooning of my heart that makes me feel complete and full.

I climb the steps onto the bus and find a seat on a bench, where I put my headphones in and stare out the window at the world cast in the sun's golden net.

Two months ago, I tried to look into what St. David's did with my old heart, to make sure it'd been destroyed. The best guess they could give me was that it'd been sent to a medical school in California for teaching purposes. Someday I'll work on figuring out exactly which one, and I'll make sure that the end for me will be the end.

Because even though hearts don't run on love or affection or fondness or devotion, I've found that they're more than just a compilation of veins and arteries. Researchers have discovered that a human's DNA is actually capable of passing down learned information from traumatic or stressful experiences that take the form of fears and phobias, and as I rub the scar that splits my rib cage in half, I wonder what else it can pass down.

I sway in my seat as the wheels of the bus veer out of the city and the coastline passes out of view. A pinch of worry hits me. This is the farthest I've been from the water since my surgery. I don't know why I survived when the odds were against me. I don't know why I made it off the list when so many others have died waiting for the gift that could save them. And I don't know how one girl and her friend could defeat the thing that was determined to take it away.

What I know is that the universe is not a Rubik's Cube, and I'm glad I'll never be able to figure it all out.

ACKNOWLEDGMENTS

This book would not exist without the help and support of countless friends along the way, so with all my heart, I extend these thanks...

To my agent, Dan Lazar, for sticking with me through thick and thin, and to Torie Doherty Munro at Writers House, for many hours of behind-the-scenes work. To my amazingly talented and insightful editor, Laura Schreiber, who has helped to shape and improve every aspect of this manuscript; to Emily Meehan for giving me my first "yes"; and to the rest of the unparalleled team at Hyperion, along with my copy editor Polly Watson, publicist Jamie Baker and cover designer Tyler Nevins, for turning this story into a book.

To Nick Harris, for your creative partnership and unwavering belief in Stella since the beginning.

To Dr. Arielle Lutterman, for acting as my medical consultant when needed.

To my YA author debut groups, the Class of 2k15, the Fearless Fifteeners, and especially my beloved Freshman Fifteens, your friendship and humor have been invaluable this year; to my trusted confidantes Lee Kelly and Virginia Boecker; to my smart and supportive writing buddies Kim Liggett, Lori Goldstein and Jen Brooks; to Shana Silver, who has listened patiently to every plot problem I've ever had; to Charlotte Huang, for endless emails of encouragement and for acting as my daily sounding board; to Kelly Loy Gilbert, for sharing the journey; and to Jen Hayley, Emily O'Brien, Christine Bassham and Kelley Flores, for listening.

To my colleagues, who granted me the generous gift of time and space to write, with special thanks to Dee Kelly, Jr., David Cook, Cal Jackson, and Mike Moan.

To my parents, for instilling in me a love of books that has lasted a lifetime and for always being my biggest fans.

And lastly, to my husband Rob: For taking on more than your fair share of our daily challenges so that I can pursue my dream, but also for always being the one to pry my fingers from the keyboard when I'm clearly in need of a break. You are my favorite person in the world and I couldn't accomplish anything without you.